BITTEN

BY

NOELLE MARIE

TABLE OF CONTENTS

CHAPTER ONE

Middletown, for all intents and purposes, was just as dull as its namesake implied.

In fact, located on the northern edge of Iowa and surrounded almost completely by corn fields, it wasn't unusual for passersby to completely miss the tiny town on their way to more grandiose cities.

And honestly, they weren't missing much.

The extent of Middletown's attractions included a modest-looking school, a meager city hall, a bank that doubled as a post office, two bars, a church, a small grocery store, and a decrepit, worn bowling alley in which half of the lanes didn't even work properly.

Perhaps the only place of true interest in the entirety of Middletown was the old, abandoned house on Miller Road.

The house was located on the very fringe of the minuscule town at the end of an otherwise forsaken dirt road and was subject to many a ghost story. Terrifying tales of ghouls and malevolent spirits were passed down from generation to generation as not even the oldest residents of Middletown had any memories of the house ever being anything but empty – at least of the living.

With nothing else to do on the weekends – especially on Sundays, as the bowling alley was closed – it was common for the youth of Middletown to disregard their parents' cautionary warnings and pay a visit to the broken down house in hopes of an adventure.

This was exactly where Katherine Mayes found herself.

In the midst of a small cluster of other teenagers – after all, no one was as brave alone as in a group – she was walking along the winding dirt road that led to the house in question. The full moon was out, its natural glow acting as her guide in the otherwise dark of night.

Even as she hiked the pothole-filled road, face sent into a mask of indifference, she couldn't help the awful feeling of foreboding from rising up in her gut. *Why, oh why, had she allowed herself to be talked into doing this?*

Truth was, Katherine had always been just a little bit uncomfortable with the presence of the house at the end of Miller Road. That's not to say she believed the numerous horror stories about the place – not in the least. It was something else. Some strange, deep-rooted feeling of *something* – uneasiness maybe – filled her whenever she thought of the old, decaying house and as such, she had always adamantly refused to go whenever her best friend had tried to nag her into tagging along with the rest of the neighborhood gang. She honestly couldn't explain why she had agreed this time. After all, she had made it sixteen years living in Middletown without visiting the run-down house once.

She was already regretting her senseless decision when the house finally came into view and the terrible feeling in her gut grew in intensity. It was much worse up close than the glimpses she had caught of it at the other end of Miller Road. From there, the house was barely visible, nearly completely hidden by the overgrown trees and bushes that surrounded it. Up close, Katherine could see the rotting rafters sticking out in spots where the roof had caved in, the twisting vines creeping up the walls, and the shutter or two that still managed to hang crookedly from glassless window frames.

More terrifying than all of that, however, was the faint light that seemed to be peeking out through one of the main floor windows.

When Katherine saw it, she immediately jerked to a stop and tried, without any luck, to prevent a shiver of apprehension from running through her. The others in the group, her best friend Abigail Gallagher – or Abby, as the redhead preferred – and three other girls her age that Katherine didn't particularly care for, but that Abby got along with, seemed to have also seen the eerie light and stopped their movements as well.

Katherine heard Abby shift next to her and couldn't prevent a surprised flinch when the animated girl grabbed her left wrist in a tight, excited grip. "This has never happened before," she whispered eagerly.

Katherine couldn't help but to inwardly curse her bad luck.

Before the group could continue onto the property, she quickly made her opinion known. "I think we should leave."

Mallory Flanders, the blonde girl who had stopped directly in front of the Katherine and Abby, smirked over her shoulder at the hurried comment. Jacqueline Smith and Heather Nelson, the other two girls who made up their small group, copied her actions. "You're not scared, are you, Katherine?"

"No," Katherine immediately bit back. And it was mostly true. She wasn't scared, per say. It was just that the terrible feeling that had originated from the bottom of her belly had grown and spread to the rest of her body, making her feel positively heavy with tension. "I just don't think it was a good idea to come here."

"Then I don't know why you came," Mallory replied scathingly.

"We certainly didn't invite you," Jacqueline added.

While Katherine remained unaffected by their comments, only too used to the other girls' cattiness after having put up with it for years, Abby bristled angrily, her grip on her friend's wrist tightening. "I invited her," she protested heatedly, "as you all very well know."

Her angry words merely earned rolled eyes and sneers from the other three girls.

"Whatever," Jacqueline retorted dismissively.

An uncomfortable silence descended after that. Whether the discomfort stemmed from the small disagreement or the light still eerily peeking out at them through the window of the abandoned house, Katherine didn't know. Eventually, Abby hesitantly broke the uneasy silence. "Well, are we going to check it out or not?"

Despite the forced casualness of the question, Katherine could still detect the slight anxiety in her best friend's voice. The other girls were not hiding their nerves very well either. While their expressions remained nonchalant, Katherine could easily see the hidden tension in the rigid way they held themselves. Heather seemed to be the worst off, fidgeting restlessly with her long hair.

Although Abby had aimed the question at all of them, it was Mallory who eventually answered. After glancing once more at the faint light and smirking spitefully in Katherine's direction, the blonde responded. "Why doesn't Katherine go? She says she isn't scared after all."

She stiffened slightly at the taunt. It was true. She *had* said she wasn't scared. And honestly, she still wasn't. The anxious feeling was still there in her gut, but she wouldn't describe it as fear. Trepidation, she supposed, was a more fitting word for it.

"Fine," she retorted curtly, before she had the chance to change her mind. "I'll go." If that's what it would take to convince them to leave, she would sneak a quick look in the light-filled window.

"I'll go with you," Abby assured her, finally letting go of Katherine's wrist so they could comfortably walk together.

The girls had spotted the light thirty yards from the house so it took a moment for them to reach the property and even longer to quietly navigate through the overgrown greenery that thickly surrounded the place. Eventually, Katherine found herself crouched securely below the intended window, Abby right beside her.

After sharing a quick glance with her friend, during which the redhead nodded encouragingly, Katherine carefully straightened up, trying desperately to ignore the tension in her stomach. Her eyes peeked over the sill and… nothing.

Katherine saw nothing more interesting than a dirty floor made of rotting wood and cement walls coated with grime and dust. There were two lumps – undoubtedly pieces of furniture – covered by sheets that may have been white at some point, but that was it.

The light was coming from further within the house, shining through an open entryway leading into some other room. "Abby, I don't see anything." Katherine whispered.

There was no response.

"Abby?" she tried again.

Silence greeted her.

Frantically trying to calm the awful feeling now crescendoing within her, Katherine cautiously glanced down at her friend, who was staring wide-eyed at a patch of bushes directly behind them. Goosebumps forming on her taut arms, Katherine forced herself to look too. She felt her breath catch.

There, not five feet away, two intense blue eyes peered out at her from within the undergrowth. When their gazes met, Katherine froze. She didn't dare move. Her stiff friend beside her seemed to be suffering the same problem.

Both remained frozen as the large figure emerged, but Katherine certainly felt her heart rate pick up when it stepped into the faint light still exuding from the window and she caught her first real look at it.

The creature was massive – all dark fur and sharp teeth. Its strong jaw was easily capable of tearing her small body to pieces. Still, she couldn't bring herself to move. It wasn't until Abby jerkily grabbed her hand and the wolf – for that's what the large animal in front of her was – released a dangerous growl that she felt her senses return to her.

"What do we do?" Abby whispered fervently into her ear.

Katherine, her eyes still locked with the blue ones in front of her, breathed back softly, "Run."

Not giving her friend a chance to react to the command, Katherine took off, dragging Abby roughly by the hand as she desperately searched for a way out of the overgrown greenery that suddenly seemed more like a vicious trap than innocent shrubbery. In her zealous bid for escape, she violently swatted away branches, not caring as the course bark dug into her hands. Abby joined her, both girls frantically trying to make their way through the thick underbrush.

She had heard the beast's enraged howl when they'd run and knew it had to be following them. Somehow – and Katherine had no idea how, for an animal like that had to be dreadfully fast – the two girls made it out of the cruel foliage without the wolf catching them and raced madly towards the three girls still waiting for them a short distance up the dirt road.

"Run!" Katherine yelled to them, repeating what she had earlier whispered to Abby. Her friend screamed warnings alongside her.

At first, the three girls ignored their frantic calls. Quite suddenly, however, they were screaming and running too. Mallory managed an impressively high shriek before turning tail and Katherine just knew that the monstrous wolf had burst out of the trees behind them. Knowing that looking behind her would cost her precious speed, however, she resisted the temptation and instead concentrated solely on the sound of her feet rapidly hitting the ground as she ran, urging her aching legs to somehow carry her faster.

The only warning she got before hitting the ground hard was an infuriated snarl.

The pain hit her immediately.

It wasn't the fall that had hurt her, though she knew she had banged her elbow rather badly. No, the sharp sting was coming from her right ankle and rapidly spreading up her leg. Ignoring the pain, she whipped her head around only to once again come face to face with dark blue eyes. They were frightening in their intensity, but what truly alarmed Katherine was the wolf's jaw clamped tightly around her ankle.

She heard a terrified scream and for a second thought it had emerged from her own throat. She was quickly proven wrong, however, when she caught sight of the horror-stricken Abby who had stopped running as soon as she had heard her friend hit the ground.

In an act of reckless bravery, Abby began racing back towards her fallen friend. She didn't make it more than a foot, however, before Katherine felt an agonizing tug on her ankle, and before she knew what was happening, her body was being dragged backwards – the wolf's jaw still clenched around her, its eyes still intent on her face.

Not knowing what else to do, Katherine frantically thrashed her body about, trying to wrench herself free. Not only did this *not* help, but it intensified the pain in her ankle tenfold.

She could hear her friend yelling her name behind her and didn't think the situation could get any worse when another enormous wolf materialized out of the looming foliage and began sprinting towards them. While not as large as the massive animal dragging her, it was menacing in its own right. No longer able to contain her fright, she clenched her eyes shut tightly, fully expecting the creature to attack her as the other held her down.

She was shocked when instead of feeling sharp claws or teeth dig into her body, she heard a surprised grunt and furious cry before her ankle was freed. Snapping her eyes open, she was stunned to discover the two wolves brutally fighting each other. She watched as the larger wolf – the one that had been dragging her – delivered a particularly violent swipe to the other's face before she remembered that she could move.

Ignoring the excruciating throb of her ankle, she forced herself to her feet and hobbled as fast as she could towards her best friend, who had stopped running and was staring in shock at the warring wolves.

By the time Katherine reached her, Abby had come back to her senses and quickly moved to help her hobbling friend. Within a few minutes, the two had managed to travel up the length of Miller Road and were back in the relative safety of town.

Looking behind her and seeing nothing but darkness, Katherine finally collapsed onto the ground. She could hear her heart beating loudly in her ears as she tried to calm herself. Abby threw herself down next to her. The other girls were nowhere in sight.

For a while, neither could do anything but catch her breath. Eventually, Abby spoke. "Are you alright?" she inquired, looking at the bloodied ankle Katherine had stretched out in front of her.

Wondering the same thing herself, Katherine finally looked at the aching injury. The first thing she noticed was that her sneaker was gone – probably completely torn off her foot by the animal. The second was that it didn't look nearly as bad as it felt. Her sock hadn't even bled all the way through. Taking a deep breath, she brought the foot up closer to her face and carefully pulled off the ruined sock.

It was hard to inspect in the dark of the night, even with the bright moon still gleaming above them, but she could still clearly see the four puncture marks around her ankle, two on the left side of her foot and two on the right. They were slowly oozing blood.

She carefully rotated her ankle, trying to determine if it was broken or even sprained, but quickly realized it wasn't. Surprised, but not ungrateful, she answered her friend. "Actually, I think I'm okay."

Abby heaved a sigh of relief and Katherine managed a small smile when she was pulled into a tight hug. After a few seconds of basking in the knowledge of each other's safety, they pulled away. Abby stood up and offered a hand to Katherine. "You say you're okay now, but wait 'til your parents see you," she joked, voice still trembling a bit from the ordeal they had been through. "After a brutal lecture, they're bound to take you straight to the hospital the town over and get you tested for rabies or whatever."

Katherine groaned at that *very likely* possibility, but grasped the proffered hand. Once she was on her feet, she allowed Abby to slowly help her make her way towards her parents' house. "The lecture I could do without," she agreed quietly, "but the doctor is probably a good idea." She grinned in a self-depreciating manner. "Knowing my luck, I've probably caught something."

CHAPTER TWO

From out of the darkness, two piercing blue eyes stared. Their azure color was just as striking as she remembered. She could feel the intensity exuding from the stare, the sensation causing her skin to tingle. The eyes were demanding – almost begging – something of her.

But she didn't know what.

She was lost in the captivating stare and could only gaze back blankly, her own eyes silently asking the other pair what it was she was supposed to be doing. But she didn't receive an answer. The blue eyes just continued to stare at her, their intensity never wavering.

"Katherine."

She was becoming more and more frustrated with the demanding eyes. Wasn't it obvious that she didn't know what it was that they wanted from her? Even if she desired to do what they begged of her and softly assure the hard eyes, she couldn't. She had no idea what they wanted.

"Katherine."

Helplessness nearly overwhelming her, she silently pleaded with the azure gaze to give her a hint, a clue, anything.

"Katherine!"

Katherine woke with a start, her heart pounding loudly in her ears as she snapped her eyes open. It took a moment for them to settle on the figure in front of her, and she was flooded with relief when she recognized her mother.

Elaine Mayes, in appearance anyway, was perhaps the complete opposite of her teenage daughter. Although well into her forties, the woman didn't look a day older than thirty-five. She was tall, regal and the epitome of aged beauty with long, blonde hair and soft gray eyes. Perhaps the only physical trait that the mother and daughter shared was a pale, smooth complexion.

"Are you alright, Katherine?"

Pulled out of her reverie by her mother's concerned inquiry, Katherine realized she'd been staring and quickly averted her gaze. "Yeah, I'm fine."

Elaine didn't look convinced, a deep frown marring her otherwise pretty features, but wisely chose to let the matter drop. "Alright, but it's already past seven. You should probably be getting ready for school."

Taken aback, Katherine hastily looked at the alarm clock on her night stand. She groaned aloud when she saw the time – 7:13 – blinking innocently back at her. She had overslept.

"Thanks, Mom, I'll be downstairs in a minute."

Acknowledging her daughter with a nod, Elaine left the room.

Katherine fought for a moment to untangle herself from her bed sheets. In her restless sleep, she had somehow managed to wrap them around herself in a complicated cocoon. Once up, she quickly stripped off her pajamas – an old, discarded shirt of her dad's and a pair of too big sweats – and hurried across the room to the small adjoining bathroom. Ignoring the chill that swept through her as her feet hit the cold, tiled floor of the room, she hopped into the shower. She knew she was already running late and probably should have foregone the quick wash, but after waking up in a cold sweat with pieces of her long, brown hair sticking to her damp forehead, she felt the shower was needed.

After fiddling with the silver knobs of the rather ancient-looking shower, Katherine breathed a sigh of contentment when warm water finally burst from the worn shower head. Relaxing under its spray, she allowed her mind to wander.

It had been three days since she had been attacked by that wolf on Miller Road, and she doubted she would be forgetting the incident anytime soon. After Abby had helped haul her home that Friday night, she had been bombarded by her worried parents, made even more frantic after the two girls had explained what had happened. As predicted, Katherine was immediately driven to the hospital of the town over – Hayfield Medical – to have the wound looked over.

In a turn of good luck, which Katherine still had trouble believing, the wolf bite was found to be clear of any infection, and she was sent back home, ankle bandaged in soft, white wrappings, in less than an hour. In the weekend of rest that followed, the pain of the wound had slowly subsided into nothing and she found she could walk and put pressure on the limb without feeling any discomfort at all – almost like she hadn't been mauled by a wolf just three days ago.

No, the only side effect that Katherine seemed to be suffering from was the dreams.

Every night since the attack, the intense blue eyes of the dark wolf had haunted her sleep. They weren't nightmares – she didn't feel the least bit afraid in them – but they were bizarre, and not just a little unnerving.

After waking from them, she'd always feel guilty that she couldn't understand what the blue eyes were trying to tell her – like she was failing the owner of the eyes in some way. Katherine sighed softly at that thought, scolding herself for thinking something so absurd.

She grabbed the shampoo and began working it through her thick hair. *Why should she feel guilty about upsetting a wolf – one that had attacked her, no less?*

Now that she was out of immediate danger and far away from the violent beast and its strong jaw and sharp claws, Katherine often caught herself looking back on Friday night and admiring the beauty of the animal that had attacked her. Both of the wolves she had seen had been remarkable, but the blue-eyed one especially had left an impression on her. Its body had been huge and powerful, and its dark – almost black – fur had been sleek and beautiful. Even the snarl that had dominated the wolf's face had done little to take away from the animal's handsome features. He – Katherine was almost positive the wolf had been a male – had truly been a magnificent creature.

Katherine shook her head a little at the direction her thoughts had taken. *Was she really describing the ferocious animal that had attacked her as magnificent?*

Perhaps she had been infected by the wolf's bite after all and one of the side effects of said infection was slowly going batty.

Reaching for the knob to turn off the warm spray, Katherine forced herself to stop thinking such thoughts.

Quickly wringing out her hair of excess water, she stepped out of the shower and grabbed a towel to dry herself off. After wiping herself down, she used the same towel to clear away the condensation that had formed on the bathroom mirror during her brief shower.

Katherine sighed when confronted with her reflection.

She had never been particularly impressed with her looks. Growing up with an exceptionally beautiful mother and older sister, she had always thought that she herself was rather plain looking. Her pale face was mostly unremarkable with a small nose and nondescript pink lips. Big, wide eyes dominated the majority of it, their color an odd mix of green and gray. Neither color really overpowered the other, giving them a rather murky appearance overall – almost like mud. Unlike her mother and sister, who both had beautiful – not to mention manageable – blonde hair, Katherine's mane was a dark chocolate brown and refused to lie straight no matter what she did with it.

Deciding that she didn't have time to blow dry the dark mass atop her head, she grabbed another towel and dried the wavy hair as best as she could before reentering her bedroom and quickly throwing on a fresh outfit – a pair of black skinny jeans and a simple white t-shirt. She snatched up her blue and green plaid jacket from atop her desk and her book bag from where it sat abandoned on the floor before opening and closing her bedroom door and rapidly descending the stairs.

Following the smell of burnt toast into the kitchen, Katherine immediately spotted her father near the toaster, cursing as he attempted to remove the blackened bread from the small machine's still hot slots.

Benjamin Mayes, Katherine supposed, was a handsome man for his age. His head was still full of brown, though graying, hair, and his dark eyes were easily capable of charming anyone – even the meanest of old spinsters in Middletown.

Elaine was seated at the kitchen's center island, chuckling at her husband's antics as he attempted to free his burnt toast with a fork. They both turned their attention to their daughter as she entered.

"Good morning," Katherine greeted them before making a beeline for the cold cereal. She had had enough of her parents' concerned lectures the past weekend to last a lifetime and hoped to escape the house that morning before being subjected to yet another one.

"How's your ankle feeling?" her dad asked as she sat across the island from her mother, placing a bowl of corn flakes on top of the dark wood.

"Okay," she answered. "It doesn't hurt anymore."

She tried to ignore the pointed glances her parents gave each other. "That's good news," Elaine finally offered. After a brief pause she added, "Does this mean you still plan on trying out for cheerleading?"

Katherine tensed slightly at the question. Sometimes it felt like her parents were always pushing her to join the same extra-curricular activities, like cheerleading, for example, that her older sister Samantha had been a part of when she was still in high school. Katherine didn't mind some of them and actually enjoyed the book club she was a member of and the track team that she would be joining again in the spring.

Cheerleading, however, she despised.

It mainly had to do with the fact that most of the other cheerleaders – Mallory Flanders, for instance – seemed to enjoy making her life miserable. It didn't stop her from trying out every year though. She knew that her parents would be let down if she didn't. "That's the plan," Katherine answered her mother.

"That's great," Elaine encouraged with an enthused smiled. "I'm sure you'll make the squad. You always do."

Katherine didn't bother to point out that everyone who tried out always *did* make the squad. With a town as dinky as Middletown, coaches couldn't exactly afford to be picky.

Benjamin, unlike Elaine, wore a concerned frown at his daughter's answer. "Are you sure you're up to that? That ankle of yours is still healing and I don't want you injuring yourself any more than you already have."

Katherine clenched her teeth, a little irritated at what her father's words had implied. "Right. Because it's always been a dream of mine to become the chew toy of a rabid wolf," she bit out testily before standing up and dumping out her half eaten bowl of cereal into the kitchen sink. "I have to get to school."

Benjamin cringed at his daughter's harsh tone. "That's not what I meant," he immediately began to explain, but Katherine had already been told enough times by her parents how reckless her actions had been on Friday night and was in no mood to hear more on the subject. Sometimes it felt like they just wanted another perfect Samantha clone and it made her feel like such a disappointment. She knew they didn't do it intentionally, but it still hurt.

She hurriedly exited the kitchen and shoved her feet into the new pair of sneakers her parents had bought for her. After all, one of her old pair had been lost to that wolf.

Ugh.

It seemed that no matter the topic, her thoughts always strayed back to that wild animal.

Berating herself, Katherine threw her book bag over one shoulder and headed for the attached garage where her car – a beat up Chevy that used to be Samantha's – sat waiting.

Moments later, she was reversing out of the driveway and heading towards the high school that was located less than a mile away. The trip only took a few short minutes before she was carefully parking her vehicle in the student lot.

The high school in Middletown – creatively named Middletown High and home of the "fierce" bulldogs – was perhaps the biggest building in the entire town.

Which wasn't saying much.

The brick structure was a mere three stories high, and combined with the teacher and student parking lots, took up a little over half of the small block it was located on.

It was only the second week of the new school year, but to Katherine it felt like school had already been in session for months.

She entered the school from the south side doors, the ones nearest the student parking lot, and swiftly made her way to the junior hallway where her locker was located. She was relieved to see teenagers still mulling around, indicating she had made it on time. She was even gladder to see Abby waiting for her by her locker.

"Hey, Abby."

Startled by Katherine's greeting, the redhead nearly dropped the bedazzled cell phone she had been furiously texting away on. "Katherine!" Abby exclaimed excitedly. "You're not going to believe this!"

"What-" Katherine began to ask, but was abruptly cut off as her arm was grasped by her worked up friend. She was hastily tugged into the nearest girls' restroom.

"You're not going to believe this," the girl repeated more quietly after checking the stalls of the room and making sure they were all empty, "but the rumor mill is going absolutely berserk with stories about you!"

"What? Why?" Katherine instantly responded, incredibly confused. She stubbornly ignored the butterflies that had suddenly sprouted wings in her stomach, firmly telling herself that she didn't care what other people were saying about her.

"Somehow the fact that you were attacked by that rabid wolf on Miller Road is going around the school," Abby explained intently. "Half the students who've heard the story apparently thinks you're dead and the other half thinks you've been mauled so badly that you've lost a limb or that your face has been deformed or something."

Katherine fought the urge to roll her eyes at the dramatics of the student population. "Let me guess," she replied. "Mallory started these rumors."

Abby winced slightly at that. Despite Katherine's contempt for the snobby blonde girl and her gang of friends, Abby got along with them all rather well. "It's possible," she admitted, looking a little sheepish.

Katherine sighed. She determinedly repeated to herself that she didn't care about stupid rumors – especially about any concerning her.

"It's fine," she breathed out, forcing the tension to leave her body. "They'll all have seen that I'm alive and well by the end of the day. Let them talk until then if they want to."

"If you're sure," Abby replied, still looking concerned, but letting the subject drop. She glanced down at her cell phone. "Shoot, it's already past eight. We only have three minutes to get to Pre-Calculus." She made a face, her opinion of the math class obvious.

The bell rang immediately after the girl's announcement, almost as if in support of her assessment. "I'll meet you there," Katherine quickly assured her friend as they left the restroom. "I still have to drop by my locker and grab my books."

Abby nodded and bounded off to class, leaving Katherine on her own by her locker.

She was all alone in the hallway, the other students having set off for their own classes. After what the animated redhead had told her about the latest gossip, Katherine was relieved. She wasn't looking forward to the stares and prying questions that she knew would be thrown her direction all day long. After all, an animal attack was big news in Middletown.

She was actually surprised Abby had gotten the chance to warn her about all the gossip before she'd been stopped and questioned by other students on her way into the school.

Dreading the rest of the morning, but already on the verge of being late to class, Katherine forced herself to speedily enter the combination of the padlock protecting her locker. Snatching the lock off the metal handle, she opened the slotted door. With a startled gasp, however, she banged it shut again.

What the...?

She felt as if her heart had leapt into her throat and was now lodged there, pounding hard. After taking a moment to calm its erratic beating, she carefully reopened the locker door, convinced she had been mistaken. Cautiously peeking into the metal box, however, she quickly realized she had not been.

For there, sitting innocently on the top shelf of her school locker, was the sneaker she was sure had been lost forever on Miller Road.

Katherine wasn't sure what to think.

Was this some sort of prank? Perhaps, but she was almost certain that except for herself and her parents, only Abby had been aware that she had lost a shoe on Friday night.

And she had literally just unlocked her locker two minutes ago. It had been locked all weekend and no one, not even Abby, knew the combination. Maybe her friend had told others that she had lost a shoe, but that still left the question of how whoever had planted the shoe had gotten into her locker in the first place.

She was getting nowhere with these thoughts.

And worse, that familiar feeling of awful foreboding was rising in her gut.

Taking a deep breath, Katherine forced herself to calm down. *There's no point in panicking*, she told herself firmly. It was probably just a dumb prank. Deciding that it was best to forget about it for now, she quickly gathered her books.

She firmly closed her locker and double-checked to make sure the padlock was fastened correctly. Then, pushing thoughts of the shoe steadfastly to the back of her mind, Katherine made her way to Pre-Calculus.

Despite what she had been trying to prevent all morning, she was five minutes late for class.

Katherine noticed the looks in Pre-Calculus, but didn't let them get to her. It helped that she shared the class with the rambunctious Abby, who was not-so-secretly doing her best to distract her – both from the stares and the class itself. Abby absolutely detested math in all its forms.

Her next class, English, passed in much the same manner. In fact, it wasn't until Katherine's third period class, the one directly before her lunch break, that she was even questioned about the animal attack.

The class in question was American History. Katherine could swear that the class had been covering the same information since she had first had it in fifth grade. Every year, the teacher spent way too much time on the Revolutionary War and the class would end with the students barely having touched upon the Industrial Revolution. Forget anything that had happened after that. Katherine seriously doubted any student in the school knew much of America's history past the early 1900's.

As it was, Mr. Jeffers was in the midst of explaining how the British government had formed the thirteen colonies – something Katherine had heard a dozen times before – when it happened. A neatly folded piece of notebook paper was placed atop her desk.

She looked questioningly at the girl who had put it there – Beth Sanders – who, in turn, gestured across the small, clustered classroom until her finger was pointing directly at one Brad Thompson.

Brad was perhaps the most popular boy in the entirety of Middletown High. Like Katherine, he was only a junior, but he was both the quarterback of the football team and the point guard of the basketball team.

In addition to his prowess in sports, he was also considered to be very good looking. He was tall and muscled with dirty blonde hair and supposedly irresistible blue eyes. That thought made Katherine reflect briefly on the intense eyes of her dream wolf. And she couldn't help but think that, in comparison, Brad's eyes were rather dull. Said eyes suddenly caught her staring, and Katherine quickly looked away.

Crinkling her forehead in confusion, she wondering why Brad Thompson of all people was sending her a secret letter in class. She hesitantly unfolded the paper note. *Are you okay? Mallory told me what happened.*

Now she was even more baffled.

Why did Brad care? He was Mallory's boyfriend – had been since junior high – and the blonde had undoubtedly told him many nasty stories about Katherine.

Like how the brunette had stolen her favorite marker from her in third grade or something equally as stupid.

Not wanting to give Mallory yet another reason to dislike her, she wisely chose to ignore the random note. Unfortunately, she couldn't escape fast enough when the bell signaling the end of class rang.

"Katherine!"

She winced at the loud call, but had no choice but to slow her pace to allow Brad to catch up – there was no way she could have pretended to not have heard *that*.

"Hey, did you get my note?" he asked eagerly.

He had obviously seen that she had. Katherine sighed, hugging her history book closer to her chest. "Yes, and thank you for your concern, but as you can see, I'm perfectly fine."

"Are you sure?" he asked imploringly. "Mallory made what happened sound really bad, like, I don't know, your eyes had been gauged out or something."

Katherine fought the urge to roll her supposedly gauged out eyes. "Nope. Both still here and accounted for."

Brad laughed a little at that, rubbing the back of his neck sheepishly. "Yeah, I can see that."

Either not noticing or choosing to ignore her obvious discomfort, Brad trailed Katherine all the way back to her locker. He seemed nervous for some reason. Maybe because she was refusing to make eye contact with him. But she didn't want to encourage him, she reasoned with herself.

"So, uh, Katherine," Brad began when it became clear she wasn't going to say anything more on the subject. He was leaning against the locker next to hers as she put away her books and grabbed her lunch money – stubbornly ignoring the object on her locker's top shelf as she did so. "I know that we don't really know each other all that well, but, uh, do you want to sit with me and my friends at lunch today?"

Katherine was surprised by the strange request, but recovered quickly and responded to his question in a firm voice. "Look, Brad, I'm sure you're a nice guy and all, but you're Mallory's boyfriend and, no offense, but I have no desire to make my life any more difficult than it already is."

Brad looked a little uncomfortable at her mention of the blonde girl. "Actually, uh, Mallory and I broke up this weekend."

Katherine couldn't say she was shocked. Brad and Mallory had been dating for years, but their relationship had been notoriously on-again-and-off-again.

At least now she knew why the popular boy was talking to her. Everyone at school knew that she and Mallory didn't get along and what better way to get his ex-girlfriend fuming with anger than to ask Katherine to sit with him at lunch? Well, too bad for Brad that she had better things to do than be a pawn in some immature attempt to make Mallory jealous.

"I'm sorry to hear that," Katherine eventually replied, her tone still unyielding, "but I don't think it's a good idea to upset her, and I'm sure we both know that me sitting with you at lunch would do just that."

Brad looked genuinely surprised by how she'd interpreted his request. "But that's not-"

Katherine interrupted him before he could say anything more. "I've got to go. I'm meeting up with Abby and I'm sure she's wondering where I am."

Refusing to let Brad get another word in, Katherine hurried down the hallway, leaving the boy to watch her as she left, completely flabbergasted at what had just occurred.

Katherine told Abby what had happened as soon as they found a secluded area in the cafeteria where they could privately eat their lunches. Abby was astonished to say the least and had instantly demanded why she hadn't taken Brad up on his offer. "Have you gone 'round the bend?" she asked hysterically. "Refusing Brad is, like, committing social suicide. He's the Edward Cullen of Middletown High."

Katherine couldn't help but be entertained by her friend's antics, but quickly explained herself nonetheless. "No amount of popularity is worth Mallory's scorn. She already hates me. I can only imagine what she'd do if she thought I was moving in on her ex-boyfriend." She rolled her eyes, emphasizing the silliness of that notion.

Abby begrudgingly conceded the point. "I guess."

"Besides," Katherine continued, smiling amusedly at her friend, "the look on Brad's face when I said no was totally worth it."

Abby let out a startled bark of laughter at that and shook her head incredulously. "Only you would think something like that."

The rest of the school day passed basically uneventfully for Katherine. She still received some odd looks, no doubt due to the circulating rumors, but Brad didn't approach her again. And she had even managed to successfully keep the mystery of the shoe still sitting in her locker banished from her mind. Katherine would go as far as to say that her afternoon had been positively dull until the final school bell of the day rang and cheerleading try-outs began.

She picked up on the negative energy as soon as she entered the locker room to change into her work-out clothes.

Mallory, Jacqueline, and Heather, who were whispering conspiringly to each other in a corner of the room, immediately became silent when they spotted her. She could feel their glares on her back as she quickly tugged on her shorts and loose-fitting t-shirt.

Abby, who had entered the locker room with her, looked nervously at the group of girls. Katherine could only assume that someone had told Mallory about Brad inviting her to sit with him at lunch, and that was what had the girl so aggravated.

Mallory's anger became more and more obvious throughout the try-outs. She had to have purposefully bumped into Katherine half a dozen times while they were being taught routines to memorize, and she was fairly certain her toes were bruised from being stomped on. The blonde had even completely knocked her off her feet once, immediately offering a falsely sweet apology after doing so, but it had obviously been more for Couch Benson's sake than Katherine's.

Just as Katherine had expected would happen, everyone made the squad and the coach let them go after announcing that voting for team captain would take place at the end of the week.

It was only after try-outs were over that Mallory finally confronted her.

Katherine was one of the last girls left in the locker room, having opted to wait to use one of the more private stalled showers rather than the large communal one. She had just tugged on her shirt and was about to pull her gym bag out of her locker when the metal contraption was slammed shut. Startled, Katherine turned around to come face to face with the furious Mallory.

"I always knew you were pathetic Katherine, but I didn't think you'd stoop so low as to go after someone else's boyfriend."

Katherine sighed. *She just knew something like this was coming.* "I don't know what you're talking about."

Mallory's face twisted into a mocking smile. "Really?" she asked, sarcasm dripping from her voice. "Because Heather told me you were talking to Brad today before lunch."

"So?"

"So?" she repeated indignantly. "So what makes you think you're allowed to try to seduce my boyfriend?"

"I'm not trying to seduce anyone's boyfriend!" Katherine immediately retorted, beyond irritated by the other girl's totally off base assumption.

"Then why were you talking to him?" she demanded, not looking like she believed Katherine's claim for a minute.

"*He* was talking to me. He invited me to sit with him at lunch! And he said you two broke up so don't start in on me about going after *your* boyfriend."

Mallory's face paled at that, her angry expression deflating a little. After a moment, however, her scowl quickly snapped back into place, and she looked twice as livid. "Don't think that just because he's talked to you it means he's interested," she bit out cruelly. "Why would Brad want someone like you, a desperate little nobody, when he could have someone like me?"

Katherine's shoulders slumped a little at the hurtful comment despite the voice in her head telling her that the blonde was just lashing out at her due to her own insecurities. "Look, Mallory-"

"No, you look," she rudely interrupted. "If I find out you talk to, or even look at Brad again, you'll regret it. Keep your grubby paws to yourself." Warning given, Mallory stomped furiously out of the locker room.

Katherine sighed. *Why did Mallory have to be so dramatic?* She tried to shake off the confrontation, choosing instead to concentrate solely on packing up her gym bag.

It wasn't until Katherine left the locker room and began walking back towards her hallway locker to grab her homework that she finally allowed her mind to return to the shoe. She had almost been able to forget about it with all of the Brad and Mallory drama.

Almost.

Making the quick trip to her locker after try-outs was forcing her to once again confront that particular issue, however.

After packing her books and homework into her book bag, she finally made herself take a good look at the shoe. The sneaker, which had been white not more than three days ago, was now a dingy-looking gray and covered with filth.

Cautiously picking up the shoe, Katherine could see that the tongue was in tatters and that its sole and red laces were missing.

Katherine startled and almost dropped the grimy sneaker when she saw what appeared to be a crumpled piece of paper shoved deep into the toe of the shoe.

What in the world?

Taking a moment to remind herself to breathe, Katherine immediately recognized the feeling rapidly growing in her gut. It was the same feeling that had plagued her three nights ago at the old, abandoned house on Miller Road and again this morning when she had first seen the shoe.

Forcing herself to push past the horrible feeling of apprehension, she carefully slid her trembling fingers inside the decrepit sneaker.

Plucking out the small, crumpled ball, she slowly straightened out the shabby piece of paper. Sloppy cursive stained the paper in black ink.

You are in danger. If you value your life, meet me tonight at the house at the end of Miller Road. I'll be waiting.

CHAPTER THREE

Blue eyes were staring at her again. They were more zealous than ever, almost urgent in their intensity. The eyes were begging her to listen, to do as she was told. But what do you want, she felt like screaming. What could you possibly want?

Katherine woke with a start, gasping for air and drenched in a cold sweat. After taking a moment to calm her erratic breathing, she slowly relaxed her fingers from where they were clenching her bed sheets in tight fists. Untangling herself from the blankets that she had managed to twist around herself, she sat up tiredly.

Katherine blearily looked at the alarm clock on her nightstand. It informed her that it was barely past five in the morning and she sighed, knowing there was no way she'd be able to fall back asleep.

Ignoring how stiff her body felt, she pulled herself out of bed, intending on going for a brisk morning run. She hoped the exhilaration she usually experienced while running would serve to relax her frayed nerves.

However, even as she prepared herself for the planned run – changing out of her pajamas and throwing on a tank top and a pair of loose athletics shorts – she couldn't stop her mind from drifting back to her dream.

It had happened again.

Every night since the events of the Friday last, the stubborn wolf – or the animal's penetrating eyes at least – had haunted her dreams, and every night the eyes were getting more and more insistent. But she still had no idea what they wanted.

The dreams were slowly wearing on her and she often woke up feeling more tired than she had before falling asleep. As a result, she felt more exhausted than she had in a long time and didn't need to look in the bathroom mirror to know that there were dark circles under her eyes.

A suppressed shudder wracked her body as she thought of the intensity at which the blue orbs had stared at her. The dreams didn't frighten her exactly, but she was becoming increasingly unsettled as they grew in both frequency and intensity. They were a constant distraction and she was spending more and more time daydreaming about what they could mean.

She had gotten so desperate for answers that she had even checked out a book – *The Hidden Meaning Behind Your Dreams* by Stephanie Crown – that had been tucked away in a secluded corner of the school library. Upon reading it, however, she quickly realized it would be little use to her. The only thing she could find about eyes appearing in dreams was a passage describing interpretations of what it meant when dreamers dreamed of their own eyes.

According to the book, seeing one's eyes in a dream represented unconscious or repressed thoughts, often hidden desires of the soul, that were breaking through the surface of consciousness.

It sounded like a load of tripe to Katherine.

Not that it mattered.

She wasn't dreaming about her own eyes. She was dreaming about someone – something – else's.

Shaking herself out of her thoughts, Katherine snatched a hair tie from her night stand so she could quickly pull back her wavy hair – made even more unruly after having slept on it – into a messy ponytail. She grabbed her MP3 player on her way out of her bedroom before quietly tiptoeing down the stairs, not wanting to wake her parents. She made quick work of tugging on her sneakers – their stark whiteness a constant reminder of their newness – before letting herself out the front door.

After finding an energetic song to run to, Katherine plugged the MP3 player's buds into her ears and started up the driveway. Soon she was jogging at a comfortable pace, the slight morning breeze cooling her face as she ran.

It was still rather dark out, the sun just barely peeking through the horizon, but Katherine knew Middletown like the back of her hand and could have easily navigated the small town even if it had been completely black out.

The brunette was slowly able to unwind as the run had the invigorating effect she had hoped it would. Unfortunately, as her body relaxed, her mind began to wander, the music blaring in her ears gradually becoming more like background noise.

As was typical of late, when Katherine's mind wasn't preoccupied with thoughts of the strange dreams she'd been having, it turned to thinking about the note she had found in her tattered shoe.

She still didn't understand it. Not only did Katherine have no idea how whoever had planted the shoe had managed to get into her *locked* locker, she had no idea why they would *want* to do it. The only explanation she could come up with was that it had been some sort of prank – a prank that had failed when she didn't show up on Miller Road that Monday night.

It had been five days since then – it was Saturday morning – and nothing had ever come of her not going.

But that didn't mean that strange things weren't happening.

Katherine was sure that her body was changing in weird ways that had nothing to do with puberty, but she was the only one who seemed to notice it.

When she had brought it up with her mom earlier in the week, Elaine had been quick to assure her daughter that she was merely experiencing the "natural changes" that all teenagers went through. Insert shudder here.

Katherine severely doubted that all teenagers went from being able to run a mile in about six and a half minutes to running it in about five and a half. She didn't know anyone who could increase their speed and endurance that quickly without some serious training. She hadn't even felt winded after she had finished that mile either.

It wasn't just that.

In cheerleading practice, she was more flexible and graceful than she had ever been before. She was doing handstands and toe-touches as she had never been able to do them. She thought puberty was supposed to make teenagers awkward and clumsy, not whatever *this* was.

Katherine supposed most people would be grateful for the changes, not questioning them as she was, but her sudden aptitude in athletics was not the only thing she was concerned about. Her body temperature had been inexplicably warm lately – like she was running a fever without the other symptoms of illness. It seemed that no matter what she did, she couldn't stay cool for long. This, unfortunately, had gotten her into quite a bit of trouble in the past few days.

In an effort to keep herself as cool as possible, Katherine had taken to wearing as little as possible. She never wore anything vulgar, but for someone like Katherine, who rarely wore revealing clothing, showing up at school in short shorts and tank tops was apparently enough to cause a small scandal.

The resulting confrontation with Mallory was still at the forefront of her mind.

She had been sitting with Abby in the cafeteria on Thursday when the blonde and her gaggle of impersonators had approached their table.

Mallory sneered at Katherine before grabbing the edge of the tabletop and leaning towards the unimpressed brunette in an intimidating manner. "I sure hope it's not Brad you're trying to impress with that appalling outfit," she bit out snidely, "because I happen to know that he doesn't go for desperate sluts."

She'd spoken loudly enough for her sidekicks to hear and they snickered at the comment.

"Funny how he ended up with you then," Katherine retorted before she could think better of it.

Abby, startled by the unexpected comeback, began choking on her laughter.

Mallory immediately flushed at the retort and glared at the laughing redhead until she managed to get herself under control, looking a little sheepish as she finally did. Then the blonde trained her eyes back on Katherine. "I'd watch yourself if I were you," she warned before stomping off.

Katherine snorted as she pulled herself out of the memory. *What was it exactly that Mallory was threatening to do? Spread rumors? Pull her hair?*

She had much more important things to worry about. Like her sudden improvement in athletic ability. Like her sudden spike in body temperature. Like the strange cravings she'd been having for red meat.

It was perhaps the oddest of the changes she had been going through and the sudden cravings had come completely unexpectedly. It had first hit her on Tuesday evening.

She had gotten back from cheerleading practice and was working on her biology homework – explaining the difference between mitosis and meiosis – when she'd smelled the steaks cooking in the kitchen. The aroma had been so enticing that she'd abandoned her homework halfway through a sentence and had followed her nose to the kitchen where her dad had been cooking up a half dozen steaks over the stovetop. Before Katherine was even aware that she'd intended to speak, she had opened her mouth and blurted, "Can you make mine rare?"

Looking back, she was fairly certain that she'd looked as surprised as her father had at the request. Katherine had never asked for her meat to be anything but well done in the past. Nonetheless, the man had agreed and half an hour later she had devoured the best steak of her life. It had been so tender and pink – not to mention juicy – that she'd managed to polish it off in record time, finishing her meal well before her parents.

Since that night, all she had been craving was meat. She preferred red meat, but poultry was okay as well. Other foods, however, had lost their appeal to Katherine. The smell of the cabbage casserole her mother had made the other night, for example, had smelled so terrible – so rancid – that she had been sure her mother had used bad cabbage. Both of her parents had assured her after trying it that it tasted perfectly fine. Still, Katherine refused to touch the stuff, opting to make herself a quick hamburger – meat still a little pink in the middle – instead.

It wasn't just cabbage either. An assortment of other foods – mostly vegetables like broccoli and asparagus, greens that she'd always enjoyed in the past – were now completely unappetizing to her.

Food wasn't the only thing her suddenly enhanced sense of smell picked up on either.

For the first time in her life, Katherine realized that people had *scents*. She wasn't referring to the funky smell that always followed around her history teacher, Mr. Jeffers, or even the flowery perfumes that Abby often saturated herself in.

No, people had scents beneath all that. Like her dad, who smelled a bit like worn leather, or her mom, whose natural fragrance more closely resembled lilacs. Not everyone had a pleasant aroma, however. Mallory's smell, for example, was putrid – not unlike the stink of sour milk.

No one's scent was overpowering and she often only caught whiffs of people as they walked by – and that was only when she put her mind to doing so. It was when she spent a lot of time with people, like her parents, or even Abby, who smelled a little like freshly cut grass underneath her heavy lavender perfume, that she really noticed it.

Katherine sighed, forcefully pulling herself out of her daydreams. She couldn't be certain, of course, but none of the books her parents – mostly her mom – had bought for her and her sister about puberty mentioned the strange ability to *smell* other people.

Frankly, Katherine thought it bizarre.

Realizing that as she had daydreamed, her MP3 player had played through quite a few songs and was in the midst of a particularly sappy ballad about unrequited love – not a good song to run to – she reached down to the device in her pocket so she could change the sound track to something a little more upbeat.

It was because she was looking down that she completely missed the man who had suddenly appeared in front of her. By the time she looked up, it was already too late and she collided full speed into him, eyes wide as she glanced up just in time to crash into his solid mass.

She was shocked that she didn't plow him down, despite their rather substantial size difference. Instead, she practically ricocheted off him, her body flying backwards. It was a battle to stay upright on her two feet – a battle she was losing – until firm hands grasped her hips and righted her, allowing her equilibrium to return to her.

An embarrassed flush rising up her neck and spreading to her cheeks, she quickly stepped out of the man's grasp. "I'm so sorry," she immediately apologized, refusing to look up at his face as she did so – too mortified to, really. "I wasn't looking where I was going."

"Are you alright?"

Katherine froze at the question. Not because it was unusual – she would probably ask the same thing if someone had crashed into her running as fast as she had been. No, her body had stiffened so quickly because she immediately recognized that she did *not* recognize the voice.

No one in Middletown had such a cultured timbre.

Curiosity nearly overwhelming her, Katherine looked up despite her embarrassment. And what she saw stole her breath away. *Those eyes*. They were a familiar and intense blue – remarkably similar to the pair that had been haunting her dreams for over a week now.

The same, her subconscious screamed at her, *they're the same!*

Katherine didn't even realize she was staring – quite rudely, she imagined – until the man cleared his throat. "Well, are you alright?"

Katherine quickly commanded control of herself. "Yes," she managed to respond, voice not the least bit shaky, she noticed proudly. She pulled the MP3 player's buds out of her ears, quickly putting the small device back in her pocket. "I apologize for nearly running you down. I was distracted and didn't see you."

The stranger – and he was certainly a stranger, for Katherine had never seen him before – didn't respond right away, and it allowed her the opportunity to really look at him now that her eyes weren't glued to his in shock.

He looked a lot younger than she had originally thought, his somber voice making him seem so much older than he must have been.

In fact, Katherine wouldn't say he was much more than two or three years older than herself.

He was also astonishingly handsome – the best looking male Katherine had probably ever seen. He was tall – well over six feet – and though he was somewhat lanky, he had an obviously muscular build. His angular face was perfectly symmetrical and framed by dark, disheveled hair that suited him entirely. He had an attractive nose and strong jaw, which Katherine had to admit made her heart start beating a little faster than it should have been. And of course, there were his blue, blue eyes, which were currently studying her as indiscreetly as she was him.

Both of them averted their gazes, however, when a rather loud *bang* sounded to the right of them. Katherine looked over her shoulder at the noise, and saw that the elderly Ester Johnson, one of Middletown's most notorious gossips, had stepped out of her house and onto her front porch, unashamedly watching them as she settled into a rocking chair.

Shaking her head at the blatant invasion of privacy, Katherine turned back to face the man she had run into only to find that he was once again looking at her, this time, though, with a furrowed brow and a frown pulling at his mouth. Katherine tried not to take the stranger's less than friendly expression personally, but couldn't help her heart from sinking a little, though she had no idea why.

Finally he spoke, an obvious dismissal, as he turned his back on her. "Be more careful next time," he bit out gruffly before taking his leave.

Katherine watched him as he stomped away, torn between feeling disappointed that the stranger who shared her dream wolf's eyes was such a prick and anger that he had so rudely dismissed her – like she was a mere annoyance for him. A bothersome little girl.

Katherine grit her teeth at that thought and even sent a small glare towards Mrs. Johnson, who was still watching her rather interestedly. She was positive the stranger wouldn't have been so coarse with her if the old coot hadn't so tastelessly announced her presence.

As Katherine jogged away from the spot of the collision, she berated herself for taking the stranger's rejection so personally. So what if the man – whatever his name was – had been handsome and made her heart race a little? So what if she felt an odd connection with him? He was obviously a jerk and she would never waste her breath on someone like that.

It wasn't until Katherine returned home from her jog and was in the middle of having breakfast – she had made herself a few sausages, as that's what she was craving – that she realized she had crashed into the man almost directly in front of Miller Road. A chill rushed through her when she realized it, a too familiar feeling of trepidation flooding her.

Almost immediately, however, she resolutely pushed the feeling away. She wasn't going to waste her weekend lost in thoughts of the wolf attack, Miller Road, the note, or the strange changes her body was experiencing. They would only lead her in circles, anyway, and give her no solid answers.

With that in mind, Katherine opted to shove her realization about where she'd collided with the stranger to the back of her mind, determined to examine it at a later date – preferably, a *much* later date.

For the majority of the weekend, Katherine was successful in her endeavor to forget her latest worries. It was Sunday evening, however, that everything came to a head.

She had just gotten out of the shower and was critically inspecting herself in the mirror. Despite her sudden improvement in all things physical, her body looked much the same as it always had. She was still slender – no sudden protruding muscles – and still rather on the short side. Gazing at her face, however, she could see one noticeable difference in her appearance.

Her eyes.

For as long as Katherine could remember, they had always been a sort of muddy combination of green and gray. Now, however, they seemed much brighter – the green, more vivid than she could ever recall, almost completely outshined the gray, which was only present in a small ring around her pupil.

Not only were her eyes brighter and more noticeable, but they seemed more alive, sharper somehow than they had ever been. And, oddly, they looked more dangerous as well. Like they belonged in the face of some spirited dare devil, not her – average little Katherine Mayes. The dark circles under them – largely the result of her restless sleep – only served to emphasize them more.

Even Abby, who was normally about as observant as a small child, had noticed them and asked where she'd gotten the sweet contacts.

Forcing herself to look away from the eyes reflecting back at her from the large, glass mirror, Katherine quickly pulled on her normal oversized sleepwear, intending on going to bed early in a bid to catch up on some of the sleep she'd been missing lately. Her plans were thwarted, however, when she heard her mother calling her from downstairs.

"Katherine!"

Sighing loudly – and a bit obnoxiously, she could admit – she forced herself to exit the bathroom and make the trek down the stairs. She first checked the living room, but upon finding it empty, made her way to the dining room. "Mom? What do you need?"

When her mother smiled mischievously at her from where she was standing next to her dad – who was looking vaguely amused himself – she knew that she should have just stayed upstairs and pretended to not have heard.

When her mother didn't immediately answer her question, Katherine quickly grew impatient. "What?" she asked again, her irritation showing through a bit.

Her mom's smile didn't fade, however, and her dad looked no less amused.

"With a temper like that, it's a wonder that you even managed to get an admirer," Elaine finally replied teasingly.

Katherine frowned in confusion. "What are you talking about?" she asked once it became clear she wasn't going to elaborate.

Her dad laughed a little at her question, his loud chuckle filling the room. "You don't have to hide it from us," he said through a grin. "I promise not to be too hard on him if you bring him around for dinner."

Katherine's frown grew and she crossed her arms over her chest defensively, trying to ignore the heat she could feel creeping up her neck. She would *not* blush. "I really don't know what you're talking about."

Elaine lifted her hand, revealing that she held something in it. A crumpled paper note. Katherine immediately tried to squash the apprehensive feeling that threatened to overwhelm her at the sight of it. "What's that?" she demanded.

"You don't have to be embarrassed, Kit," her mother replied, smiling even as her daughter cringed at the *special* nickname that she and her father had bestowed upon her as a child. "You're turning into a beautiful young woman. It's only natural that others are starting to take notice. You're sixteen after all. I remember Sam having already had a few boyfriends by your age."

Katherine would have been surprised if her face wasn't completely red by that point. Not only was she terribly uncomfortable with the compliment, but she hated being compared to her sister.

"Hey!" Benjamin objected good-naturedly. "I'll be perfectly happy if Katherine chooses to remain single through her thirties," he told his wife in a playfully stern voice before smiling at his daughter.

Torn between embarrassment and anger at her parents' antics, Katherine impatiently bit out her next words. "I told you that I have no idea what you're talking about!"

Elaine's smile finally deflated a bit and Benjamin frowned at his daughter. "Katherine, there's no need to get so worked up. You have to expect a little ribbing if you allow your parents to find a love letter."

Katherine glowered, still not knowing what in the world they were talking about. Elaine sighed and held out the piece of paper to her daughter. "I found this in one of your pockets," she explained. "You always forget to clean them out before putting your shorts in the dirty laundry."

She quickly snatched the note from her mother, hoping her blush was beginning to fade a little.

Before her parents could tease her anymore, she pulled open the crumpled paper.

What she saw made her temporarily lose her ability to breathe. She felt the blood drain from her face as she recognized the sloppy cursive. This time, the message was actually addressed to her.

Katherine,

We need to talk. You know where. Sneak away as soon as you can. Please.

Like the first note, it was not signed. Before Katherine could react – though she had no idea how she was *supposed* to react – she felt a hand on her shoulder, jolting her out of her distressing thoughts.

"Are you alright?" Elaine asked.

Katherine glanced up at her parents, both of whom looked concerned. Her reaction to the note must have startled them.

"I'm fine," she choked out. But she wasn't fine. Not even close. "Just tired."

"It better not be because you've been sneaking out to see this boy," Benjamin pointed out, and in her numb state, she couldn't tell if he was joking or not.

Katherine immediately shook her head. "Of course not," she managed, barely hearing herself above the sound of her heart palpitating in her chest. She quickly shoved the note into a pocket of her pajamas. "I'm going to bed," she informed her parents. "I need to catch up on some sleep."

"You have been looking awfully tired lately," her mother agreed, seemingly willing to let the subject of the love letter go for now. Katherine allowed herself to be pulled into a brief hug. "Sleep well."

When her father had also bid her good night, she quickly left the dining room, barely able to stop herself from rushing up the stairs.

Once in her room, Katherine immediately took out the piece of paper and began to study it. The handwriting definitely matched the one on the note that had been planted in her locker. But just as she had no clue how that note had gotten into her locker, she had no idea how this note had made its way into one of her pockets. She felt like she should know – like all the clues were there – but she was coming up empty.

Perhaps because she didn't truly want to examine her thoughts too closely. She was almost afraid to. Because if she did and found the answer to all of the questions that had been plaguing her, she didn't think she'd like what that answer would mean for her. She didn't think she'd like it at all.

CHAPTER FOUR

Katherine couldn't believe that she was actually going to go through with this.

Staring at the boy in front of her, however, she didn't really see what choice she had.

Her parents were completely convinced that the note they had found last night had been written by her "boyfriend" and despite her insistence that it had not been, and no real evidence pointing to the contrary, they had been adamant that she bring him to supper that evening.

Her first instinct had been to refuse, but she didn't particularly want to deal with the consequences of that. Her dad, in fact, had threatened to investigate the situation for himself if she didn't bring the boy over.

The problem with that? There was no boy. Only some whack-job leaving her weird messages in which he insisted she meet him.

And her parents definitely didn't need to know *that*.

So there she was, about to do something she knew would have some very unpleasant consequences. All because of that stupid note.

"Hey, Brad."

A small *bang* and muffled curse greeted her. The blond boy looked irritated as he pulled himself out of the confines of his locker, a rapidly growing red mark on the center of his forehead where it had connected the metal. The annoyed expression was quickly wiped from his face, however, when he saw her. He offered her a flustered smile. "Hey, Katherine."

She took a deep breath. It was now or never.

Oh how she wished she could pick never.

"Are you busy tonight?"

Brad looked surprised by the inquiry and Katherine could hardly blame him. It was only last week that she had turned down his offer to sit with him at lunch, after all. He quickly recovered, however, and asked her a question of his own. “Why do you ask?”

Reminding herself that it had to be done, Katherine plastered on the friendliest grin she could manage. “Well, I was wondering if you wanted to come over later.”

Brad’s earlier surprise was nothing compared to the astonishment he showed now. His eyes were the widest she had ever seen them.

“You know, to my house?” she clarified, hoping to jolt him out of his shocked stupor.

It seemed to work and he let loose a bit of an embarrassed laugh. “I figured that.” To her frustration, however, he still didn’t answer her question.

“Well?” she persisted, trying not to let her exasperation show through.

“I would like to go,” he admitted. The hesitancy in his voice, however, didn’t exactly encourage her. “But I can’t help but wonder why you’re inviting me. You didn’t really seem interested in hanging out the last time we talked.”

“Only because of Mallory,” Katherine immediately objected, though it wasn’t exactly true.

Brad must have known because he didn’t look convinced. “Well, nothing’s changed on that front,” he pointed out. “Mallory would still probably freak if she knew we were spending time together.”

Katherine sighed, resigning herself to telling Brad the truth. She supposed it was better this way anyhow. She didn’t *really* think he was interested in her, but she’d still feel better about the whole thing if she was honest with him.

“The truth is I’m in a bit of a bind and need a favor,” she confessed. “Some idiot thought it’d be a good idea to write me this silly note and my parents found it and for some crazy reason are convinced that it was some sort of love letter. They’re insisting I bring whoever wrote it to supper tonight.”

Katherine did her best to ignore the strange guilty feeling that swelled within her as Brad's expression dimmed at her explanation. "You want me to pretend to be this person?" he questioned, having worked out her intentions.

"Yes," she confirmed, despite the guilt that continued to gnaw at her. "You're the only one I feel comfortable asking," she added, though she wasn't sure why because it wasn't exactly true.

She didn't feel comfortable asking anyone.

Brad just happened to be the most convenient. She was almost positive he'd agree, if only to rile up his ex-girlfriend. It was the reason he'd ask her to sit with him at lunch last week, after all.

"Okay, I'll do it."

Immediately relieved by his positive response, the inexplicable guilt Katherine had been feeling all but dissipated. "Thanks, Brad," she replied, truly grateful. "You're really helping me out. Supper's at seven. Does that work for you?"

Brad's face brightened a little at her obviously heartfelt gratitude, the smile he was sporting looking a bit more genuine. "I'll be there," he quickly assured her.

Katherine offered him a few more words of thanks before turning and walking away, feeling mostly satisfied with how her conversation had gone with Middletown's most popular jock. Though, to be honest, she was dreading the unavoidable confrontation with Mallory that she knew was coming later.

She had almost reached her locker to unload her history book when Brad called out to her. "Katherine!"

The small brunette stopped and turned, hoping the boy hadn't changed his mind *already*.

"Just so you know," he half-shouted across the busy hallway, "whoever wrote that note probably wasn't joking around like you think. A lot of people like you, Katherine – they can tell there's something about you. Something special."

Katherine could feel her whole face heat up at the comment and knew that she was probably red enough to put a tomato to shame. She had no idea how she was supposed to respond to something like that.

Luckily, Brad didn't wait around for a response, opting instead to offer her one last smile before turning away.

Special?

Katherine snorted in disbelief.

Unless he was talking about *that* kind of special, she couldn't help but think that he was wrong.

She didn't give much more thought to Brad and their upcoming "date" until nearly noon when Abby bombarded her at lunch. The blond boy must have told his friends about their plans because there was no other way the redhead could have found out.

"Is there something you need to tell me?" her friend demanded as soon as they had found somewhere to sit. Despite her harsh tone, the girl looked positively giddy.

Weighing her options carefully, Katherine decided that denial was her best bet. "No."

Abby blinked, looking rather dumbfounded at the unexpected response. "No?"

"No," Katherine repeated, fighting off the smile she could feel trying to emerge, as she took in her friend's flummoxed expression.

Abby caught on rather quickly, however, and smacked Katherine playfully on the arm. "Don't you lie to me, Katherine Elizabeth Mayes! Why didn't you tell me you liked Brad?"

Katherine paused, wondering how she was going to explain herself. "I don't, but-"

"And here I thought you were the only girl in the whole school who *didn't* like him," Abby continued, ignoring Katherine completely. "Why, all this time you've just been hiding your true feelings!"

"But I don't-"

"I knew there was a reason you've been dressing differently at school," she went on, talking more to herself than Katherine at that point. "Showing off your legs and all that."

"*What?!* I haven't-"

"Na-ah-ah," Abby interrupted, finally acknowledging her friend's protests. "You don't have to explain anything to me, Katherine." Her eyes glazed over a bit. "I can't believe it. My best friend. Going out with Brad Thompson."

"Look, I don't like Brad that way," Katherine tried again, attempting to get through to the redhead. But it was to no avail. It was like she didn't even hear her.

"I'm so jealous." Abby sent her disgruntled friend a mock glare. "I wish I could get Brad to notice me."

Just then, loud yelling from across the cafeteria caught both the girls' attention. Turning to the sudden noise, Katherine winced at what she saw.

She immediately spotted Mallory, who was jabbing an angry finger into Brad's face. Brad wasn't reacting – just sitting there and looking unsure as to what he should do. The blonde girl caught Katherine staring and glared wrathfully in her direction. If eyes could kill, Katherine would already be six feet under. She quickly looked away.

Abby, who suddenly appeared rather pale, the freckles splattered across her nose more prominent than ever, caught her eye from across the table. "Perhaps I don't envy you as much as I thought," she joked weakly, sneaking another glance at the quarreling couple across the cafeteria. "Come to think of it, I'm glad Brad doesn't notice me."

Despite Abby's following premonition of Katherine's gruesome death by Mallory's hands, however, she didn't see the blonde – not even during a shared class, British Literature – until cheerleading practice. To her surprise, Mallory steadfastly ignored her in the locker room and throughout most of the practice.

Unfortunately, that didn't stop Mallory's friends – Heather and Jacqueline mostly – from making awful faces at her and constantly tripping her when the coach wasn't looking. Not even her newfound grace could help her and she lost track of how many times she ended up on the ground.

Katherine was finally given a reprieve around six when Coach Benson blew her whistle, signaling the end of practice. She was sitting on the floor next to Abby, stretching her legs and arms with the rest of the squad, when the coach made an announcement.

"I've tallied the votes for team captain that you girls cast last Friday," she informed them as she clasped her hands together excitedly.

Katherine saw Mallory straighten up from where she was sitting across from her and squashed the urge to roll her eyes. Everyone on the squad, including Mallory, knew the blonde was a shoo-in for the position.

"And the captain of the bulldog cheerleaders this year, as voted in by her peers is," Couch Benson paused, trying and failing – at least in Katherine's opinion – to create a sense of anticipation. "Mallory Flanders!"

Katherine clapped politely with the rest of the girls as the blonde's name was announced, though certainly not as enthusiastically as Mallory's sidekicks.

"And Katherine Mayes!" the coach declared abruptly, catching everyone by surprise. "It was a tie! Looks like this year, the squad will have co-captains!"

Abby squealed and slapped her on the back excitedly, but Katherine was ignorant of her friend's reaction and the other congratulations she received. She couldn't take her eyes off of Mallory, who's previously pleased expression had quickly turned sour.

Katherine didn't understand it.

Why did so many of the squad vote for her to be captain? She wasn't even that good at… *Oh.*

She *had* been doing really well in practice the past week – she was more nimble and agile than she'd ever been before.

She felt the sudden urge to scream. *Great. Just great.* Another reason for Mallory to hate her.

Suddenly, Abby's premonition of her death wasn't looking all that unlikely. She hoped Mallory didn't have any sharp objects handy – like a pair of tweezers or nail clippers – in the huge purse she liked to haul around.

"I'll need both of you girls to stay after practice so we can discuss some of your responsibilities as co-captains."

Coach Benson's instructions jerked Katherine out of her morbid thoughts. She glanced at the clock and just barely suppressed a groan. It was already twenty minutes past six. If the coach was as long winded as she normally was, there was no way she'd be able to shower and make it back to her house before Brad arrived for supper.

Half an hour later, she and Mallory were finally dismissed. Katherine forced herself to keep her shower brief – a mere five minutes – before she quickly dried her hair with one of the coarse towels the school provided and made her way to her locker to change into a fresh set of clothes. Mallory, too, had finished showering, and the atmosphere was tense as they both dressed, the only two left in the locker room.

"Going to be late for your little date with Brad, aren't you?" Mallory asked coldly, breaking the silence.

Katherine debated if she should even bother responding before deciding she could probably save herself some trouble by telling the girl the truth. "Mallory-"

"Forget it," the blonde briskly interrupted. "I give up. You win, Katherine."

Katherine was truly perplexed. Mallory sounded tired, an almost defeated quality in her voice. "What's that supposed to mean?"

"Don't act innocent. You know," Mallory accused. "You have Brad. You have captain. You have *everything* I want. So congratulations. You win. You've managed to completely ruin my life."

"I don't-"

"Save it," Mallory snapped before slamming her locker shut and storming out of the room, leaving Katherine alone in the empty space. Something resembling guilt began to form in the pit of her stomach. She scolded herself as soon as she identified the feeling. Mallory had always been horrible to her and she had absolutely no reason to feel bad for the girl.

She pushed the feeling away. Just like she had to so many of the other negative feelings she'd been experiencing lately.

Katherine caught a glance of the clock on her way out of the gym and clenched her teeth in frustration when she saw the time. It was already past seven. All she could do was hope that Brad's football practice had run late and that he hadn't shown up at her house yet. She wasn't optimistic, however, when she didn't see his car in the near-empty student parking lot.

She forced herself to drive a little faster than she usually would have on the way home and hurriedly parked her car in the garage when she saw Brad's Ford pick-up sitting in front of her house. She entered the house through the door connected to the garage.

"Mom? Dad? Brad?" she called as she haphazardly shucked off her shoes.

She didn't receive a response, but didn't think much of it as her attention was immediately consumed by the awful smell permeating the air. She followed the odor down the carpeted hallway and into the kitchen where she immediately spotted the large pot of stew on the stovetop. She quickly turned off the burner it was sitting on and lifted the pot's lid, only for her nose to be further assaulted by the horrid, burnt smell.

She grabbed a nearby spoon to mix the lumpy concoction, but quickly realized that it was a lost cause. Blackened meat and potatoes stuck stubbornly to the bottom and sides of the pot. The stew was completely ruined.

"Mom?" Katherine yelled from the kitchen, surprised that her mother had forgotten about food on the stovetop when she knew there was a guest coming over for supper.

When she once again didn't receive a response – from her mom, dad, or even Brad – an uneasiness began to settle in her gut. The house was almost *too* quiet.

And her mom would never allow the stew to burn this badly.

Where was everyone?

Determined to put her foolish fears to rest, Katherine quickly dropped her book bag off on the counter and exited the black and white tiled kitchen in search of her parents. As soon as she entered the next room, however, she froze.

For there, lying prostrate on the floor, was her father. Thick blood gushed from a deep wound on his side and even more of the red substance was trickling down from his forehead.

Around him, what used to be the dining room lay in shambles. The table and chairs were in pieces and lay haphazardly around the room. Broken glass from her mother's china cabinet was everywhere. A vase that just that morning had held a dozen daffodils was smashed near her father's head. And under a large pile of rubble, made up mostly of pieces of the wooden table, Katherine could make out a shoe-clad foot and part of a leg. The shoe she vaguely recognized as one of the pair that Brad had been wearing that morning.

"Dad!" Katherine shouted frantically, not thinking twice before running – feet protected only by thin socks – across the floor covered in jagged wood and sharp glass. The pain didn't register as she knelt by her father's side – small pieces of glass digging into her knees – and gently grasped his face in her hands. To her immense relief, he blearily opened his eyes.

They widened in alarm, however, when they focused on her. "Kit," he rasped and managed to weakly grab onto one of her wrists. "You have to leave."

"What happened?" she demanded, choking a little on the tears gathering at the base of her throat as she took in the total destruction of the room around her. "Who did this?"

"Run," her father insisted, ignoring the question completely. "Please. You have to run. They're here for you."

Katherine felt the blood freeze in her veins. "Who's they, dad?" she asked desperately. "Are they still here?"

He nodded feebly, looking as if he was on the cusp of losing consciousness. "Have to run, Kit. *Please*."

"Where's Mom?" Katherine asked, shaking her father a little in an attempt to keep him awake. "Do they have her? Is she hurt too?" She was all too aware of her mother's absence.

Benjamin tried to answer his daughter, but a harsh coughing fit consumed him before he could. Katherine absentmindedly noticed the red spatter that resulted from the coughing, half of which ended up on her shirt.

To her horror, her dad's eyes closed after that, and worse, his grip on her wrist went lax. In her panicked daze, she couldn't tell if he was still breathing or not.

Forcing herself to get up, Katherine rushed into the adjoining living room and headed straight for the phone, intent on calling for help. When she lifted up the receiver, however, she quickly realized there was no dial tone. "Damn it!" she cried, slamming down the phone in helpless fury.

Immediately catching her mistake, however, she whipped out her cell phone from her pocket.

But before she could dial 9-1-1, it was smacked out of her hands. She was grabbed from behind and didn't even have the chance to scream before she was slammed to the floor and the breath was stolen from her lungs. "Don't even think about shouting for help, little girl," a big man wearing a ski mask warned from where he stood above her.

Another masked man, this one shorter than the first, clucked disapprovingly at his partner from where he casually lounged against a wall. "This ain't no little girl," he pointed out nastily before stomping a boot-clad foot down on her cell phone, destroying it beyond repair. "This here is just a dirty, rotten creature that needs to be put down." The man's beady eyes glinted cruelly at her from the holes in his mask.

"Who are you?" Katherine demanded, ignoring the sharp pain in her side from being thrown to the ground as well as the fear that enveloped her at the shorter man's words.

"You aren't in any position to be demanding things, little beastie," the same man retorted. Her fear only intensified when he pulled a small, but sharp-looking knife out of his jacket and pointed it at her threateningly.

Katherine took a deep breath and forced herself to remain calm. When she opened her mouth again, her voice came out as soft and submissive sounding as she could make it. She didn't want to give the man a reason to use that blade. "What do you want?" she asked delicately. "Why are you here?"

"We're here because monsters like you don't deserve to live," he bit out snidely.

"I don't know what you're talking about," Katherine pointed out sensibly. She was frantically trying to think of a way out of the situation she'd found herself in. "I'm not a monster. I'm a person, just like you."

The man paused at that, seeming to think about what she said.

"Think she knows, boss?" the taller man asked.

The beady-eyed one only snorted at the question. "Doesn't matter," he said indifferently. "She still has to die."

Katherine clenched her fists in frustration at his callous response. She knew then that there was no reasoning with either of the men in front of her. They were insane – completely and utterly mad.

"Why are you doing this?" she yelled angrily, any attempt at appearing meek and compliant forgotten. "I've never hurt anyone! My dad's never hurt anyone!"

The taller man sneered at her. "Maybe not yet, you've never hurt anyone, but it's only a matter of time. Your dad was just collateral damage. It's really too bad you dragged him into this."

Did they not realize that they sounded more and more unhinged with every word that came out of their mouths?

"I still have no idea what you're talking about! You haven't explained why you're here – why you're doing this. And where's my mom?"

"Dead," the smaller man replied unsympathetically, shrugging his shoulders a bit. "Just like your little boyfriend. Your dad's dead too – or at least, he will be shortly."

And Katherine finally cracked. Knife or no knife, she flung herself at the smaller man. She hit and kicked and clawed at him everywhere she could. The suddenness of the attack worked to her advantage and she was winning the physical battle until the man's bigger partner once again seized her from behind and threw her brutally to the floor.

It was just as the disheveled and infuriated man looked ready to pounce on her that a loud *crash* – the unmistakable sound of a window breaking – alerted Katherine to the fact that another person was about to join the fray.

And join he did, immediately distracting both men as he sprinted into the room and slammed into them. Although she'd seen him only once, she immediately recognized her rescuer – the wild, black hair was a dead give-away. "Run!" he bellowed at her.

She didn't need to be told twice.

Katherine bolted from the room, trying to ignore the colossal shame she felt at having to leave her dad and Brad. But she knew she wasn't physically strongly enough to drag either of them with her and still get away in time.

She was getting help, she reminded herself firmly. She wasn't leaving them there. She was getting help.

Because the front door was blocked off by broken furniture, Katherine was forced to head back to the door connected to the garage, intent on running to a neighbor's house and calling the police.

She had just opened the door when she heard it. A deep howl of pain.

Katherine paused her hurried movements, concerned for the first time that if she left the stranger with those men, he could get hurt or worse, die. *Should she stay and try to help him?*

Her indecision cost her precious time and before she could dodge the masked man who suddenly appeared, she was thrown violently into her car, the back of her head smacking hard against unyielding metal. "You're not getting away, you little monster!"

Following her instincts, Katherine kneed the man where she knew it would hurt the most. When he buckled, but didn't go down, she swung her fist wildly, ramming it right into his nose. She heard a satisfying crack before he finally toppled over.

Wasting no time, she threw herself into her car, her original plan of running to a neighbor's house dashed. She jammed the key, which she thankfully still had in her pocket, into the ignition, twisting it and bringing her car to life.

The man forced himself up as soon as she'd revved her engine and began violently banging on her driver's side window. She didn't have time to open the garage car door, so slamming her Chevy into reverse, she drove straight through it.

She managed to get the vehicle onto the street, the furious man chasing her down the driveway, screaming obscenities at her as he did. Katherine hoped that the commotion would alert someone to what was happening.

Somehow, despite her trembling hands, she was able to maneuver the car past the man. Looking into her rearview mirror, however, she could see him jumping into a black BMW that was parked across the street from her house. She berated herself for having missed it when she had gotten back from cheerleading practice. She had been too focused on Brad's truck.

The BMW sped off the curb and was soon on her tail. Katherine raced through town, but to her distress, couldn't shake the man. Praying that her parents would forgive her, she whipped her car out onto the highway, hoping she'd be able to lose the BMW in time to get them some help.

CHAPTER FIVE

For the first time in nearly two hours, Katherine thought she may have finally lost the black BMW. She hadn't seen it emerge from the last back road she had taken and could only hope that the masked man driving it had made a wrong turn somewhere on the twisting gravel.

Until now, he had been on her tail the entire time, even threatening to run her off the road on one occasion. After that, she'd been forced to abandon the much too open straightness of Highway 67, continuously turning off onto rarely used back roads in attempts to lose the crazed man.

She had somehow made her way back onto the main highway a few minutes ago and had seen no sign of the black BMW since. She remained suspicious, however, and couldn't stop herself from glancing into the rearview mirror every few seconds, expecting to see bright headlights every time she did so.

Despite her fears that it was some sort of trick, she knew she'd have to pull over somewhere soon. Every time she looked at the gas gage, the pointer got closer and closer to E.

Empty.

She was almost out of gas and she'd have to stop whether she thought she'd truly lost the black BMW or not.

Katherine had thought she'd be relieved when she finally lost the fanatical man chasing her, but the truth was, as the adrenaline she'd been running on for the past few hours began to fade, so did whatever was keeping her together. She felt more and more nauseous as the true horror of the situation she had found herself in sunk its claws into her.

All she could think about was her dad bleeding out onto the dining room floor, blood gushing from his side. Her mom, scared and hurting somewhere. Brad, unconscious and suffocating under a heavy pile of rubble.

And the man who had so fearlessly come to her rescue. The howl of pain she had heard before getting away. Was he going to be okay?

Were any of them going to be okay?

Dead. That's what the cruel man had told her in his cold, emotionless voice. *They were dead.*

But Katherine couldn't bring herself to believe it. She knew that if she did, she'd completely lose whatever strength she had left. She'd surrender to the terrible pounding of her head and give up. But if that happened, those evil men would win. And Katherine couldn't allow that. She *would* get help for her parents, for Brad, and for the man who had saved her.

So many emotions filled her as she thought of them – especially her mom and dad. She'd been so defiant and disrespectful to them lately. Now the frustration that usually enveloped her when she thought of her parents was replaced with burning regret. All she wanted was to be able to apologize for every hurtful comment she'd ever directed at them.

And then there was Brad, who had been so kind to her despite the rudeness she had shown him just the week before. Cold, hard guilt nearly consumed her as she thought of how he wouldn't have even *been* at her house if she hadn't asked him to come over. It was all her fault that he was hurt – or worse, *dead.* She had dragged him into this, whatever *this* was.

That thought triggered something within her and the words that the malicious men had spewed at her returned at full force.

"It's really too bad you dragged him into this."

Like it was somehow *her* fault that they had attacked her dad. Her mom. Brad. Like *she* was responsible. Katherine's grip on the steering wheel tightened as more of the men's words resonated in her head.

"This ain't no little girl."

"This here is just a dirty, rotten creature that needs to be put down."

"We're here because monsters like you don't deserve to live."

Monster? She wasn't a monster. There were no such things... *were there?*

For a moment, the evidence nearly overwhelmed her. The wolf attack. Her increased prowess in all things physical. Her improved sense of smell. Her sudden cravings for red meat. The notes. The dreams of nothing but blue, blue eyes.

But... but that was preposterous! It couldn't possibly be true!

Katherine quickly regained control of her thoughts and shoved the ludicrous theory as far back into a dark corner of her mind as possible. *No.* None of that had anything to do with what was happening. Those men were just crazy. Plain and simple. They had to have been. Monsters like that weren't real. They didn't exist!

And Katherine refused to believe even for a moment that they did.

Because if they did... then that would make what was happening completely her fault. And she couldn't handle that. So if she felt a painful twinge in her chest as she denied *their* existence, well, she'd just have to chalk it up to her imagination.

Forcing herself to concentrate on more pressing matters, Katherine glanced down once again at the gas gage. She couldn't suppress the panic that rose when she saw that the indicator was now pointing firmly at the E. If she didn't reach a town soon, her car would break down, and she'd be a sitting duck. She couldn't let that happen. She needed to get help – not only for herself, but for Brad and her parents. *They're still alive*, she told herself firmly. They had to be.

The problem, however, was that Katherine had no idea where she was.

She had never taken most of the back roads she'd forced herself to brave and didn't recognize the section of Highway 67 she had ended up on. To be honest, she wasn't even completely certain what direction she was going.

Was it really just a few hours ago that she'd been worried about hurting Mallory's feelings? It seemed like a lifetime had passed since then.

All of her earlier concerns – like her parents' reactions to the true nature of the note they had found, or how to best avoid Mallory's wrath – seemed so trivial. So insignificant. Especially when she couldn't get the image of her dad choking on his own blood out of her head. Or the grotesque picture Brad's leg had made sticking awkwardly out of that pile of debris.

It took all of Katherine's will power to push those memories aside. She needed to focus solely on driving and looking for any farm houses that she might be able to spot from the highway. She needed help and would take it from anyone at that point. Unfortunately, she had yet to spot a residence.

She was losing hope of finding help before her car ran out of gas when she saw it. About half a mile up the road was a gas station. The shabby-looking building stood alone and for one horrible second, Katherine thought it had been abandoned. As she drove closer, however, she could see that the lights were on, and that a glowing, neon sign – though only three of the letters lit up properly – proudly proclaimed the place to be Gary's Rest Stop.

Tears of relief flooded her eyes when she saw the lights and sign, but Katherine refused to let them fall. She hadn't cried yet and couldn't afford to give into the temptation now.

As she sped closer to the gas station, she could see that it even had a pay phone located only a few feet from the right side of the building. It was practically screaming for her to use it. Glancing once more into the rearview mirror and seeing nothing but the darkness of night behind her, she hastily pulled into the gravel lot that surrounded the building and parked near one of the gas pumps.

Finally.

She could get help.

Katherine looked once more at the phone. Should she head straight for the little booth or ask for assistance from whoever was running the station? She shifted her gaze to the building's entrance. She frowned when she noticed the group of rough-looking young men lounging against the brick wall near the double glass doors, a rusty white van parked not far away. How could she not have seen them before?

There were five of them, all wearing beat-up jackets. Even from a distance, Katherine could see that they were filthy. They were laughing uproariously as one of them – the tallest one of the group, who had a red bandana wrapped around his greasy-looking hair – pointed in the direction of her car. In essence, they were exactly the type of men her mother had always warned her to stay away from.

Her mother. *Dead.* No! No, she was not dead and she was going to get her help right now! Decision made, Katherine grabbed the spare change she would need to be able to use the pay phone.

She glanced once more at the suspicious-looking men by the station's door, and seeing that they no longer seemed to be paying her any mind, she quickly opened and closed her car door and rushed to the pay phone. When she got there, however, she couldn't stop herself from letting out a curse. "Damn it!"

The cord connecting the phone to the booth had been completely severed – no doubt bitten through by animals of some sort. She took a deep breath to calm herself. It was fine. So what if the phone didn't work? Surely the gas station manager would help her.

Katherine hadn't taken more than a few footsteps toward the building, however, when she realized something important. She was covered in copious amounts of blood. Who knew how whoever was running the station would react upon seeing her?

Katherine saw the restroom attached to the side of the building and made the split second decision to use it. She was certain she could get at least some of the blood off. She hurried to its entrance, determined to be in and out in less than a minute.

The room was positively grimy. The walls and floor were encrusted in dirt and other disgusting muck. The smell was even worse – a rancid odor originating from the door-less stalls and encompassing the whole room. Katherine forced herself to ignore the unsavory conditions of the dank place, however, and headed straight for the single, cracked mirror. She cringed when she saw herself.

She looked absolutely horrid – like something out of a horror movie. Her hair was a mess, wayward waves going in all kinds of directions and a part of it plastered down with dry blood. She gingerly touched the spot and flinched at the unexpectedly sharp pain. It was definitely where the throbbing in her head was originating from. It must have happened when her head had been thumped against her car.

Her clothes were in even worse shape than her brown locks. The jeans she wore weren't too bad, but her blue top was covered in dark stains that she knew to be blood. Katherine didn't even hesitate in tugging the shirt off. She turned on the sink's faucet and waited a moment for the brownish-yellow water to run clear before sticking it underneath the stream. After rubbing out the stains as best as she could, she used the drenched shirt to wipe the dried blood from her face and scrub at her matted hair despite the dull pain it caused her.

Once finished, she rinsed the once-blue shirt out again before yanking it back over her head. She felt the goosebumps rise on her arms as the damp, cold shirt stuck to her skin.

Katherine then spent the next half a minute roughly washing her hands, desperate to get the blood off her arms despite the absence of soap or hot water. It was a difficult task as the pink stains extended all the way up to her elbows. She knew where they had come from. Her father. He had looked so lifeless when she had last seen him. But she refused to believe she had her *dead* father's blood on her hands. Just absolutely refused to acknowledge the possibility.

Knowing that she'd done the best she could do, and not wanting to waste any more time, Katherine swiftly exited the unsanitary restroom, relieved to be rid of its odor. Taking a deep breath to calm her nerves, she marched determinedly around the corner of the station and headed straight toward the building's entrance.

She had resolved to ignore the men still loitering near the double doors. They were even grubbier up close – all five of them with sweat and grime caking their faces. And some even smelled worse than the restroom she'd just come from. She didn't react when the bandana-clad man whistled and called out to her. "Hey, doll face. What brings ya 'round these parts?"

Katherine quickly pulled the glass doors open, not turning to acknowledge the man. Relief flooded her senses as the doors closed behind her, making a resounding *ding* as they did. She was so close to getting help.

The noise should have announced her presence to the manager, but no one greeted her as she walked up to the counter, and there was no one behind the cash register either.

"Hello?"

Katherine didn't receive a response. Not even the sound of shuffling feet. In fact, the place was entirely too quiet. An empty sort of quiet. Katherine felt her stomach plummet as realization dawned.

She hadn't seen any other vehicles parked out front except for her own and that rusty van. One of those thugs – maybe all of them – was running the place. Fantastic. And she had just snubbed one of them.

Reminding herself that those men were the only chance she had of getting help for her parents and Brad, she forced herself to go back outside. The *ding* of the door, which had served to relieve her a mere minute ago, suddenly seemed more ominous as she exited the building.

The group of men eyed her as she came back out, the one who had spoken to her looking especially smug. She approached them as confidently as she could manage in her soiled clothes and ignored the snickers she heard as they found amusement in her predicament.

"What do ya know, boys? Looks like the little princess realized I'm the one runnin' this place."

It was the bandana-clad man who spoke, sharing a dark grin with his companions before turning his eyes back on her. They were gleaming with something she didn't want to identify. "It's okay, doll," he said condescendingly, his voice full of false understanding. "I'm sure ya can make it up to me somehow."

Katherine steadfastly ignored the clashing emotions – hot anger and cold fear – that rose within her. *Be polite*, she reminded herself firmly. *You need help and it looks like this is all you're going to get.*

She clamped her jaw shut and swallowed down a scorching retort, knowing her conversation with these men would end badly if she let her mouth get the best of her. "I'm sorry to bother you," she bit out as civilly as she could manage. "But do any of you have a cell phone I could use?"

One of the men – the scrawniest of the bunch – strutted forward and smiled yellow teeth at her. "I have a phone, sugar, but I can't just let ya go using it for free."

Katherine clenched her fists – whether it was due to indignation or fear, she wasn't certain. "I have money," she pointed out reasonably, hoping her voice didn't betray the emotions swirling within her. "I'll pay you whatever you want if you let me use it."

The rat-faced man smirked. "Oh, sugar, I don't want your money. Ya got somethin' else more to my likin'."

Katherine knew all too well what he was referring to when his eyes swept up and down her body. Aware that her wet shirt was clinging to her skin, she quickly folded her arms across her chest.

The men sniggered at her actions.

"A credit card then," she offered, refusing to acknowledge the man's disgusting leering. "I have one in my car if you want it."

Before he could answer, the tall man with the bandana pushed him back and took up the space he had been occupying, his own phone gripped between his fingers. He was clearly the leader of the little group as Rat Face didn't protest to the rough treatment.

He grinned predatorily, but Katherine refused to be intimidated despite the spike of alarm that traveled up her spine. "I don't think so, doll face. How 'bout some lovin' instead? I haven't had a thing as pretty as you in… well, ever."

Behind him, his friends laughed. Katherine searched their faces for empathy, but couldn't find any – though the scrawny one looked a bit put out. She quickly came to the conclusion that none of them were willing to help her. If anything, they thought the whole situation rather entertaining. Suppressing her disgust, she realized what she'd have to do if she wanted that phone. Forcing what she hoped was a friendly smile on her face, she stepped a bit closer to the man. His grin widened.

"I don't know," she bluffed, glancing coyly at him from under her lashes and playing shyly with a loose thread on her sleeve.

She successfully prevented a flinch when her wrist was abruptly grabbed and the man dragged her closer to him. He leaned into her until his body was pressed against hers. Stale breath hit her nose as he whispered huskily into her ear. "Let me convince you, dollie."

Knowing that she'd been given the opening she'd been looking for, Katherine swiftly kicked the man in the shin. He yelped in a mix of surprise and pain and she quickly snatched the phone from his loosened grip before turning and running back towards her car. She'd just reached the driver's side door and was working to unlock it when the man caught up to her. Large hands seized her arms and in one swift motion, he had her turned around and slammed up against the car, the side mirror digging painfully into her back.

The sense of déjà vu was strong.

So was the nausea the jarring action had caused.

She felt the vomit rising, but could do nothing but clench her eyes shut as foul liquid burst from her mouth and nose and splattered on the gravel and the shoes of the man holding her. When she opened her eyes, her vision was a little fuzzier than it should have been, but she could still clearly see the rage-induced flush covering the bandana-clad man's face.

"Ya shouldn't have done that, princess," he hissed. "I was gonna make this fun for ya, but now you've asked for it."

Still clutching the phone in an unyielding grip behind her back, Katherine tried to focus on the words the man in front of her was saying. But the pounding in her head was rapidly getting worse and she couldn't concentrate. The man's features were growing blurrier as well. *No*, she thought desperately, *not when she was so close to getting help.*

Before she could bring herself to react – to somehow escape the clutches of the threatening thug – she heard it. A car engine. A vehicle was on the highway. She and the men surrounding her looked to the source of the sudden noise and Katherine nearly died of relief when she saw that it wasn't a black BMW, but a huge, dark green SUV. The man holding her against her car backed off a little as the vehicle turned into the gravel lot of the station, though he was still much too close for comfort.

To Katherine's shock, she immediately recognized the man who stepped out of the SUV. Tall, muscular build. Wild black hair. Intense blue eyes. It was the stranger she had run into outside of Miller Road. The same man who had rescued her at her house. He was okay!

But… what was he doing here?

The man – as young as he looked Katherine couldn't bring herself to call him a boy – didn't hesitate in making his way over to them. The tense manner in which he held himself and the way his biceps strained against his shirt gave him away. He was furious. "What's going on here?" he asked coolly.

One of the men – the scrawny one with the rat-like face – sneered at him. "None of your business. Now get out of here, boy. There's another gas station twenty miles up the road."

The man ignored the thug completely, choosing instead to focus his attention on Katherine, who was still feeling rather lightheaded. "Are you okay?" he asked gently.

Gently? The last time he'd spoken to Katherine, the man had been downright cold to her. But then he'd rescued her from those delusional men who'd hurt her parents. And now these ruffians.

Who exactly was this guy?

Katherine wetted her lips and opened her mouth to respond, but the bandana-clad man still standing next to her roughly grabbed her wrist, stealing her attention away from her rescuer.

As it so happened, however, she didn't need to answer Blue Eyes

– she still had no idea what his name was, but Blue Eyes seemed fitting – because as soon as he saw the man grab her, he quickly stepped forward so that he was nose-to-nose with the thug. "Let go of her," he ordered.

The man scoffed in response and refused to relinquish his grip on her arm. "Oh yeah, and what are you gonna' do about it if I don't?" To emphasis the control he thought he had over the situation, he tightened his hold on her arm and yanked her closer to him. The unexpected jerk caused Katherine to stumble and another wave of dizziness washed over her.

Before she could even attempt to regain her bearings, Blue Eyes had physically removed the man's hand from her arm by throwing him against her car. The strength behind the shove dented the Chevy's hood. "I said to keep your hands to yourself!"

The man was clearly surprised by the attack, but quickly recovered and shoved Blue Eyes back, a disgruntled expression on his face. "Mind your own business, boy, or blood's gonna spill," he threatened.

Katherine felt her nausea return at the mention of blood, the last time she'd seen her father once again flashing in her mind. She almost missed it when her rescuer glared contemptuously back at the man and spat out, "Only yours."

The man chuckled at the response. He glanced at his friends before turning a sardonic grin loose on his challenger. "You guys stay outta this," he commanded his gang. "I wanna take this smartass down myself."

Katherine stood silently by her car door, uncertain as to what she should do. The phone was still tightly clasped behind her back, but she couldn't use it with the bandana-clad man's friends still surrounding her. Should she try to help Blue Eyes take the man down? She had a feeling if she did that she'd be more of a hindrance than help. Before she could decide for sure, the thug threw the first punch – or tried to, at least – and the fight started.

It became obvious that Blue Eyes most definitely did *not* need her help.

He took the other man down easily. He was swift and brutal in his attack, sending powerful jabs to the man's face and stomach before pouncing and instantly knocking him to the ground. Once he had him on the gravel, his hands immediately went for the man's throat. His biceps bulged as he squeezed. The man underneath him flailed and struggled to take in air. Soon, however, the thrashing stopped and he lay limp. If Katherine couldn't clearly see his chest still rising and falling, she'd have thought the man was dead.

Blue Eyes picked himself up off the ground, showing not a bit of remorse over his actions. He looked to the man's friends, who suddenly seemed to have lost their swagger. "Who's next?" he demanded, a dark edge to his voice.

The grubby men bolted, leaving their fallen comrade where he lay on the gravel.

As soon as they'd run off, he turned his attention back to Katherine, who was still watching the scene numbly, unsure as to how she was supposed to react. *Thank him*, a voice inside her head insisted. He'd saved her life twice now, after all. But her thoughts were fuzzy and her mouth was refusing to work. Blackness, too, was slowly creeping into the sides of her vision.

"Are you alright?" Blue Eyes asked softly, repeating his earlier inquiry.

But Katherine never heard the question. The pounding of her head became too much and she felt the sensation of being caught by strong arms before everything finally went black.

CHAPTER SIX

Blue eyes again. A dark and blazing azure that threatened to consume her very being. Except... the eyes were no longer hard and demanding, but sad. Apologetic even.

As awareness flooded Katherine's sore body, she was conscious of little but her aching head. A sort of haziness blanketed her thoughts and she couldn't quite conjure the energy to open her eyes. Instead, she devoted herself to lying as still as possible to avoid jarring her head.

As she lay there, she slowly became more cognizant of her surroundings.

She was resting on something soft and though she felt somewhat cramped, she was comfortable enough. Something warm – probably a blanket – covered her body. She was aware of multiple scents permeating the air around her too. There were many, but the sweet smell of sugary vanilla was the strongest.

And then, voices.

As the thick haze that seemed to suspend her thoughts lifted, the clear sound of voices rang though. Katherine didn't recognize the noises for what they were at first. They were merely muffled, jumbled sounds. After struggling to push the pounding in her head away, however, she could focus and identify the strange sounds for what they were. She realized at once, though she didn't physically react, that she didn't recognize them.

"-don't understand why we're going through all this trouble. Look at her. She's a runt – basically worthless to us." The voice was distinctly male and its owner sounded furious.

Another voice, this one just as angry but obviously female, was quick to counter. "She needs us! She's a part of us now whether you like it or not so get used to it."

Katherine vaguely wondered who the "she" they were talking about was. Her heart nearly jumped out of her chest when she realized that it was probably her.

"She's only a girl, Markus." *Another voice*, Katherine thought dazedly. *Who are these people? And how many of them are there?*

Markus revealed himself to be the owner of the first voice she had heard when he heatedly responded. "Shut it, Caleb. No one asked you. And she isn't *only* a girl. She's damn trouble. All she's going to do is attract the wrong sort of attention."

"Like you care about attention! You're just looking for an excuse to dump her somewhere." It was the female voice again.

"We wouldn't have to dump her anywhere if we would have just left her where she was!"

"And what do you suggest we had done, Markus? Just leave her there with those men?"

That seemed to have done the trick as silence was the only response to the woman's question. For a moment at least.

"She took care of that hunter just fine."

His remark was met with an indignant gasp. "You're heartless," the woman spat.

"And you're pathetic," the man flippantly responded.

There was more silence as a sort of invisible tension began to grow. Even Katherine, whose eyes were clenched tightly shut, could feel the air thickening.

"He has a point, Sophie. The odds of her even surviving…"

The new voice – *there's at least four of them*, Katherine thought numbly – didn't get a chance to finish before another one – *five!* – interrupted.

"That's enough."

It wasn't a yell, but certainly wasn't spoken gently either. And its power – for the voice couldn't be described as anything less than powerful – demanded immediate obedience.

Silence followed and Katherine realized that she was holding her breath, waiting for someone to dare disobey what was obviously an order. No one did and she feigned unconsciousness for what seemed like hours, but was probably only minutes, before anyone risked speaking again. And even then, it was the same powerful voice – a low timbre that sounded oddly familiar – that broke the quiet.

"You'll wake her if you keep yelling like you do." The words were spoken softly this time, but the roughness in his voice still promised violence to anyone who dared to disregard its owner.

Katherine heard a derisive snort. "As if a stampede could wake sleeping beauty back there," Markus mumbled under his breath.

If anyone else heard the comment, they declined to respond.

More minutes passed, though they were distinctly more comfortable than the last. Katherine had almost allowed herself to lower her guard when she felt the breath on her ear.

"I know you're awake."

Katherine, though startled by the voice, refused to open her eyes. She tried to keep her breathing even, hoping to convince the owner of the voice – who she believed to be the one they had called Caleb – of her continued unconsciousness.

"There's no use in pretending. It's only a matter of time before the others will know you're awake too."

Figuring the jig was up, Katherine braced herself before slowly opening her eyes and tilting her head up slightly to look at the man who had addressed her.

He wasn't what she had expected. But then again, what *had* she expected? Some mean-looking brute?

How cliché.

No. This man's face matched his voice – he looked kind. Dirty blond hair sat atop his head in a sloppy-looking cut, but his wide brown eyes looked honest and only the slightest hint of stubble covered his cheeks. *He's young*, Katherine realized with a jolt. He looked about the same age as her. Maybe only a year or two older.

Regardless of how non-threatening he appeared, however, she still immediately sprang back when the man attempted to lay his hand on her forehead.

"Don't touch me!"

Katherine's nerves were shot and despite the instincts that urged her to remain calm, she was anything but. Her memories of the past twenty-four hours were slowly coming back to her and she forced her aching body to move and pushed herself as far into the corner of the back seat – she was in a vehicle of some sort, Katherine numbly took note – as she was physically able.

Her panicked shrill and hurried movements immediately caught the attention of the rest of the vehicle's passengers. Her eyes shot from face to face and she quickly realized that as the voices had indicated, there were five other people in the spacious SUV. Like Caleb, they all looked young. She could feel their eyes on her as well – pinning her into place.

She immediately recognized the driver as her eyes connected with the intense blue of his.

"Who are you?" she demanded, addressing her entire unwanted audience, but keeping her eyes locked on the familiar stranger's.

When she didn't receive an immediate response, her agitation only grew stronger, brought on no doubt by a deeper emotion – fear.

"Who are you?" she asked louder, clutching the blanket that had been covering her closer to her chest. "Why have you taken me? What do you want?"

The muscular, brown-haired man sitting in the seat in front of her snorted and she immediately recognized him as Markus when he opened up his mouth. "Cut the dramatics, princess."

Princess.

Images of the disgusting men from the gas station filled her head. She remembered their grotesque appearances. What they had wanted to do to her. Being slammed up against her car – no wonder her head hurt so much – and the man arriving to help her.

Katherine kept her gaze fixated on the driver, who seemed torn between watching her and the road in front of him. "Have you been following me?" she demanded, unsure whether she should be angry or frightened. Or even... *flattered.* She immediately shot that thought down, deeming it ridiculous.

But the man didn't even deign to respond. Markus, however, snorted at the question. "That's one way of putting it."

Katherine struggled to wet her suddenly dry lips. "Are... are you with those men? The ones who attacked my house?" Visions of blood and a dismantled dining room table momentarily obstructed her vision. Her stomach lurched.

"No," the driver immediately spat defensively, turning hard blue eyes on her in obvious anger.

The only other female in the vehicle turned her own glare loose on the man before peeking around the passenger seat to offer Katherine a more sympathetic gaze. "We're not here to hurt you, honey."

Katherine was taken aback by how Amazonian the woman appeared. She didn't even acknowledge Markus's next comment. "Speak for yourself, Sophie."

Katherine hadn't gotten a good look at her until now and even sitting, she could tell the long-haired blonde – this Sophie – was tall. And her solid body, though obviously feminine, spoke of strength and athleticism. If her eyes weren't radiating warmth, Katherine would probably have been more afraid of her than the four men in the vehicle.

She knew how vicious females could be, after all.

While Blue Eyes, Markus, the other nameless male, and even Caleb – who was noticeable scrawnier than the others, but a far cry from puny – had powerful bodies, Katherine was much more impressed by this woman.

What was with these people? Why were they all so strong and... *good looking?* Being in their presence was making her feel small and, truthfully, down-right pathetic.

Still, she wasn't one to let others intimidate her – at least, not let them know that they did. "I'm only going to ask you once more," she bit out steadily. "Who are you?"

The question hung in the air. Katherine could vaguely feel the painful sting radiating from her palms as she fisted her hands and dug her nails into the skin there, waiting tensely for a response.

She watched as Blue Eyes made eye contact with Caleb, the man she was stuck sharing the back seat with. Katherine realized bemusedly that the smell of vanilla was radiating off of him. She forced her own eyes to turn away from blue and meet brown. The man took a deep breath before exhaling. "We're your pack."

Caleb seemed to want to put his hand on her shoulder as he announced this, but kept it cautiously by his side when his first attempt led to her flinching away from him. Katherine was sure that her turbulent emotions must have been playing out across her face.

First, bewilderment. "My *what*?"

But, of course, Markus had no patience for her utter confusion. "We're your pack," he spoke slowly as if talking to a small child. "Your unwilling and resentful pack, but your pack nonetheless."

That hardly helped ease the confusion. "Pack?"

Finally, the nameless dark-haired, dark-eyed man spoke up. "Werewolf pack."

Katherine's racing thoughts stilled.

"That's not funny," she managed to choke out.

"It wasn't meant to be," was the man's calm response.

And then came the denial. "Right," Katherine managed, stressing the disbelief in her voice. "You're werewolves."

"No. *We're* werewolves."

And then she could feel the beginning of panic build up in the pit of her stomach. Because even though it was so ridiculous... it also made so much sense. It was the same absurd idea that had been plaguing her for the past week. Ever since that gigantic wolf had seen fit to take a bite of her ankle.

Katherine found she couldn't talk around the sudden lump that had formed in her throat.

Markus had no such problem and spoke up, a definite sense of mocking present in his voice. "Been experiencing any weird changes lately? Changes you can't explain?"

And *of course* she had. The warmer body temperature. The improved speed. The sudden skill in cheerleading. The way she had been devouring meat. The damn dreams.

"For me, the change in diet was the worst. I was a vegetarian before... well, *before*," Caleb added in a sincere attempt to be helpful.

But to Katherine, his words were like poison – proof that the changes her body had been experiencing weren't all in her imagination. And she just couldn't accept the alternative that he – that each one of them – was offering her.

"Werewolves aren't real," she finally managed to bite out. "They don't exist."

Katherine ignored the hurt look that spread across Caleb's face and dismissed the ache in her chest that her own words seemed to cause her.

She also refused to acknowledge how her current company tensed at her response. Markus was the least affected. He merely rolled his eyes. "She's a goner."

"Shut up, Markus," Sophie immediately spat at the rude man. But Katherine found the driver's response – Blue Eyes, as she'd christened him – much scarier. His glare – though directed at Markus and not her – sent a thrill of chills through her body. Markus, catching sight of the look on Blue Eye's face, immediately bowed his head and shut his mouth.

An uneasy silence descended upon the vehicle, but Katherine was far from satisfied with the answers that had been given to her and was quick to break it. "Where are you taking me?"

Blue Eyes, who Katherine had discerned was the leader of this pack – *group*, she corrected herself fiercely – sighed at the question. As if answering it was somehow a huge bother. "Canada," he said shortly.

Canada? Katherine blanched. Why were they going to Canada? She didn't want to go anywhere with these people. And besides, she'd never traveled outside of the U.S. in her life and didn't have a passport.

She quickly blurted this out, as if it would change their minds. Stop them from taking her.

Right.

The dark man who was still nameless merely glared and condescendingly explained that she wouldn't need one where they were going.

"And where exactly is that?" she demanded. "And why are you taking me there?"

"Why, to a werewolf colony, of course. Honestly, where else would we be taking you?" The dark man's tone made it clear that she should have known that. Said tone, of course, only served to make her angrier than she already was.

"I thought I already said that I didn't believe in that garbage. Now take me home this instant!"

Markus apparently couldn't keep his mouth shut for long. "Splendid idea. You heard the girl, Bastian."

So that was Blue Eyes's name. Katherine had been wondering what it could be.

Bastian. It was a strong, handsome name. It fit the man.

Katherine quickly snapped herself out of such thoughts, annoyed with herself for even caring what his name was in the first place.

"How can you possibly expect me to believe in something as crazy as werewolves?" she asked. "If such... *creatures*... existed, then how could people not know about them?"

"People did used to know about us," Sophie explained from the passenger seat. "But during the seventeenth century there was a... misunderstanding of sorts... and let's be honest, communication between normal humans and werewolves had always been strained anyway. They hunted and killed so many of us that we were forced into hiding."

"Right." Katherine wouldn't have been able to keep the disbelief out of her voice even if she had wanted to.

"It's true," the still nameless man insisted. "Our existence has been reduced to inaccurate legends of monsters. And how else do you think stories of such beasts came to be? The people who lived in that time told of our existence to their children, and them to their own young, and so on."

"What do you mean, inaccurate legends?" Katherine demanded,

stuck on that phrase. "Do werewolves not turn into huge, hairy wolves on the full moon?"

*Not that they exist*ed, she added inwardly.

Nameless looked annoyed. "Yes," he agreed, "but that is perhaps one of the few grains of truth the legends still have."

"So what are these nefarious legends so wrong about then?"

"Well, the most important fact that they're missing," Sophie once again took over, "is that there are two types of werewolves. Born and changed."

Caleb piped up from his seat beside Katherine. "Born werewolves are those who are born with the gene. It's recessive, so both parents must be werewolves for the child to be one as well. Changed werewolves are humans born without the gene, but who've exchanged fluids with a werewolf during a full moon."

"Exchanged fluids?" Katherine questioned incredulously, a dark pink slowly staining her cheeks.

"Being bitten," Caleb quickly explained, "is usually how it happens."

Oh. Katherine fought the blush off her face.

"People aren't changed often," Sophie immediately assured her from her seat. She turned and Katherine was forced to meet her cerulean eyes. "And even when someone is bitten, it usually-"

"Stop," Bastian immediately demanded and the blonde did, but she continued to gaze at Katherine like she wanted to say more.

Katherine glared at the man. Why was he denying her information?

It doesn't matter, she assured herself when it became clear that Sophie wasn't about to finish her sentence. It wasn't like she believed the other girl. Not really.

"I still don't understand," Katherine muttered. "You say you're in hiding, whatever that means, but how is it that no one has ever seen you? It's not as if you can disappear." Katherine thought for a moment. "Can you?"

Nameless snorted. "No, I'm afraid invisibility is not one of our many talents."

"And besides," Markus added, sneering, "There *are* some people who know of our own existence. Hunters."

Katherine felt Caleb tense up next to her. She glanced at him. His hands were trembling. Katherine immediately turned her attention back to the brawny man.

"Hunters?"

"The men who ambushed you at your house," he explained, ignoring the dirty looks he was getting from the majority of the vehicle's occupants, "are prime examples."

Katherine could feel her lungs constrict and for a moment, oxygen was denied from her.

Markus didn't seem to notice and he continued to talk. "Still don't know what hunters are? Here's a hint, princess. Instead of out shooting pheasants in the fields, they're after us. You. And they don't kill clean."

Katherine desperately wanted to punch the jerk, but was beaten to it when Sophie reached back and slapped him clear across the face.

"What the hell, woman?"

The blonde just glared. "You just be glad it was me who did it," she growled back and Katherine noticed her eyes flicker to Bastian. He looked furious. Markus must have gotten the hint because he shut his mouth. But Katherine was already getting a sense of his personality and knew without a doubt that he'd be back to harassing her soon enough.

Sophie smiled apologetically. "Sorry, sweetie. We keep meaning to get him fixed."

The glare she received in return from the man would have sent people with weaker constitutions running. But she just ignored him. "Hunters are one of the many reasons we keep to ourselves. Obviously, there aren't many of us or we wouldn't be able to hide like we do. In fact, there are only four werewolf colonies in all of North America. The one in Canada is the biggest. It's made up of a dozen or so packs and we're one of them."

"So you're a pack?" she asked skeptically.

Nameless sighed, clearly exasperated. "Didn't we already explain this?"

Katherine glared. "I just meant aren't you kind of... you know... *small* for a pack?"

"A pack can be anywhere from two to a couple dozen wolves," he immediately protested. "As long as, of course, they have an alpha. Bastian is our alpha." He nodded towards the blue eyed man. "Markus is our beta, or second-in-command." He pointed towards the man in question. "There's also Sophie, whose Bastian's sister." He gestured towards the blonde. "And Caleb, who you're stuck sharing the backseat with." He paused for a moment. "Oh, and my name's Zane by the way."

Not so nameless after all then.

"Well, if you're one of these so called packs, then why aren't you at your colony in Canada?"

"That is none of your business," Bastian immediately interjected from his place behind the wheel. His eyes met hers through the rearview mirror and the warning they contained made her want to claw his face.

If she had claws.

Which she didn't.

"None of my business?" Katherine demanded. "I'm the one who was bitten!" And with that, realization dawned.

"Which one of you did it? Which one of you bit me?" Judging by the nauseous feeling in her belly, she already knew.

It was only quiet for a moment before he opened his mouth. "It was me."

Bastian.

Katherine wanted to throw up. But even more than that she wanted to yell – to scream at the man who had done this to her. "This is your entire fault," she managed to choke out. "You... how could you do this?" Her voice only increased in volume as she continued. "I hate you!"

Katherine was vaguely aware of Markus rolling his eyes at what he probably thought was girlish dramatics. But she was too caught up in her rage and devastation to even acknowledge him. "My parents…" she mumbled under her breath.

And how could she have forgotten about them even for a moment?

She didn't even know what those hunters had done to her mother. And her father. She had left him broken and bleeding in what had once been the dining room of her home. Brad too, she reminded herself. He was buried under a pile of rubble.

"My parents," she repeated. "And Brad. They're hurt. And it's all because of you!"

And then another realization dawned. *And, oh God, how could she have forgotten it?*

"I never got them help," she whispered to herself.

"It's too late for them," Bastian said softly.

Katherine glanced up at him, denial gleaming in her eyes. "What do you mean it's too late?" she demanded, spitting his words back at him. "It's not too late! What if no one knows that they're hurt? How long have I been out? Turn this car around. I need to get them help!"

"I said that it's too late," Bastian barked, though his voice was devoid of anger. "They... when we left the house after you... they were already gone."

"Gone? What do you mean *gone*? They were injured. It's not like they could've just gotten up and walked out of there!" She didn't care how obtuse she was purposefully being, she was not about to accept that they were… that they were…

"Katherine." Bastian's voice demanded her attention. She numbly acknowledged that it was the first time any of them had said her name. She didn't want to think about how they knew it. And then, with finality, he said, "They're dead."

Katherine could feel the tears gathering in her eyes even as she began chanting the mantra… *he's lying, he's lying, he's lying...* in her head. She wanted to scream those words at him, inform him that he was nothing but a dirty liar. But even in the midst of her despair, she couldn't deny his words and the conclusiveness in which he'd said them.

"I'll never forgive you." She didn't recognize her own voice, thick with tears as it was.

His eyes left hers as he looked away. "I know," he whispered.

Katherine, who was usually embarrassed by tears, couldn't stop them from falling.

"So you believe us then?" Markus asked callously, seemingly unaffected by her sorrow.

"What choice do I have?" Katherine knew her words were bitter, but she couldn't find it in herself to care.

She curled up into a ball and using the blanket she had woken up with to hide her face, she sobbed. She was sure, though, that they could still hear her ugly cries. Her parents. Brad. They were all dead because of her.

No, because of *him*.

She didn't know how long she had been curled up when she felt a hand on her shoulder, but she immediately tensed. "If you need to talk," she heard Caleb's kind voice inform her, "I understand what you're going through."

And that was it.

Katherine whipped the blanket away from her face, not caring that her cheeks were covered in tear tracks and her nose was red and running. "How could you possibly understand?" she shouted at him, ignoring the pang of guilt she felt as his face crumbled. "How in the hell could you know what I'm going through?"

She didn't wait for a response. She wrapped the blanket around herself once more as uncontrollable sobs wracked her body. Right then and there she made a vow to get away from these people. These people who had ruined her life.

And whether it was the anguish of losing her parents or just pure exhaustion, she slowly managed to cry herself to sleep.

If she hadn't, perhaps she would have heard Sophie turn on the radio.

"And this just in, folks. It seems as if a small family living in Middletown, Iowa, was attacked in their own home earlier this evening. While Elaine Mayes remains unharmed, Benjamin Mayes was rushed to Hayfield Medical and is listed in critical condition. It also appears as if their teenage daughter, Katherine Mayes, is missing and is presumed to have been kidnapped by the home invaders. If anyone has any information about the girl's whereabouts, they are encouraged to contact the proper authorities. As for Brad Thompson, a teenage boy who was also in the home when the attack took place-"

Bastian quickly cranked the knob of the radio, stopping the reporter mid-sentence.

Four pairs of accusing eyes landed on him.

Oddly, it was Markus who spoke up. "I still don't think you should have told her-"

"It was for her own good. Don't question it."

Caleb wasn't so sure. "But Bastian-"

"Katherine's parents are dead. No one is to tell her otherwise."

Sophie glared. "Brother-"

"That's an order," Bastian interrupted, his voice stern and leaving no room for any arguing.

No one did.

CHAPTER SEVEN

The next time Katherine awoke, daylight was shining through the car window her cheek was pressed against, and through her blurry vision she could make out a sign welcoming them to River Valley, Population: 937.

The billboard was so similar to the one welcoming people to Middletown that Katherine was almost able to convince herself that she'd never left. But she was seeing the sign through the window of an unfamiliar SUV. And after a subtle glance around the vehicle, she could see she was still surrounded by the same strange people from the night before.

Any remaining hope that yesterday had just been some terrible nightmare immediately dissipated.

Katherine wanted nothing more than to close her eyes and pretend she'd never woken up – pretend that last night had never happened. So she did just that – closed her eyes. But her stomach gave her away with a very unladylike growl and though it seemed ridiculous to be concerned about something so trivial, she couldn't stop the involuntary blush from spreading across her cheeks and down her neck at the sound.

"Good. The princess is awake. Now can we finally stop for some grub?"

That was Markus, of course.

Katherine's insides clenched at the thought of food. Although her stomach was rumbling like she was starved, it was impossible for her to feel anything but nauseated with the grotesque picture of her father lying in his own blood permanently etched in her brain.

"I think I saw an advertisement for some sort of diner about a mile back."

As soon as Katherine heard Sophie's suggestion, she knew she had to intervene.

Ignoring the protests of her sore throat, she parted her dry lips and objected. "I'm not hungry."

Markus snorted. "Yeah? Well, according to your stomach, you are."

"I don't care," Katherine shot back – though she wasn't exactly sure what it was that she didn't care about. Being hungry. The crazy situation she had found herself in. Or just her life in general. What did it matter now that her parents... now that they... *Oh God.*

"Well, I don't much care whether you eat either, your majesty, but we had to wait hours for you to wake up just so the rest of us could. So suck it up and take one for the team. Or *pack*, rather." He sneered at her, an infuriating smirk plastered to his face.

Markus's words managed to pull Katherine from her quickly darkening thoughts. She didn't know if she had ever met such an aggravating person before. But she was grateful for the distraction. "I wouldn't have cared if you had stopped," she insisted.

The muscled man's smirk transformed into a sour frown. He glanced from her to Bastian, who was still occupying the driver's seat. Katherine's eyes followed his. "Bastian refused to stop for anything but gas until you had woken up," he informed her. "Said he didn't want to wake you up, or worse, have you wake up all alone if the rest of us stopped to eat."

It was obvious to her that Markus did not agree with the man's decision. And frankly, neither did she.

If she would have woken up alone, she'd have bolted – taken a chance and tried to get away from the people who were trying to convince her of the impossible. Now, however, she'd have to wait it out – be patient until another opportunity for escape arose.

The sound of Markus's voice once again forced Katherine to concentrate on the present moment. "Can we please stop somewhere to eat now?"

Coming from his mouth, the "please" sounded more belligerent than polite.

"I'm rather hungry myself," Zane added.

Katherine's eyes once again wandered to Bastian's. His forehead was creased in uncertainty, but when Katherine's stomach traitorously growled once more, he reluctantly gave in to the requests to stop and eat.

"Fine, but we'll have to make it quick. We still have over a day's worth of travel before we reach Haven Falls."

Haven Falls. It sounded too *pleasant* to be a werewolf colony or wherever it was they thought they were taking her.

Sophie was proven correct about the advertisement she'd seen when within minutes they were pulling up to a brick building with the words Betty's Diner sprawled across the front. It was an establishment that apparently made "Minnesota's Best Fried Chicken."

Katherine couldn't bring herself to be surprised that they'd already crossed state boundaries and were getting steadily closer to Canada. *Katherine, we're not in Iowa anymore*, she thought to herself ala Dorothy in *Wizard of Oz*.

She'd always hated that movie.

Once Bastian had parked, Markus and Zane practically flew out of the vehicle and Sophie wasn't far behind. Caleb started for the door, but hesitated and looked back at her with an inquisitive expression.

"Aren't you coming?" he asked.

Katherine could feel the intensity of Bastian's stare as he gazed at her through the rearview mirror. He hadn't left the SUV either.

Ignoring how the blue eyes lingered on her, she shook her head. "I'm not hungry."

"You're eating," the man ordered from the driver's seat.

Katherine bristled at the authoritative tone, but she didn't have time to form a retort before Bastian stepped out of the vehicle and slammed the door. She turned her incredulous expression towards Caleb, who was looking at her sympathetically.

"Is he always like that?" Katherine demanded. "Bossing people around?"

Caleb shrugged helplessly. "It's his job. But, no, he's not usually so..." he seemed to struggle to find the right word, "harsh. He's actually very lenient in comparison to most other alphas."

Katherine ignored the blatant reference to werewolves, but begrudgingly unbuckled her seat belt and exited the SUV when it became apparent that she would not be left alone even if she did refuse to go into the diner. She'd have to make her get-away some other time – sometime soon. Knowing that they were already in Minnesota made her nervous.

It was still early morning so the restaurant they'd stopped at was only serving breakfast – something no one in the group seemed to mind. But Sophie had chosen to sit at a booth instead of a table – something Katherine *was* bothered by.

Markus and Zane had already crammed into one side of the booth with the long-haired blonde, leaving Katherine stuck sitting across from them. She was directed to the very inside of the less-than-cozy booth. Bastian slid in next to her and Caleb sat quietly beside him.

She felt distinctly uncomfortable by Bastian's proximity despite the fact that he was keeping a more than respectable distance – practically forcing poor Caleb to sit on the floor as a matter of fact. Along with feeling uncomfortable, Katherine also felt unjustifiably hurt.

Did she smell or something?

Bastian certainly did.

She hadn't been close enough to the others to peg their individual scents just yet – besides Caleb, who inexplicably smelled of vanilla. It wasn't exactly a masculine smell, but it was nice enough. Very sweet, like the man seemed to be.

Bastian, on the other hand, smelled like... it was hard to explain. He smelled earthy – like the smokiness of a campfire, the pine of an evergreen tree, and the freshness of rain all rolled into one. It was far from an unpleasant smell and actually very, very enticing.

Katherine tried to distract herself from it and listened to the others make small talk as they glanced through their menus. She glared across the table at Markus when he made a particularly disgusting joke about sausage. He smirked back at her, but Sophie was quick to scold him. "Really? Can you be more immature?" She paused. "Or unoriginal for that matter? Surely you could rub your two remaining brain cells together and-"

"Good morning! And what can I get for you lovely folks today?" The waitress's animated greeting cut Sophie off mid-rant. Katherine looked at the woman. She was older – mid-fifties probably – and smacking loudly on her gum. Her name tag identified her only as Andrea.

For a split second Katherine considered crying out to the woman – and the rest of the people sprinkled throughout the diner – that she'd been kidnapped by crazy people who thought they were werewolves. But even in her thoughts, the idea seemed ludicrous. She was more liable to get herself locked up in a nuthouse than her companions. And besides, she was fairly certain that Bastian could have dragged her out of the diner and thrown her back into the cramped SUV before the word "werewolves" ever left her mouth.

Forcing herself to concentrate on what was going on around her, Katherine quickly realized that everyone had turned their attention towards Bastian when the waitress had finished asking her question. She fought the urge to roll her eyes when she realized that they waiting for him to order first. He was their so called alpha after all. *Ugh.*

But Bastian surprised her – and the others too if their gobsmacked expressions were anything to go by – when he looked in her direction. It was clear that he was offering to let her go first.

When Katherine stubbornly kept her mouth shut, however, his eyes narrowed in frustration. As the silence stretched on, his shoulders tensed and she could clearly see that he was clenching his jaw.

"Well?" he demanded shortly.

Katherine pursed her lips, suspicious of the respect he was showing her. Was this an odd sort of attempt at chivalry? She hadn't forgotten how he'd treated her thus far. Or *before* for that matter. *Before everything that had happened.*

Katherine bit her tongue and forced herself to blink away the tears that immediately sprang into her eyes as the image of her bleeding father once again assaulted her vision. She didn't even want to think of her mother and how she... how she had possibly *gone*.

How could she eat when her insides were such a jumbled mess?

"I'm not hungry," she managed to spit out. She felt stupid that she had to keep repeating herself, but she wasn't about to attempt to eat. Her stomach quivered at the very thought of food – and not in a good way.

"What was that, dear?" the waitress asked as she leaned forward, straining to hear.

The sight of Bastian's balled up fists was the only indication that he, at least, had heard her – though Katherine had no idea why her refusal to eat upset him.

"I said," Katherine enunciated loudly, both for the waitress's benefit and for the sake of riling Bastian, "that I'm not hungry."

The woman shrugged before turning her attention towards Bastian. "And for you, honey?" she asked, her voice developing a more flirtatious inflection. She blinked furiously in a way Katherine suspected she thought to be attractive, but Bastian missed it, his blue eyes refusing to remove themselves from Katherine's form. Eventually, he turned to look at the bottle-blonde grandma.

"She'll have the ham and eggs special – extra ham – with a large glass of milk," he ordered smoothly. "As for me, I'm keen on…"

Katherine didn't hear the rest because she was too busy staring at the man in disbelief that he had the gull to order for her. A sort of self-righteous fury began to build in the pit of her stomach and she knew her heated cheeks must have been painted an angry red.

If he felt her accusing eyes fixated on the side of his face, Bastian made no effort to acknowledge them. Was the man deaf? She had said countless times that she wasn't hungry!

Katherine waited tensely for the others to order their food. When the waitress sashayed away, she immediately addressed the man. "What was that?" she demanded.

"What was what?" he asked, feigning ignorance.

"You know what! Why did you order for me? I said that I wasn't hungry."

The man's dark eyebrows rose incredulously. "Of course you're hungry."

Before Katherine could retort, Zane interrupted their argument from his spot across the table. "He's right you know. By my calculations, you haven't eaten anything in nearly twenty-four hours. And those inflicted with our... well, our *condition*... have particularly ravenous appetites."

Zane's words only angered her further. He – no, *they* – were not supposed to make sense. But the cold rationality of Zane's statement could not be denied. And that, coupled with the smugness she could practically feel coming off of Bastian in waves, was quickly making Katherine see red.

She was only vaguely aware of Sophie clearing her throat across the table over the ringing in her ears. "Bastian," she spoke quietly, "you have to understand that Katherine has been through quite the ordeal. It probably feels like all of her choices have been stripped from her. And when you took away yet another one by ordering for her-"

Katherine had enough of being talked about like she wasn't even there. "Stop trying to psycho-analyze me!" she shouted across the booth, not caring if she was drawing attention to herself. "I'm sitting right here!"

"As if we could forget," Markus snorted, apparently not satisfied until he'd inserted himself into the argument as well.

Katherine turned her heated glare onto him, but said nothing more. She was too pissed to even open her mouth.

Her angry stare, however, spoke volumes.

The next few minutes passed tensely. Everyone was quiet, and it seemed to Katherine as if they were merely waiting for her next outburst. Their silence, however, wasn't as gratifying as she'd thought it might be. Instead of feeling proud that she'd managed to shut them up, she only felt more weighted down. And disappointed in herself that she was letting them get to her.

When Katherine heard the footsteps of the waitress returning, she was almost relieved to see the gum-smacking flirt.

Or she would have been if the footsteps had belonged to her.

Instead, when she looked up from uncomfortably studying the table, she was forced to meet the eyes of a stranger.

The man was tall with wild-looking hair that was pulled back into a sloppy ponytail at the nape of his neck. Despite his casual lean against their table, his leer caused Katherine to discreetly pull herself closer to the booth's padded wall. She estimated him to be around Bastian's age, maybe a bit older. And she wasn't sure how, but as soon as she saw him, she knew. He was one of *them.*

Maybe because it was how they all reacted when they saw their unexpected company.

Although she couldn't see Caleb's reaction over Bastian's dominating form, Sophie and Zane immediately tensed. Markus glared. And Bastian – well, he edged himself closer to her in an unexpectedly protective gesture. So close that that his muscular thigh pressed firmly against her slender one. She was also fairly certain she heard a low growl originate from deep within his chest.

The strange man only seemed amused, however, and actually chuckled at the less than welcoming reception – though it was clear that his laughter didn't stem from true mirth. "Honestly, a simple hello would have sufficed."

"What are you doing here, Rogue?" Bastian snarled and Katherine found herself thankful that she wasn't on the other side of the man's deadly glare.

This Rogue person, however, merely raised an eyebrow. "I see your manners remain as appalling as ever, Bastian. Color me surprised." His wandering eyes met Katherine's. "But surely you're not so impolite as to not introduce me to your new... *friend.* Who might this young lady be?"

Katherine wanted nothing more than wipe the fake smile straight off the man's face. His eyes were bright with something dangerous and the dark orbs disconcerted her more than she was willing to admit.

"You could use a little work on your manners yourself," Sophie snapped at the man at the same time that Bastian informed him that Katherine wasn't any of his damn business.

The man's smile only widened in response to their outbursts. "Now, now. I was only asking an innocent question."

Innocent? The man came across as anything but.

"So did Bastian," Markus pointed out coldly. "Why don't you answer *his* question and tell us why you're here?"

"Council business," the man quickly responded. "I'm afraid I can't divulge the details. You know the rules." They may have, but Katherine certainly didn't.

"Did Cain tell you to trail us?" Bastian demanded, not sounding particularly enthused about the possibility. Not that Katherine had any idea what it meant.

The man, completely ignoring the question, inclining his head towards her. "Does she know-"

"Yes," Bastian snapped, not allowing Rogue to finish his question. But Katherine knew exactly what it was going to be. *Does she know about us?*

"Is she-"

"Yes," Bastian repeated sharply. *Is she one of us?*

Katherine didn't know what possessed her to open her mouth. "*She* is right here," she informed both men, though she immediately regretted it.

It was one thing to throw the snarky words at Bastian and the others, but quite another to throw them at this man.

Rogue's eye lit up with a positively feral glint. "Of course you are," he agreed with her. "And your name?" The man leaned over their table, reaching out to her with his hand as if offering her a handshake.

Before the man's limb could get near her, however, Bastian was up on his feet and this time Katherine knew she wasn't imagining the threatening growl. Rogue quickly snatched his hand back, but instead of looking startled or frightened – as any sane person would – his eyes gleamed with excitement.

"I see," he murmured to himself, eyes glancing from Bastian to

Katherine and then back again.

Bastian looked ready to throw himself at the man, but before whatever was happening could escalate any further, the waitress reappeared, balancing two large trays in her hands. She spared Rogue an interested glance. "Is there a problem here?" she asked between gum smacks.

The man flashed a smarmy smile at her – though Katherine was sure the woman thought it charming. "Of course not, ma'am. I was just leaving." He locked eyes with Bastian's once more before turning and making his way toward the door.

The waitress – Andrea, Katherine reminded herself as she once again spied the name tag – shamelessly watched the man's backside as he left. Then she turned her attention back on the men at the table – Bastian, in particular. She not-so-subtly winked as she placed his overflowing plate of bacon in front of him. "Big boys gotta' eat," she simpered.

After asking if the group needed anything else and getting a negative response, the waitress reluctantly took her leave.

Katherine glanced down at the plate in front of her and felt her mouth begin to salivate at the sight of thick slices of greasy ham. But despite her stomach's demands for sustenance, she couldn't force herself to take a bite.

She looked across the table at the others, but watching them stuff themselves only churned her stomach. "Is anyone going to tell me what that was all about?" she demanded, determined to avoid eating the food in front of her.

"Eat," was the only response she received. It came from the man next to her and she realized quickly that no one was going to answer her.

She glowered at Bastian.

"I said eat," he repeated himself.

"No."

"No?"

"Are you deaf?" Katherine provoked, spitting out the words

she'd only thought earlier. "*No.* As in I already told you I'm not hungry and am not going to eat just to please you."

The man swiped a hand through his hair in obvious frustration and grinded his teeth together as if his next words – or word, rather – took a lot out of him. "Please."

Katherine wasn't moved. And was about to inform the man thusly when an idea came to her. "A compromise."

"What?"

Katherine almost didn't realize she had spoken aloud. "A compromise," she repeated. "I'll eat, but only if you tell me who that man was and why you all seem to dislike him so much."

Across the table Katherine could see Sophie attempting to smother a grin as she watched their interaction. Zane, too, looked somewhat amused, though Markus just looked irritated. Caleb was hard to see over Bastian's tall form.

Bastian himself looked somewhere between bemused and annoyed. Katherine wasn't surprised. If how the others acted was any indication, he was used to his word being law. Well, Katherine was only all too happy to play the role of the *out*law.

"Fine," he man eventually exhaled. But, of course, he didn't elaborate.

"Well?" Katherine demanded.

"As I'm sure you could surmise, the man's name was Rogue."

Katherine narrowed her eyes at Zane, not finding the tan man's interjection amusing in the least.

"A dirty scoundrel is what he is," Markus spoke up from his spot, stabbing a sausage smothered biscuit with his fork.

Yes, because that cleared everything up.

It seemed that Sophie was just as exasperated as she was because she sighed before quickly explaining what the others had not. "Rogue's another alpha from Haven Falls. He's only a little older than Bastian, who's the youngest alpha of our colony." She smiled proudly at her brother, who only ignored her. "Unlike Bastian, however, Rogue doesn't have a pack."

Katherine furrowed her brows in confusion. "But you just said he was an alpha. I thought-"

Zane quickly interrupted her. "Alphas without packs are known as lone wolves," he condescendingly explained.

"Rogue's always been jealous of Bastian."

Katherine shot Sophie a quizzical look. "Why?"

"Because Bastian's important. And Rogue... well, you heard Zane; he doesn't even have a pack."

Bastian looked uncomfortable as soon the word "important" had left his sister's mouth. "Sophie," he warned with a frown.

"I don't know why he's jealous because *all* alphas are important." She gave Bastian a pointed look. "They have places on the council."

Katherine couldn't help but feel that they were keeping something "important" from her – if Bastian's reaction to the word meant anything anyhow. Nonetheless, she trudged on with her questions. "The man – Rogue – mentioned something about that. He was talking about council business?"

Bastian sighed in a resigned manner before explaining. "The council acts as overseers of the colony. Its members make and enforce rules."

"And you're one of these members?"

"Yes," he replied stiffly.

Katherine raised an eyebrow, irritated at the one word answer.

Glancing at her untouched plate, Bastian offered her more information, though it was clear that he wasn't eager to do so. "There are sixteen of us – all alphas – who make up the Council. We all, with the exception of Rogue and one other, have packs."

"It's not unusual for young alphas to go packless for a while," Sophie added. "In fact, it's the norm. Bastian here is just special." She threw him a grin.

Markus spoke through a mouthful of meaty gravy. "Ha! Everyone knows that an alpha is only as good as his beta."

Bastian rolled his eyes before turning them back onto Katherine. *Why did they have to be so blue?* "There, you've heard enough. Now eat."

"Not yet," Katherine immediately disagreed, not able to resist voicing another question – a very significant question, at least to her. "Like I said, Rogue mentioned something about council business. Is that..." she hesitated, "is that why were you in Middletown the night that you… bit me?"

Katherine's inquiry was met with an uncomfortable silence.

After a few moments, however, Bastian responded. "Yes. Though it doesn't happen often, the head of the council sometimes sends packs to complete certain tasks – missions – outside of Haven Falls."

"Head of the council?"

"The head alpha is the leader of the council," Zane quickly elaborated when Bastian didn't, "and ultimately of all of Haven Falls. Bastian and Sophie's uncle, Cain, is the current council head. You'll meet him eventually I'm sure."

"He shouldn't be head," Markus grunted. "He's only in the spot he's in because-"

"I think we've said enough," Bastian interrupted what was sure to turn into a tirade.

Before he could command her to eat again, however, Katherine opened her mouth. "Why do we have to go back there? To Haven Falls, I mean? Can't we just stay in the states?"

She didn't want to leave the country – go to some place she didn't know where people thought they were fictional creatures. A colony ironically named Haven Falls that was apparently run by Bastian's uncle – a man named after the wicked son of Adam.

"We have to go back eventually. It's our home. Besides, it's best for new werewolves to be around others of their kind."

Katherine just barely bit back her immediate response, which was to deny the existence of werewolves. "But it's not *my* home," was what came out instead, "I don't want to go there."

Sophie shared a look with Bastian before forcing Katherine's eyes to meet hers. "I can't imagine how hard this is for you Katherine, but *we* are your home now."

Katherine knew if she'd responded to the blonde, she would have regretted the fierce show of emotion. So instead, she bit her tongue and forced herself to eat a few bites of her food, which had long turned cold – much like her entire body had at the prospect of considering *these* people her home.

She only managed to finish half the eggs and one slice of ham before her stomach threatened to protest in a violent way. Instead of nagging her, Bastian merely requested the leftovers to be packed in Styrofoam on the off chance that Katherine would find her appetite and eat the rest later.

When the others had finished and the group was on their way out the door, Katherine was stopped by the enamored waitress who had served them. After nudging her in the side with a sharp elbow, the woman whispered in her ear. "I wouldn't let that one out of my sight if I were you, dear." It didn't take a genius to figure out she was referring to Bastian.

Uncomfortable with the woman's assumptions, Katherine hurriedly walked away.

Minutes later, she was ushered back into the SUV and they were on the road again.

As Bastian drove, Sophie's words repeated themselves over and over again in Katherine's head. With her parents gone, she didn't know where her home was anymore. But of one thing she was certain – it was *not* with them.

CHAPTER EIGHT

When Katherine was eight years old and her sister Samantha was fifteen, she could vaguely recall staying at a Motel 8 with her parents. Her father had gotten them lost on the way to visiting one of her mother's many eccentric aunts. Minnie was her name – though Katherine couldn't remember if it was her given name or an unfortunate childhood nickname that had stuck.

Either way, when the sun had set and it became obvious that Benjamin had no idea where they were – let alone if they'd made it to Nebraska, where Minnie had lived at the time – he'd finally conceded defeat and pulled into the nearest motel.

The room they had been given by the motel staff had been the definition of run-down. She didn't think she'd ever forget the lumpy mattress, peeling wallpaper, or her sister's ungodly scream when she'd discovered the hand-sized spider in the motel's rusted bath tub.

Apparently, the motels in Canada weren't built much differently than the ones in the good old U.S. of A.

Musty smell. *Check.* Suspicious stains on the carpet. *Check.* Creepy paintings hanging from the walls. *Check.*

While Sophie had protested as soon as Bastian had pulled into the motel's parking lot, Katherine had kept her mouth firmly shut, and she wasn't about to open it to complain now.

In the SUV, her reasoning had been that she was tired, her body ached, and she honestly didn't think she could spend another minute being stuck in the same enclosed space as Markus. The man positively infuriated Katherine. However, even she could admit that there was a silver lining to his blatant dislike of her – it made for a wonderful distraction. It kept Katherine angry, and she'd much rather feel anger than the grief that she knew was lurking underneath.

Still, Katherine needed a break from the man and wasn't about to ruin her chances of that by complaining about the dingy room. At least, not out loud anyway.

So, reminding herself that staying at the motel was better than sleeping in the SUV again, Katherine retreated to a corner of the room, where she could lean comfortably against a wall and ignore the others' loud chatter.

Markus had plopped down on one of the beds as soon as Bastian had jimmied open the door. He was engaged in a boisterous conversation with Sophie, who had sat in an uncomfortable looking chair next to a small desk. Caleb was sitting quietly beside her on a similar chair and Zane was on the phone, apparently making good on his promise to order some hamburgers as soon as they got a room.

Bastian, after thoroughly inspecting the room, had relaxed on the bed adjacent to the one Markus had thrown himself on. Her eyes followed his movements as he set his car keys on the night stand. If only she could find a way to snatch them. But Katherine wasn't stupid. She knew that there was no way she could outmaneuver five people who were infinitely stronger – and probably faster – than she was.

Tearing her eyes away from the keys, Katherine took a moment to really look at Bastian. Even sitting, his form seemed so solid. His black hair was in a state of disarray. That, combined with the brightness of his eyes, made him look wild – almost feral, really. And for a second, Katherine could nearly make herself believe that he... well, that he was...

"Hey, princess!"

Tensing at the disrespectful nickname that the jerk had been insistent on calling her since she'd woken up in the SUV that morning, Katherine turned her attention towards Markus. "What?" she spat back at him.

Rolling his hazel eyes, the man gestured at Zane, who was staring at her expectantly. "He just wanted to know how you like your burgers."

Ignoring the heat spreading across her cheeks, Katherine managed a nonchalant shrug. "Lots of ketchup," she muttered. "Oh, and rare, I guess."

Markus gave her a knowing look at that particular specification. The raised eyebrows practically begged for her to smack the man. So what? What did it matter if she liked her meat bloody? That didn't prove anything – certainly not that she was some mythical creature.

Turning away before she actually *did* give in to the urge to hit him, Katherine examined the painting on the wall nearest to her.

It was a portrait of a woman in a lacy, off-white gown. She appeared to belong in the eighteenth – maybe nineteenth – century. The painting itself was done well, Katherine supposed, but the way the woman's dark eyes – dead eyes – peered out at her made it impossible for her to look at it for long.

"Are you going to sit?"

Katherine spared a glance at Bastian, who was observing her from his spot on the bed. In response to his question, she looked pointedly at the chairs of the room – both of which were occupied. Even just sitting, she wasn't about to share a bed with Markus. Or Bastian.

"Where?" Katherine demanded, ignoring the way the man's eyes flickered to the empty spot next to him.

Before he could suggest where she should sit, however, Sophie leapt from her chair and linked her elbow through Katherine's. The woman ushered her to the bathroom door. "I'm sure you could use a shower, honey. You haven't had the chance to clean up since... well, in a while anyway."

Thankful for the opportunity to escape Bastian's observant eyes – at least for a few minutes – Katherine immediately agreed and practically slammed the door in the helpful blonde's face.

She took a moment to savor the feeling of being alone before turning to look in the mirror. She wasn't able to withhold the gasp that escaped her lips when she saw her reflection.

Her chocolate-colored hair was a dark and greasy tangle. Her face was smudged with dirt and grime. And a large bruise had blossomed half-way across her forehead.

Looking as she did, she could hardly believe she had been let into the diner they'd stopped at earlier. But she supposed she had been practically hidden behind Bastian the whole time she was there.

It wasn't her filthy appearance that most bothered Katherine, however. It was her eyes. In the past week, they'd gained a certain gleam – a sparkle. Which was now noticeably absent. They looked murky again – dead. Disturbingly similar to the woman's in the portrait.

Tearing her eyes away from her reflection in disgust, Katherine quickly stripped off her clothes – a pair of sweatpants and an oversized shirt.

She hadn't even noticed that she'd been changed out of the sullied clothes Bastian and the others had found her in until earlier that day, shortly after they'd stopped at Betty's Diner. But she supposed that she had more pressing matters on her mind at the time. Like the idea of werewolves. Like the death of her parents. Katherine swatted those thoughts away.

Still, she'd been distressed when she had found out that Sophie had undressed her during her first stint of unconsciousness – and in the SUV in front of the others, no less. But the blonde had insisted that she hadn't let the men see anything. And she guessed that *that* was the least of her worries anyway.

Once undressed, Katherine carefully examined her body and was surprised by the lack of bruises or other wounds. Besides the purple lump on her forehead and a few cuts on her knees, the only noticeable discolorations on her body were the four small puncture marks on her ankle from when that wolf – *not a werewolf, just an ordinary wolf* – had bitten her on Miller Road.

Forcing herself to concentrate on the task at hand, Katherine laid a couple of white towels – those small ones provided by all motels – on the rack next to the shower before stepping into the bath tub. The cold porcelain immediately caused her skin to erupt into goosebumps, but the tub was surprisingly clean. Pristine really. No spiders, anyway.

Adjusting the metal knobs, Katherine turned on the water and quickly cranked up the faucet labeled "hot" when a cold spray erupted from the shower head. In a few moments, the water was near scalding, but it felt good on her aching body and Katherine couldn't be bothered to adjust it.

Quickly locating the shampoo and conditioner provided by the motel, she emptied the tiny bottles. She scrubbed her scalp with both, anxious to get her long locks clean. Once finished, she chose to forego the cheap razor altogether and unpackaged the unscented bar of soap she had spotted while conditioning her hair. She scrubbed her body until her skin began to tingle – though she still felt unclean.

She stood under the hot water for a while longer after that, her mind pleasantly blank.

She refused to acknowledge that some of the droplets of water rolling down her cheeks were silent tears and not the water from the showerhead.

Twenty minutes later, Katherine finally found the will power to turn off the water and step out of the tub. She used one towel to quickly dry her body – she noticed immediately how red her skin was from the hot water – and the other to wrap up her dripping hair. She was reaching down to grab the pair of sweatpants she'd shed a half hour earlier when she heard the voices coming from the other room. She wasn't surprised – motel walls were notoriously thin – but the words themselves gave her pause.

"-don't even understand why we're bothering with her. She's nothing but a spoiled brat."

It was Markus, once again complaining about her. He'd said similar things to her face, but she was a little surprised that he was also spouting off insults behind her back. She actually felt somewhat hurt.

"Her attitude has been atrocious."

And there was Zane chiming in. Katherine couldn't say she was surprised. His condescending attitude thus far had made it clear that he didn't particularly like her either.

"Oh? And you two have been perfect gentlemen? *Please.* You calling that girl out on her attitude is laughable."

It seemed that Sophie, at least, was sticking up for her, and Katherine couldn't help but feel a twinge of gratefulness towards the other girl.

Caleb spoke up next – in what was perhaps the sternest voice she'd heard from the seemingly timid man. "At least she has an excuse for her unfriendly disposition. Being attacked by those hunters and then again by those men at the gas station, and now this huge, life-changing revelation."

The death of her family, Katherine mentally added to the list. She clenched her fists tightly as a spasm of anguish rocked her body at the traitorous reminder.

"What's your excuse?" she heard Caleb demand and forced the pain to the deepest recesses of her mind. She didn't want to think about them – her parents.

"Are you trying to say that our lives haven't been affected by this? Bite me."

"Too late!" she heard Markus mock loudly in response to Zane's comment. "Bastian's already bitten her!"

"Precisely, and it's changed everything for us."

"Would you two shut your mouths?" she heard Sophie snap. "For God's sake, we don't even know if... well, if she'll even..." Katherine pressed her ear to the bathroom door, but couldn't make out the rest of the woman's words as her voice trailed off weakly.

"An even better reason to ditch her – to let her find her way back home!"

"Her home is in shambles! Besides, I told her earlier that *we* are her home now. And I meant it."

"Oh please, she doesn't even want to be here!"

"Shut up, Markus!"

"And we don't want her here either! So what's the problem?"

We don't want her. Katherine could feel her stomach flip as the words reached her ears, but she refused to identify the feeling in her gut as hurt. After all, what right did she have to be upset when everything Markus and Zane had said was true? She didn't want to be there with them. And they... well, they'd made it clear that they didn't want her around either. That was just fine with her. If everything went her way, she'd be gone come morning anyway.

"Stop." Even Katherine's thoughts obeyed and ceased at the command. She couldn't prevent a shiver of *something* from rushing through her body at the sound of Bastian's low timbre. "I think we've all put up with your vulgar mouth for long enough, Markus. It doesn't matter if you don't want her here. It doesn't matter if *I* don't want her here."

This time, Katherine couldn't deny that the words stung – hit her hard where her heart was supposed to be. But after a moment, she was able to brush the comment off and concentrate on an emotion more productive than hurt – anger.

"No amount of yelling and complaining from you – or her for that matter – will change what has been done. She stays."

Bastian's words sounded final, but Katherine still waited for more protests from Markus. When only the quiet sound of the television met her ears, however, Katherine backed away from the flimsy bathroom door and quickly dressed.

Looking for an excuse to remain in the privacy of the bathroom for at least a few minutes longer, she searched the cabinet under the sink and found some travel- sized toothpaste. She squirted some onto her finger and used it as a tool to rub the mint concoction against her teeth. Avoiding looking into the mirror, even as fogged with steam as it was, she rinsed and spit. Then, taking a deep breath to compose herself, she stepped out of the bathroom.

She saw that a chair was now available – Caleb was currently sitting on the same bed as Markus and Zane, though none of the trio looked too happy about the arrangement. Deciding not to question it, she immediately made her way towards the open seat.

Before she'd taken more than two steps, however, Bastian was in front of her, inspecting her critically.

"Why is your skin so red?"

Katherine used her hands to try to cover up the exposed skin of her arms. "The water was hot," she mumbled before stepping around him.

Her back was turned so she couldn't see how the man frowned at her answer, but his tone made it obvious enough that he was displeased with it. "And what? You didn't notice it scalding your skin?"

Katherine rolled her eyes as she settled herself into the chair, but managed to withhold the sarcastic response that was on the verge of escaping her mouth.

"You need to be more careful," Bastian continued despite her silence.

"Or what?" Katherine snapped. "You'll send someone in to supervise next time?"

A tinge of red spread across the man's face, but Katherine couldn't tell if it was from anger or embarrassment. Maybe a combination of both. "Don't think that I won't," he threatened under his breath.

Katherine pretended not to hear. In fact, she spent the next few minutes trying to mentally drown out all of their voices. She refrained from socializing except for a small "thank you" when Caleb answered the door for the delivery man and handed her one of the hamburgers that Zane had ordered.

Although the thought of food still didn't appeal to her, she couldn't resist devouring the entire burger within minutes when its delicious scent hit her nose. She ignored the look she got from Bastian – though judging by his expression, he was just pleased to see her eating.

As the others ate and chatted, Katherine silently observed them. They all seemed so content. Even Caleb, who Katherine noticed was picked on by Markus and Zane whenever they weren't targeting her, seemed happy. Bastian, perhaps, was the only melancholy one. He was a brooder, Katherine supposed. She knew that a lot of woman probably liked that about him. He was the embodiment of tall, dark, and mysterious, after all. Not to mention handsome.

All of them were good-looking.

So good looking, in fact, that a rampant thought of how they could all still be single crossed Katherine's mind before she forced herself to remember that they were all *insane.*

But were they really?

Why would anyone make up the existence of werewolves? A whole society of them with leadership and rules and all of that?

Knowing that her thoughts were headed into dangerous territory, Katherine forced herself to concentrate on the television.

Two hours' worth of *I Love Lucy* later, Katherine could barely keep her eyes open. She'd caught herself drifting off more than once, but forced her eyes to remain open and glued to the television set. She just needed to wait for the others to fall asleep and then she could act upon her plan.

She wasn't counting on Bastian rising from the mattress he was lying on and unceremoniously shutting off the television. He cut Lucy off midway through one of her infamous schemes.

"Oh, come on Bastian! Turn it back on. Lucille Ball is hot. So is that chick who plays Ethel."

Sophie scrunched up her nose at Markus's remarks. "Um, ew. Don't you know that the women who played those characters are dead?"

Bastian didn't bothering commenting on Markus's taste in women. He just gave the hazel-eyed man a pointed look. "No. We all need our rest."

It was clearly non-negotiable and the man begrudgingly agreed after shooting a glare in Katherine's direction. Katherine stuck out her tongue at him as soon as he turned his head back around. *Ass.*

But she couldn't find it in herself to be upset. The pack deciding to sleep was exactly what she wanted and needed to happen. She'd only have to wait until they were all out to take off.

They'd only crossed the border into Canada mere hours ago – with no border patrol in sight. Katherine had been paying attention to the roads Bastian had taken and was fairly confident she could find her way back into the states. She'd been thinking about it all day. She'd only have to drive a few hours after hitting the border to make it to Duluth, Minnesota. It was where her sister had settled down with her husband after attending college there. She could already picture Sam's surprised face in her mind.

"I'm sleeping here," Markus gruffly announced, pulling Katherine out of her thoughts. He buried his head into the pillow of the bed he'd been lounging on.

Katherine couldn't quite stop the corner of her lips from lifting into a smile of amusement when Bastian stood up and brusquely ripped the sheets off the man's form.

"What the hell?"

Bastian merely raised an eyebrow at the man's irritated expression. "Markus, Zane, you've got the floor." He ignored the immediate shouts of protest. "Sophie and Caleb, you've got this bed." Bastian turned his blue eyes on Katherine. "And you. You're with me."

Her amusement quickly faded.

In fact, she temporarily lost control of her motor functions and actually allowed her jaw to drop.

"You ought to shut your mouth before you catch flies," she heard Markus scoff from somewhere to her right, but she didn't bother to acknowledge him.

"Wait," Katherine demanded, sitting up higher in her chair. She suddenly felt more awake. "What do you mean I'm with you?"

"It means we'll both be sleeping here," Bastian informed her, gesturing towards the bed he'd been occupying all night.

"I'm not sharing a bed with you," Katherine immediately objected. She hadn't even wanted to *sit* on the same bed as the man. She was certainly not *sleeping* on one with him!

"Yes, you are," he corrected her, completely disregarding what she'd just said.

"Actually, no, I'm not," she snappishly retorted.

"In case you haven't noticed, you don't exactly have a choice." Katherine ignored Zane much like she had Markus.

"Why? Why would you want that? To share a bed with me, I mean?" she demanded of the blue-eyed man, who was paying her no mind as he straightened up the bed he had demanded she share with him.

"Stop acting like you're getting gypped, princess. Zane and I are stuck on the floor," Markus grumbled.

A wave of irritation washed over her and Katherine couldn't stop herself from verbally attacking the man. "Don't you ever shut up?"

Markus's eyes lit up in surprise for a moment before they darkened and he glowered at her. "I don't know. Don't you ever stop being a bi-"

"Enough Markus. You too, Katherine." Her heart skipped a beat at hearing Bastian say her name. It was only the second time she'd ever heard him say it.

Wait.

Why did she know that?

"Now get over here."

Katherine had never met so many maddening people in her entire life. Did he seriously think that she'd just obey him? *Really?*

"Why are you insisting we share a bed?" she demanded again.

"So you don't get any stupid ideas, that's why. Someone needs to babysit you tonight."

Katherine saw red at the word "babysit."

She was so mad that she almost didn't hear Sophie's mumble. "Sure, that's why."

The blonde's comment prompted Katherine to take note of her. Wouldn't *she* make a much more appropriate bedmate?

"If you really think I need to be *babysat*," Katherine spat the word out, "then why can't I sleep with Sophie?"

Zane's amused snort made Katherine turn her eyes on him. "Yeah, perhaps that'd be possible if the woman didn't sleep like the dead."

The man was smacked across the head by the woman in question, but she offered Katherine a sheepish shrug. "It's true. I'd be little use as a babysitter."

Katherine continued to seethe. "Why not Caleb then? Zane? Even Markus?"

Bastian tensed as soon the name "Caleb" had spilled from her mouth. His hands clenched at "Zane". And by the time "Markus" had been said, a dark red color was slowly creeping up his neck.

"No," the man answered through his teeth.

"Why not?" Katherine commanded Bastian to tell her despite the voice in the back of her head telling her not to mess with the man who looked mere moments away from having steam burst from his ears.

"They're men!" he exploded, his eyes fierce as he glared at her.

"So are you!" Katherine shouted back.

"It's different with me!"

"How?" Katherine demanded incredulously.

"It just is!"

Katherine made a face, pushing a lock of dark hair behind her ear. Then she crossed her arms, making it very clear that she wasn't going to move unless she got an explanation.

In response, Bastian took a deep breath, seemingly trying to get a hold of his wiry temper. "Just get over here," he finally ordered after a minute of silence and neither of them moving.

"Make me," Katherine shot back, not backing down for a minute.

"Fine," the man rumbled before stalking over to her. "Have it your way."

Katherine froze at the predatory growl sounding from the man's chest and couldn't quite react in time to dodge him as he lifted her by the waist and threw her over his shoulder. It was like she weighed nothing.

After letting out a surprised squeak, Katherine was able to contain her shock. "Put me down!" she yelled, absolutely infuriated. She also landed a few forceful punches to his back – which she couldn't help but notice was very firm. The punches, in fact, probably hurt her more than him.

Within moments, she was rudely tossed onto the mattress of the bed in question. It was surprisingly comfortable. But that didn't stop Katherine from immediately sitting up and glaring at Bastian, who remained towering over her, his arms crossed over his chest. It was eerily similar to the pose she had held not two minutes earlier.

Katherine was only vaguely aware of their audience, having almost completely forgotten about the rest of the people in the room, who were no doubt more amused by than sympathetic of her situation.

"Why are you doing this to me?" The words were supposed to come out as an angry demand, but came out sounding defeated to even Katherine's own ears.

"Because I don't trust you to stay," Bastian said simply.

And what could she say to that? He was right. Her intentions were to leave – to escape from these peoplc as soon as she was given the opportunity.

"I don't like you," Katherine snarked, for lack of anything else to say. But even she could tell the words lacked any real malice.

Bastian must have known as well because he remained unimpressed. "You've made that perfectly clear. Now scoot over and lay down."

Rolling her eyes, Katherine finally did as she was told and perched herself at the very edge of the queen-sized mattress. She buried herself under a blanket. Her whole body tensed when Bastian lay beside her, but she relaxed when he remained on top of the covers.

She stubbornly faced the wall, but could hear the others as they made themselves comfortable – with lots of groaning from the two men forced to brave the floor.

Katherine couldn't help but think it ironic that they were as jealous of her sleeping arrangements as she was of theirs.

Soon the man beside her shut off the lamp on the nightstand and the room was cast into darkness.

Despite her exhaustion, Katherine forced herself to keep her eyes open. She wasn't willing to believe that her plan had been completely thwarted. She concentrated on breathing as evenly as possible, hoping to be able to convince Bastian of her slumber. She nearly dozed off twice, but managed to keep herself awake by pinching her arm whenever she felt like falling asleep.

After what had to have been close to an hour had passed, Katherine finally put her plan into action. She slowly shifted her body until she was on the verge of falling off of the bed. Then, holding her breath, she carefully sat up. The bed frame squeaked when she moved and she immediately tensed. And waited. When nothing happened, she let out a soft sigh of relief and continued.

She placed one foot on the carpet. Two.

And then a hand latched onto her wrist.

Katherine just barely managed to swallow a scream. Her eyes immediately turned to meet those of the man who'd grabbed her. Much like the long fingers engulfing her small wrist, the man's eyes were gentle.

His words, however, were as stoic as ever.

"Nice try. Now go to sleep. You've been keeping me up."

His indifference only added to her embarrassment of being caught. "I was just going to the bathroom," she managed to mumble angrily, denying the man's unspoken accusation.

Bastian raised an incredulous eyebrow, but didn't call her out on the obvious lie.

"Fine, so maybe I wasn't," she admitted.

Tearing her eyes away from his face, she peeled back the sheets and climbed back under them. She usually wouldn't sleep under the covers, but despite her warm body temperature, the room was chilly. Under the sheets, however, was *...nice.*

And the bed was actually pretty comfortable. The mattress was soft and nothing like the one she'd been forced to sleep on when she'd stayed at that Motel 8 with her family. Even the pillow was fluffy.

And the weight on the other side of the bed, the dip that Bastian's body made and the warmth it created... well, it was cozy. Even the gaze she swore she could feel on the back of her head wasn't unpleasant. It was reassuring. And she felt warm. *Safe.*

And despite her best intentions not to, Katherine slowly drifted off into a dreamless sleep.

CHAPTER NINE

Katherine woke up cold. Even tangled in a thick blanket, she could feel the chill.

After a particularly violent shiver, she managed to force herself to sit up. Sluggishly rubbing the sleep from her eyes, she glanced at the other side of the bed. It was empty. She absentmindedly touched the pillow that *he* had been laying on last night. It was cool to the touch.

"He left."

Startling at the sound of Caleb's soft voice, Katherine jerked back her hand. She turned to see that the brown-eyed man was sitting on the bed that he and Sophie had shared the night before. Unlike the mess of sheets she was lounging on, the bed he sat on was neatly made – the blankets were tucked in and even the pillows looked as if they had been fluffed.

It couldn't have been more obvious that Caleb had been awake for a while.

And to Katherine's surprise – and not-so-secret delight – the others were nowhere in sight. She subtly peeked at the night stand between Caleb and herself.

And promptly felt her heart skip a beat.

The keys to the SUV were still there!

Where had everyone gone? Surely Bastian hadn't left her alone after meticulously *babysitting* her the night before.

Had he?

Was Caleb really the only person between her and the keys to a potential getaway car?

It wasn't as if Katherine had scruples against stealing it. She'd been kidnapped, after all.

"Where is everyone?" Katherine asked, the question flying past her lips before she could taper her excitement.

"Bastian and Sophie went to the supermarket we saw on the way into town," Caleb explained. "It's only about a half mile from here and Bastian thought it'd be a good idea to get you a few things. You know, necessities – some clothes, a toothbrush, deodorant," he hesitated a moment, a light pink staining his cheeks, "...other feminine products. He wasn't sure what you'd all need – that's why he brought Sophie with him."

"I see," Katherine said, working to hide her enthusiasm. She hoped Caleb assumed the red she could feel creeping up her neck was from embarrassment at the mention of "feminine products" and not the result of her suddenly racing heart.

"And the others? Markus and Zane? Are they gone too?" she asked, trying her best to sound nonchalant.

Caleb furrowed his brows, looking distinctly uncomfortable at the question. "Well, they weren't *supposed* to leave, but Markus wanted to get something to eat. Both he and Zane took off a few minutes ago."

"Why weren't they supposed to leave? Babysitting duty?" Katherine couldn't stop the knee-jerk anger from briefly clouding over her excitement.

Caleb cringed and Katherine almost felt bad for taking her irritation out on the man.

Almost.

"In a way," he admitted. "Bastian did say were all to wait here for him to return." He hesitated, "And he also said that we weren't supposed to let you out of our sight."

Katherine rolled her eyes, completely unsurprised by the revelation. Caleb seemed apologetic about his friend's behavior, but she couldn't help but notice that the man's eyes *were* glued to her. He was clearly taking the order seriously – which left her in quite the predicament.

How could she get away with him watching over her like this?

Despite his seemingly docile nature, Katherine knew she could never take Caleb in a fight. He may have been smaller than the other men in the so called pack, but he was still much larger than her. He'd win a physical battle every time and easily be able to restrain her.

Katherine tugged a hand through the knotted mess of hair on her head, anxiously trying to think of a solution to the situation she'd found herself in.

Why, oh why, did that infuriating man have to leave her with a babysitter?

She didn't even notice the frustrated growl building in the back of her throat until it had escaped.

"Are you okay?"

Katherine spared a glance at the blond man who was *still* watching her.

"Why?" she demanded, the question exploding from her mouth before she'd even had the chance to form it in her head.

Caleb was clearly taken aback – and more than a little weary at the sudden outburst. "Why what?" he asked delicately.

"I don't know. Why everything?" Katherine licked her lips before asking the real question – the one that had been on her mind for days now. "Why'd he do it? Why… why did Bastian bite me?"

If Caleb had looked weary before, his hunched shoulders screamed that he was uncomfortable now. "That's something that he should explain to you."

Katherine was far from satisfied with that answer. "Just tell me," she insisted, the desperation she could hear in her own voice taking her by surprise. She sounded absolutely pathetic.

Caleb must have thought so too because she could practically see his resolve start to crack. He opened his mouth, hesitated, shut it, and then with a seemingly resigned sigh, opened it again. "Since you've been bitten, have you noticed that your senses have been enhanced – made better? Especially your sense of smell?"

Katherine immediately nodded. "People have scents," she blurted.

"Yes," Caleb agreed before pursing his lips, seeming to consider his next words carefully. "People have scents and somehow, in his wolf form, Bastian sensed... well, he *smelled* you."

Katherine was affronted and couldn't have stopped the offended words from flying past her lips if she'd wanted. "And what?" the angry brunette demanded. "I smelled so horrible that he couldn't stop himself from assaulting me?"

"No!" Caleb immediately denied. "I think that his wolf must have… *liked* it – recognized something in it that made him-"

"What? *Attack me?*" Katherine was adamant in her incredulity. "He liked my scent so much that he mauled me?"

Caleb seemed to sink into himself. "This is why he should be the one to explain it to you." He sighed. "I don't think he was attacking you."

Katherine's eyebrows shot up. "Then what?" she demanded, disbelief saturating her voice.

Caleb frowned, his eyes finally leaving her form as they drifted down to the floor.

In response to the man's dejected posture, she could feel the hard ball of anger in her gut soften to something more closely resembling shame. She sighed. "I'm sorry," she managed to bite out. "I never should have asked you to try to explain *his* actions."

Caleb glanced up at her. A slight frown was still tugging at the corners of his lips, but he looked grateful that she would no longer be interrogating him.

Still feeling guilty, Katherine offered him a small smile. She hoped it didn't look as forced as it felt because she thought that, deep down, she might actually *like* Caleb. He really did seem like a good person, and she could tell that his kindness wasn't manufactured.

But she knew she couldn't afford to feel anything but animosity towards the people who had kidnapped her.

"I was bitten too."

Katherine almost didn't hear the softly spoken confession. But the words *did* reach her ears and Katherine couldn't withhold a small gasp.

What?

"Bastian attacked you too?" Katherine couldn't even begin to name the fierce emotions she could feel threatening to surface. Shock. Anger. Even jealousy, strangely enough.

The expression on Caleb's face quickly assured her that she'd assumed wrongly, however, and the intense emotions disappeared as quickly as they had come, leaving Katherine feeling disoriented. She forced herself to concentrate on Caleb's voice.

"Truthfully, I don't know who bit me, but I *do* know that it wasn't Bastian. It happened over five years ago when he and the others were still in school. Whoever did bite me... he didn't stick around like Bastian did for you."

For a moment, Katherine forgot that she wasn't supposed to believe and was horrified. "Five years ago?" she asked faintly. "You couldn't have been more than what? Fourteen?"

"Thirteen," he correctly gently. The man's brown eyes met her green ones squarely. "I know it's hard to feel anything but anger and grief in your situation, but Bastian – he really did do the right thing by taking you. I know it doesn't feel like it, but you have all of us in your corner. *Especially Bastian.* I didn't have anybody."

For the briefest of moments, Katherine considered pointing out that she'd overheard them talking last night – that she *knew* they didn't want her. But something – tact, or maybe empathy for the man in front of her – made her keep it to herself. Instead, when she opened her mouth, an apology spilled out. "I'm sorry."

Caleb waved the words off. "What happened to me wasn't your fault. I've learned to accept it."

Katherine was suddenly struck by the absurdity of what they were discussing. "Accept being a *werewolf*?"

Caleb's half-smile faltered. "I didn't believe it either until I changed."

"Into a *werewolf*?" Katherine repeated. Her tone made her skepticism obvious.

"Yes," he insisted. His eyes begged her to believe him. "I had no one to help me through it. I don't want to scare you, but it was terrible. I was so frightened – terribly confused and in so much pain – I had no control over myself. I thought I was going mad and," he paused, taking a deep breath, "Katherine, I almost *killed* someone."

The intensity of Caleb's words resonated with Katherine. The unassuming man in front of her – boy, really; he was only two years older than her – had almost killed somebody?

Caleb must have mistaken her shock for fear because he looked away from her in shame. She didn't know what to say to comfort him so she just let the man keep talking.

"Word of the attack got out and werewolf hunters showed up."

Katherine tensed, quickly finding her voice. "Stop," she demanded, knowing the moment he mentioned hunters that his story was too similar to hers. It would be too agonizing to hear.

Caleb startled at the sound of her voice, almost as if he'd forgotten she was there as he relived his memories. He nodded solemnly, however, and obeyed the order. He quickly ended his story, only adding that he'd been rescued from the hunters by someone from the colony – he didn't say who – and that was how he'd met Bastian and the others.

Katherine couldn't help but notice the irony – whereas Caleb had considered himself rescued, she felt as if she'd been kidnapped.

Kidnapped.

Katherine nearly choked on the air she was breathing. *What was she doing?*

She glanced at the clock on the nightstand – it was tantalizing close to the SUV's keys. The time – 9:37 – glared back at her. Why was she wasting precise time *talking* when she could have left – escaped – by now? The others could be back any minute!

Panic caused something in her chest to tighten and before Katherine could even really think about what she was doing, she was flinging the bed sheets off her body. She stood and began tugging frantic fingers through her long, wavy hair, trying futilely to make the knotted mess lay straight.

Caleb stood with her, looking confused by her sudden actions and more than a little nervous. "Are you okay, Katherine?"

"I'm hungry," she blurted. It was the first excuse she could think of to get Caleb to agree to leave the motel room. And he'd have to leave – at least for a minute or two – for her half-cocked plan to have a chance of working.

The man's eyebrows shot up. "You are?"

His astonishment was downright comical.

"Yeah, I thought we could join Markus and Zane for some breakfast."

Caleb's eyebrows rose even higher – almost disappearing into his hairline. "You want to go eat with *Markus* and *Zane*?"

"Yes," she snapped, glancing back at the clock. 9:41.

Caleb seemed to recover from his surprise. He subtly – though not subtly enough for Katherine not to notice – put himself between her and the exit. "Bastian ordered that we stay here," he reminded her – *as if she needed reminding*. "Maybe we can order some food?"

"Breakfast food?" Katherine questioned incredulously. "I doubt anyone delivers eggs."

Caleb grimaced. "Can't we just wait until Bastian and Sophie get back? They should be here soon. You could even change clothes and-"

"But I'm hungry now," Katherine immediately objected. She gazed at Caleb imploringly. "Please."

"I don't think-"

"Markus and Zane left. Why can't we?"

"Yes, but Bastian-"

"Bastian," Katherine stressed, "will be so pleased that I'm eating that he won't even care that we left."

The man frowned, but seemed to be considering her argument. "Maybe," he conceded.

Katherine could sense victory and wasn't above begging. "*Please*," she repeated.

Caleb examined her for a long moment before sighing. "Okay," he agreed, "I know Zane said something about a cafe a few blocks from here. I think that's where he and Markus were going. We could meet them there."

"Sounds great," Katherine immediately agreed despite having no intention of walking any further than the parking lot. "Just let me use the bathroom real quick. Meet me outside?"

Katherine prayed her plan would work.

But Caleb looked reluctant. "Bastian said not to let you out of my sight."

Bastian. Bastian. Bastian. Katherine was so sick of hearing about *him* and what *he* wanted. She crossed her arms, hoping she looked more nervy than nervous. "I assure you that I don't need any help in the bathroom. A little privacy please?"

Caleb flushed. "I'll wait outside."

Yes.

Katherine wasted no time scurrying to the bathroom. Once she'd locked herself in, however, she did little more than anxiously trail her fingers through her hair, waiting to hear the sound of the motel room's front door closing. It was her signal that Caleb had, indeed, left.

When she heard the squeaky hinges, she only waited a heartbeat before hurrying out of the bathroom. She quickly made her way to her backpack – she'd discovered yesterday that Bastian had grabbed it from her car when he'd snatched her – and pulled out her wallet. The leather folds contained a few bills, but more importantly, a silver Visa credit card. To be used only in emergencies, as per her father's instructions.

If *this* didn't qualify as an emergency then Katherine didn't know what did.

She shoved the wallet deep into one of the pockets of her overly large sweat pants, strode across the room to the nightstand, brazenly grabbed the keys to the BMW, and shoved them into the same pocket. Then, talking a deep, calming breath, she walked across the room, opened the door, and peeked outside.

So far, so good.

Except that Caleb was leaning against the SUV.

Damn it.

She'd have to get him away from it.

The blond man smiled as she closed the door behind her, which assured Katherine that he didn't sense that anything was amiss.

"You can do this," she reminded herself under her breath before striding up to Caleb as confidently as she could manage. She walked halfway across the parking lot with him before she began her quickly improvised act.

She stopped and started patting her pant pockets anxiously. "Caleb, I forgot my wallet!"

The man's brow wrinkled in bewilderment. He laid a concerned hand on her shoulder. "Don't worry about it. Bastian would never expect you to pay for anything."

"I know," Katherine quickly agreed, hoping she sounded appropriately distressed, "but I wanted to pay for breakfast. It – It'll make me feel a little less helpless."

Katherine could see Caleb's eyes soften in sympathy, and for a second, shame assaulted her. But like she did with so many others feelings, she pushed the uncomfortable emotion away.

"I'll go get it for you," Caleb offered. *Just as she knew he would.*

Katherine nodded, not trusting herself to speak.

She waited until he disappeared back into the room before making a mad dash towards the SUV. She fished the keys out of her pocket and quickly pressed the unlock button. She hoisted herself up, immediately relocking the doors behind her. Then she took half a minute – though to her frenzied mind it seemed closer to ten – to adjust the seat so that her petite feet could at least touch the massive pedals.

She had just shoved the key into the ignition and revved the engine to life when Caleb stepped out of the motel room, confusion etched onto his face. He obviously hadn't been able to find her wallet, but how could he have? It'd been in her pocket.

Katherine met his eyes from her seat behind the vehicle's protective windshield. For a second, he didn't seem to register what was happening. Then she watched as panic warped his face. He made a move towards the SUV, but before he could reach the car, she jerked it into reverse and peeled out of the parking lot.

It wasn't until she had maneuvered out of the small Canadian town they'd spent the night at – Linburg, the sign had read – that she could feel her heart's rapid pace begin to slow.

But she didn't feel as relieved as she thought she would have to be out of the pack's company.

In fact, Katherine felt positively heavy with guilt. She felt terrible, like she'd betrayed the only person who had been unwaveringly kind to her throughout the entire, horrid ordeal she'd been through. Would Bastian blame Caleb for letting her escape? Would he punish the man for losing his hostage?

Had she truly been a hostage in the first place?

They'd never hurt her.

What in the hell was she thinking?

Of course she had been a hostage! Who cared about Bastian? Or Caleb? Or what the former would do to the latter when he discovered she'd gotten away? She shouldn't be picturing Caleb or Bastian or – oh God, Markus – in her head. She should be thinking about her sister – Samantha – and how happy she'd be to see that Katherine was okay. How they'd hug and cry and... talk about mom and dad.

Katherine could feel the moisture begin pooling in her eyes, but she stubbornly rubbed out the tears before they had a chance to fall.

She spent the next hour trying – and failing – to replace the picture she had in her head of Bastian's face with Samantha's. When nothing she tried worked, she spent the remainder of the trip trying not to think at all.

It was, perhaps, the longest twelve hours of her life.

By the time she finally reached Duluth, it had long since turned dark. Her hands were shaking with exhaustion as she crookedly parked in her sister's driveway. It was curiously empty.

Katherine only took a moment to stare up at the dark house before stumbling out of the vehicle and up the front steps. It was raining, but she cared very little about how quickly her clothes became soaked or how wet strands of her hair immediately began clinging to her face and neck.

She pounded on the door. "Samantha!"

The yell came out hoarser than she would have liked.

"Samantha!" she tried again, pounding harder.

No lights came on in the house. Silence – the too quiet kind that sent chills through her body – was the only response to her hollering.

"Sam!" she cried, her fists growing more desperate as they hit the wooden door. *Thwack. Thwack. Thwack.*

"Sam!" *Thwack.*

"Sam!" *Thwack. Thwack.*

"Sa-am!" She choked half-way through her sister's name, something that felt a lot like panic restricting her lungs.

"Sam!" she tried once more time before finally grabbing the door's brass knob and tugging. It was locked. She twisted and shook the thing, but the door wouldn't budge.

All the same, Katherine wasn't ready to give up – wasn't ready to accept that Samantha wasn't... that she wasn't home.

Katherine ripped the welcome mat off the steps, even smashed the flower pot by the door and dug through the soil that stained the cement. She was trying desperately to find a spare key – praying that Samantha kept one somewhere.

And then lights came on.

But not the ones Katherine wanted to see.

It was the neighbor's bright lights that illuminated her form from across the yard. She froze as a man – she'd guess by his white hair that he was at least in his sixties – from next door stepped out onto his porch. He was peering at her suspiciously. "Hi, there!" he shouted over the pitter patter of the rain.

Though the words were friendly, Katherine knew the man must have thought she was deranged. She managed to swallow the lump in her throat. "Hi," she croaked back.

"If you're here looking for Chad or Samantha, they aren't home."

Katherine forced her breathing to remain even. She wouldn't allow her panicky thoughts to overtake her common sense.

"Any idea where I can find them?" She could only hope she didn't sound as desperate – or look as crazed – as she thought she did.

"Why, didn't you hear?" The man sounded incredulous. "They left for Iowa days ago – won't be back 'til next week at the earliest. Poor Samantha – word is that there was a home invasion at her parents' house down in Middletown. Her sister's missing."

Katherine had never felt like a bigger fool.

Of course. Of course, Samantha wouldn't be here. Why would she be? It was only logical that she would be in Middletown – picking up the ruins of the house, trying to find Katherine, planning their parents' burial...

Katherine's breath hitched. "Oh," she murmured, but she doubted that the hushed word of realization reached the man's ears. He was still looking at her – openly concerned.

"Can I help you with anything else?"

Katherine did her best to regain her bearings. She shook her head. "No. No, I was, uh, I was just leaving."

She walked down the steps and numbly made her way back to the SUV, feeling the man's curious eyes on her until she was back behind the wheel of the vehicle.

She watched as he disappeared back into his house and the porch lights were turned back off.

But she couldn't bring herself to start the SUV.

She sat there, her oversized shirt drenched and sticking to her body, staring up at her sister's house.

How could she have been so stupid?

She wanted nothing more than to collapse in frustrated tears, but she couldn't allow herself that luxury. Instead of breaking down, she began assuring herself that Middletown wasn't *that* far from Duluth – that she could make it there in a day or two. She had her credit card, after all. She could afford as much gasoline as she needed.

But none of her reassurances distracted her from the fact that she couldn't keep driving. Not tonight.

Her body ached with fatigue and her head was throbbing. Not to mention the fact that she couldn't stop her hands from shaking – no longer from exhaustion, but from the cold. Digging for that nonexistent spare key seemed nothing short of idiotic now. She was in no condition to drive.

So instead of throwing the car in reverse and beginning the journey back to Middletown, Katherine tucked her hands under her armpits, trying to warm the freezing extremities. And somehow, despite the chill, she managed to drift off, curled up in the front seat of the SUV.

Her wolf.

She hadn't realized she had missed him until now that he'd returned. As always, he was staring at her – his deep azure eyes ridding her mind of all other thoughts. In his presence, they were inconsequential.

Today his eyes were sad – intense as ever, but missing a certain glint that had been present before.

And for the first time ever Katherine reached out to touch him. She kneeled and placed a bold hand on his head, petting the ferocious animal's fur.

"Hey," she whispered, "it'll be okay."

In response, the wolf pressed his snout into her hands, obviously enjoying the soft touch. But his eyes remained distraught. "What's wrong?" she murmured absentmindedly.

"Katherine."

Her heart jolted and she jumped away from the wolf. What the-?

"Katherine."

But the wolf's jaws weren't moving.

Of course, they weren't moving! It was a wolf.

"Katherine."

She snapped her eyes open.

Only to once again meet the blue eyes of her wolf. But they were in a different face – a human face.

Bastian.

He was standing outside of the open car door, looking at her with a grim expression. It was still raining and his shirt was drenched, his wet hair plastered to his forehead.

It took Katherine a few moments to realize that she was no longer dreaming. That she was still sitting in the SUV in front of her sister's house instead of on her way to Middletown. That she'd been caught.

But instead of feeling upset, or even angry, she only felt sick. She – she felt horrible.

Her heavy head was pounding, and it was all she could do to lift it up and look at the man. And there was a gigantic pressure on her chest trying to prevent her from breathing.

Katherine was half-delirious when she opened her mouth and asked Bastian, "Are you mad?"

He must have known she was unwell because he didn't immediately begin berating her – yelling at her for running from him. Instead, he grabbed her gently by the waist and cradled her body to his chest as he walked around the vehicle to deposit her into the passenger seat. His chest was warm and Katherine absentmindedly clutched his soaked shirt with her fists as he moved her. She was much too exhausted – *much too sick* – to protest being carried.

She allowed her eyes to drift shut and as sleep pulled her back into oblivion, she swore she could feel the faintest press of lips to her forehead and a quiet voice whisper, "I could never be mad."

CHAPTER TEN

Three days passed before Katherine woke from her fever induced slumber. In her state, however, it felt as if mere hours had gone by – hours she spent curled around her dream wolf, his fur covered body pressed against her own frail form as it was wracked by violent shivers.

When she did finally manage to peel her heavy eye lids open, she found that she was lying on a large bed – in an *unfamiliar* room. She probably should have been more concerned, but was getting awfully used to waking up in strange places with only hazy memories to remind her how she'd gotten there. She was numb to the experience.

In this particular instance, she remembered very little. She knew she had tricked Caleb – stolen the keys to the SUV and taken off in the gigantic, green vehicle. She also recalled arriving at her sister's house in Minnesota – how she'd banged desperately on Samantha's front door and broken one of her flower pots.

Her last memory was of Bastian showing up. His wet shirt clinging tightly to his sculpted chest as he stared at her with his too blue eyes was one of the few things she could remember vividly.

Katherine supposed that he was the one who had brought her here.

But when? And how?

She licked her dry lips and worked a hand through her hair – the dark curls were as wayward as ever – as she attempted to recall *exactly* how it was she'd ended up here – wherever here was.

Try as she might, however, she just couldn't remember. She had been sick, she thought. There had been a horrible pressure on her chest – a tightness that threatened to squeeze the very oxygen from her lungs. She'd had a headache too – could still feel faint traces of pain in her temples, in fact.

Perhaps she really had been as weak as she had been in her dream.

But sick enough to sleep the day away and not remember how she'd gotten here?

She could think of no other explanation.

But that still didn't answer the question of *where* she was.

Even the room she was in was veiled in darkness. The lights were off and the blinds on the windows were seal shut with no rays of daylight peeking through the gaps. There was no clock in the room so she could only assume it was night.

Though she felt far from tired.

And now that she was up and *aware* that she was in an unfamiliar room – in an *unfamiliar bed* – she couldn't very well just go back to sleep.

She was just itching to explore.

Katherine was hesitant to do so, however, as she very much doubted that she'd truly been left to her own devices. She knew that Bastian must have been nearby. He wouldn't leave someone else to watch over her. Not after the last time he'd left and put others in charge of *babysitting* her.

Ugh. Babysit. She despised the word.

Suddenly paranoid that she was being watched from the shadows of the room, Katherine reached over and flicked on the lamp she spotted on the nightstand.

The lamp's light cast an eerie glow on the rest of the room, but quickly revealed that no one was spying on her from the darkness. She would've heaved a sigh of relief if her breath wouldn't have caught in her throat as she got her first real look at the room she was in.

It was beautiful.

The room was decorated in rich shades of brown with little accents of green – like the curtains on the tall windows or the silken sheets of the bed. It was sparsely decorated – the bed, nightstand, and mahogany dresser were the room's only furniture – but that only served to draw attention to the gleaming hardwood floors.

But it wasn't the shiny floor or five drawer dresser that caused

Katherine to lose her breath.

It was the splendid fireplace that took up half the wall opposite the bed. It was magnificent – gloriously rustic with an abstract design of some sort looping around its golden frame. The pile of logs in its pit weren't currently burning, but she knew it'd make an even more awesome sight when they were.

Not able to resist the temptation to examine the fireplace more closely, she untangled herself from the comfortable sheets of the bed and knelt on the fur rug – if she had to guess, she'd say the pelt used to belong to a bear – that lay directly in front of the fireplace.

Up close, she could see that the frame wasn't painted gold as she'd first thought, but truly seemed to be made of the expensive material. She could also see that the looping design wasn't made up of vague shapes as it had looked like from her place on the bed, but detailed figures.

Detailed figures of wolves.

Katherine felt her stomach clench when she noticed, but she couldn't find it in herself to think the design any less beautiful for it. She idly traced the indented gold with her fingers before the desire she felt to explore the rest of the room could no longer be ignored. Hands on her knees, she pushed herself off the floor.

She'd noticed earlier – when she'd turned on the lamp – that the room had three doors. Briefly glancing at the other two, she hesitantly headed towards the one closest to the fireplace.

She opened it to reveal an immaculate bathroom.

Its decor matched that of the bedroom. The walls were painted a pale green color and the tiled floor was a checkered brown and white. Serving as the room's center piece was an enormous whirl pool bathtub. The large rectangular mirror above the sink was very impressive as well.

Unfortunately, she caught a glance of herself in its reflective surface.

She looked like a heathen.

Sweat coated her forehead and the greasy mop of hair on her

head was managing to both stick to the slick skin as well as defy gravity and stand on end.

She was sorely tempted to make use of the tub behind her – If only to wash her demented hair. Despite how the white porcelain beckoned her, however, she didn't feel comfortable using it. She didn't even know where she was for God's sake – or who the tub belonged to for that matter.

Determined to rectify that, Katherine swiftly exited the bathroom and closed the door behind her. She made her way towards the next closest door – the one a few feet from the mahogany dresser.

She opened the shuttered door and immediately recognized the adjoining room as a closet – a huge, spacious closet.

Or it *would* have been a spacious closet if it wasn't half full of clothes.

Men's clothes.

Pants, t-shirts, and a few dressier collared shirts filled the shelves and hangers. Katherine gnawed at her bottom lip.

Was – could it be possible that – was she in *Bastian's* room?

Had she been admiring *his* possessions?

Sleeping in *his* bed?

Katherine probably shouldn't have been as affected as she was – she'd already slept in a bed *with* the man after all. But she couldn't stop the swarm of butterflies from materializing in her stomach – their wings flapping frantically against her insides.

The air in the room was suddenly too thick.

She had to leave.

Not leave *leave*, of course. She'd been there, done that. It didn't work out so well.

But she had to get out of this room – out of this house.

She shut the closet door – perhaps more noisily than she should have – and made a bee line for the last unexplored door. She tugged on the knob, pulled it open and escaped the room.

The dark hallway she found herself in was as sparsely decorated as the room she'd come from. No picture frames or other hangings were nailed to the walls, but the beige carpet under her feet was plush.

Katherine didn't take the time to observe much else, however, as she was anxious to find an exit. She rushed by a staircase in her search as well as two open entryways leading to other rooms when she spotted a pair of sealed double doors.

The doors' locks made it obvious that it was the way outside.

An irrational thought ran through Katherine's mind. *What if the locks were in place more to keep her in than others out?*

But realizing that the thought probably wasn't so irrational only made her more desperate for some fresh air. She slid one lock open and jimmied another free.

"Making another escape attempt?"

Katherine froze.

Bastian.

The low timbre undoubtedly belonged to the man, but there was something in his voice – something menacing – that made the hair on the back of her neck stand up. Ignoring the last remaining lock, she slowly turned to face him.

He was sitting in a large dining room – apparently, it was one of the rooms with a gapping entryway that she'd thoughtlessly ignored on her way to the locked double doors. Bastian was bent over in one of the chairs surrounding the table in the center of the room, his stiff shoulders betraying his otherwise casual posture.

He was nursing a mug of some sort – the steam rising out of the cup and the bitter smell permeating the air leading Katherine to suspect the liquid to be coffee.

It was painfully obvious the man was standing guard.

But she wasn't trying to escape, Katherine thought defensively. She only wanted to breathe in some of the crisp night air – to calm her nerves.

And she wasn't about to be intimidated into doing otherwise.

But instead of opening her mouth to explain this to the brooding man, when her lips parted, what came racing out was a loud question. "Where are we?"

Bastian eyed her before taking a long swig from his mug. “My house.”

“Your house?” she echoed numbly. Did that mean that the room she’d woken up in *did* belong to him? Were they… had they already arrived in-

“Yes, in Haven Falls, Canada – just in case your memory has been impaired along with your common sense. I can think of no other reason for you taking off at the motel in Linburg.”

Katherine could think of plenty – like the fact that the man before her was a complete prick, for one.

But she was more concerned that she didn’t have any memories of the trip to Haven Falls – and it was a long journey from Duluth.

“How long was I out?” Katherine questioned.

Bastian stared at her for a tense moment, his mouth set in a stoic frown. And for the first time Katherine noticed how haggard he looked. There were dark shadows under his eyes and he didn’t look like he had shaved the entire time she’d been unconscious. His hair, too, was a mess and could have easily given her own wavy locks a run for their money in terms of chaoticness.

And yet… he was still probably the most handsome man she had ever met.

It wasn’t fair.

Eventually Bastian answered her. “Three days,” he bit out, twirling a finger around the rim of his mug. “This is the first time since I picked you up in Duluth that you’ve been lucid.”

Katherine’s eyes widened in surprise. *Three days?*

“How are you feeling?”

She fought the urge to childishly demand why he cared. It wasn’t like he’d worried himself about her health when he’d *kidnapped* her. Except that he sort of had, she acknowledge to herself, remembering all the times he’d forced her to eat.

“I feel better,” Katherine answered honestly. While it was true that she still had a bit of a headache, the unbearable pressure she could vividly remember squeezing her chest was gone.

Bastian inspected her face intently, searching her eyes with his – most likely trying to determine if she was telling the truth or not. Katherine fought the urge to squirm and instead crossed her arms defensively in front of her chest, determined to continue boldly meeting the man's stare until he'd finished.

After what seemed like an eternity, he tore his eyes from hers. "Good," he grunted, "then we can talk about punishment."

"What?" Katherine blurted in surprise, further confused when a vague memory of Bastian saying he could never be mad at her reverberated in her head.

Huh?

"For running away. You get punished and you learn not to repeat mistakes," Bastian reiterated and Katherine pushed the memory – or figment of her imagination, whatever it was – to the back of her mind. She allowed anger to consume her as she understood the meaning of his words.

"Who do you think you are? My mother?" Katherine could feel tears briefly cloud her vision as her own words caught up with her. Of course he wasn't her mother – she was *dead.*

But Katherine was quickly distracted from her own angst when Bastian abruptly grabbed the mug he'd been from drinking from off the table and launched it at the wall. It shattered upon impact and shards of glass fell to the floor. Brown liquid splattered the wall.

Katherine jumped in surprise, but held her ground even as the man slammed his hands on the table and pushed himself up to his full height. The chair he was sitting on clattered to the floor and he towered over her. Blue eyes captured green ones, and she couldn't bring herself to look away from his fierce stare.

"No," the man snarled. "I'm not your mother. I'm your *alpha.*" His voice was lethal and Katherine fought the urge to tear her gaze from his, but his blue eyes had mesmerized her – they almost seemed to be *glowing* with power. "I'm your leader and you have no other duty – *no other purpose* – than to obey me."

Katherine's body hummed with tension – with disagreement. She wanted to open her mouth and yell back at the man – tell him that she was her own person and that her life did have purpose. That it had meaning that went far beyond his own selfish plans. But she found that she couldn't – she could feel that intense weight on her chest again. It hurt – made it hard to breathe, let alone talk.

But Bastian was oblivious to the effect his words were having on her and continued his tirade uninterrupted. "Don't you get it, you stupid girl?" he demanded. "If you don't stop this foolishness, you're going to die!"

The man abruptly shut his mouth – clearly as shocked that he'd said what he did as Katherine.

"What are you talking about?" she asked faintly, finally finding her voice.

Katherine could vaguely remember wisps of other conversations, the nagging feeling that he and the others were keeping something from her. Markus exclaiming that she was a goner when she'd first met him – immediately after she'd denied the existence of werewolves – suddenly had new meaning.

Could – could she really die?

Katherine wasn't sure if it was her stricken expression or her softly spoken question that caused the change in Bastian – perhaps he had just worn himself out – but his face softened and picking up his fallen chair, he sat back down. Refusing to meet her eyes, he gestured towards the chair on the opposite side of the table with a flick of his hand.

For perhaps the first time ever, Katherine obeyed him without question and sat. She needed an explanation and probably would have sat on the floor if he'd demanded it.

Katherine considered her admittedly stubborn nature.

Or perhaps not.

She forced her wayward thoughts to quiet so she could listen to Bastian's explanation.

"Many people, especially females, don't survive the first change." He said it quickly, the words rushing past his lips.

As if saying it faster would cause her less panic, less pain – like pulling off a band-aid.

Katherine forced herself to remain calm. "What does that mean – the first change? The first time someone… that they turn into a…" she hesitated, her tongue and lips nearly refusing to form the word, "a *werewolf*?"

The man nodded his head, his dark, shaggy hair bobbing with the motion. "Yes. Some die during the change itself and others days, or even weeks, before – usually of illness."

Katherine's eyes widened.

Did… did that mean she had almost… died?

"Is that what happened to me?" she asked as his words registered.

Bastian finally looked at her and up close Katherine could see that the dark shadows under his eyes were more pronounced that she had first thought. "I don't know," he admitted seriously. "People who fall ill – it usually happens because their minds refuse to accept the changes their bodies are going through. You… you seemed to be having a difficult time believing in the existence of us so we thought that maybe you were… *fading*."

"I'm not," Katherine immediately assured the man – then wondered briefly why she was the one comforting him when *she* was the one who had a chance of dying.

She thought maybe it had something to do with wanting to erase *that particular* look on his face. She wasn't sure if it was pity or something else entirely, but she wanted it gone. "I'm not fading as you said. I feel much better."

Bastian nodded, but his solemn expression remained.

Katherine licked her lips nervously, knowing she'd have to voice her next question or allow it to go unasked and drive her mad. "So what are my odds here?"

Bastian's eyes locked onto hers. "Your odds?"

"Of surviving," she clarified, wondering why she didn't sound or feel more upset. Perhaps the fact that she might die hadn't sunk in yet. But more likely, she acknowledged, it was that she knew she could survive this – knew that the man in front of her, as much as she disliked him, wouldn't allow her to die.

Bastian hesitated to answer her question, running an agitated hand through his already wild-looking hair. "Only about half survive the change," he finally said.

Half. So her odds were fifty-fifty. *It... it could be worse*, she fought to assure herself.

"Most are men," Bastian continued, catching Katherine off guard. "They're strong and in peak physical condition. Women – they have less of a chance. Only a few can handle the physical and mental strains of the change."

Katherine bit the inside of her cheek, clamping down on the sensitive flesh there between her teeth. "So… less than half of women make it?"

Bastian looked away from her. "Less than a fourth."

The panic Katherine suspected she was supposed to feel earlier began to hit her – forming a hard, uncomfortable knot in her stomach. "Oh."

Oh? Was that all she had to say? Bastian had just told her she may— probably would, in fact – die and the only reaction she could conjure up was, "Oh"?

"Your odds of surviving are much higher," he hastily explained upon seeing her expression. "You're in good physical shape, barring your recent bout of illness, of course, and have been exposed to the company of werewolves almost since the day you've been bitten."

"If my odds are so much better, then why'd I get sick?" Katherine demanded.

Bastian's eyes hardened at her question and Katherine knew almost immediately that she'd asked the wrong thing. "You got sick because you were out gallivanting around in the rain and decided to sleep in your wet clothes. You got sick because you disobeyed orders and ran away."

Bastian's eyes had regained their earlier glint and as much as Katherine wanted to challenge his brazen assumptions and remind the man that he'd just told her he didn't know how she'd gotten sick, deep down she suspected he was right. She'd done it to herself – gotten herself sick.

"Now about your punishment," Bastian continued and she clenched her teeth together in an effort to stay quiet. "You and Caleb are responsible for preparing and serving meals for the next week – meals, I assure you, that you will eat."

That actually didn't sound so bad. She wasn't exactly the best cook, but she could make do. But there was one thing Katherine couldn't allow.

"Don't punish Caleb. It's not his fault that I ran away. I tricked him." She still felt guilty about it too.

Bastian was unrelenting, however. "I'm well aware of what happened, but whether you tricked him or not, Caleb knew better than to go against my direct orders."

"Markus and Zane did too," Katherine snipped before she could stop herself.

Bastian glared at her and she almost gave into the temptation to sink into her seat. "They've been dealt with," he promised darkly before pushing back his chair and rising to his feet. "Caleb will wake you up at dawn tomorrow to help him prepare breakfast."

Dawn? As in five o'clock in the morning?

Fabulous.

Bastian walked away from the table and was nearly out of the room when he abruptly jerked back around and looked at her. Except that he *wasn't* looking at her – not really. His eyes were focused on a spot above her right shoulder. "If you leave again," he warned, voice unwaveringly firm, "I won't come after you."

The *I'll leave you to die* was heavily implied.

Then he turned away and left her sitting in the dining room alone. His harsh words echoed in her ears.

But she hadn't once thought about leaving since she'd woken up, she wanted to argue to the unoccupied chair across from her. She hadn't been trying to escape earlier – just go outside.

But why not?

She had been desperate to escape before.

As crazy as it seemed, Katherine knew the answer. "Because I believe," she whispered to the empty room.

She sat in the dining room a few minutes longer, stewing in her realization. Feeling utterly drained, she rose from her seat, relocked the two locks she'd popped opened earlier, and made her way back into the bedroom she'd ran from not an hour earlier.

She knew now that the room must have been Bastian's. But he wasn't there. And Katherine no longer cared that the room belonged to the infuriating man – at least, tonight she didn't. She buried herself under the bed covers – the sheets pleasantly cool against her warm skin – and closed her eyes. Within minutes, she was asleep.

She didn't dream.

CHAPTER ELEVEN

Punishment.

Katherine realized quickly that it wasn't going to be as easy as she had first assumed.

In fact, it only took about five seconds after being roused at the crack of dawn by a wide-eyed Caleb for her to understand that cooking wasn't Bastian's *real* punishment for her.

No.

The true torture was being woken up so early to do the said cooking that it was still dark outside, only the faintest beams of pinks and oranges peeking in through the windows' blinds.

And Caleb's real punishment, apparently, was having to put up with her.

She'd been jostled awake by the man shaking her shoulder and startled, Katherine managed to nail him in the nose with a sharp elbow.

The force of the blow caused Caleb to stumble backward and a completely mortified Katherine tore the sheets off her legs and shot out of bed. "Crap! Are you okay, Caleb?"

"I'm fine," he immediately assured her. He was holding one hand to his injured appendage, however, and the words were somewhat muffled as they traveled between the cracks of his fingers. "I'm sorry for startling you. I called your name, but you wouldn't wake up so I grabbed your shoulder."

She had just smacked Caleb in the face with her elbow and *he* was sorry?

"Don't apologize. I'm the one who should be sorry. I shouldn't ha-"

"It's alright," Caleb interrupted. He removed his hand from his nose. While she was glad to see it wasn't bleeding, she couldn't help but notice how red and tender it looked.

Katherine bit her lower lip, gnawing at the plump flesh, before hesitantly approaching the man. "I actually meant that I'm sorry for the stunt I pulled back in Linburg. Not that I'm *not* sorry for hitting you," she assured him when she saw his brow furrow in confusion, "but back at the motel, I shouldn't have tricked you."

She hoped Caleb would be able to hear the sincerity in her voice.

He must have because he graced her with a smile. "It's okay," he assured.

Katherine had hoped that apologizing to Caleb would have made her feel better and ease the guilt she still felt about the incident, but his easy forgiveness only served to make her feel worse.

It was maddening.

"No, it's not," she insisted, the words thoughtlessly spilling from her lips. "I made you go against Bastian's orders and now you're being punished. It's completely my fault. I tried to tell Bastian that it was all my doing and that you didn't do anything wrong, but he wouldn't listen to me. He never listens to me!"

Caleb's eyes widened as the words continued to pour out of her mouth, her verbal filter apparently experiencing a glitch of some sort. "Katherine, it's okay. *Really.* I don't blame you for what you did. I've been in a position similar to yours and I can't begrudge you your actions. And as for Bastian, well, I mean, he's right. I knew better than to disobey his orders, but I did anyway."

The man's brown eyes were earnest and Katherine didn't know whether to be relieved that the only person in her pack she considered a friend had forgiven her or angry that he was insisting Bastian was right and that letting said man dictate his life was "okay.".

"But Caleb-"

"Besides, I like to cook," he interrupted her protests once more. "I'm usually responsible for the meals anyway."

Katherine frowned, not knowing if Caleb really did usually do all of the cooking or if he was just trying to pacify her.

If he was, it was working.

"Okay," she sighed in defeat before running a hand through her hair. And was abruptly reminded of the horrendous state it was in. She groaned. "Do you mind if I take a quick bath before meeting you in the kitchen?"

The man laughed, but she wasn't sure if it was due to the question or the twisted grimace her face had undoubtedly transformed into as she'd attempted to untangle her knotted mess of hair with her fingers.

Katherine eyed him. *Probably the grimace.*

She glared until his laughter subsided.

"Sure," he agreed, a smile stretching across his face, "but, no offense, you look like you might need to upgrade that into a *long* bath."

"Ha ha," Katherine muttered, rolling her eyes. She perked up, however, when she remembered the whirl pool bathtub she'd discovered while she'd been exploring the bedroom the night before. "Actually, I might take you up on that offer. If it's okay with you, I'll meet you in the kitchen in twenty minutes. It's connected to the dining room, right?"

Caleb nodded, though he looked confused as to how she could have known that. Apparently Bastian had informed him that she was awake, but not about the conversation – and she used the term "conversation" lightly – she'd had with him a few hours earlier. Good. She'd like to keep it that way.

"Alright, I'll see you in twenty then."

Caleb agreed and swiftly exited. Katherine took the time to stretch before making her way towards the door she knew led to the bathroom.

The tiled room looked even more exceptional than it had the previous night. The tub especially. She twisted its glass knobs and shucked off her clothes without a second thought. She avoided gazing into the mirror as the porcelain bathtub filled with water, weary of the disheveled girl that had greeted her the last time she had looked into its reflective surface.

She filled the tub as high as she dared before turning on the jets and allowing her tense body to sink into the pool of warm water. Her muscles relaxed immediately and she couldn't stop an appreciative groan from escaping. She only allowed herself a few minutes of relaxation, however, before reaching for the hair products she'd snatched from a cabinet before getting into the bathtub.

Katherine thoroughly washed her dark locks before treating her body to the same treatment via soap. A few minutes later, she reluctantly unplugged the tub and shut off the jets. She used a thick, fluffy towel – she'd found it in the same cabinet as the shampoo and conditioner – to pat her wet hair dry before wrapping it around her torso.

Once completely dry, Katherine reluctantly pulled back on the sullied pair of sweatpants and oversized t-shirt she'd been stuck wearing the past few days. Then she combed through her hair with her fingers – a task made infinitely easier after said hair had been eagerly conditioned – before finally leaving the bathroom in favor of finding the kitchen to help Caleb with breakfast.

Katherine found the man standing over one of two metal stoves, a white apron tied neatly around his waist. She wasn't sure what she was more impressed by – the massive kitchen and its state of the art appliances or the heavenly aroma that permeated the air of the room. Katherine followed her nose to the source of the smell that was causing her mouth to salivate. She looked around Caleb's shoulder to see that he was scrambling a dozen or so eggs in a frying pan. There was also a large pot of delicious smelling white gravy coming to a boil on a separate burner.

The brown-eyed man must have sensed her presence behind him because he turned to greet her. "Oh, good, you're here. I was just about to start the bacon. I'm nearly finished with the eggs and the biscuits are in the oven."

"You're making more?" Katherine questioned, mouth slightly agape.

There was enough food on the stove to feed a small army.

Caleb laughed at her expression. "Yes, *we're* making more. You have seen Markus eat, haven't you?"

Katherine felt the heat blossom across her cheeks. Yes, she *had* seen the man eat. Or rather, she'd seen him stuff himself with enough food to feel a *not-so-small* army. "You're right," she conceded, "we need to make more."

"Exactly," Caleb agreed before handing her the spatula he'd been using and heading over to the large freezer pushed up against the far corner of the room. He dug around for a moment before pulling out a large zip lock bag filled with thick-cut strips of bacon.

"Here," he said, tossing the bag over to Katherine, who deftly caught it. "Could you start frying these on the griddle? It should be warm enough by now."

She glanced at the griddle set up near the second stove before turning her attention back to the bag of bacon in her hands. "All of it?"

"All of it," Caleb confirmed, digging another spatula out of a cabinet drawer – the cabinets were beautiful, a similar wood to the mahogany of the dresser in Bastian's room – before turning his attention back to the eggs.

"I hope you prefer your bacon crispy," she muttered, having never really cooked it before.

Caleb offered her a bemused grin. "Crispy is fine. The bad news about cooking for the pack? A ton of food needs to be made. The good news? No one's picky. Sophie can be particular about some things, but trust me, the others will eat anything."

Ten minutes later, Katherine had finished the bacon – it was only a little burnt – and Caleb was pulling the biscuits out of the oven. She helped the man transfer the food they had made onto large serving platters.

As she was setting a tray of bacon on the dining room table, she absentmindedly noticed that the mess Bastian had made by throwing the mug against the wall last night had been cleaned up. The sharp shards of glass had been cleared from the floor and the brown stain on the wall had been wiped clean. Katherine wondered if Caleb had been the one stuck cleaning the mess and berated herself for not having the sense to do it the night before – even if Bastian was the one who had chucked the unoffending mug at the pale-colored wall.

She had just set the plate of biscuits on the table – Caleb was searching the refrigerator for some butter – when a bright-eyed Sophie bounded into the dining room. "Something smells divine," she greeted Katherine, offering her a cheerful smile. "I can't tell you how happy I was when Bastian told us you were feeling better."

Before Katherine could respond to the exuberant blonde – she was clearly one of those obnoxiously happy morning people – Zane, too, came striding in the room. "Good morning," he greeted amicably enough before taking a seat on one of the six chairs set around the table.

Any latent fear Katherine may have felt at having to face the rest of the pack after having run away – *and failing rather spectacularly at it at that* – slowly dissipated.

And then Markus walked into the room.

As soon as the brawny man spotted her, his eyes hardened and a sort of disgusted grunt escaped him. *Good morning to you too*, Katherine thought sarcastically, unable to withhold the urge to roll her eyes. Before she could confront Markus about his attitude problem, however, she noticed the discolored purple and yellow skin surrounding one of the man's hazel eyes and another bruise that had flowered along the sharp edge of his jaw. The sight of them made her hold her tongue.

What had happened to him?

She was debating whether or not she wanted to ask the man what he'd done to earn his face such a beating – though she suspected it had something to do with Bastian's promise that Markus, too, had been punished for Katherine's little disappearing act – when the man in question entered the room. He strolled right past her – saying nothing and making no gesture to acknowledge her existence – and sat in the seat at the head of the table.

And just like that Katherine no longer thought that Markus's grunt was quite so rude. He, at least, hadn't blatantly ignored her. She viciously bit down on her bottom lip to prevent herself from saying something she'd probably regret and reluctantly took the last available spot at the table – on the chair directly on Bastian's left. Caleb was on her other side, at least, which *almost* made her closeness to the blue-eyed man bearable. Unfortunately, she was also seated straight across from Markus.

Ugh.

Katherine observed as Bastian filled his plate with a copious helping of bacon and eggs before the others began hastily taking their fill as well. Trying not to watch Markus mash his food together in his open mouth, a dribble of the gravy Caleb had made making its way down his chin, Katherine helped herself to some bacon and snatched up one of the delicious smelling biscuits. She spread some butter on the still steaming bread, which immediately melted.

A heavy sort of silence fell as everyone concentrated on their food, silverware scraping against plates the only sound that permeated the quiet dining room.

"Who made the bacon?"

Katherine glanced across the table and met the hazel orbs of the man seated across from her.

"I did."

Markus snorted. "Figures."

She tensed, her eyebrows furrowing together. "What's that supposed to mean?"

"It means," he spoke slowly, as if talking to an exceptionally dim-witted person, "that it tastes more like charred ash than anything resembling food."

Katherine immediately felt an angry blush burst across her cheeks, heating her pale skin. *What a prick!* She opened her mouth to call him exactly that – and a few more colorful names, if she was honest – but wasn't even able to get out the soft sound of the "p" when a fist came down on the table, the force of the blow causing more than one plate to rattle.

She immediately turned her attention to the man who'd slammed down his fist – it was still clenching a fork that had speared two slices of bacon – onto the wooden table. He looked more than a little frustrated, the muscle on the right side of his strong jaw twitching noticeably.

"Enough," Bastian spat through clenched teeth.

Katherine fought the urge to talk back. She hadn't done anything! It was all that stupid bully of a man.

"Yeah," Sophie immediately agreed with her brother, though her glare was aimed at Markus and not Katherine. "Wouldn't want another black eye to match your first one, would you?"

So Bastian *had* been the one to rough up Markus.

"Anyway, Katherine, I've been thinking," Sophie announced, interrupting the tense quiet that the room had once again fallen into.

"Didn't hurt yourself, did you?"

A spark of annoyance crossed the blonde's face, but neither girl made an effort to acknowledge the belligerent man who'd spoken – Markus, again, of course.

"Yes?" Katherine inquired politely.

"If you're feeling up to it, I was hoping you'd let me show you around Haven Falls today. We can kill two birds with one stone and do some much needed shopping too. I'm sure you're getting sick of having to wear Bastian's shirt."

Katherine was thankful her cheeks were still an angry red from squabbling with Markus as she was sure a wild flush would have taken hold of her otherwise. She hadn't known she'd been wearing Bastian's shirt. Though now that she knew, it made sense – the thing nearly hung to her knees after all.

She couldn't stop her curious eyes from glancing at the man sitting on her right. He was staring resolutely at his plate of food, however, and refusing to look at her. He shifted awkwardly, perhaps uncomfortable with her scrutiny.

Unless his discomfort stemmed from the fact the she was wearing his shirt.

Well, it wasn't like she'd had a choice, Katherine thought angrily. She hadn't been the one to pick it out – or even put it on for that matter!

Unconscious people didn't exactly have superb fine motor skills.

"It's okay if you have something else planned..." Sophie trailed off, sounding confused. Her voice brought Katherine back to the present and the small brunette abruptly realized that she'd taken too long to answer the girl's question, having been staring unabashedly at Bastian instead.

"No, um," she responded, unbelievably flustered and desperately searching her mind for an excuse to say no. She wasn't exactly a huge fan of shopping. But the fact of the matter was that she *was* in desperate need of some new clothes. And she couldn't help but be curious about Haven Falls. If it was truly where she would be staying for the foreseeable future, she'd need to learn all that she could about the place. "That plan sounds good," she finally hedged hesitantly.

"Great!" Sophie agreed exuberantly. "We can go as soon as breakfast's cleaned up. It's a bit of a trek into town, so by the time we get there the shops should be open."

Katherine nodded complacently, impaling a bit of biscuit with her fork and popping it into her mouth.

But, of course, Markus had to put a damper on their plans.

"What about the lunch she's supposed to be making?" he demanded, pointing a butter knife in her direction, though his eyes were on Bastian and the question was clearly meant for him.

"God Markus, don't you ever stop?" Sophie scowled, clearly annoyed.

"It's fine," Bastian immediately assured her before another argument could break out. "I'll be at a council meeting anyway and since Sophie and Katherine will be gone, everyone can be responsible for their own meal."

Sophie smiled triumphantly at the news while Markus positively scowled.

Katherine's attention, however, had been diverted from the excursion into town Sophie had planned to the council meeting Bastian mentioned. She was curious – too curious to keep her mouth shut. "What's the council meeting about?"

Bastian seemed surprised by the question, though perhaps that had more to do with the fact that she had asked nicely than the inquiry itself. If the silence from the others was anything to go by, they seemed rather shocked by her civil tongue as well.

Katherine supposed that was fair. She hadn't exactly been very respectful up to that point. But after her talk with Bastian the night before, she'd come to the realization that she couldn't remain angry and combative forever. She needed to learn from these people, after all. Learn to get along with them, too – even Markus.

Bastian recovered from his surprise rather quickly and tersely answered her question. "The meeting's about you."

Katherine's eyes widened, but before she could respond to his blunt answer, the man stood up, scrapping his chair across the floor as he did so, and stomped out of the room. Sophie sent her an apologetic look before taking off after him.

Great. What faux pas had she committed this time?

Her mood didn't improve when she caught sight of Markus's mocking smile. She wondered if the responding scowl on her face matched his from earlier.

The rest of breakfast passed in silence – at least, from Katherine's end. Markus and Zane discussed something about hunting elk by a nearby stream, with minimal input by Caleb.

When everyone was finished eating, Katherine and Caleb gathered the dirty dishes – Bastian's plate still half-full of eggs stared at her accusingly – and set up an efficient system for cleaning them. She washed, and he dried and put away the clean glassware as she'd yet to learn where everything went.

They were just finishing up when Sophie entered the kitchen and hastily pulled her away from the sink. A fluffy, purple coat that was probably only two sizes too big – which meant it definitely belonged to Sophie, even if the thought of Bastian or Markus wearing it brought an amused grin to her face – and a pair of oversized boots were shoved into her arms.

"I know it's only early October, but there's definitely a chill in the air. Our kind isn't super affected by the cold, but you aren't a full-fledged werewolf quite yet so you should probably put that stuff on."

She couldn't hide her skeptical glance at the purple monstrosity, but she obediently tugged the thing on anyway.

Sophie sniggered. "Don't worry, you can pick out a new coat and other winter gear in town." She pulled a shiny plastic card from a tote bag she had slung across her shoulder. "And don't hold back on getting what you want. Everything is going on one of Bastian's many handy dandy credit cards."

Before Katherine could properly process that, Sophie had a firm arm wrapped around her elbow and was forcing her out the front door. As soon as they reached the outside, however, Katherine jerked to a stop, forcing the blonde to tarry as well.

It was so *green.*

The color absolutely dominated the landscape.

Towering spruce and pine trees were everywhere, emerging from the thin fog that did little to hide the grass and greenery on the ground. Even Bastian's house, composed of beautiful burgundy bricks, was being overtaken by the green. Thick vines crawled up the walls and wound up the columns of the wrap-around porch.

It was so different from the yellow cornfields of Iowa.

Katherine's stupor was broken by Sophie when she draped a friendly arm around the dazed girl's shoulders and guided her off the creaky porch. She led her to a dirt path just barely peeking out of the huge forest surrounding the house. The path wasn't very big – just wide enough for one vehicle to make it through safely.

"It's a bit overwhelming, I know."

Katherine nodded, unable to stop herself from repeating her initial impression. "It's just so green."

Sophie laughed before removing her arm from around the smaller girl's shoulders. "Yeah, just be happy it hasn't snowed yet. In the winter, everything turns white. I much prefer the green of spring and summer."

Katherine nodded genially, clutching the borrowed coat closer to herself when a strong breeze whistled through the trees and ruffled her still damp hair.

They'd been walking a good fifteen minutes before Katherine

noticed how anxious Sophie seemed to be. The older girl kept giving her furtive glances, like she was aching to say something, but wasn't sure if she should.

This, of course, did nothing but make Katherine uneasy. Sophie seemed nice enough, but she was reluctant to trust her. She *was* Bastian's sister after all.

"Katherine, look, about my brother." *And there it was.*

"What about your brother?"

"I know you don't have much reason to believe me, but he's not as bad of a guy as you probably think he is. Hell, he's not as bad of a guy as *he* thinks he is. He's just under a lot of stress right now."

Katherine just barely resisted the urge to snort. *He* was under a lot of stress? If she wasn't so young, she was convinced she would have died of a stress-induced heart attack days ago.

Sophie must have sensed her skepticism and kept on talking. "I know that seems like a silly excuse, but it's true. He was very worried about you when you were sick. He wouldn't even let you out of his sight long enough for me to change you into something a little more comfortable than his grimy sweats."

Katherine vividly recalled Bastian standing guard the night before. But to her, it seemed more like he did it to thwart another escape attempt than out of actual concern for her well-being.

His words from the night before – *"I won't come after you."* – reverberated in her head.

Then again, maybe that *wasn't* the reason.

But Katherine wasn't about to attempt to get inside the man's head. She could admit, however, that is was fairly obvious that Bastian felt responsible for her. Probably because he was the one who'd bitten her. That being as it may, the man certainly didn't *like* her. If Sophie thought he did, then the blonde was delusional.

Realizing she'd been quiet for too long, Katherine voiced her thoughts. "I suppose he feels responsible for me. He is the one who bit me, after all."

Sophie frowned. Whether it was due to Katherine's not-so-friendly tone or the reminder of her brother's imperfections was anyone's guess. "You have to know that he didn't mean for this to happen. He never meant to hurt you-"

"Yeah," Katherine quickly cut her off, not in the mood to hear the blonde make more excuses for her brother. "Caleb explained it to me. Something about my natural scent... calling to him?"

Sophie froze, her eyes wide, and Katherine was forced to stop beside her. "What? What's wrong?"

"What else did Caleb tell you?" Sophie immediately demanded.

Katherine scrunched her brow in confusion, but answered anyway. "Nothing really. And to be honest, what he did say – you know, about me smelling good to Bastian – sounded like a load of tripe to me."

Sophie's tense shoulders relaxed as she realized that Caleb hadn't told her anything more – though it was obvious to Katherine that her so called pack was hiding something, probably multiple somethings, from her.

"Katherine, you have to know that Bastian would never purposely do this to someone. His will is stronger than anyone's I know. For him to have bitten you, I mean..." she trailed off, losing some of her gusto, "he wouldn't have had a choice."

Katherine didn't buy it for a minute. There was *always* a choice. She didn't care how tasty she'd smelled or how many inhibitions were dropped when one was forced to turn into an animal – and, dear God, her mind still couldn't quite grasp that insane concept.

"Things will work out."

Katherine managed a weak smile for the girl walking on her left, but seriously doubted that was true. Still, she managed to keep her mouth shut about the subject.

A few more minutes were spent walking in an amicable silence before they came to the end of the dirt road. Sophie brushed aside a low hanging branch of a trembling aspen tree – one of the few deciduous trees speckled throughout the coniferous – and finally, the heart of Haven Falls was revealed.

Katherine wasn't sure what she was expecting, but this – this *quaint* little village – wasn't it.

Most of the buildings spread out before her were made of wood – possibly from the trees that must have been cleared away to make room for the tiny town that couldn't have expanded more than a half a mile in any direction. Most of the cabin-like buildings were bunched together, separated only by dirt roads a little wider than the one she and Sophie had traveled to get there. There were a few houses, some made of a similar brick as Bastian's home, further out in the distance. She suspected they served as the homes of other inhabitants who lived in the town.

"So, what do you think?"

She glanced at the blonde next to her. Sophie didn't seem too put out by Katherine's lack of reaction.

"It's small," Katherine said tactfully.

Sophie nodded, a smile spreading across her face. "Yeah, it makes your Middletown look like some bustling city. Haven Falls isn't much, that's for sure, but it is home."

She began walking again, straight towards the cluster of buildings located in the center of the town. Katherine trailed behind her, continuing to take in her surroundings. "Why's it called Haven Falls?"

Sophie slowed her pace, allowing Katherine to catch up. "It's named after a nearby waterfall. It's absolutely dazzling and close to our house actually. I can take you to see it later this week if you want." She paused. "Or maybe Bastian could take you."

Katherine frowned. "Maybe *you* can take me," she hesitantly agreed.

Sophie led her past two buildings, but dragged her to the wooden door of the third. The sign above the entry way proclaimed the small shop to be The Closet.

Hesitating outside of the boutique, she couldn't help but wonder how the people of Haven Falls – or, the creatures, rather – would react to seeing a fresh face. No one would attack her.

Right?

As if sensing her distressed thoughts, Sophie turned to face Katherine, her blue eyes – so different from her brother's with his darker colored irises – exuding comfort. "It's still early in the day, so it's likely the only person in there will be the shopkeeper, but you still ought to know that anyone who sees you today will probably stare and ask questions."

Katherine felt her stomach drop, landing somewhere near the oversized boots cladding her feet. She'd almost prefer to be attacked than be on the receiving end of any sort of attention or scrutiny.

"What are they going to ask me?" she immediately demanded, her mind whirling with possibilities. *Who are you? Where'd you come from? What sort of pathetic werewolf are you supposed to be*?

"It doesn't matter what they ask. You can't answer their questions. We need to keep to ourselves as much as possible today."

"Why?" Not that she was complaining.

"Remember Bastian explaining how the council meeting today is about you?"

How could she forget? "Yeah."

"Well," Sophie explained, twirling a piece of her long hair around her finger, "he and the other alphas are deciding what to do with you and until they came to a conclusion today, Bastian wants to shield you from the rest of the community. I had to practically beg him to take you out and only managed to convince him because you were in need of so many supplies."

They were deciding what to do with her? That sounded ominous.

"Anyway," Sophie continued, oblivious to Katherine's inner dialogue, "the council members are the only ones who know of your existence so far, so it's best that we keep as low a profile as possible while we're out. Just ignore the looks I'm sure you're going to get and I'll deflect any questions that come our way, okay?"

Katherine took a deep breath and slowly let it out. "Okay," she agreed before allowing Sophie to drag her into The Closet.

The rest of the morning and afternoon passed in a blur of cotton, lace, and chiffon. After spending over two hours trying on clothes in

The Closet – the shop sure had a lot of merchandise for such a tiny establishment – Sophie dragged her to another shop clear across town called Vintage Underground.

Here, the blonde convinced her to buy what Katherine had to admit was a phenomenal leather jacket. She also manipulated her into buying a little black *thing* – Sophie insisted it was a dress – with way too many frills and a complete lack of fabric in the back.

The conversation had gone a little something like this:

"Oh! How about this? Every girl needs a little black dress. You never know when a special occasion will come up."

"I don't know. Isn't it a little, well, skimpy?"

"Yeah. Bastian would hate it."

"...I'll try it on."

Apparently, Sophie knew just what to say to get those around her to do as she pleased.

After they were finished there, the sun was high in the sky and they stopped to eat at a restaurant, creatively named The Bistro. Katherine supposed it didn't really matter what it was called though, because according to Sophie, it was the only eatery in town.

Once they finished scarfing down their lunches – Katherine had ordered a steak and it'd been pink, juicy, and delicious – Sophie showed her the locations of the butcher shop and what she referred to as the grocery store, though it was more of a farmers' market than anything.

Finally, they stopped at an apothecary where Katherine purchased some locally brewed shampoo and conditioner, some soap, a package of razors, and deodorant.

She'd never been so happy to see a roll-on.

Of course, the shopping spree wasn't a completely fun experience. Both shopkeepers and the apothecary owner had stared at her without shame, only forcing their eyes to leave her form after catching sight of Sophie's responding glare. The waiter at The Bistro had been even worse, but Katherine couldn't find it in herself to be too upset with the dark-haired young man who looked to be about her age. He'd flushed and seemed embarrassed when Sophie had called him out on his aberrant gawking.

Despite the stares and her general aversion to shopping, however, Katherine discovered that she rather enjoyed Sophie's company, and it was with reluctance that she returned to Bastian's house with her late that afternoon.

Katherine figured her lack of enthusiasm had a lot to do with having to once again deal with the temperamental owner of said house.

For all her foot-dragging, though, she didn't see Bastian until supper, and the man didn't even deign to speak to her until she and Caleb had begun clearing away the remains of the meal – scalloped potatoes and ham, which had contained more ham than potato.

"We need to talk."

Katherine forced herself to look up from the stack of dirty plates in her arms and meet the man's eyes. "About what?" she demanded.

His eyebrows rose in response to her abrasiveness. What did he expect? For her to fall over herself for the mere opportunity to speak with him?

Maybe when hell froze over.

"I think it'd be better if we discussed that alone. Follow me. You can leave those dishes for Caleb."

Rolling her eyes at the blatant order, Katherine allowed the brown-eyed man to take the plates from her. She ignored a sneering Markus and followed Bastian out of the dining room. He led her down the hallway to a sturdy door opposite Bastian's bedroom. Opening the door, he gestured for her to enter. Despite her reservations, she did so.

Katherine couldn't help but be impressed by the room he'd led her to. Books were overflowing from shelves that nearly reached the ceiling and the lights of an extravagant glass ceiling fixture reflected on gleaming hardwood floors. A worn, plush-looking chair pushed into a corner of the room looked immensely comfortable and inviting.

She suspected that she'd been led to Bastian's study.

Her observations of the room were cut short, however, by the sound of the door clicking shut behind her. Bastian stalked past her before sitting atop a cherry wood desk that served as the center piece of the room. Wordlessly, he invited her to have a seat on a chair opposite the desk.

Katherine ignored the invitation completely. Instead, she remained standing, pulling her arms across her chest defensively.

"What am I in trouble for now?" Katherine couldn't be bothered to beat around the bush. She had no desire to be in the overbearing man's presence any longer than absolutely necessary.

Bastian released a weary sigh before swiping a hand through his already disheveled hair. "Nothing as far as I know. I actually wanted to talk to you about what the other alphas and I discussed at the council meeting today."

Oh.

Did they decide what they were going to do with her? Katherine tightened her arms around her torso. "You already told me that the meeting was about me," she reminded Bastian.

"I know," he agreed, "but what I didn't tell you was that we were deciding whether or not you were fit to attend school."

Wait. Haven Falls had a school?

"School?"

The corners of Bastian's lips dipped to form a frown. "Yes, werewolves…" he paused as if feeling out her reaction to the word. She forced herself to remain impassive. "Werewolves," he continued, "typically attend school until the age of seventeen. It's considered the age of majority."

"I'm sixteen. I'll be seventeen this spring. That's close enough."

Bastian pinched his nose between the thumb and fore finger of his hand. "Not according to the council. They've decided that you'll go until you've turned seventeen. They went as far as to say it'd be inappropriate to *not* send you there – that the school is the best place for you to learn about our culture."

Katherine was incredulous – and completely unwilling to accept that premise.

"But can't you teach me? You and the rest of the pack? I don't want to go to school! I don't know anyone and everyone will stare – it'll just be an all-together uncomfortable situation."

Bastian shook his head. "I can assure you that they don't particularly care about your comfort."

"But…" Katherine searched her mind for more reasons that sending her to school was a terrible idea. "But I haven't even survived the change! What if when the full moon rises in a few weeks, I die? Making me go will have been pointless!"

"Don't say that!" Bastian spat, his face turning nearly as blue as his eyes. "You're not going to *die*," he insisted through clenched teeth before roughly rubbing the palms of his hands deep into his eye sockets. "They know you haven't been through the change, but they're set in their decision."

Katherine waited a minute for the man to regain control of himself before opening her mouth again. "You keep saying *they*," she noted shrewdly. "Not *we*. Does that mean you agree with me? That you don't support their decision to send me to school either?"

For a long moment, Bastian refused to meet her eyes. When he finally did, they shone with an emotion she couldn't identify. "No, I don't. But they're convinced that this is the right course of action and there's nothing I can do about it short of disappearing with you and the rest of the pack in the dead of night."

If Katherine didn't know any better, she'd say the man seriously considered that an option.

But she knew it wasn't.

And as Bastian confessed that he didn't want to send her to school any more than she wanted to go, she felt the fight drain out of her.

"Fine, I'll go."

Bastian's eyebrows rose in surprise at her sudden compliance. "Really?"

"I said I would," she snapped. "It's not like I really have a choice in the matter."

He smiled at her words, but the sardonic grin that stretched across his face was anything but happy. It was dark. Self-depreciating. "No,

I suppose you don't."

Katherine shifted her weight from one foot to the other as an uncomfortable silence descended upon the study. "Is that all you wanted to talk about?"

Bastian shook his head. "No, actually, there's more – something else."

Katherine was quickly growing impatient. "What else is there to discuss? I already said I would go!"

Bastian sighed in frustration, but didn't answer her question.

"Well?" she demanded when the man refused to open his mouth and explain himself. "What else do we need to talk about?"

"You're an unmarked werewolf." The words escaped the man's mouth seemingly without his permission.

She continued to gaze at him with incredulous eyes. "What?"

Bastian scratched the back of his neck in obvious discomfort, a faint red color creeping up his neck. "Are you aware that certain animals like to… *mark* their territory?"

Katherine's confusion continued to grow. "Like dogs? That pee on fire hydrants?"

"Yes," Bastian immediately agreed, his relief apparent. The tense lines that had formed on his forehead disappeared at her understanding. "Yes, like that."

But the problem was that Katherine *didn't* understand. And she was fed up with his cryptic crap.

"What does this have to do with school?" she demanded.

The tense lines made a reappearance. "I can't – that is to say, I *won't* – allow you to attend school as an unmarked wolf."

Katherine threw her arms in the air in utter exasperation. *Honestly, couldn't the man have just said that?* "How do I go about getting marked then?"

Bastian shifted in obvious distress, and she couldn't deny that she took some perverse pleasure in seeing the usually so put-together man squirm. Even if she didn't know what it was he was so embarrassed about.

Finally, he opened his mouth. "Your example was actually a rather good one." He paused. "The one about the dog."

Katherine felt her whole body stiffen as realization dawned. But there was *no way* she was understanding him right. "Are you trying to tell me that you need to mark me as your territory by *peeing* on me?!"

Bastian sighed wearily. "I knew you'd be unreasonable about this."

"*Unreasonable?* Are you kidding me? I am *not* going to let you pee on me!"

"You don't have a choice in the matter," he repeated her earlier words.

"No," Katherine snarled. "This, at least, I have a choice in. Hygiene issues aside, I am not *your territory.*" She was disgusted by the concept. "I'm *no one's* territory and I refused to be treated as such!"

Bastian crossed his powerful biceps over his chest, clearly unimpressed. "I can't let you go to school unmarked. It would be an absolute catastrophe."

"Why? Who cares if I'm marked or not? Why do I even need to be marked?"

"Wolves are marked so that other wolves know they belong to a pack. All pack members smell like their alpha; it's just the way it is. If I left you unmarked, no one would respect my pack's claim on you."

"So?" Katherine goaded the man, knowing she was being childish, but not liking the fact that he thought he had a claim on her any more than she had appreciated being referred to as territory.

Bastian's eyes narrowed and his arm muscles bulged under his shirt sleeves. "Don't you understand?"

Katherine pursed her lips. "Understand what?"

"The dangers of attending school unmarked! If they – the students, the teachers – don't smell me on you, there are bound to be unpleasant consequences."

She snorted derisively. "Like what?"

"You could be attacked!" Bastian softened his tone when he spied the astonished look on her face. "But for the most part," he admitted,

"I'm worried about you being recruited. No one will mess with you if you're marked by me."

Katherine wasn't sure exactly what sort of recruiting he was talking about, but the way he spat out the word made it clear that it was nothing good. "Why would anyone attack or… *recruit* me?"

Bastian relaxed his arms and swiped a hand through his hair. "Plenty of reasons. You know turned females are rare. You'll cause a stir – interest those you shouldn't."

Nothing the man was saying was making her feel any better about having to attend school. "I'll blend in."

Bastian looked at her like she'd just announced she was a unicorn. "Impossible. Haven Falls is too small a community for any new additions to go unnoticed. I'm sure you've already realized that after touring the town with Sophie. Besides, no one could *not* notice you."

Katherine had no idea what *that* was supposed to mean.

"But aren't there other ways to mark me? I mean, did you have to pee on the others too?" She couldn't stop the corner of her lips from lifting into a small smirk at the image that assaulted her brain – Markus in the same position that she was currently in.

"No," he admitted, causing Katherine to deflate as the hilarious image she'd concocted disintegrated. "By the time we formed the pack, we'd all spent enough time together that they smelled like me already."

It was true, Katherine knew. Although the members of Bastian's pack all smelled differently, the same underlying scent clung to them all.

"What about Caleb?" she asked. "I mean, he told me he's not a born werewolf."

Bastian's reaction to her question surprised her. His eyes hardened and his lips straightened into a hard, unyielding line under his mouth. "Yes, he told me he shared that with you, but no… it was my father who marked him."

Recalling the story Caleb had told her, a light bulb went off in Katherine's head. "Was it your father that saved him?"

"Yes," Bastian divulged, but looked away from Katherine's piercing eyes before she could ask any more questions. It was clear that he didn't want to reveal anything else to her.

She couldn't help but wonder where he – Bastian's father – was. And his mother for that matter. Obviously, Bastian was old enough to be considered an adult in were culture – he wasn't in school, after all. Her curiosity got the best of her. "How old are you?"

He furrowed his brows at the abrupt subject change, but answered her anyhow. "Eighteen."

So he was an adult according to her culture too. But that still didn't explain his absentee parents. A horrible thought occurred to her. *What if they were dead?* She clamped down hard on her lower lip. It was possible by the way Bastian was acting. He never mentioned them.

She was torn out of her thoughts by Bastian's voice. "I assure you that I'll make this experience as comfortable as I can for you. I'll do it right before you go to bed tonight and you can shower right after. I'll even transform into my wolf form if it makes you feel better."

What?

"Your wolf form?" Katherine deadpanned.

Bastian looked thoroughly annoyed. "What? Don't tell me you still don't believe?"

"No," she snarked, then immediately backtracked. "I mean, yes, I believe, but it's not the full moon."

"Though it can be difficult, once one experiences the change, it's possible to transform at any time," he explained.

Katherine desperately tried to stop her temper from erupting. "Then why didn't you just do that to prove your existence to me?" she asked in disbelief.

Bastian grimaced as he realized she had made that connection. "I thought it might do more harm than good. You already didn't believe in werewolves. It would have been a shock I wasn't sure your fragile psyche could handle if one of us morphed into a giant beast in front of you."

Fragile psyche? *Fragile psyche?!* She'd show him a fragile psyche!

"You're excused, by the way."

Katherine's body, which was trembling in anger at the insult, abruptly stilled. "Excuse me?"

The corner of Bastian's lips jerked, as if he was fighting off an amused smile. "Exactly – you're excused. You may leave."

Who did he think he was?

She fumed silently, glaring at the brazen man, but the sight of his twitching mouth only served to infuriate her more. She marched out of the study, making sure to slam the door behind her.

Katherine was marked later that night. It was a wholly foul experience as far as the small brunette was concerned, and she scrubbed her body down for an entire hour afterwards.

The only thing remotely pleasant about the ordeal had been once again seeing Bastian's wolf form, though she'd nearly had a heart attack when he'd bounded into her room on all fours. He'd called himself a gigantic beast earlier, but she couldn't help but think the creature he transformed into was majestic and even beautiful.

She just really wished she didn't.

CHAPTER TWELVE

Katherine was *not* nervous.

She could not feel what seemed like hundreds of tiny butterfly wings flapping in her stomach. And she had certainly not had trouble sleeping last night or forking down her breakfast that morning due to said butterflies.

She wasn't nervous and those stupid butterflies didn't exist because she didn't care what any of the people attending *a frickin' werewolf school* thought of her.

Really, she didn't.

Katherine could almost have convinced herself that it was true. If only she hadn't spent over half an hour picking out what to wear and a further fifteen minutes gazing into the mirror in the bathroom, inspecting her appearance for imperfections.

The outfit she had finally decided on was a simple pair of jeans and a long-sleeved, black V-neck shirt. She'd also shoved a glittery headband that Sophie had insisted on buying for her at The Closet into her hair in a desperate attempt to tame the mass of brown waves. Katherine was no fashionista, but she thought she actually looked half-way decent.

Unfortunately, no amount of primping and preening at herself in the mirror would calm those inanely persistent butterflies.

Knock. Knock.

"Katherine, are you ready to go? Bastian's waiting for you in the SUV."

Katherine released a small lungful of air she hadn't even been aware she'd been holding before leaving the bathroom attached to Bastian's bedroom. She had absolutely no idea where the tall man had been sleeping the past two nights. Not in his room, obviously. She'd been taking up his bed.

Which was really weird now that Katherine thought of it.

She'd even put away her new clothes in the room's spacious closet, which, bizarrely enough, had been cleared of the shirts and pants that had occupied it earlier.

"Are you excited about your first day of school?" Sophie accosted Katherine as soon as she exited the room.

"Sure," she agreed half-heartedly, retreating down the hallway to the front door and tugging on her knee high boots. She wasn't about to admit how nervous she was to the blonde. Besides, Sophie seemed excited enough for the both of them.

She had one arm through her leather jacket and was reaching to pull open the door with the other when a hesitant hand landed on her shoulder. Katherine turned to face Sophie, who was gnawing on her upper lip in a seemingly anxious gesture.

Maybe she wasn't so excited after all.

The blonde released her tortured lip. "Katherine?"

"Yeah?"

"Bastian's told you about recruiting, right?"

Katherine couldn't stop her forehead from creasing and the edges of her mouth from forming a frown. There was that word again. Recruiting. Bastian had briefly mentioned it the other night, but as for explaining it? "No, not really," she admitted.

Sophie huffed. "That just figures," she muttered, visibly annoyed by Katherine's answer. She threaded an aggravated hand through her blonde strands before meeting the curious girl's eyes. "Recruiting," she explained, "is how werewolf packs are formed. I *assumed* that my idiotic brother would have told you that considering recruiting, for most wolves anyway, begins and ends during their last year of school – right before they turn seventeen."

Well, that was certainly interesting. But Katherine failed to understand how it applied to her. Wasn't she already a member of a werewolf pack – *this* pack, in fact? Wasn't that the whole point of – Katherine scrunched her nose in revulsion as she remembered – being marked by Bastian the other night?

Katherine voiced her thoughts. "I thought I was already a member of this pack."

"You are," Sophie rushed to assure her. "Most werewolves are born into packs and remain members of them until they reach the age of seventeen – it's the age of majority for us. As soon as they turn seventeen, however, they are free to choose their own packs after competing in a tournament known as the Recruiting Rites. They may decide to remain members of their current alpha's pack or attempt to gain the attention and favor of another alpha. Unless they've been recruited by that specific alpha in the Rites, though, they are usually forced to prove themselves in some other way to become members of his pack – typically by completing a task or trial of some sort. If they fail, they're almost always rejected by the alpha and have to approach a new alpha for another chance to prove their worth."

Katherine's head ached as she attempted to retain all of the information Sophie was spewing forth. "What exactly is recruiting then?" she asked, still not quite grasping the concept.

"It's when an alpha," Sophie paused, clearly searching for the proper word to use, "*woos* a werewolf – tries to convince him or her to join his pack."

Having finally managed to shove her second arm through her jacket, Katherine crossed said appendages over her chest. "If recruiting and all this other crap is inevitable – and you seem to be under the impression that it is – then why did Bastian insist on," she pursed her lips, willing herself not to blush, "*marking* me last night?"

Katherine glowered at Sophie when she grinned. "Yeah, *that*. Bastian seems to think that if he makes his claim obvious, the other alphas of Haven Falls will be more hesitant to recruit you."

Katherine furrowed her brow. "Is he right?"

Sophie sighed, her amused smile drooping. "I don't know," she admitted. "I just wanted to make sure you knew exactly what kind of situation you were walking into today. Nearly every wolf your age is looking to be recruited. It's very competitive and, by nature, we werewolves are very prideful creatures. Just… be careful."

Well, wasn't *that* wonderful?

As if the butterflies in her stomach weren't enough, Katherine now felt as if a full-blown dragon was flying around in there.

A blaring car horn sounded from outside.

Sophie rolled her eyes. "Sounds like he's getting impatient. You'd better get going."

Katherine nodded, but didn't make a move for the door. Despite the gigantic beast now taking residence in her stomach, her curiosity had been roused. "Hey, Sophie?"

"Yeah? What is it?"

"Why… I mean, did Bastian… how was this pack formed?" she finally managed to spit out.

A sad smile enveloped Sophie's face. "Well, when our parents died, Bastian was sort of forced to become the new alpha of the Prince pack. Prince. That's our last name."

Katherine's stomach dropped as her suspicions were confirmed. Bastian's and Sophie's parents were dead. *Just like hers.* She unconsciously clenched her hands into fists, her blunt nails digging into the soft skin of her palms.

"Bastian was only fifteen when it happened, and Caleb and I were the only members of the Prince pack who chose to stay under his leadership. When Bastian finished school with Markus and Zane, they both joined. I wasn't shocked when Zane approached Bastian; he and his family were in the Prince pack before my parents died. But Markus," she shook her in fond exasperation, "*he* was a bit of a surprise."

Katherine listened as Sophie explained how Zane and Markus had joined Bastian's pack – the Prince pack, apparently – but she was stuck on the fact that their parents were dead. Morbid curiosity demanded that she ask how they'd died, while empathy – some strange sort of kinship due to what had happened to her own parents – insisted she keep her mouth firmly shut. Before one could win out over the other, the sound of a loud car horn once again pierced the air. She groaned. "I should go."

Sophie nodded. "Good luck and have fun at school."

The luck Katherine was sure she would need, but based on what Sophie had said about recruiting and competing, she was fairly certain that fun was out of the question. Nevertheless, she grabbed the satchel Caleb had borrowed her, walked out the door, and clambered into the passenger seat of the running SUV parked in front of the porch.

Bastian didn't acknowledge her, but waited for her to strap in, before taking off down the same dirt road she and Sophie had traveled yesterday morning. Neither Katherine nor Bastian broke the heavy silence as they cruised through Haven Falls and took a left onto a slightly wider road. Within minutes, they arrived at a large brick building with a small collection of rusted cars parked haphazardly in the tall grass on its right.

Katherine could only assume this was the school.

Bastian stalled the SUV in front of the building's white double doors. As subtly as she could, she turned and glanced at the man. She didn't know what she was waiting for. Some sort of instruction? A wish of good luck similar to Sophie's? Heck, even a simple good-bye? Whatever she was expecting, it wasn't for the man to be directing his blue eyes forward, resolutely refusing to meet her questioning gaze.

Katherine sighed. He was intent on throwing her to the wolves then.

Har. Har. Get it? *Throwing her to the wolves?*

Apparently, the higher her anxiety, the lower her standards of humor.

Katherine reached for the passenger side door handle, readying herself to exit the vehicle, when Bastian finally spoke up. He grabbed a red folder she hadn't even noticed had been lying on the dash and shoved the stapled papers inside of it under her face. "Here."

Startled, Katherine took the papers. She looked down at them. The piece of paper on top appeared to be her class schedule.

Werewolf History	*8:00AM – 9:00AM*	*Room 112*
Algebra	*9:00AM – 10:00AM*	*Room 204*
Free Study	*10:00AM – 11:00AM*	*Library*
Lunch	*11:00AM – 12:00PM*	*Cafeteria*
Pack Dynamics	*12:00PM – 1:00PM*	*Room 210*
Mating Rituals	*1:00PM – 2:00PM*	*Room 106*
Physical Education	*2:00PM – 4:00PM*	*Gymnasium*

Katherine gaped for a solid minute. Pack Dynamics? Mating Rituals? How sick was it that the only classes similar to those she'd been taking at Middletown were Algebra and P.E. – her two least favorite subjects. And apparently, P.E. was *two hours long* here.

If only Katherine was narcissistic enough, she'd almost believe the universe was conspiring against her.

She forced her eyes to abandon the schedule Bastian had handed her and turned towards the man. She must have looked *really* pathetic because he actually attempted what she suspected was supposed to be a reassuring smile. Even if it did come across as more of a grimace.

"You'll be okay."

Katherine couldn't help but cling to those words and repeat them in her head in an encouraging mantra. *You'll be okay. You'll be okay. You'll be okay.*

"Just to the right of the entrance is an office. Go there. The school's secretary – her name's Juliana – has arranged for another student to give you a tour of sorts."

Katherine waited a few more seconds to see if Bastian had anything else to tell her. Sensing the dark-haired man was done talking, Katherine nodded jerkily and shoved the schedule and other papers into her bag. "Thanks," she said, finally opening the car door and stepping out of the SUV.

Before she could fully shut the door behind her, however, Bastian leaned over the passenger seat and stopped the heavy metal from closing. "Markus will drive you home at four," he informed her gruffly.

Katherine froze, her mouth half-way open and her eyes wide in a wonderful impression of a deer caught in headlights. Or, at least, she assumed it was a wonderful impression based on the way Bastian's lips quirked in amusement before he finally allowed the door to shut, revved the engine, and took off.

Katherine's incredulous expression slowly transformed into a glowering frown.

Well, wasn't that just *grand*?

Forcing herself to concentrate on more pressing matters than *Markus*, she hesitantly trudged up the walkway – actual concrete – to the school's double doors and proceeded to follow Bastian's instructions.

To Katherine's shock, the inside of the school looked like… well, *a school*. Linoleum floors, narrow hallways crammed with pale blue lockers, and open doors that led to classrooms full of desks. The smell of Lysol, chalk, and teenage hormones permeated the air.

A few kids secreting said hormones – they looked a bit younger than her, maybe thirteen or fourteen – blatantly stared as she entered the building and made her way to what was apparently the school's main office.

A tall redhead with severe eyebrows greeted her as she entered the room's glass doors. "You must be Katherine."

"And you must be…" Katherine frantically tried to remember the name Bastian had given her,"…Juliana!"

The woman smiled, but it looked painful – forced. "I prefer Mrs. Wright actually."

Katherine felt the blood rush to her face, and she cursed Bastian in her head. Before she could apologize or embarrass herself any further, however, she heard another person shuffle rather hurriedly into the small office. Mrs. Wright tore her eyes from her form as she shifted to welcome the newcomer. Her smile, though, remained just as insincere.

"Melanie, there you are. I was just about to send out a search party."

Katherine turned to face this Melanie person. The first thing she noticed – to her utter delight – was that she actually appeared to be normal-sized. She was lithe and Katherine's height – maybe even a bit shorter, though it was hard to say for sure. Katherine was wearing heeled boots in a desperate attempt to boost her meager stature.

"Sorry I'm late," the girl immediately apologized before her eyes wandered to meet Katherine's. "Hi," she offered, her lips stretched into a friendly smile.

"Hey," Katherine responded, still taking in the girl before her. She was pretty in an understated way. Her dark hair was parted in the middle and cut into a chin length bob. The style suited her thin face, out of which her equally dark eyes shone intelligently.

"Melanie," Mrs. Wright addressed the girl, "this is Katherine. Katherine, Melanie. She's going to show you around the school today."

"Come on," Melanie insisted as soon as the woman finished introductions, grabbing Katherine's elbow and dragging her into the hall. "I'll show you to your first class before the bell rings."

Before Katherine could ask the girl how she even knew what her first class was, Melanie was rolling her eyes and gesturing towards the office with her free hand. "Evil old witch," she muttered.

Katherine immediately snorted – equal parts amused and shocked. Once she recovered from the surprising comment, however, she pulled her arm out of the girl's vice grip. "How do you know where my first class is? I haven't even shown you my schedule."

Melanie's eyebrows inched upward. "I know because your schedule is the same as mine. All sixteen and seventeen year olds have the same one. It makes sense since there are not even twenty of us."

"Oh," Katherine said faintly.

And she'd thought Middletown High was a small school.

Melanie reclaimed Katherine's elbow and, ignoring the strange looks they were getting from their peers, led her down two hallways to Room 112.

"History's not so bad," the girl assured her as they entered the tiny classroom that was packed with books. "Mostly, Mr. Sinclair just likes to rant. As long as you look like you're actually paying attention and nod when he starts getting especially loud, you should be alright."

That sounded somewhat ominous.

Before Melanie could impart any more advice, however, the bell rang – its loud *bbrriinngg* causing Katherine to jump – and the skinny girl pulled her towards one of the desks in the back of the room and sat next to her.

Apparently, there were no assigned seats. That, at least, Katherine could appreciate about this school.

She sat tensely as she watched teenagers that she knew to be her age – even if most of them were much bigger and taller than she was – enter the room. A few didn't seem to notice her, but most immediately spotted the new face in their mist. Of those who noticed her, some immediately dismissed her. Others let their eyes linger over her form with curiosity.

Fabulous.

Katherine felt as if she had the words "fresh meat" branded on her forehead. Uncomfortable with all the scrutiny, she ducked her head and used her curtain of hair to hide as best as she could. Not before she saw a particularly tall girl with long platinum blonde hair sneer at her though.

For a second, Katherine could have sworn it was Mallory Flanders. The girl's eyes were too blue, though, and her cheekbones too sharp.

It was a crazy thing to think anyway.

Before she could dwell on it further, Mr. Sinclair plodded into the room. Like everybody else she'd encountered thus far in Haven Falls – with the exception of Melanie – he was tall. He wore a plaid shirt with its sleeves rolled up, exposing his hair-covered forearms. "Hey, guys," he greeted amiably enough before searching the sea – okay, more like a puddle – of faces before him. As soon as he spotted her, he grinned. "Ah, Katherine, isn't it? Why don't you come up here and introduce yourself to the class."

Katherine glared at Melanie, who shrugged. She had failed to mention that Mr. Sinclair was a sadist.

Hoping to get it over with as quickly and painlessly as possible, Katherine reluctantly made her way to the front of the classroom. "Hi," she greeted the room with a sad little wave, "my name's Katherine." Having no idea what else to say, she just sort of stood there awkwardly.

Mr. Sinclair, obviously not appeased by the lackluster introduction, began asking questions. "And where are you from, Katherine?"

"Iowa."

"Oh, and what's Iowa like? That's in the states, right?"

"Yes, and it's dull," Katherine answered monotonously, knowing she wasn't making Mr. Sinclair's job very easy, but not particularly caring either. She had no interest in sharing her life story.

"Come now! I'm sure it's more interesting than you're letting on. What'd you do for fun there?"

She didn't want to think, let alone *talk*, about Iowa. If she did, she knew an avalanche of depressing thoughts and emotions would overwhelm her. So instead of politely answering the man, Katherine crossed her arms and remained stubbornly silent.

Flustered by her lack of response, Mr. Sinclair began to fidget. "Er, okay," he stammered. "Why don't you grab a textbook from the shelf in the back – it's the green one entitled *The Effects of History on Modern Day Werewolves* – and grab a seat."

Refusing to meet anyone's eyes, she did as she was told and sat back down in her seat next to Melanie. The girl looked like she was holding back snickers at the disastrous introduction. Katherine couldn't blame her. The look on Mr. Sinclair's face when he'd realized she wasn't going to answer his questions had been pretty funny.

The rest of history class passed quickly. Melanie was right about Mr. Sinclair and his propensity to rant, but he seemed harmless enough. Algebra went by in a similar fashion – without, thank God, Katherine having to make another embarrassing introduction.

During Free Study, Melanie introduced Katherine to her circle of friends. There was Mack and Jonathan, who, like herself and Melanie she assumed, were both changed wolves. They were the two shortest boys in their year. There was also Leander, a skinny boy with shaggy auburn hair. And Agnes. Agnes was a bit… *blunt*. Katherine supposed that was the polite word to use. Melanie explained that everyone in Agnes's pack acted in a similar fashion. It was the only pack in Haven Falls that was strictly made up of females. Even the alpha. Apparently, female alphas were rare and positively disgraceful in the eyes of the community, and Agnes was essentially shunned by most of the other werewolves at the school.

Katherine, naïve as she was about the culture of werewolves, simply couldn't process what was so outrageous about having a female alpha.

In turn, Agnes took an immediate liking to her. Katherine had yet to decide if that was a good thing.

She also met the blonde girl who'd so thoroughly remaindered her of Mallory. She approached the table that Katherine, Melanie, and her four friends had sat at in the library and introduced herself as Priscilla Wright, with the fakest, most patronizing smile she'd ever seen on a person. As soon as she said her name, Katherine knew immediately that she must have been the daughter of Mrs. Wright, the red-headed secretary.

At lunch, Katherine met even more people. She was shocked to find out that in addition to teaching werewolves, the school also taught non-werewolves. Just in separate classrooms. The non-werewolves consisted entirely of family members of changed wolves. They'd been brought to Haven Falls with their changed parents, children, or siblings to protect them from hunters. Katherine tried hard not to think too much about that.

There were only two non-werewolves in the school who were close to her age: a sixteen-year-old named Nathaniel and a fifteen-year-old named Penelope. She immediately recognized Nathaniel as the nosy waiter at The Bistro. Both joined Melanie and her group of friends – and by association, Katherine – at one of the small plastic lunch tables in the cafeteria.

Katherine realized pretty much immediately that she'd somehow been thrust into a group of outcasts – people who didn't fit in with the other werewolves of Haven Falls and were basically ignored by their peers.

She didn't think she'd ever been so pleased.

After lunch, Pack Dynamics passed without incident. Katherine actually took an honest interest in the class. Proper interaction between pack members was discussed and she was looking forward to better understanding the duties of the alpha, beta, and even omega of a pack.

And then came Mating Rituals.

It wasn't until it rolled around at one o'clock that Katherine's day really took a turn for the worse.

Katherine understood quickly that it was really just a sophisticated sex ed. class. In essence, she'd be learning how werewolves courted one another. Apparently, werewolves mated for life and some pairs were so deeply connected that when one died, the other soon passed. There was even such a thing as destined mates, who were apparently werewolves that just knew they were supposed to be together forever as soon as they saw – or rather smelled – each other. Soul mates, basically, as far as Katherine could discern from the syllabus she'd been handed.

After briefly going over the different aspects of werewolf courtship – from choosing to canoodling, as the teacher had charmingly put it – she had informed the class that she was going to pair up all the female students with male students so they could discuss the first stage of courtship amongst themselves – choosing a mate. Basically, Katherine had been told to tell her partner what she was looking for in a husband.

How awkward.

And then she'd been paired with Rip Briggs. Rip, like most born werewolves, towered over her and weighed close to twice as much as she did. It was all muscle too – that much was obvious under the boy's tight, practically see-through, white shirt.

"Alright, little girl," he greeted Katherine, sauntering over to her desk. "Let me guess, you're looking for a strong," he flexed an admittedly impressive bicep, "handsome," he grinned, running his fingers through his cropped hair, "protector who can provide for you."

Katherine positively scowled as Rip pulled an empty desk next to hers, plopped down, and proceeded to lean into her space. She immediately moved her desk a good foot away from his. *Jerk.*

He just smirked at her. "No? Why don't you tell me then? What are you looking for in a man?" He waggled his eyebrows as he asked her.

Katherine didn't think people did that in real life. Didn't he know he looked like an imbecile?

"For your information," she snapped at him, "I'm *not* looking for a man. I can take care of myself. But even if I was intent on finding one, he'd have to be intelligent and unpretentious. And in case you were wondering, no. I don't think you embody either of these particular traits."

Rip clutched both his hands to his chest. "You wound me."

Apparently, however, she hadn't wounded him enough. The irritating boy kept talking. "Anyway, you forgot patient. I don't care how hot you are, a man would have to have the tolerance of a saint to put up with your smart mouth." He leered at her. "Don't worry, though, I have more than one idea on how to put it to better use."

There was a delayed pause as she processed that.

Then an angry red blush burst across Katherine's cheeks, spreading down her chest and up to the very tips of her ears. "*Excuse me?*" she demanded, glaring at Rip.

"Aren't you going to ask me what I look for in a girl?" he asked, ignoring her furious response to his words.

Katherine scowled. "I don't give a-"

"I like all kinds," he told her, pretending like he hadn't heard her at all. "I could have any girl here, you know. All the girls in this class want me."

She rolled her eyes. *Yeah, all eight of them.*

Rip continued. "Just now, though, I'm craving a feisty little brunette who doesn't know when to shut up."

Katherine gasped and parted her lips, prepared to show Rip just how feisty she was. "You-"

Bbrriinngg.

The bell signaling the end of class rang, denying her the opportunity to ream the cocky boy. Rip stood up and casually walked out of the classroom. Like he hadn't spent the past ten minutes openly harassing her.

Katherine seethed in her chair a full minute before forcing herself to get up and follow Melanie to the gymnasium. "Are you okay?" the girl asked, eyeing the surly scowl that was undoubtedly painted on her face.

"I'm fine," she muttered.

But when they entered the brightly lit gym, Katherine's day got even worse.

It was Markus. There. In the gym. Wearing blue athletic shorts, a gray t-shirt, and a whistle wrapped around his neck.

"What are *you* doing here?" Katherine demanded rudely, unable to stop the question from flying out her mouth.

Melanie glanced wearily from Markus to Katherine, obviously confused by her outburst.

Markus's responding grin was borderline demonic. "What? Didn't Bastian tell you? I'm the P.E. teacher."

Katherine was going to kill him. *Them.* Both Bastian *and* Markus.

Though this did explain why it was Markus who would be driving her home at four.

The man in question threw a pair of black shorts and a gray shirt similar to the one he was wearing at Katherine's head. She fumbled to catch them. "What's this?"

"Gym uniform," he answered before jerking his head in the direction of a door with a female stick figure painted on the outside out it. "Now get into the locker room and change. I don't stand for tardiness."

Katherine ground her teeth together, doing her best to stomp down the irritation that speaking to Markus always seemed to cause. Begrudgingly, she clutched the uniform to her chest and allowed Melanie to show her to the girls' locker room.

Quickly picking a locker, Katherine stripped and tugged on the clothes Markus had flung at her. The shorts were a little big, but the elastic held around her waist at least. She borrowed an extra pair of sneakers from Melanie. She couldn't exactly run or do much else in heeled boots.

She was shoving her boots into her locker when she felt someone tap her shoulder. Assuming it was Melanie, she was a bit shocked to turn around and come face to face with Priscilla. Much like earlier, she was wearing a phony smile.

"Do you need something?" Katherine asked when the girl didn't say anything.

A few snickers sounding behind Priscilla alerted Katherine to the fact that the locker room was still full. Most of the girls were looking on in interest. Melanie, standing near the door, looked furious with the platinum blonde cornering her against her locker.

"Look, Katie…" Priscilla began.

"Katherine," she immediately corrected, crossing her arms over her chest.

Her smile only widened. "Like I said, Katie. You seem like a," she paused, "*nice* girl."

The way she said "nice" made Katherine suspect she meant something a little more *not* nice.

"It's because of that that I'm going to give you a fair warning, but keep in mind that I'm only going to tell you once."

Katherine raised an eyebrow, utterly unimpressed with the girl despite the fact that she had a solid six inches on her. "What?"

Priscilla's smile slowly contorted into a sneer. "*Stay away from Rip.*"

Katherine was flabbergasted. Of all the things she'd expected to come out of the blonde's mouth, *that* was not one of them. She didn't need to be told even once to stay away from that arrogant boy. She'd sooner spend the day with Markus, for God's sake. "You're kidding, right?"

"I don't kid," Priscilla assured Katherine, condescendingly patting her cheek. "You're new here so I know you didn't realize, but Rip and I are mates. We've been together for years. So *don't* go getting any ideas." Flicking her hair behind her, she sauntered out of the room.

Oh. *Oh.* Rip was Priscilla's boyfriend.

Well, wasn't that just dandy? Priscilla reminded Katherine even more of Mallory now. Though Rip was nothing like Brad.

Katherine scolded as soon as her mind conjured his name – Brad. She wasn't supposed to be thinking of him or her parents today.

Realizing that Melanie was waiting for her by the door, a seemingly apologetic grin on her face, Katherine hurried to join her.

"Sorry about that," Melanie said, opening the door for Katherine, "Evil witch seems to be a genetic condition around here."

Katherine smiled at that.

When they exited the locker room, however, something that had nothing to do with Priscilla or Rip caught Katherine's attention. Not only were Markus and her classmates in the gym, seven or eight men – the youngest perhaps in his mid-thirties and the oldest well into his fifties – were scattered along the wall opposite the locker rooms. Some were chatting quietly to each other while others were merely observing silently.

Noticing where Katherine's eyes had been drawn, Melanie gently elbowed her in the ribs to get her attention. "Those are some of the alphas of Haven Falls," she explained. "Usually only a handful show up on any given day to watch P.E. They do it so they can see our physical strengths and weaknesses. Someone's explained recruiting to you, right?"

Katherine nodded jerkily.

Smiling conspiringly, Melanie leaned over to whisper in Katherine's ear. "Three guesses as to why there are so many here today."

Before Katherine could respond to that, Markus blew his whistle and the two girls rushed to where the others were gathering at the center of the gym. Before they had even got there though, Markus blew the infuriating whistle again. "Twenty laps, ingrates!" he howled.

Katherine was immediately relieved. Yes, twenty laps were a lot. But running, at least, was something she could do. Running, she enjoyed.

Katherine paced herself the first ten laps, sticking with Melanie for the most part. Soon, however, her pent up energy – it'd been weeks since she'd run last – demanded that she go faster. The dark-haired girl didn't seem to mind when Katherine left her in her dust. She quickly passed two other girls, one boy, and Melanie's friend Agnes. By the time she'd finished all twenty laps, she was somewhere in the middle of the pack, but she'd beaten Priscilla by a good thirty seconds at least.

When everyone had completed all twenty laps, Markus once again blew his whistle. This time, he allowed everyone to reach center gym, where he told them to line up. "What a disappointing performance," he immediately criticized. "I ask you to run a measly two miles and the last of you clocks in at over fifteen minutes."

No one said a word.

"Vincent," Markus snarled, turning to the boy who had finished with the fastest time. "Why is this unacceptable?"

"A pack is only as strong as its weakest member," he immediately answered.

It was obvious to Katherine it was a slogan that had been drilled into him and the rest of her classmates.

"That's right," Markus agreed. "My own pack, in fact, has recently gained a new member," he continued, causing Katherine to tense. Nearly all of her classmates turned to look at her. Some were subtle about it. Others, not so much. She was hyperaware of the alphas near the wall eyeing her as well.

What in the hell was Markus doing?

"She is, by far, the weakest of us."

Katherine's face burned. Her fingers itched to ball into fists and punch the man, but somehow, she managed to control herself.

"As beta of the Prince pack, it is my job, of course, to strengthen her – to strengthen my pack." Markus finally met Katherine's eyes. "I want a hundred push-ups, princess. Now."

It took a moment for Katherine to get her body to move. When she finally managed, it was an even greater struggle not to pounce on the man. But she refrained. She wouldn't give him the pleasure of knowing he was rattling her.

Trying her best to ignore the eyes on her, she slowly got on her hands and knees and began doing the push-ups. She knew that there was no way she'd be able to do close to a hundred of them. Not even half probably. She was tired from running and pure strength was in no way her strong suit.

Katherine was right. She collapsed onto her stomach after thirty-seven.

After a bit of yelling from Markus, she was able to handle ten more. But that was it. Forty-seven out of one hundred. If it had been some sort of test – and it was Markus, so it undeniably was – Katherine had failed. Spectacularly.

He had no sympathy for her, of course. "Pathetic," he muttered under his breath – but certainly loud enough for her to hear – before gesturing for her to get up. Using her shaky arms to push herself off from the floor, she stood.

Many of the alphas, Katherine noticed, were talking quietly to each other.

Great.

Once she was back on her feet, Markus informed the class that they'd be playing dodgeball for the rest of the period.

As if the man hadn't already punished her enough.

Markus split them up into two teams and sent them to opposite sides of the gym before setting an array of balls – some small and squishy looking and others large and rubbery – near the center of the gym. Once everyone was ready, he blew his whistle.

Katherine didn't think she'd lasted more than two minutes in the first game. She'd been pelted by three balls at once. She hadn't fared any better the second game.

Then the third game began.

Katherine didn't know how she'd managed it – probably a mixture of quick reflexes and sheer luck – but she was one of the last two members of her team still standing. Then Vincent chucked a ball into the chest of Agnes – a member of the other team – at the same time that she hit him in the leg.

And it was only Katherine. Katherine and the last remaining boy on the other team. Rip.

He immediately began hurling balls at her. Katherine was able to dodge them all, but just barely. As he bent down to pick up yet another one, she took her chance. She grabbed a ball from the ground and channeling all her inner fury – directed towards both Rip and Markus – she lobbed it at him.

And the ball hit him. Right smack in the face. It even left a red mark.

For a moment, the whole gym was silent. Then her entire team cheered and with a gigantic smile glued to her face, Melanie wrapped her arms around Katherine's torso and squeezed.

The girl could hug, that was for sure.

They played one more game of dodgeball after that – Katherine was out almost immediately – and Markus sent them back to the locker rooms to clean up.

There were no stalled showers, only a large communal one, so Katherine hung back fifteen minutes before finally stripping and quickly hopping under the spray.

Over the sound of the running water, she heard Priscilla talking about her near the lockers. "Poor girl," she said, "I don't even know why Bastian is bothering with her. She's a weakling. Even Markus thinks so. There is no way she'll survive the change."

"I know," a voice Katherine didn't recognize agreed. "It's a disgrace that they even let her attend the school before her first full moon. They're only encouraging her to get her hopes up and well, *you* saw her performance in the gym."

Fuming, Katherine bit down hard on the flesh of her inner cheek and cranked the handle of the shower to shut it off. She quickly tied a towel around herself and stomped back to her locker.

Both girls immediately shut up and took off when they saw her round the corner.

What did they know anyway?

Katherine had the now empty locker room to herself so she took her time changing back into her regular clothes. Ten minutes later, she put the pair of sneakers Melanie had loaned her back into the girl's locker before grabbing her bag and finally leaving.

She wondered where she was supposed to be meeting Markus.

She didn't have to wonder long. He was waiting tensely for her right outside the door.

"What took you so long?" he immediately demanded.

"I wasn't aware I had a time limit," she snapped back. *Not that she would have abided by it even if she did.*

But he didn't need to know that.

"Whatever; let's go."

Katherine reluctantly followed him to the grassy parking lot. He hopped into a crimson truck that she could only assume was his so she climbed into the passenger seat.

As soon as he pulled out of the lot, Katherine let loose her tongue. "Did you have to embarrass me like that today? Push-ups, *really*? Christ, you are such a prick!"

Markus, maddening as always, merely rolled his eyes. No doubt he thought that she was just being dramatic. "Why do you even care what your classmates think? Most of them are as pathetic as you."

Katherine ignored the insult. "I don't," she insisted, "but a bunch of alphas were there and recruiting is-"

Markus jerked his truck so hard to the right, they nearly crashed into a tree. "*You* care about recruiting?" he immediately demanded, turning to face her, only keeping half an eye on the dirt road.

Katherine was startled by his intense reaction. Then debated baiting him. She decided against it. "No," she admitting with a sigh.

"Good," Markus growled, directing his eyes back to the road.

"Bastian would never let you go without a fight."

She snorted derisively.

"If I were him, I wouldn't either."

Katherine risked a glance at Markus, wondering what he could possibly have meant by that. But his eyes were still burning holes through the windshield, and he wouldn't look at her.

CHAPTER THIRTEEN

The next two weeks passed by in a senseless blur.

Despite Katherine's initial reaction to Bastian forcing her to attend the werewolf school in Haven Falls, she quickly found that it served as an excellent distraction to the absolute wreck her life had become.

She thought less of her parents.

Of Brad.

And even the ever-looming date of the next full moon.

Instead, Katherine concentrated on learning all she could in her classes and getting to know her new friends. Although she was at first reluctant to befriend the gaggle of teenagers she'd met on her first day, Melanie made it near impossible for Katherine to ignore them. The black-haired girl had dragged her to sit with them at lunch every day she'd been at the school. She reminded her a great deal of her best friend Abby. That, of course, only made it more difficult for Katherine to resist her charms.

She was warming to the others as well. Of Nathaniel and Mack, Katherine had grown especially fond. She couldn't explain why exactly – the boys were virtual opposites. Despite the incident at The Bistro, Nathaniel was quiet and unassuming, whereas Mack was loud and often obnoxious. If pressed, Katherine supposed she'd say it was because both had wound up in Haven Falls through rather tragic circumstances and she could sympathize.

She'd learned Nathaniel's story on the Friday of her first week of school.

"Christ, Katherine, what'd the asparagus ever do to you?"

Katherine ignored Melanie's question, continuing to crush the steamed stalks with the blunt side of her fork. She thought if she pulverized the vegetables enough, then the awful smell coming from them would somehow cease to exist.

She was wrong – the resulting green sludge proved to be just as nauseating.

Why the lunch ladies even bothered to serve vegetables in a werewolf school, Katherine didn't know. Potatoes were the only kind she'd encountered thus far that didn't make her want to barf. And judging by the untouched asparagus on the rest of her classmates' plates, they felt the same way.

With a sigh, Katherine gave up attempting to annihilate her asparagus and tuned in to the conversation going on around her.

"Oh my god! Did you see the shirt that Rip is wearing today? It's practically translucent! I swear I can see his-"

"Penelope," Katherine interrupted sharply, immediately wishing she hadn't tuned in. "I cannot be held responsible for my actions if you finish that sentence."

She did not want to know what Penelope could see under his shirt.

And Katherine had endured enough of the girl going on and on about frickin' Rip, of all people. Every time Katherine saw Penelope, she was talking about him – usually gushing about what he was wearing on that particular day.

Penelope just rolled her eyes at Katherine's outburst. "I don't know why you dislike him. He's so hot!"

"He may be hot," Melanie pointed out, "but he's a complete jerk. If you had to attend classes with him, you'd know that."

"Uh, do you guys really have to discuss how dreamy you find another dude in front of us?" Jonathan spoke up. "It's kind of emasculating."

"Kind of?" Mack interjected loudly. "I'd like to at least be able to pretend I'm still the proud owner of a pair of testicles, thank you very much."

Penelope completely ignored both of them. "Rip's not a jerk! He's a normal hot-blooded male. I'm sure that as soon as he dumps Priscilla and actually finds a nice girl to be with, he'll settle down."

Katherine could understand Penelope's abhorrence of Priscilla easily enough. But her mammoth-sized crush on Rip was downright irritating.

"You do realize that he'll never go for you, don't you?" Agnes addressed the girl frankly.

Penelope's face reddened and became pinched. "What are you saying?"

"I'm saying that you're not a werewolf! And Rip is. Your infatuation with him is inconsequential because werewolves don't mate with humans. You know that."

"Yeah, well, maybe I don't plan on remaining human forever. Ever think of that?"

Her announcement was met with tense silence.

Katherine was surprised when it was Nathaniel who broke it. "How could you possibly want that?" the usually quiet boy demanded angrily. He was the only other non-werewolf at the table. "You know the risks! The odds of a girl like you surviving the change are abysmal."

Katherine winced, but Nathaniel didn't even glance at her. He quickly snatched up his still half-full plate and marched out of the cafeteria.

A few moments later, Melanie nudged a baffled Katherine with her elbow. "You know he wasn't talking about you when he said that, right? He probably wasn't even thinking-"

"What was that about?" Katherine demanded, cutting the other girl off.

Melanie sighed and gestured for Katherine to join her in the hallway outside of the small cafeteria. Katherine immediately obliged. Once there, the black-haired girl told her all about how Nathaniel came to live in Haven Falls. Apparently, his older sister was bitten by a werewolf a little over three years ago. She, Nathaniel, and their parents were immediately taken to Haven Falls for their own protection. It was all for naught, however, as the girl didn't survive her first transformation. Regardless, Nathaniel and his parents were stuck at the colony as they already knew of the existence of werewolves.

It was a heartbreaking story. And when Nathaniel approached her later that day to apologize for his thoughtless words, Katherine surprised even herself by pulling him into a tight embrace.

She'd learned how Mack ended up in Haven Falls the Monday immediately after. He'd told her during P.E. It was on the day that Markus, the tyrannical brute that he was, had the class playing flag football in the haphazardly mowed grass behind the school.

Katherine was appalled when Markus announced they'd be playing flag football after she and the rest of her classmates had finished running their daily laps in the gym.

Half an hour into it, however, she was mostly just bored.

Katherine realized quickly that the boys in her class considered football a man's sport and thus, only allowed other males to ever actually touch the ball. As a result, most of the girls in her class had been reduced to playing defense and pulling on the red or yellow flags hanging from the boys' hips – usually, in ill-disguised attempts at groping said boys.

Okay, so maybe Katherine was still a little appalled.

"You throw like a girl, Collins!" Mack shouted at the gangly boy currently acting as their team's quarterback. He'd just thrown two incomplete passes – both of which had landed far short of their intended receivers.

"Excuse me?" Agnes exclaimed from her spot beside Katherine. "What's that supposed to mean?"

The quarterback – Collins – turned to her. "What do you think?" he asked snidely. "Girls can't throw – they shouldn't even be allowed to play football as far as I'm concerned."

"I can throw better than you, you dunce."

Katherine believed it too. Collins really did throw like a girl – a prepubescent girl at that.

"Oh yeah? Let's see it then," he taunted, shoving the pigskin into Agnes's arms.

"Gladly," she sneered before leaning over slightly to murmur

softly to Katherine. "Get open. Twenty yards or so down the field and to the left."

Katherine grinned and immediately agreed. She was all too happy to help Agnes show Collins and all the other sexist pricks in her class what girls were really made of.

Hint: It wasn't sugar, spice, and everything nice.

Maybe a little spice, though.

Markus blew his whistle and the two teams quickly lined up. Mack hiked the ball to Agnes. Following the other girl's instructions, Katherine ran about twenty yards down the grassy field before angling her body slightly to the left. As promised, Agnes threw the ball right at her. And because no one was covering her, she had no trouble catching it.

Katherine turned to run towards the make-shift touchdown area. She didn't get five yards, however, before a colossal weight slammed into her. She immediately fell to the ground. Whatever – or rather, whoever – had crashed into her, landing on top of her back. Oxygen was forced from her lungs and for one terrifying second she couldn't breathe.

Then a familiar voice whispered in her ear. "You'd better get used to this position, little girl. If you survive the change, you'll learn to love being under me."

It was Rip.

And Katherine was disgusted.

Before she could draw a breath and respond, the weight was yanked off her. "This is flag football, you imbecile! What are you doing tackling her? She's not even a full-fledged werewolf! You could have crushed her!" Markus was furious.

"I tripped. It was an accident," Rip insisted.

"Get your ass back in the school and wash up. I don't want to see your face for the rest of the afternoon." Markus ended his tirade, turning his attention to Katherine. "Are you alright?" he demanded, his eyes still bright with obvious anger.

"I'm fine," Katherine assured him, allowing Mack to help her off

the ground. He and her other classmates had gathered around as soon as Markus began wailing at Rip.

"You sure?" Markus asked doubtfully.

"Yeah. I'm just a little winded."

"Whatever then," he sighed, running a tired hand over his face. "Why don't you sit on the sidelines for the rest of the game, just in case?"

"I'll sit with her," Mack immediately volunteered, surprising Katherine.

Markus grunted in acknowledgement. Katherine and Mack both took it to mean that he approved of Mack's suggestion.

Minutes later, the football match had resumed. The two friends watched from the shade of a nearby pine tree. Katherine had to fight the urge to roll her eyes when Priscilla started shooting her dirty looks from the field.

"Don't let them get to you," Mack advised from his spot to her right.

Katherine furrowed her brows, turning to meet his so-light-blue-that-they-were-almost-gray eyes.

"Those popular jerkoffs, I mean," he clarified. "You can't let them get under your skin. Believe me, you're not the only new kid they've tortured."

Katherine frowned. "You?" she guessed.

"Yeah. I was dropped off here when I was fifteen. Don't remember my life before I was bitten. Have no idea who bit me. It was... hard when I first got here. People like Rip only made it worse for me. Don't let them make it worse for you too."

Katherine had no idea how she was supposed to accomplish that. But Mack's words had affected her – made her chest swell with compassion for the boy – and she shifted her body so she could sit just a little bit closer to him.

Looking back on that particular day of P.E. class, Katherine was still a little surprised that Markus had reacted so violently to Rip tackling her.

He had actually seemed genuinely concerned for her. He'd even asked her if she was okay.

Perhaps Katherine wasn't really all *that* surprised though.

After all, she knew that Markus had it in his head that Bastian would be upset if she got hurt.

And she was beginning to suspect that he was right.

Bastian's behavior over the past two weeks had been odd to say the least. Half the time, he blatantly ignored her – acted like she didn't even exist – and the other half of the time, the man was completely overbearing.

He was at his worst during meal times when the pack gathered around the dining table to eat Caleb's delicious food. He always inquired about her day at school. Whenever it had been bad, Katherine had simply lied to him about it. She certainly hadn't told him about Priscilla threatening her on her first day or Rip tackling her the week after. Bastian didn't seem like he knew she was lying so she could only assume that Markus hadn't told him about the difficulties she was experiencing either. Not that the other man knew anything beyond what happened in P.E.

Anyway, after grilling her about her classes, Bastian would proceed to make sure she stuffed herself – practically demanding that she eat twice her weight in food. No matter how much she ate, however, he was never satisfied. He was constantly adding more food – and in particular, meat – to her plate when he thought she wasn't looking.

She was a little insulted that the man truly thought she was that unobservant. The reality was that Katherine just knew how to pick her battles.

His erratic behavior only worsened as the date of the next full moon grew nearer.

And then, before Katherine knew it, that date – October 29, 2012 – had come.

After spending the morning getting barked at by Bastian to eat her eggs, she'd had to endure Caleb, Sophie, and Zane explaining to her what to expect that night when the full moon rose. Zane had wanted to transform in front of her so she could see exactly what it was that would be happening to her, but Bastian had adamantly refused.

Apparently, he thought it would freak her out too much.

Which, of course, only served to freak her out.

Funny how that worked.

It wasn't until late that afternoon that Bastian informed Katherine they'd be hiking to a remote location in the forest for her to experience her first transformation.

Only Bastian and the others in the pack would be around to witness it.

After he'd made the announcement that they'd be traipsing out into the woods, Katherine learned from Zane that the rest of the werewolves of Haven Falls would be going to some monthly celebration called a moon gathering. According to Zane, moon gatherings took place every full moon and were basically how all the packs in the small community stayed connected to each other.

Katherine was glad she didn't have to attend *that* at least. She doubted any of the other werewolves in Haven Falls would have wanted her there anyway. The distinct possibility of her dying would have put a bit of a damper on things.

Anyway, within an hour of Bastian notifying Katherine of his plans, they'd left. She found herself trailing slightly behind the rest of the pack as they trekked through the tall grass and avoided the low-hanging branches of the trees in the section of forest behind Bastian's house. Only Caleb had slowed his pace enough to stay close to her. Bastian glanced back every so often to make sure they were still following the path that he and the others forged as they trudged on ahead of them.

It was just cold enough outside for Katherine to see her breath as it was expelled from her laboring lungs. She pulled her leather jacket a little more snugly around her torso, trying to ignore the way the cotton mittens Bastian had forced onto her hands before they'd left his house largely failed at keeping her fingers warm.

She couldn't help but wish that she'd prepared herself more for this.

Not for the hiking or the frigid air. But for the distinct possibility of death.

Death.

It was too nice a word for something so inherently frightening. People were right to be afraid of it, Katherine thought. Had every reason to fear it. The pain associated with the act of dying itself. The unknown that came after it.

But even as she thought it, Katherine didn't *feel* afraid. She felt almost removed from the situation.

Situation.

Katherine snorted.

Who called what may be imminent death *a situation*?

She did, apparently.

Probably because the thought if it – that she might very well die tonight, probably in less than an hour from now, in fact, when she felt perfectly fine – seemed absurd.

She couldn't die. She was only sixteen.

And it was a Tuesday. For God's sake, who died on a Tuesday?

At least she hadn't been made to go to school earlier that morning. *That would have been torture.*

Katherine was forcibly pulled from her increasingly irrational thoughts when she tripped over an overgrown tree root, nearly losing her balance and pulling Caleb down with her.

"Are you okay?"

"Fine," Katherine managed to force out between her teeth. She wasn't about to point out that the only reason she hadn't been able to see and avoid the root was because it was starting to get dark outside, the gray color of the sky slowly turning a navy blue.

They resumed walking.

What couldn't have been twenty minutes later, Bastian and the others ground to a halt ahead of them. Katherine and Caleb quickly caught up. She could see that they had stopped at the edge of a clearing.

The clearing was small and the grass in it so tall that it nearly reached her knees, but the ground seemed stable enough, and it was the first time that Bastian had stopped since they'd began their impromptu hike. Katherine suspected that they'd reached their destination.

She was proven to be correct when he led their small group into the center of the clearing before turning to face them – turning to face her. "Now we wait."

So that's what they did. They waited.

Katherine observed quietly as the blue of the sky darkened into a purple and then a near-black. She didn't say anything when Caleb placed a hand on her shoulder or when Sophie grabbed her forearm and squeezed. She did nothing to acknowledge the others' stares.

And then she saw it – the moon. The pale, bright orb was slowly rising in the eastern horizon. Caleb let go of her shoulder and Sophie released her arm, but everyone's eyes remained on her form.

That was when she finally felt it. The fear. Within moments, she went from feeling detached to nearly being overwhelmed by such an intense fear that she almost stopped breathing entirely. She could feel her heart jackhammering in her chest, like it wanted to burst free. She knew if she reached her fingers up to the pulse point at her neck, she'd have tangible proof of it. Her racing heart. No amount of sarcasm, anger, or forced apathy could hide it.

She didn't want to die.

Not even if it meant joining her parents in the afterlife.

If there even was one. Katherine didn't know for sure. How could she? But she liked to believe there was a God, and that there was *something* that came after life.

For the first time since she'd been bitten and her parents had died, Katherine contemplated praying.

Then the moon's light filtered through the towering trees surrounding the clearing where she stood, and Katherine could focus on little but the heat.

Her whole body warmed. At first, it was just her chest, but it quickly expanded to the rest of her body. Her freezing fingers were suddenly burning.

And then, when the moon reached its peak in the sky, the pain.

It wasn't so terrible right away – a small, but sharp twinge in her lower back. But like the heat, the pain soon spread. And intensified. Her entire body throbbed. Even her bones ached. And Katherine knew it was because they wanted to move around – *shift* within her.

She instinctually fought it. Was hardly even aware of the movement going on around her – that the places where Markus, Zane, Sophie, and Caleb had once stood were now occupied by massive, four-legged creatures. Was hardly even aware that she was trembling violently and mewing softly in pain.

A large hand encircled the back of her neck and Katherine forced herself to look up and meet blue eyes set in an angular face. *Bastian*, some still logical part of her brain recognized.

And then he was pulling her close, ramming her face into his expansive chest and holding her there.

A moment later, he hauled her away again, but left his hand on her neck. Katherine dazedly realized that his mouth was moving. He was saying something – yelling something at her – but she couldn't hear it over the rushing in her ears.

The pain got worse. She was vaguely aware of someone screaming. Was that awful sound coming from *her*?

Bastian pulled her forward again, crushing her small body to his larger form, but she somehow found the strength to yank herself away.

The man was fighting the moon's pull, Katherine knew. The same way she was. And he was shaking – must have been hurting as much as she was.

She wanted him to give in – to change.

But somewhere in her, even as the pain nearly overwhelmed her, *she knew*.

He'd wait for her. Suffer along with her for as long as it took – for as long as she chose to drag it out.

So she did it. She gave in to the infinite pain – felt something inside of her break. And then, blackness engulfed her.

* * *

Katherine had no idea how much time had passed before she was jolted back into reality.

She just knew that when she was, the pain had all but disappeared. There was still some lingering discomfort along her spine and her muscles were sore, but for the most part, she felt good.

Different, but *good.*

Except that something kept nudging her side. And Katherine didn't like it. She was trying to think – to *feel* what was different about this new her – before she opened her eyes.

She knew she'd changed – successfully transformed into a wolf – but it was more than that. It was odd. She had to slog through her thoughts, yet they were racing at the same time. She could literally feel the blood – the hormones – running through her body. She felt wild. Downright primitive.

If only whatever was nudging her would stop so she could concentrate!

Katherine snapped her eyes opened, and a low growl she wouldn't have even realized was coming from her if she couldn't feel it reverberating in her throat broke free. She picked her new body up on shaky legs and turned to face whatever it was that insisted on annoying her.

It was *him.*

Her dream wolf. Bastian. She'd already seen him in this form twice already, but it was different seeing him this way now that she was a wolf too.

He was much bigger than her – his black fur quite a bit darker than her chocolate brown. He was still handsome. She was still attracted to him. But in addition to that, she felt this strange urge to *please* him. To make him notice her – *like* her.

And that pissed Katherine off.

Before she could consider the intelligence of her actions, she found herself growling again – this time *at* Bastian. Her ears lowered threateningly against her head as she took an offensive stance.

He growled back, the loud rumbling coming from deep within his chest. He took a step towards her with a giant paw.

Katherine immediately stopped her snarling, instincts demanding that she submit to the larger wolf. She shrunk into herself, resting the majority of her weight onto her hind legs.

And wasn't *that* weird.

As soon as Katherine took the more docile position, Bastian stopped his own growling. He began nudging her on her side again, using his head to do so. She realized quickly that he was urging her to try to walk.

Figuring that it was largely instinctual – much like the growling, apparently – she attempted to walk forward. Somehow, however, her feet – or paws, rather – got tangled and she wound up on the ground in an awkward heap of fury limbs. If wolves were able to laugh, Katherine suspected Bastian would have been doing just that at the moment. His blues eyes were gleaming with amusement.

Katherine was only barely able to resist the urge to once again snarl at the large, black wolf. She was still a bit wary of how Bastian reacted the first time. There was a reason he was the alpha of the pack, after all – the power practically rolled off him.

After a few more tries – and one more mishap that resulted in Katherine being sprawled out on the forest floor – she was successfully walking. And brimming with excitement over the achievement.

Now that she knew she could walk, Katherine wanted to run. She could feel the rush of adrenaline at the mere prospect of it. She didn't even care where she was going to run – every direction seemed filled with possibilities. She just knew she wanted – *needed* – to do it.

When she tried to leave the clearing, however, the large form of Bastian stopped her. She yipped and attempted to get around him, but he blocked her again.

An indignation so strong filled Katherine that she couldn't stop a low growl from escaping her. The emotions she felt as a wolf were so much stronger – so much more extreme – than what she felt as a human. And they came and went at the drop of a hat. A moment ago, she'd been all kinds of excited. And now she wanted to rip chunks of Bastian's fur out with her teeth.

Without a second thought to the consequences of it, Katherine plowed right into the alpha wolf – not really sure if she was still trying to get past him or just engaging him in a fight.

Of course, as soon as she collided with him, Bastian used his superior strength to fling her off of him, and a moment later he pounced on her. It wasn't much of a fight. Physically, Bastian was much stronger than Katherine and after only a brief tussle, he had her restrained on her back. His large form loomed over her, and he bared all his teeth in a way she was sure was meant to be threatening.

But Katherine wasn't nearly as intimidated as she should have been. Anger surged through her, and as futile as it was, she snapped her own teeth at him.

His answering growl had nearly the same effect that his first one did. She wasn't afraid, per se. But the need to obey Bastian – to submit to him – quickly overtook the remnants of anger she still felt.

It was like Katherine's body just knew what to do. She went limp and pulled her head back as far as it could go while still keeping eye contact with Bastian. She bared her neck for him.

Just like before, Bastian's growling immediately ceased. Then, to Katherine's shock, the giant wolf *licked* her. Swiped his long tongue from the base of her throat to the tip of her snout. And then, he *nuzzled* her, pressing his face hard against hers.

Katherine yelped and tried to push the giant, black wolf off her. He didn't freely comply, however, and she found herself fighting with him once again. This time, though, their grappling was more playful. She wasn't actively trying to bite him and he wasn't using his full strength against her.

It was *fun*.

Not much later, however, a loud howl sounded through the night air, quickly overpowering the other noises of night life in the forest – small animals scurrying about in bushes and trees, the occasional bird calling out to its flock. Bastian nudged Katherine into a standing position before answering the howl with one of his own.

A few moments later, the others of the pack – *her* pack – raced into the clearing. She immediately recognized the furry white wolf that bounded up to her as Sophie. The other wolf that hesitantly approached her – his fur was darker than Sophie's, a dark gray color – she instinctually knew was Caleb.

The other two – Markus and Zane – held back a little. The former was nearly as large as Bastian – his brown fur not unlike Katherine's own, if perhaps a bit lighter in color. Zane was slightly smaller – though still bigger than Sophie or Caleb – and his coloring was similar to Bastian's.

As soon as Sophie reached Katherine and Bastian, she began barking in an animated fashion, her tail literally wagging as she gestured with her head in the direction of the forest that the pack had emerged from.

Bastian responded to the barking with a slight nod of his head. The expression on Sophie's face – wolf or not – could only be described as a grin. Then, prodding Caleb with her shoulder as she turned around, she began to run back into the forest. Caleb, as well as Markus and Zane, quickly followed her. Bastian started head butting her side again and for a second, Katherine didn't know what was going on.

And then she did.

Elation filled her. Bastian was allowing her to run with the pack.

Needing no further prompting, Katherine took off after the others. Her powerful limbs sprung her forward and she flew through the forest, avoiding trees expertly. She was fast.

She easily caught up to and outpaced the others. Only Bastian attempted to stay with her and even then, he was only a black blur she'd see in her peripheral vision every once in a while.

It was positively exhilarating. Dopamine raced through her veins. It was one of the most amazing feelings she'd ever experienced.

Katherine didn't know how long she ran, only that quite a bit of time had passed before her body finally grew tired and she stopped. She was well ahead of the others when she gave into the urge to rest. As she collapsed onto the dew covered ground, however, she heard a bit of rustling coming from a leafy bush not ten feet to her right. She turn to look at the bush, wondering what it was that could have made the noise, when she spotted it.

A rabbit.

Ravenous hunger nearly consumed Katherine. *And she hadn't even been aware that she was hungry!*

She immediately attempted to pounce on the small animal. As soon as her paws even got close to it, however, it took off, sprinting out of her reach and quickly disappearing into the surrounding forest.

Some hunter she was.

An annoyed growl emerged from her throat, only growing more vicious when she turned to see that Bastian and the others had caught up to her and had obviously seen her failure at hunting, if the amusement shining from their eyes was anything to go by.

Apparently, growling was her go-to reaction to just about everything in this form.

Before Katherine could dwell on her embarrassment, however, Bastian raced off into the forest and Sophie quickly captured her attention by rubbing up against her side and engaging her in a play fight similar to the one she'd had with Bastian in the clearing.

It was as fun as it had been earlier. Maybe even more so since there wasn't such a huge disparity in size between the two female wolves. And Sophie didn't attempt to lick her either, which was a plus.

It was just as entertaining watching Markus and Zane spar. Markus won nearly every time. At least until Sophie entered the brawl and joined forces with Zane. Katherine was only all too happy to watch Markus get a beat down courtesy of his fellow pack members.

Bastian wasn't gone long before he returned, three dead rabbits clamped between his powerful jaws.

As soon as Katherine spotted the blood-stained animals, her

stomach began to rumble beseechingly. As hungry as she was, however, she still knew it wasn't smart to encroach upon another wolf's kill.

But then Bastian set the three rabbits down directly in front of her – clearly offering them to her – and Katherine didn't hesitate. She devoured the first animal, tearing her sharp teeth into the small creature, fur and all. She took a little more time with the second one, savoring the bloody, raw meat.

There was no sense of horror at what she was doing. These weren't adorable little bunnies any longer. They were sustenance. Food. Plain and simple.

Still, Katherine's hunger had been satisfied by the first two rabbits so she used her nose to push the third one back at Bastian, who had been watching her eat with rapt eyes.

Some things didn't change, no matter what form they were in.

He didn't take the rabbit though, and when Katherine once again refused to eat it, he offered it to Sophie, who was all too willing to scarf it down.

After eating, Katherine continued to play with the others. Soon, however, the meat settled in her stomach and she began feeling tired. Her movements slowed as her limbs grew heavy with fatigue.

Bastian must have sensed her exhaustion as soon after, he began leading the pack back in the direction of the clearing. It took a while to get there as they'd run north quite a ways, but Katherine managed to keep pace with the others.

As soon as they arrived at the clearing, however, she immediately picked a spot to rest in the tall grass, lying down and resting her face on her paws. Her eyelids began to droop immediately. She was so tired that she didn't even mind when Bastian settled down next to her – even allowed her weary body to lean into his a little as sleep threatened to overtake her. Katherine could vaguely feel him once again nuzzling her face with his own when sleep finally pulled her under.

* * *

Too soon she was forced awake by a firm hand shaking her arm. "Katherine," a voice whispered urgently.

Straining to open her eyes, Katherine could groggily make out Sophie's face directly above her own. The blonde had more than a few leafs stuck in her hair and a streak of dried mud covering half her face. Katherine took the rest of her in and realized that the usually put together girl was wearing a red t-shirt that hung off her frame and a pair of loose sweatpants.

"What?" Katherine mumbled incoherently, still half asleep.

"Come on," Sophie urged, tugging on her arm again. Her *bare* arm. "We need to get you dressed before the others wake up."

Her *bare* arm attached to her *bare* body.

She was stark naked!

That certainly woke her up.

Trying not to panic, Katherine reached down in an attempt to cover her exposed breasts. As she did so, she immediately noticed Bastian lying incredibly close to her.

The events of last night came back to her.

She had done it. Katherine had survived the change. She was a full-fledged werewolf now.

And she should have been relieved. Ecstatic, even.

But how could she possibly focus on that when Bastian, like Katherine, was *completely* in the buff? He was on his stomach so she couldn't see anything *too* horribly embarrassing but that didn't stop her eyes from sweeping down his naked form – down the lightly tanned skin of his muscled back and *lower*.

When she realized what she was doing – ogling Bastian's unconscious, naked body, and right in front of his sister, no less, Katherine's face immediately reddened. She knew Sophie was getting a prime view of just how far reaching her blush really was.

Perhaps she wouldn't have been quite so mortified if Bastian was just lying next to her.

But *no*. He also had his right arm thrown haphazardly over her hips.

"Katherine," Sophie repeated herself. "You have to get up."

Katherine wholeheartedly agreed. And she tried to get up. She really did. But when she moved, the arm around her waist tightened significantly.

Katherine was positive that if one could truly die of embarrassment, she would have done so at that moment. It would have been terribly ironic. Surviving the change only to die the next morning out of complete mortification.

She glanced up at Sophie with pleading eyes, begging the blonde to somehow get her out of the predicament she'd found herself in. Muttering about what a pain her brother was, Sophie bent over and helped Katherine pry Bastian's arm off of her.

And *that* hadn't been humiliating at all.

The small brunette couldn't bring herself to feel anything but thankful towards the blonde, however, when she fished some clothes out of a bag and handed them to her. Katherine hadn't even noticed that Sophie had been wearing the backpack yesterday when they'd hiked through the woods.

But she supposed she'd had other, more pressing matters on her mind.

Katherine wasted no time pulling on the long-sleeved shirt and pair of sweats Sophie had given her. The shirt nearly hung down to her knees, but she hardly cared and quickly slipped into some sneakers that Sophie offered her as well.

She knew without a doubt that the clothes she'd been wearing last night – including her beloved leather jacket – had been shredded beyond repair.

As soon as Katherine was adequately dressed, Sophie surprised her by pulling her into a hug. She leaned into it. Now that she wasn't in danger of dying of embarrassment, Katherine allowed the relief – the joy at still being alive – to flow through her.

Sophie eventually released her, but only to clasp her hand around Katherine's elbow as soon as she did. "Come on, sweetie. There's a stream not far from here where we can wash up a bit."

"Okay," Katherine agreed and let the other girl pull her along.

After only a few minutes of walking, they arrived at the stream. The current was moving slowly, allowing Katherine to catch a glimpse of her reflection on the water's surface.

Christ. And she thought Sophie had looked haggard.

Whereas the blonde had had a few leafs tangled in her hair, Katherine was pretty sure a whole tree had somehow managed to dislodge in her mahogany locks. Or at least a large branch of some sort.

It took Katherine a solid half hour to pick all of the leaves – *and sticks* – out of her hair and wash her face clean of mud.

When she was finished, she and Sophie headed back to the clearing. "Hopefully the guys are awake and actually dressed by now," she commented idly, smirking in Katherine's direction. "Sorry you had to see that, by the way," she teased.

Katherine scrunched her nose, making sure to act properly traumatized by it all. But she couldn't exactly say she was sorry that she'd seen Bastian in his birthday suit.

It turned out that the men *were* awake and properly clothed when the two girls returned to the clearing. Katherine accepted a shy hug from Caleb and even a one armed squeeze from Zane when he spotted her. Markus, of course, didn't move to touch her, but she was more than okay with that. She took the fact that he didn't immediately begin insulting her when she entered the clearing as his way of telling her that he was glad she was okay.

It was Bastian's response to seeing her that surprised Katherine the most. For someone who'd spent half of his time avoiding her the past two weeks, he nearly crushed her in a bone-crushing embrace when he saw her. He held her in his arms for a solid minute. When Bastian finally pulled away, he kept his hands wrapped around her biceps.

His eyes roamed over her form and Katherine suspected he was searching for any visible injuries. Not that he could see much. She was practically drowning in the oversized clothes Sophie had given her. Eventually his roving eyes met hers and blue bore into green.

"You're okay," he muttered, tightening his grip on her arms for a second before finally letting them go. He rubbed the back of his neck with one of his hands. "I'm... *glad.*"

For perhaps the first time ever, Katherine smiled at Bastian.

"Me too," she said, truly meaning it. "Me too."

And for once in her life – at least, the wreck her life had become since that fateful night on Miller Road – things were looking up.

CHAPTER FOURTEEN

The immense relief – the pure joy and elation – that Katherine felt regarding surviving the change lasted for all of a day. If she thought her life would miraculously improve after she'd made it through her first full moon, well, she was wrong.

Horribly, dreadfully, irrevocably *wrong.*

In fact, it was as if changing into a werewolf – if only for one night – had somehow messed with her head and caused her hormones to go completely haywire.

She was still the same person. She could still look in the mirror and see little Katherine Mayes staring back at her. And yet…

It was like she had no control of herself.

Not two days after she'd survived the change, she burst into tears when Bastian returned from an impromptu trip to Haven Falls bearing a brand new leather jacket – an exact replica of the one she'd inadvertently torn to shreds during her transformation. To Katherine's utter mortification, as soon as the man handed her the jacket, her eyes wetted, the oncoming tears sticking to her eyelashes and clumping the fine hairs together as she frantically tried to blink them away. He also gave her a pair of fleece mittens and a matching hat with large flaps for her ears.

She barely managed to croak out a soft "thank you" before retreating to her room where the waterworks *really* started. She knew her reaction to his thoughtfulness had undoubtedly bewildered Bastian, but she really couldn't help it.

It had just been such a *nice* thing to do. And Bastian was hardly synonymous with the word "nice."

Even if she did find herself drawn in again and again by the earthiness that seemed to define his natural scent, by the lone dimple the appeared on his right cheek whenever he tried to suppress a smile, by the intensity of his dark blue eyes…

Occasionally, Katherine caught herself thinking of the firm muscles of his back – picturing the expanse of sculpted, tanned skin as she allowed her mind to wander back to how it had felt to wake up next to him on the hard, forest ground.

Despite the draw she felt towards him, however, he still infuriated her most of the time. Quite often, she had to resist the urge to punch him.

Same with Markus.

That, though, Katherine could boast she had finally done.

It happened the morning after Bastian had given her the leather jacket. Markus, who'd been in the same room as Katherine when she received it the night before, poked fun at her tearful response over breakfast. She couldn't even remember exactly what he had said – though she seriously doubted it was as offensive as some of the comments he'd made in the past. She just knew that her newly volatile temper had flared, and before she even made the conscious decision to do it, she hauled off and slugged the man right in his impertinent mouth.

Markus's reaction surprised her. After he got over the shock of being hit in the face, he *laughed*. Apparently, she didn't pack quite as much of a punch as she thought.

Sophie, at least, was impressed. She thumped Katherine on the back, congratulating her for finally giving Markus what he deserved.

Whether the man deserved to be hit or not, however, Katherine couldn't bring herself to look at Bastian after she'd done it. She avoided him for the rest of the day, afraid she'd see a disappointed frown aimed her way if she allowed her eyes to meet his.

Not that she cared what the dark-haired man thought.

Really.

She didn't.

And anyway, punching Markus was nothing compared to what happened at school three days later. Bastian finally allowed her to go back on Monday – a full five days after she'd survived the full moon on Tuesday night – and Katherine was equal parts proud and ashamed to admit that she'd gotten into a no holds barred girl fight with none other than Priscilla Wright.

Katherine scanned the books lining the shelves of the school library. She was looking for something – anything – that might pertain to the immunity system or healing process of werewolves. It was Free Study and for once, she was planning on doing exactly that – study.

When the scratches she'd obtained from running through the woods on Tuesday had disappeared by the next morning, she'd been reminded of how quickly her head injury had healed when she'd first been brought to Haven Falls. Her curiosity had been piqued, to say the least.

After a few minutes of searching, Katherine finally found something she thought may be useful – Anatomy of a Werewolf *by Harold Spalding.*

She grabbed the book, brushing the dust from its spine, before turning around.

And coming face to face with Priscilla.

The blonde had her arms folded across her chest. Her eyes were bright with anger and her pink mouth was set in an unattractive scowl. One of the girl's friends – Katherine didn't know her name – stood beside her with a similar expression on her face.

Katherine was understandably confused – and more than a little annoyed.

She hadn't been to school in nearly a week and within hours of coming back, she'd already managed to do something that ruffled Priscilla's feathers? Really?

"Can I help you?" Katherine asked tersely, irritation lacing her voice.

Priscilla stepped forward into Katherine's space, forcing her to take a step back in turn. Unfortunately, in the confined space of the library, that meant backing up into a shelf.

"Yes," Priscilla hissed. "You can help me – and yourself, for that matter – by staying away from Rip."

Hadn't they already had this conversation weeks ago?

"You tell Rip to stay away from me," Katherine retorted, in no mood to squabble with the other girl.

She could already guess what had brought about this particular outburst, but it was hardly her fault that Mr. Sinclair had put Katherine and Rip in the same small group in Werewolf History that morning. And she certainly hadn't asked for Rip to start whispering lewd comments in her ear once he'd sat next to her.

The boy was repulsive.

And Katherine was seriously beginning to doubt that even Priscilla deserved to be shackled with someone like him.

"Please. Like Rip would ever truly be interested in a scrawny thing like you," the blonde snapped. "You could never handle a real man like him."

Priscilla thought Rip was a real man? Seriously? Maybe they did deserve each other.

The blonde took another step into Katherine's space. If she was half a foot taller, they'd be nose to nose. "No one knows how you even survived the change on Tuesday. I mean, you have to know how pathetic you are. You're just like that Melanie girl – an absolute disgrace. I don't know how Bastian can stand carrying the shame of having turned someone like you. No doubt he wishes he'd have just left you to die."

Tightly clutching the book she'd picked out with one hand, Katherine shoved Priscilla away from her with the other. "You can leave me alone too," she spat, turning to leave.

Before she could take more than two steps, however, the other girl had her long fingers wrapped around her elbow in an unyielding grip. "Did you just push me?"

She actually had the nerve to sound affronted.

"That depends," Katherine replied, somehow prying her arm out of Priscilla's clutches. She dropped her book to the floor and this time she used both her hands to shove the blonde away. "Do you consider that a push?"

"You vile, little bi-"

Priscilla didn't even bother to finish the insult before vaulting at Katherine, yanking hard on the brunette's hair – almost like she was trying to rip it from her scalp.

Katherine immediately had a hand wrapped around one of the girl's wrists, her fingernails digging into Priscilla's skin as she attempted to stop her from pulling out her brown locks. She closed her other hand into a fist and hit Priscilla hard in the stomach.

The blonde let go of her hair for only a second, but that was all the time Katherine needed, and she pounced. The two girls were reduced to an undignified pile on the floor, limbs flailing as each tried her hardest to hurt the other.

Priscilla's friend, who'd been watching the entire debacle, released a loud squawk as they went down, and it wasn't long before the librarian intervened and separated them.

She and Priscilla were immediately been escorted to the secretary's office. The secretary? Yeah, Mrs. Wright – Priscilla's mom.

Mrs. Wright, who didn't bother with her usual fake smile, immediately berated Katherine, not even giving her the chance to tell her side of the story. The only upside to the entire ordeal was that apparently, the school had no principal. It was up to pack leaders – or alphas, in other words – to discipline their underlings.

Mrs. Wright told her in no uncertain terms that she'd be informing Bastian of her "atrocious behavior."

But at home later that evening, Katherine wasn't wholly convinced that Mrs. Wright had reported the events to Bastian. If she did, Bastian hadn't confronted her about it. He certainly hadn't punish her. She somehow suspected he'd be criticized for *not* punishing her, though, and kept that little tidbit of information – that she'd gotten off scot-free for tussling with Priscilla Wright – to herself.

"Katherine!"

She was startled out of her reverie by the sound of Melanie's voice. "Yeah?" she asked, quickly surveying the cafeteria and realizing that nearly everyone had left.

"Are you alright?" Melanie asked, furrowing her brow. "The bell rang a while ago. We need to get to class."

"I'm fine," she assured her friend, picking up her empty plate before following the other girl out of the room. "Just tired, I guess."

Katherine wasn't lying either – she *was* tired. It had been a long week. She was just glad it was finally Friday.

"Have you decided if you want to go to The Bistro with us to-night? We were talking about possibly going to Leander's place after-wards to watch a movie too, but I don't think you were really listen-ing."

Katherine smiled sheepishly at her friend. "Sorry about that."

"That's okay," Melanie grinned back. "But *have* you decided? Are you going to come?"

Katherine shook her head. "I don't think so. I really am exhaust-ed."

She reasoned that Bastian probably wouldn't let her go even if she *did* want to – not without a chaperone anyway. The man really could be ridiculous sometimes.

For a second, the corners of Melanie's lips slipped into a frown, but she recovered quickly. "Oh. That's understandable. I remember what it was like after I survived my first transformation. It really messed with my head."

"Yeah," Katherine agreed, her mind once again wandering back to the last week and her own erratic behavior and fluctuating emotions. Soon, the two girls arrived at their classroom.

Pack Dynamics and Mating Rituals passed without incident. P.E., too, flew by. For once, Markus had arranged for the class to play a somewhat non-violent game – badminton. She and Melanie partnered up to play against Mack and Leander until Markus dismissed them a little after three-thirty.

He pulled Katherine aside, however, before she could reach the locker room. "I have to clean up some equipment from the field behind the school before we leave. If I'm not here by the time you're done showering or whatever it is you girls do in there, just meet me at my truck, yeah?"

"I think I can manage," Katherine muttered, yanking her arm out of Markus's grip and making her way to the locker room to shower.

It wasn't that she didn't appreciate the warning – he'd been ready and waiting in the gym to take her home every day since she'd started school again. It was just that she despised being babied. And ever since she'd survived the change, that was exactly what the pack had been doing – babying her.

It was maddening.

Only made more so by the fact that she knew she was at least partially to blame for their behavior. She *did* start crying when Bastian bought her a new coat, after all. And then she went and punched Markus in the face the very next morning for making fun of her for it.

Still, the kid gloves were a little much.

"See ya, Katherine. If you change your mind about hanging out with us later, we're heading out to The Bistro 'round six."

Nodding in acknowledgement of her friend's comment, Katherine waved good-bye to Melanie and Agnes with one hand and used the other to towel dry her hair. After throwing her brown locks in a sloppy ponytail, she took advantage of the empty locker room and shucked off the towel still wrapped around her waist and tugged on her red sweatshirt and jeans. She quickly picked up her satchel and slung it over her shoulder, readying herself to leave.

It would be vindictive of her to make Markus wait for too long.

Besides, she didn't particularly want to deal with the attitude she'd catch if she *did* make him wait.

Pushing the heavy locker room door open, she stepped into the gym. She didn't make it more than a few feet, however, before something – or rather, *someone* – yanked hard on the hood of her sweatshirt, propelling her backwards.

Twisting around, Katherine glared at the perpetrator.

It was Rip. *How utterly unsurprisingly.* And he'd even brought a friend. She wasn't completely sure, but she thought his name might have been Thomas or Tommy or something.

"Hey kitty cat, where do you think you're going?"

Kitty cat? Really?

Katherine had no patience for Rip that day – or *any* day, really. And if she were being perfectly honest, the moniker he'd just bestowed upon her was a little too close to the nickname her deceased mom and dad had often used – Kit.

"Can't you take a hint, you thick-headed prick?" she spat. "I don't want anything to do with you! Why can't you just leave me alone and pay attention to *your actual girlfriend* for once? Maybe then she'd get off my back too!"

"Aw, don't be like that," Rip cooed, even having the nerve to move forward into Katherine's space.

Refusing to be intimidated, the small brunette stood her ground. "Does Priscilla know you like to spend your free time harassing other girls?"

A muscle along the meathead's jaw twitched. *Finally, a reaction!*

"Hey, man," Rip's friend injected, rubbing the back of his neck in a seemingly nervous gesture, "maybe we should go. Priscilla *would* be pretty mad."

Rip snorted. "Right. It's Priscilla you're concerned about."

Tom – she was pretty sure it was Tom – shrugged his shoulders. "Whatever, man. I don't want to be caught bugging her and get the snot kicked out of me by her alpha. His scent is all over her."

Huh. So that whole Bastian peeing on her thing was finally coming in handy.

"Yeah, why don't you listen to your little friend and run along now, Rip?" Katherine jabbed. "And get it through your head, would you? Not even if the survival of the human race depended on it would I ever even consider, and I quote," she whipped out quotation fingers, "getting down and dirty with you."

Rip narrowed his eyes at her and refused to drop his glare as he addressed his friend out of the corner of his mouth. "What are you, Tom? An omega? If you're so worried about being caught, make yourself useful and guard the gym door."

Rip's friend still looked uneasy, but did as he was told.

Katherine felt a nervous flutter in her stomach. "Why do you need someone to guard-"

Before she could finish her sentence, Rip had his strong fingers wrapped securely around one of her wrists and was dragging her back into the girls' locker room.

"Hey! What do you think you're doing? Let go of me!"

He did let go of her – practically throwing her into a row of metal lockers. Katherine carefully rubbed her tender wrist with her uninjured hand. "What's your problem?" she demanded.

"Funny you should ask," Rip jeered. "*You.* You are my problem, Katherine."

She was dumbfounded. "I haven't even done anything to you."

Rip laughed, but it was a mocking sort of sound. "Maybe not," he conceded, "but I'm getting awfully tired of you turning me down, sweetheart. You're starting to make me look bad."

"You make yourself look bad," Katherine scoffed.

Rip shook his head. "You actually think you could do better than me?" he asked, the disbelieving expression on his face matching his incredulous tone.

"Even Priscilla could do better than you," Katherine insisted – though of *that*, she wasn't completely certain.

"Priscilla knows her place. You, however," Rip took two steps forward, forcing Katherine to back up against the lockers he'd thrown her into, "apparently still need to learn yours."

Katherine put two hands up, pushing against the boy's bulging pectorals in an attempt to shove him away from her. "Back off. Right now."

Rip didn't budge. Instead, he grabbed Katherine's shoulders, holding her still. "Lesson number one," he whispered, his foul breath hitting her face and causing her nose to crinkle, "no one says no to Rip Briggs."

Without further ado, he crashed his lips onto hers.

Shocked at his audacity, Katherine gasped against Rip's lips –

which he apparently took as an invitation to thrust his tongue into her mouth.

The invasion forced her to quickly regain her bearings and she bit down on Rip's slimy tongue. *Hard.*

She may or may not have tasted blood in her mouth.

Regardless, digging her sharp teeth into his tongue had its intended effect and Rip pulled away with a snarl. He spat on the ground and Katherine couldn't say she was sorry to see that his saliva was tinged red.

Rip wiped some of the excess spittle from his mouth, and she could have sworn his hazel eyes darkened to near black as he sneered at her. "You asked for it now, you stupid girl."

It was when Rip once again began advancing towards her that Katherine finally realized she was in serious trouble. She immediately tried to sidestep him and get to the door. With a rough yank of her ponytail, however, Rip manage to simultaneously thwart her attempt at escape and slam the side of her head into the corner of a metal locker.

Pain exploded from where her temple hit the hard edge and the sensation of blood trickling down her face absolutely incensed Katherine. She tried to kick him where she knew it would hurt the most, but missed. She only managed to connect a few hits to his shins before he was able to restrain her. He easily encircled both her wrists with just one hand and pinned them behind her back. He pressed his chest flush against hers.

"Let go of me!"

Then Rip's mouth was on hers again, muffling her protests. "Don't worry, kitty cat," he sighed against her lips, "by the time I'm through with you, you'll be begging for more."

Katherine was forced to swallow an angry cry when she felt his free hand begin working its way up her sweatshirt. She tried to focus solely on her anger and not the fear causing her stomach to quiver as she attempted to somehow wiggle out of his grasp.

But the fear was winning out.

Tears were rapidly filling her eyes when suddenly, Rip was torn off of her. Katherine watched dazedly as his body went flying into a wooden bench opposite from where he'd trapped her against the lockers.

Breathing deeply and forcing oxygen into her air-deprived lungs, she turned to face her rescuer.

Markus.

But he wasn't paying attention to her. His eyes were glued to Rip. Markus didn't even let the meathead get to his feet before tackling him to the ground. He held Rip by the throat, his firm grip on the boy's neck causing him to sputter and wheeze.

With Rip sufficiently detained, Markus finally chanced a glance at Katherine. His brown eyes were the most serious she'd ever seen them. "Get out of here," he demanded, voice gruff. "Go out to the truck and wait for me there. Don't stop to talk to anyone."

Katherine couldn't make her legs move.

"I said to get out of here!"

Markus's raised voice finally forced her into action. She dashed out of the locker room and didn't slow her pace until she had reached Markus's truck, pulling on the monstrosity's rusted handle and lifting herself into the cab.

Only after leaning over the driver's seat and jabbing down the lock button did Katherine allow the relief to wash over her. She adjusted the rearview mirror so she could examine the wound on her head. There was some faint bruising and a little blood still oozed from where the skin had been broken, but it didn't look *too* terrible. Besides the small injury to her temple, the only evidence of Rip's attack was Katherine's wild hair – nearly half of the still damp waves had fallen loose of her pony tail.

Maybe Markus would keep what had happened to himself and she could just tell Bastian that she'd fallen. Katherine couldn't say why exactly she didn't want him to know what had happened, just that she didn't.

It occurred to her that she really needed to learn how to fight. Maybe then she wouldn't find herself in situations like the one that had just happened. Perhaps Bastian would teach her. She'd be able to lay guys like Rip flat on their backs with his tutelage she was sure.

Katherine was pulled from her thoughts by the sound of sharp rapping on the driver's side window of the truck. She startled, but willed her racing heart to calm when she recognized Markus. He was pointing at the engaged lock. Katherine immediately reached over and let him into the vehicle.

"For God's sake," he muttered when he spotted her bloody forehead. He pulled the shirt off his chest, ignoring Katherine's involuntary blush as he pressed it against the wound. "Hold this there until the bleeding stops," he ordered.

Despite the slight sting it caused, Katherine obeyed.

Markus started the truck, but didn't touch the clutch to put it into drive. Instead, he just sat there – his bruised knuckles nearly turning white as the grip his fingers had tightened around the steering wheel. He spared her a glance, eyeing her disheveled appearance wearily. "Bastian's going to kill me."

He seemed resigned.

Great.

Somehow Katherine knew that he wouldn't be willing to keep what had happened a secret from Bastian.

CHAPTER FIFTEEN

For all that Katherine worried about Bastian's reaction to her bruised temple, she didn't see the man at all that evening. Markus, too, disappeared soon after he'd dropped her off at the house. She was asleep by the time they'd finally returned, both with bloody, torn knuckles and Bastian still harboring a lingering rage in his eyes.

She'd foolishly deluded herself into believing that Markus really would keep quiet about Rip attacking her and that nothing would come of it.

The very next morning, that delusion came crashing down around her.

* * *

"As leader of the council, I hereby call this meeting to order."

The head alpha of Haven Falls was the epitome of intimidating. Nearly as tall as Bastian and just as muscular, the middle-aged man's very presence demanded respect.

Cain, Katherine could vaguely recall was his name. He was Bastian's uncle.

His steely gray eyes roamed up and down the long, rectangular table that easily seated all fifteen of Haven Fall's other alphas before landing on Katherine's petite form. He smiled at her. "Hello."

Attempting a weak grin in response, she couldn't help but wonder exactly how it was she'd managed to get herself into this situation.

When Bastian had jostled her awake early that morning – only the faintest beams of yellow sunlight had been filtering in through the windows – demanding that she get dressed, she'd been more than a little confused. Rubbing the sleep from her eyes, she'd immediately asked to know why he was making her get up at such an ungodly hour.

His answer had consisted of two simple words – "Council meeting."

Bastian largely ignored the barrage of questions that response had prompted from Katherine. He wouldn't answer why she was being made to come to what she understood to be private meetings, but it was obvious by the worry lines etched across his brow and the downward slope of his mouth that for whatever reason she was being forced to go, he wasn't happy about it.

Less than an hour later, they'd arrived at a building located in the very center of tiny Haven Falls. Katherine realized quickly that it was a pseudo city hall of sorts and where the meeting would be taking place.

She'd then been led to a back room in the building where a large table served as the space's center piece. Nearly a dozen other people – all alphas, Katherine had immediately noticed – were already seated around said table.

Katherine recognized a few of the alphas from their semi-regular appearance in her gym class. She also easily spotted the lone female alpha she knew to be the leader of Agnes' pack. She was tall – pushing six feet – with long red hair and an attractive smattering of freckles across her nose.

Unfortunately, Katherine saw *them* as well – Priscilla and Mrs. Wright. They stood behind one of the men sitting at the table, wearing matching smug smiles. Another non-alpha, a slightly plump woman with her arms crossed over her ample breasts, glowered at her from behind a different man.

If Katherine hadn't been feeling apprehensive before they'd arrived at the meeting, her nerves had certainly kicked in then. She was positively vexed that Bastian had refused to tell her what was going on.

Some of her anger fled, however, when he immediately offered her what she knew had to have been *his* chair at the mahogany table. She was the only non-alpha offered a seat. The other females in the room – barring the redhead, of course – were made to stand slightly behind their respective alphas.

Any good will she may have felt towards Bastian disappeared, however, as soon as Cain had stalked into the room, announcing the beginning of the meeting and addressing Katherine personally. Despite the smile stretched across the man's face – nearly all of his teeth were showing – she already knew by the presence of Priscilla and Mrs. Wright that she was in some sort of trouble. And judging by the firm grip Bastian had on her chair from where he stood behind her, he knew it too.

Unfortunately, he hadn't deemed it necessary to inform her *what* exactly it was she was in trouble for before dragging her there.

Jerk.

It was at that precise moment, as Bastian was clutching her chair, Katherine first noticed the bruises on the man's knuckles. Though they looked as if they were already half-healed, the light blue and yellow splotches still stood out starkly against the white of Bastian's fingers as they held tightly to the rungs of her chair.

The sight of the fading bruises caused Katherine's stomach to churn and the anxiety already brewing there to turn into outright trepidation.

It occurred to her that maybe Bastian didn't tell her what the impromptu meeting was about and why he was so insistent that she come along because she wasn't the only one in some sort of trouble.

What had Bastian done?

The sound of Cain's voice as he once again began to talk jerked Katherine out of her increasingly distressing thoughts. "Friends, I'm afraid I've called you here today because a rather… disconcerting matter has been brought to my attention. One of us – an alpha – has been accused of assaulting a young werewolf who is not a member of his pack."

Katherine knew, of course, even before she could feel the curious eyes wander over her form and fixate on the space above her right shoulder – the space where Bastian loomed over her – exactly who it was being accused.

"As we all know," the head alpha continued, "this is a serious breach of conduct. Before allowing the injured party to seek retribution, however, it is imperative that I – that *we* – hear exactly what took place – both sides of the story, if you will. Briggs, as it was you who made the accusation in name of your son, why don't you take the floor?"

Without further ado, Cain sat in his seat at the head of the table and the man that he'd addressed, behind whom the glaring woman Katherine didn't recognize stood, pushed himself out of his chair.

"With all due respect, Head Alpha, the story that you've alluded to is quite simple. *Prince*," the man spit of Bastian's last name like it was a curse, "unjustly attacked my son."

Murmurs broke out amongst the alphas, many of whom were sending doubtful looks Briggs's way. The female alpha was the only one who stood and challenged the man directly. "I know your son, Briggs. I find it hard to believe that if Bastian, indeed, did attack Rip, that it was completely unprovoked."

Katherine had already suspected it was Rip whom Bastian had gone after, of course, but hearing her suspicions confirmed did nothing to relieve the uneasy feeling in the pit of her stomach.

Briggs's lips curled, like he found the very presence of the red-haired woman distasteful. All the same, he addressed her scarcely veiled accusation. "Rip is a remarkable and exceptionally charismatic young man and I don't appreciate what you're implying, Atkins. Nevertheless, I, too, was skeptical and questioned my son when he insisted that the attack was unprovoked. After all, I've never known Bastian to be particularly aggressive."

Katherine fought the near hysterical laughter that threatened to bubble up her throat. *Not aggressive? Did this Briggs person not know Bastian at all?*

"But that was before it was brought to my attention that a girl was at the center of all this trouble."

The urge she had to laugh suddenly dissipated.

"These two women here – Juliana and Priscilla Wright, wife and daughter of Vance Wright – will corroborate my story. This little girl," the man actually had the nerve to point at Katherine from his place across the table, "has been infatuated my son ever since she's been brought to Haven Falls. When Rip rejected her advances, what he thought was a harmless crush turned dangerous – more along the lines of an obsession, really. When he rejected her again yesterday, she got angry and got her alpha involved. We all know that Bastian has a weak spot for the girl, and she used that weakness against him, spinning lies, and causing him to attack my son!"

Katherine was completely gobsmacked.

She suspected she was doing a rather remarkable impression of a fish, her eyes large in their disbelief as her lips formed a surprised "o", her jaw having dropped halfway through the man's unbelievably erroneous account of what had happened between Rip and her.

After a beat of silence, she recovered from her shock, sputtering as she tried to discredit Briggs's completely *fictional* story.

Before she could manage to force out a single word, however, Bastian was leaning over the table, swatting the man's accusing finger out of her face as he erupted. "Your mongrel of a son deserved everything he got. He's the one who doesn't understand the word "no." It was well within my rights to have killed him if I had so chosen!"

Briggs's face purpled. Before he could rebuff Bastian or Bastian could throw a fist – Katherine wouldn't put it past him at that point; both his hands were balled up where they lay on the table – Cain interjected, "Where is your boy, Briggs? Surely he should be here to tell his version of events – so we can better divulge the truth?"

The woman whose eyes were still glaring daggers at Katherine, finally spoke up. "Rip can barely walk! Both his hands are broken, the fingers on his right hand totally crushed!"

Bastian snarled at her, the sound originating from somewhere deep in his chest. "His hands wouldn't be broken right now if he would've just kept them to himself in the first place. You should be thankful that they're the worst of his injuries."

Briggs glared at the woman standing behind him. Katherine was certain now that she was the man's wife – Rip's mother. She reluctantly bowed her head. Briggs turned back around to face Bastian. "Rip's injuries will put him out of commission for weeks. It's recruiting season. That's a devastating amount of time to be out of the game! Furthermore, we've been told by my pack's healer that the damage done to his hands was so extensive that there's a chance they won't heal correctly."

"I, for one, can't say that I'm surprised at this turn of events."

Katherine recognized the owner of the patronizing voice immediately. Rogue.

How could she have missed him when she'd entered the room?

The scruffy-looking man's eyes were drilling into Bastian's form. "I mean, what do you expect? Giving such a young and inexperienced alpha so many charges to care for? He was foolish to think he could bring yet another person into his pack. Bastian attacking that boy just proves he has no control over himself, let alone of that little girl by his side."

"Shut your mouth, you prick."

It was the first time Katherine had spoken since the meeting had started and the words flew out of her mouth before she'd even thought them. When the eyes of everyone in the room swiveled towards her and she felt Bastian's weighty gaze on the back of her neck, she immediately wished she could've taken them back.

Rogue grinned at Katherine, seemingly amused by her brief outburst, before turning his attention back to Bastian. "Tell you what, I'll take her off your hands for you."

For a brief moment, time stood still. Then, with an almighty roar, Bastian dove across the table.

Katherine immediately leapt from her chair. Others, too, moved out of the man's way. Bastian ended up sprawled halfway across the table, one of his hands with an unyielding grip around the collar of Rogue's shirt.

Not knowing what else to do, and more than a little aware that Bastian's sudden exhibition of violence was *not* helping their case,

Katherine quickly snatched up Bastian's free hand, squeezing it as hard as she could and attempting – though mostly failing – to pull him away from Rogue.

"Order!" Cain demanded over the ruckus that had erupted in the meeting room.

Katherine's grip on Bastian's hand remained unwavering. Even as her fingers tugged on his calloused palm, however, she knew that she'd never be able to move him – not unless he allowed himself to be moved.

"Let him go," Katherine begged in a near whisper. "You'll only get us into more trouble if you don't."

Bastian glanced at her, his blue eyes dark with anger. After a moment, however, he seemed to regain control of himself, letting go of Rogue's collar with reluctance and straightening up so that the table no longer had to hold his weight.

Katherine let out a sigh of relief, but didn't let go of his hand.

Just in case he decided to take another dive across the table, of course.

Neither sat in the now empty chair between them.

After allowing everyone in the room a moment to compose themselves, Cain surprised Katherine by once again addressing her directly. "And what do you have to say about Rogue's suggestion, girl? Do you find Bastian to be an acceptable alpha?"

His question hung in the air – everyone once again turning to face Katherine as they waited for her response. She could feel Bastian as he tensed beside her, the grip his fingers had on hers becoming almost painful, but she didn't withdraw her hand. She took a deep breath and answered Cain with complete honesty.

"Without Bastian, I'd be dead."

Cain nodded once, in acceptance of her answer, but kept his eyes intent on her face as he continued to question her. "And what's all this about Bastian attacking one of your classmates? Were his actions justified?"

"Why are you asking her?" Briggs quickly demanded.

"As if the girl would actually tell the truth," Briggs's wife muttered in disbelief.

Cain held a hand up, demanding silence and their protests immediately ceased. "Well?" he asked her.

Katherine licked her lips, having no problem implicating Rip. "Yes, it was justified. Rip cornered me at school. Whatever Bastian did to him – it was only to protect me."

Cain gazed into her eyes for a good while, no doubt searching them for deception. "Very well," he announced shortly. "Briggs," he turned to the man in question, "I'm afraid that you have no proof Bastian was acting in anything other than defense of his pack when he went after your son. As such, there will be no retribution for his actions."

Katherine's shoulders sagged in relief, but she wasn't immune to the smoldering glares sent her way by the Briggs and Wright families. She was just thankful that they didn't dispute the head alpha's quick decision. She really didn't want to have to explain exactly why it was that Rip had cornered her at school – that *he* was the one with the demented crush.

Before she could completely relax, however, Cain continued speaking – and what he had to say this time was *not* what Katherine wanted to hear.

"Bastian," he addressed the dark-haired man. "I'm afraid, however, that you've proven Rogue's point about your lack of control valid when you launched yourself at him just now. Perhaps he's also correct in implying that you have too many charges to care for. I wouldn't protest if-"

He hadn't even finished his sentence when Rogue, clasping the edges of the table with both his hands and leading into Bastian's space, spoke. "I issue an alpha challenge. You and me, Bastian. Next full moon. For the girl."

What in the world was an alpha challenge? And she had better not be "the girl" he was referring to… though realistically, who else could it be?

Bastian's eyes narrowed, his mouth transforming into a hard line. "I don't think-"

"As I was saying," Cain interrupted, sending both men disapproving frowns, "I wouldn't protest if someone else wished to take Katherine on."

"You can't be serious," Bastian protested, taking the words straight from Katherine's mouth and turning his baleful glare onto the head alpha – his uncle. The man remained unmoved.

"Fine!" Bastian spat before getting into Rogue's face, enunciating his words thoroughly. "If you want a fight, you've got a fight. But I assure you that you will not win."

"So mote it be," Cain announced, a shrewd smile taking shape on his lips. "All you here are witnesses. An alpha fight between Bastian and Rogue will take place at the next moon gathering. The winner secures Katherine as a member of his pack."

Wait. *What?*

Katherine tried desperately to keep the panic she could feel rising in her gut from showing on her face.

"Is that all then?" Bastian demanded of Cain, not bothering to disguise his rude tone. "Are we dismissed?"

The head alpha didn't seem impressed with Bastian's lack of respect. Nevertheless, he nodded. "Meeting adjourned."

Not bothering to wait for further confirmation, Bastian pulled Katherine out the door. She could practically see the steam coming out of his ears as he marched her down the hallway towards the building's only exit.

"Bastian! Hey, Bastian, wait up!"

The sound of someone calling out Bastian's name caused him to abruptly spot and spin around. "What?" he barked.

It was Agnes' alpha – her long red hair in a bit of disarray as she struggled to catch up with them – who was attempting to get his attention.

"Is that any way to greet a friend?" she asked, feigning a huff. Katherine tried to recall her name. Atkins, she was fairly certain, was what Briggs had called her. Was it a last name?

When Bastian merely rolled his eyes at her question, she playfully punched him in the arm. "Quite a show you put on in there," she commented. "Lord knows it's the most entertainment I've had in a while." She finally focused her gaze on Katherine. "Quite funny, wouldn't you say?"

Katherine wasn't sure how to answer that. Because, no. To be quite frank, she hadn't found any part of the meeting funny. Confusing? *Sure.* Anxiety-inducing? *Definitely.* But funny? *No.*

And Katherine didn't like the dynamic between Bastian and this woman either. Despite his surly attitude, it seemed like Bastian was familiar with her. They were friends, no doubt. Maybe even more.

Not that it was any of Katherine's business. She didn't care what – or rather *who* – Bastian did in his free time.

Still, she couldn't help but think that the redhead was much too old for Bastian. She had to be pushing thirty. There was no way they were *together* together. Just no way.

Thankfully, Atkins didn't appear to be waiting for Katherine to answer her question. Instead, she'd returned her attention back to Bastian. "Well," she demanded, "Aren't you going to introduce me?"

Bastian finally slipped his hand free from Katherine's – seemingly startled that they'd been holding hands in the first place – before loosely gesturing towards Atkins. The small brunette ignored the pang of irritation she felt.

"Katherine, this is Gabriela. As I'm sure you've deduced by now, she's another alpha of Haven Falls and one of the town's best healers. Gabriela, this is Katherine, my… well, she's the newest member of my pack."

Gabriela offered Katherine a smile. It seemed genuine, but Katherine could only muster up a half-hearted one in return. She didn't know what was wrong with her.

Before she could dwell too much on it, however, Bastian was bidding his friend an abrupt good bye and placing a hand on the small of Katherine's back, leading her out of the building and to his SUV parked on the side of the road.

If Bastian was expecting a silent ride back to the house, however, he was in for a disappointment. As soon as he'd put the car into drive, questions were spewing from Katherine's mouth.

"Why did you agree to fight that jerk – Rogue? And what's an alpha challenge anyway? Why didn't you tell me what we were getting into before dragging me to that meeting?"

Bastian took a deep breath, running a hand through his wild hair with the hand not grasping the steering wheel. "I didn't tell you because I didn't know for sure what the meeting was about. I suspected, of course, but-"

"Then why didn't you tell me your suspicions?" Katherine demanded.

Bastian frowned at the interruption. "I didn't want to unnecessarily concern you."

"Yeah, because waking me up at the crack of dawn and dragging me to an alpha meeting didn't concern me at all," Katherine agreed sarcastically.

"I'm sorry," he bit out through clenched teeth. "In hindsight, perhaps it was counterproductive of me to keep the truth from you."

The apology – the idea that Bastian was capable of apologizing, let alone admitting that he'd done something wrong – shocked Katherine into a temporary silence.

But the silence was exactly that, temporary.

"Yes, well, thank you," she managed to sputter. "But you know, we wouldn't even have been put in that situation in the first place if you'd have just restrained yourself from going after Rip. I don't know what Markus told you, but the only injury I sustained from our little confrontation in the locker room was a cut on my forehead. Hardly worth the trouble you caused by attacking him in retaliation."

Katherine knew it was the wrong thing to say. Even as the words poured from her mouth, she could see the way Bastian stiffened at them, the way furious tremors began to take hold of the tense muscles of his arms.

He turned to face her, not at all minding the dirt road he was driving on. His blue eyes, darkened with palpable rage, were made to look nearly black. "I'm your alpha. You don't get to question my decisions. What I did, I did to protect you. You're my responsibility and you can be damn sure that I wasn't going to let that boy get away with forcing himself on you."

Katherine fought to keep her cheeks from reddening in mortification. "He was hardly forcing himself on-"

"Markus told me what he saw happen in that locker room!" Bastian boomed before snorting derisively. "*A cut forehead.*"

Katherine pursed her lips together tightly, forcing back the angry words that threatened to spill out of them. "Are you going to answer my other questions?" she asked instead of cursing him out like she wanted to. "What's an alpha challenge and why'd you agree to one with Rogue?"

Some of his anger seemed to deflate at the change of subject. He turned his eyes back to the road. "An alpha challenge is a physical fight between two werewolves wherein at least one of the contenders is an alpha."

When no further explanation was forthcoming, Katherine rolled her eyes. "Gee, thanks for that riveting description."

The grip Bastian had on the steering wheel tightened, but despite his obvious ire, he acquiesced to her less than subtle request for a better answer to her question.

"Typically, an alpha challenge – or alpha fight – occurs when the beta of a pack makes the decision to vie for the alpha position of that pack. Occasionally, however, an alpha will challenge another alpha to a fight because he has something he wants – like a member of that alpha's pack."

"And that's what happened today?"

"That's what happened today," he confirmed.

How could he be so calm about this?

"Why did you agree?" she asked, trying to mask how upset she was at that fact. *Couldn't he have just said no to Rogue's challenge?*

"I didn't exactly have a choice," Bastian replied, almost as if he could read her mind. "If I didn't agree, I feared Cain would simply order me to hand you over to him."

Katherine blanched. "He could do that?"

Bastian shrugged, but when he met her eyes a moment later, she had her answer. *Yes, he could do that.*

"But what if you lose?" Katherine demanded, fighting the near hysteria building in her chest.

Bastian looked almost offended by her question. "I won't lose," he assured her.

"But what if you do?"

"I won't," he repeated, adding a hard edge to his voice.

"You can't possibly know that!"

"Do you have no confidence in me – your alpha? I assure you that I'll win. Now this discussion is over." His words rang with finality.

But Katherine wasn't done. "You can't-"

"Be quiet!"

She snapped her mouth shut. *Chauvinistic pig.*

Katherine stewed in her anger, but forced herself to remain silent for the rest of their journey home. Within minutes, they'd arrived at the house. Feeling petulant, she ripped off her seat belt, slammed the SUV's door as loudly and obnoxiously as she could, and stormed up the porch steps to dish out the same treatment to the house's double doors.

"What's the matter with you?"

"What happened? Are you alright?"

Ignoring a bewildered Zane and Sophie, Katherine marched straight past them to her room. Once there, she paced for a minute or two, trying in vain to keep down the turbulent emotions she could feel rising to the surface.

"Stupid jerk," she mumbled to herself.

She knew better than to let him get to her like this.

When the pacing didn't help to calm her down, Katherine decided a nice, long soak in the tub was the next remedy she would try.

Thankfully, it proved to be the perfect solution for stifling her stormy emotions. Slowly, but surely, the hot water forced her muscles to relax. She felt invigorated when she stepped out of the bathtub, quickly dry her hair and throwing on a clean pair of sweat pants and a t-shirt.

As she slipped the shirt on over her head, however, her stomach rumbled grumpily, reminding her that she'd yet to have breakfast. Knowing there were bound to be left-over banana muffins in the fridge from yesterday – she and Caleb were the only ones who liked them – she left her room and headed towards the kitchen.

She hadn't quite reached her destination, however, when the sound of Bastian's stressed voice reached her ears. A peek around the corner of the hallway wall revealed that he – along with Zane and Sophie – were sitting around the dining room table. And more importantly, blocking her entrance to the kitchen stationed behind it.

Great. Hadn't she dealt with Bastian enough for one morning?

Katherine was debating what was more important to her, retrieving that delicious, crumbling morsel of banana heaven stowed away in the fridge or avoiding Bastian for another couple of hours. That was when Bastian's words – what he was actually saying, not just the vague impression of his tired voice – registered.

"-made me look like a fool in front of the entire council."

"Forget him, Bastian. Everyone knows what a parasite Rogue is." Sophie's voice was a bizarre cross of sympathy and impatience. Clearly, he'd been unloading on them for a while – probably since they'd gotten back.

"Sophie's right," Zane agreed. "No one on the Council even respects Rogue. Don't let his antics get to you."

"Regardless on his esteem with the Council, I played right into his hands."

"Bastian-"

"And you know what the most infuriating part of it all is?" he asked, ignoring his sister entirely. "He was right."

Silence met his assertion. If the sound of her own heartbeat wasn't hammering in her ears, Katherine would have been certain that the organ had disappeared altogether – broken and disintegrated at the meaning behind the man's hastily spoken words.

"Come on, Bastian," Zane interjected.

"That's not true!" Sophie insisted.

"No," Bastian disagreed, "Rogue was right – *is* right. Katherine – she's a distraction."

Katherine desperately fought back the tears gathering in her eyes. *She was a distraction, was she?*

"She takes up so much of my attention that I've been neglecting my other duties."

"What other duties?" Sophie demanded.

"You know what other duties," Bastian shot back, using the same tone he'd used with Katherine in the SUV. "She's a weakness, Sophie – a weakness that I can't afford. Most days I wish I'd never laid eyes on her."

I wish I'd never laid eyes on her.

I wish I'd never laid eyes on her.

I wish I'd never laid eyes on her.

Katherine had heard enough.

Trying her hardest to smother the sob that threatened to reveal her position, Katherine pushed herself away from the wall she was hiding behind, her footsteps falling heavily on the floor as she raced past the dining room to the doors leading to the outside.

She needed to get away.

"Katherine?"

Bastian's voice sounded disjointed to her ears. She didn't process how shocked – dismayed – it sounded. She didn't even bother to put on her shoes before she flew out the double doors. She ran barefoot through the lawn, heading towards the surrounding trees without thought.

"Katherine!"

His voice was more panicked now, but she didn't acknowledge it – didn't acknowledge *him*. She zigzagged around trees, running as fast as her legs could take her. She ignored the cold wind that nipped at her nose and paid no attention to the sharp rocks and thistled shrubbery that dug into the soft soles of her feet.

She just knew that she needed to be alone – to get away from Bastian. So she ran – she ran until she couldn't run anymore, collapsing atop a large tree stump. She pulled her knees up to her face, trying to catch her breath. But it was made nearly impossible by the tears that had gathered at the base of her throat, choking her.

"Katherine, please. You need to calm down. Just breathe."

Of course. Of course he had followed her.

"Shut up," she managed to snap at him between hitched breaths. She refused to pull her head up and look at him. "I don't know why I'm crying. I don't even like you!"

Katherine knew, even as she forced the words out, that it was the most pathetic lie she'd ever told.

"You can not like me all you want. Just please calm down. You're scaring me here."

Couldn't he tell she was trying? It's not like she wanted to have a mental break down in front of Bastian of all people. It was humiliating.

"What happened to not coming after me if I ran away?" she demanded, though the words were garbled by tears and hiccups.

She remembered the promise he'd made vividly – though it'd been over a month since then. It had hurt her at the time – the idea that he would leave her to die if she ran away. Now, she just wished that he'd kept his promise.

Katherine tensed when she felt him tentatively place a hand on her upper back, rubbing it in slow circles between her shoulder blades as he spoke. "Just breathe."

She was torn between ripping the hand away from her and shifting closer to him so he'd have easier access to her back. Eventually, though, when she got her breathing under control and had managed to subtly as possible swipe the tears from her cheeks, she forced herself to move away from him and his soothing fingers.

"Are you okay now?" Bastian asked hesitantly.

"What other duties am I distracting you from?" Katherine didn't know why she picked that question from the dozens of others buzzing in her brain, but as soon as she'd asked him it, he tensed.

When his eyes met hers, though, they were the clearest blue she had ever seen them. "I didn't mean it," he told her, voice rough with an emotion Katherine couldn't place. "You're not a distraction – a weakness – or whatever you heard me say in there."

What he'd said was that he wished he'd never laid eyes on her.

"That doesn't answer my question."

Bastian looked away from her and for a long moment, Katherine didn't think he'd answer her. Then, just as she was about to get up and stalk away from him, he took a deep breath and turned to face her again.

"I lied to you earlier," he announced, startling and confusing Katherine all at once, "when we first met and you asked me why we were in Middletown. I let you believe we were there on council business, but that wasn't true."

Katherine blinked. "Okay…" she trailed off, not understanding what that had to do with her question, but assuming that he'd explain.

"We had Cain's permission, of course, but we were there because I – my pack – we," he paused, as if struggling to get the words out, "well, we were tracking my parents' killers."

Katherine inhaled sharply. "What?"

Bastian's eyes bore into hers. "The same hunters who went after you and your family… they murdered my mother and father."

Katherine was vaguely aware that she was trembling – from the bitter wind or the new piece of information revealed to her, she didn't know. "I'm sorry," she whispered, truly meaning it.

"Don't be sorry," he muttered, once again looking away from her. "You have nothing to be sorry for. It's I who should be apologizing. It was because of me – my vendetta – that we were even in Middletown to begin with. I bit you – changed you. Probably even led the hunters right to you and your family with my carelessness. I as good as killed your parents. Nearly got you killed too. I'm the one who's sorry."

The mention of her family stung, but Katherine kept the tears at bay. "It's not your fault."

The speed at which Bastian jerked his head around would have been funny in any other situation. His expression was beyond incredulous. "Did you not hear a word I just said?"

"I don't care why you were in Middletown that night, and Caleb and Sophie – they told me why you bit me. They said your wolf – that he… he was attracted to my scent." Katherine was glad that her face was already red from crying. "They said it wasn't your fault. And I believe them. Those hunters – the ones who killed your parents – they're the only ones responsible for what happened to my mom and dad."

Even after all this time, she couldn't bring herself to say it – that they were dead.

It looked like Bastian wanted to argue, but thought better of it when she jutted her chin out at him, just daring him to disagree with her. "Anyways," he muttered, rubbing the back of his neck, "the other duties I was talking about, was tracking those hunters. Well, the remaining one anyway. I killed one at your house in Middletown. I've hardly even thought of how to get my hands on the other one since you've joined our pack."

"Oh," Katherine muttered and bit her bottom lip. She wondered if she should be concerned that she *wasn't* concerned with the fact he'd killed someone – a nasty, vile someone who's had a hand in killing her parents, but still.

"That wasn't the only time I've lied," Bastian continued, surprising Katherine.

She released her tortured lip. "Is that so?"

"Yeah," he admitted, the corners of his mouth inching upward. "You obviously remember I told you that I wouldn't go after you if you'd run again. Clearly, that was a lie."

Katherine fought the urge to smile. "Clearly."

He grinned at her reaction, but too soon his mouth leveled into a straight line. "But that's not the worst or most hurtful lie I've ever told."

"No?"

"No," he agreed.

When he didn't elaborate, she crossed her arms over her chest. "Well?" she asked. "Are you going to tell me or not?"

For a moment, Bastian seemed uncomfortable and glanced away, but when his eyes met hers again, they were once again the honest blue they'd been since he'd chased her out there. "One of the worst lies I've ever told is that I wished I'd never laid eyes on you."

Katherine's breath caught in her throat.

"It makes me a truly awful person because I know that my actions – biting you, taking you away from your home – have caused you so much pain. But I'm ashamed to say that despite it all, I'm glad – so very glad that you're here with us – with *me*. And I'm terribly sorry that I feel that way."

Katherine didn't know what to say, but Bastian's words… they made her feel warm all over. She was both elated and… uncomfortable. She cleared her throat. "Wow. What is that? Three apologies in one day. Must be a record for you."

Bastian seemed disappointed at her flippant response to his declaration. Katherine nervously chewed the flesh on the inside of her cheek. "Well, I've lied to you too, if it makes you feel better," she finally volunteered.

Bastian glanced at her curiously – hopefully, even. "Oh yeah?"

"Yeah," she admitted, forcing herself to keep her eyes locked on his. "That whole 'I don't even like you' thing? It wasn't true." For a moment she lost her nerve and looked down. When she peeked up again, she was glad she did. The smile on his face was glorious.

"Katherine?"

"Mm-hm?" she asked, slightly dazed.

"I like you too."

Moments after his confession, he was hauling her from the mossy stump she'd perched herself on. She released a surprised squawk, but he just laughed and started heading in the direction she assumed was home.

"I can walk, you know," she pointed out indignantly.

Bastian grimaced. "Your feet," he said.

Katherine glanced down – they were in rather bad shape. "Oh."

They'd almost made it back to the house when Katherine was reminded of something she'd been meaning to ask the man. "Hey, Bastian?"

"What is it?"

"Will you teach me how to fight?"

His response was not what Katherine expected – anger saturated his voice. "What? Why would you want to learn how to fight?"

Katherine frowned. "Well, I figured that the whole incident with Rip could have been avoided if I had just known how to defend myself."

"No." His voice was hard. Final.

Katherine was flabbergasted. She had thought for sure that he would agree to her idea. Especially if she brought up Rip. "No? But why? I need to learn. Even forgetting what happened with Rip, you never know when I might need to-"

"I said no, Katherine. It's my duty to protect you – to protect all the members of my pack. You don't *need* to learn anything."

She tried once more. "But-"

"No."

Knowing not to push Bastian – she certainly didn't want to ruin their newfound truce – Katherine agreed to drop the subject.

* * *

Later that night, when Bastian had enclosed himself in his study, Katherine approached Markus, who was idly napping on the coach in the living room. "Markus?"

He cracked one hazel eye open, gazing at her questioningly. "Yeah?"

"Will you teach me how to fight?"

CHAPTER SIXTEEN

"Oomph."

Katherine landed on her butt. Hard.

But that was okay. *Really.* The shooting pain stemming from her tail bone would complement perfectly the dull ache that encompassed her right knee and the small but smarting finger-shaped bruises encircling both her wrists. She was fairly certain she'd managed to wrench her shoulder as well.

"You're doing it wrong."

If Katherine heard that one more time, she was going to rip the smug prick's head off. And by smug prick, she meant Markus. Not for the first time, she questioned her decision of asking him to teach her how to fight.

"Maybe I wouldn't keep doing it wrong if you'd stop throwing me to the floor every time I *tried* to do it right," she grouched. Despite its fluffy appearance, the carpet in the living room was abysmal at softening the blows her body took as she was constantly tackled to the ground. "I'm hardly going to be able to flip you over my shoulder if I can't even *feel* said shoulder."

"Right. Because your opponent will be terribly apologetic if he accidentally hurts you while you're sparring," Markus drawled. "Oh, I'm sorry. Did I knock you over? Here, let me help you up and make sure you're okay before we continue to try to maul each other."

Katherine gnashed her teeth together in an effort to stop from laying into the sarcastic man. After all, as much as she hated to admit it – and she truly did *hate* to admit it – Markus had a point. If she was in a real fight, she couldn't expect whoever she was facing to go easy on her.

With more than a little effort, the small brunette was able to pull herself off the floor. She briefly attempted to rub the pain from her backside before squaring her feet and once again turning to face her pugnacious teacher. "Okay, let's try again."

Before Markus could charge her, however, an exasperated groan from the couch caught both of their attention. "You two are insane. I'm not going to sit here and watch you get thrashed *yet again,* Katherine. I mean, come on, Markus, how do you think Bastian will react when he finds out you've been manhandling her?"

The owner of the voice was Zane, of course. He'd been moaning all afternoon – and all the previous afternoons they'd held these little sessions – about how careless the both of them were being. He was convinced that Markus would take it too far at some point and since their pack didn't have a designated healer, he would be the one to end up having to cart Katherine to the town's general healer – Bastian's friend, Gabriela Atkins – and have to explain to her and their alpha what exactly had happened to land her there.

Truth be told, Katherine could understand Zane's concerns. She didn't think that Bastian would take too kindly to the fact that they – she, Markus, and Zane – were going behind his back this way.

Okay, so she *knew* he wouldn't.

But Katherine was certain that she needed to learn how to fight! And since Bastian had adamantly refused to teach her, she'd felt like she had no other choice but to turn to Markus for help. And to be fair, she'd told him upfront that Bastian would be none too pleased if he ever learned of what they were doing.

She'd originally only intended to involve Markus in her little scheme. However, he'd quickly persuaded her into including Zane in their lessons. Apparently, he was the first of the pack to master voluntary transformation, and Markus couldn't exactly teach her how to fight in her wolf form without her learning how to change into it first.

A fun fact Katherine had learned? Born werewolves didn't actually transform into their wolf forms until after they hit puberty. There would be no puppies running around at the upcoming moon gathering.

The moon gathering – it was the first one she was to attend and taking place the very next night. Her pack would be there with her, but

Katherine couldn't deny that she was nervous. Bastian would probably be too busy with the Rogue situation to guide her through it like he had her first transformation.

Rogue. Despite whatever Bastian believed, Katherine *did* have the utmost confidence in his fighting prowess. Logically, she knew he could easily beat Rogue in a battle of strength, endurance, or even intelligence. But that didn't stop the slight nausea from rising in her gut whenever she thought of what could happen to her if by some twist of fate, he did lose to Rogue. For Bastian's sake, though, she'd been doing her best to hide her increasing anxiety as the day – or rather, night – of the fight loomed nearer. She and Bastian had actually been getting along ever since their rather intense talk in the forest, and she didn't want to destroy the tentative peace they'd established.

In fact, earlier that week he'd even taken her to the waterfall that Haven Falls was named after. She didn't know how it looked in the spring or summer time, but in the winter, it was a breathtaking sight – absolutely worth the hike through the snow that they'd had to take to get there.

"How much longer?"

Katherine couldn't believe that she'd actually been excited when it had started to snow two weeks earlier. The fat flakes had been so white and pretty falling from the sky. She'd watched from the house's windows as they began to build up on the ground and didn't stop building until at least a foot of the stuff covered the once green grass. It wasn't until she'd had to walk through the heavy snow the day after that her disdain for it had begun to grow.

And after a nearly mile long hike where she'd had to bring her boot-clad feet up to nearly her knees to get over the drifts? Well, that disdain was quickly growing into contempt.

"We're nearly there – just a few more minutes. Are you sure you don't want me to carry you the rest of the way?"

It would be easy for Katherine to be offended by Bastian's question if he didn't sound so genuinely concerned for her. As it was, she was huffing and puffing to keep up with the tall man whose powerful legs easily maneuvered through the wet sludge and snow.

"I'm fine," she managed to force out between breaths.

Bastian looked doubtful, but trudged forward. Katherine trailed behind him. And then, just as he had promised, they were there. Surrounded by pine trees with branches that were heavy with snow, was the most magnificent waterfall she had ever seen. Huge icicles hung from the contours of a cliff – like the rushing water had literally frozen as it had cascaded down the dark hunk of rock.

Katherine was speechless.

"Pretty, isn't it?"

The sound of Bastian's voice quickly snapped her out of her daze. She turned to face her companion – and he looked just a little too pleased with himself.

"It's gorgeous," Katherine agreed honestly.

Bastian grinned, his upturned lips bringing out the dimple on his right cheek. "I knew you'd like it," he muttered, seemingly to himself, before gesturing widely towards the west, beyond the trees surrounding the waterfall. "The moon gathering always takes place a few miles from here. Before the full moon rises this Wednesday, that's where we'll need to be."

As soon as he mentioned the moon gathering, his smile drooped, disappearing entirely until nothing of it remained but the hard, somber line of lips that Katherine was too used to seeing on Bastian's face.

Wanting to bring his smile back, Katherine acted impulsively. She bent down low and gathered a wad of snow between her hands. She hastily packed it into a ball before letting loose and chucking it right at the distracted man's head.

Her aim was true and the ball of wet snow smacked into Bastian's cheek with a splat. The look of shock on his face was so hilarious to Katherine that she couldn't stop an undignified bark of laughter from escaping.

And then she got her wish. Bastian smiled the biggest smile she'd ever seen – from him, at least. His eyes sparkled and the white of his teeth gleamed in the sun shining overhead.

Katherine's only coherent thought was that the beauty of the frozen waterfall had nothing on his smile.

"Oh, so that's how you want to play it, huh?" he asked, wiping the remains of the snowball from his face. "You know what this means, right?" He paused. "War."

Katherine knew he was going to lunge at her only a moment before he actually did. She tried to dodge him, but was too late and could only shriek in surprise as he wrapped his arms around her waist and tackled her to the ground. She retaliated the only way she could, grabbing a fistful of snow and smashing it into Bastian's face. In no time, however, he had her arms pinned and was demanding that she apologize for her dastardly deed. "Come on, say you're sorry."

Eventually, between peals of laughter, she did. "Okay, okay! I'm sorry... I'm sorry I didn't think of doing that sooner."

Bastian's grin sharpened into something positively diabolical. "Hm, not exactly the apology I was looking for," he said, using his free hand to gather a large snowball and hold it threateningly over Katherine's form. "Don't make me do it," he warned.

"I'm sorry," Katherine squealed. "I'm sorry!"

"I'm not sure if I believe you" he teased, bringing the snowball back behind his head as if to throw it down.

Katherine had resigned herself to a face full of snow when at the last second he changed his trajectory, hurling the sludge at a nearby tree. Chuckling at her slack-jawed expression, Bastian released her arms.

Unfortunately, it was at this time – as they were smiling at each other, both of their faces tinged red from the cold – that Bastian seemed to realize the rather compromising position they were in and quickly pulled himself off of her. He helped her up, but refused to meet her eyes as she patted the snow from her coat and pants. He jerked his head in the direction they'd come from. "We should head back to the house."

Katherine sighed, knowing that Bastian was planning on forgetting that their brief snowball fight had ever happened. "Okay."

"Oomph."

Katherine was literally knocked out of her thoughts as she was thrown to the floor. Again.

"I wasn't ready!" she cried, wincing as a sharp spark of pain, originating from her tail bone, once again shot up her lower back.

Markus didn't seem at all apologetic. "Oh yeah? And what's the first rule of fighting that I taught you?"

Katherine rolled her eyes, but begrudgingly answered. "Always be aware of your surroundings."

"Exactly," he agreed condescendingly. "You should constantly be prepared for an attac- Ow!"

Zane guffawed and Katherine couldn't have stopped the haughty smirk from emerging if she'd tried. "You were saying?" she asked.

The glare she received in return to her question was enough to make her immediately regret the hasty decision she'd made to test Markus on his own rule. She supposed she shouldn't have kicked the man in the knee cap as hard she could from her place on the floor. But he'd been the one preaching about vigilance!

"You're lucky I don't throttle you," he muttered, yanking his pant leg up to examine his knee. It looked fine to Katherine.

"It's not my fault that you weren't prepared for an attack," she pointed out, repeating his earlier words. "If I have to follow your rules, shouldn't you be following them too?"

He must have come to the same conclusion as Katherine – that his knee, while obviously hurting a bit, wasn't seriously wounded – because he allowed his pant leg to fall back down. "I suppose I should just be thankful you actually remembered one of the body's five weak spots."

"Eyes, nose, throat, groin, and *knees*," Katherine obediently reiterated what Markus had told her many times by then. He'd made it clear their very first lesson that her small size would be a disadvantage in any fight she partook in and thus, she was to immediately go for her opponent's weak spots – areas where he or she would be most susceptible to injury.

Markus had shown her how to straighten her thumbs to jab them into an attacker's eye sockets as well as the proper way to butt her head to smash into the nose of anyone who might grab her from behind. Katherine had drawn the line at practicing groin grabs, however. Neither Markus nor Zane had protested.

One armed shoulder throws, however, were something they'd both insisted she learn. Markus had been trying to teach her the move for the better part of the afternoon, but every time she'd try to execute them on him she ended up on the floor.

Like now, for instance. Though, this time, she truly just hadn't been paying attention.

"How is it that you can remember all that, but this move – this *simple* move – is too much for you?"

"It's not simple," Katherine disagreed, forcing her battered body to stand. "And even if it was, I just *can't* do it. You're too heavy and my arms aren't strong enough to lift you."

"It's exactly because strength isn't your strong suit," Zane interjected, grinning a little at his pun, "that you need to learn this. The move uses your opponent's strength – their momentum, if you will – against them."

"…Oh." It was the first time either man had explained it that way.

"Get in the position Markus showed you," Zane ordered, leaving his perch on the couch to maneuver Katherine's limbs how he wanted them. "Spread your legs further apart. Okay. And keep your hips centered under your torso. Make sure your head stays straight. Your body will always follow your head."

Once satisfied that Katherine had taken the correct stance, Zane gave Markus the okay to move backward a few feet and get ready to charge.

"Alright," Zane spoke softly in her ear, "instead of stepping forward when he comes at you, step backward. Use *his* power to throw him over your shoulder, not your own."

Katherine nodded that she understood and Zane shifted out of the way. As soon as he moved, Markus rushed at her.

Ignoring the instinct to brace herself for impact, Katherine kept her body loose and just as Zane instructed, stepped backward when Markus got close enough. She grabbed just above the elbow of his right arm with her left hand and twisted underneath him so that his front was flush against her back. Then, reaching around with her other hand, she seized the collar of his shirt and with one mighty heave, flipped Markus right over her shoulder. He landed flat on his back in front of her.

For a moment, Katherine could only stare at the fallen man, shocked that she'd managed to pull it off. As soon as Zane broke out in applause, however, she could no longer contain her grin.

Markus scowled at her from his place on the floor, but she could clearly see the pride in his eyes. "Not bad, princess," he complimented her. "Not bad at all."

* * *

The next day came and passed too quickly.

Before Katherine knew it, the sun was setting and she – along with the rest of her pack – had been forced to set out for the moon gathering. It was a long walk from Bastian's house – though *trek* may have been a better word for it. There had to have been close to two feet of snow on the ground!

At least once they'd reached the frozen falls, a somewhat decipherable trail had been created by other wolves whose heavy footsteps had packed down the white stuff as they'd made their way to the moon gathering earlier in the day.

Katherine followed her pack – their alpha leading the way, of course – as they journeyed through the snow, marching straight by the cluster of pine trees surrounding the waterfall and continuing onward until they'd reached the top of a small hill, under which lay a large clearing.

It was quite crowded.

Amidst the throng of people, Katherine could make out a large fire pit where red and yellow flames licked at the sky. The smell of smoke and incense was heavy in the air.

She hadn't taken more than two steps towards the fire and surrounding mob, however, before she spotted a cluster of her friends huddled together near the tree line far east from the soaring blaze.

"Can I?" she asked, turning to face Bastian, whom she'd noticed follow her gaze.

He seemed uncomfortable with the idea of her letting her leave the safety of the pack to go meet her school friends, but reluctantly nodded regardless. "Just make your way back to me at the first sign of moonlight. I'll be near the fire pit."

"Alright," she quickly agreed and took off before he could change his mind.

"Katherine!" Mack, the first of her friends to see her approaching, greeted her enthusiastically. "We didn't know for sure if you were going to make it."

Katherine frowned. "Why wouldn't I?" she asked tucking a wayward strand of dark hair behind her ear as she came to stand beside him. "I thought going to these gatherings was kind of required."

"It is," Melanie quickly interjected. "What Mack meant was that it's only your second full moon and well, we all know how," she paused, her cheeks reddening a bit as she seemed to search for a word, "protective of you Bastian has been since you've been here. And with his fight with Rogue tonight, well…"

"The fight's going to be epic!" Jonathan exclaimed, eyes alit with excitement, before Katherine could protest to Melanie's assertion that Bastian was protective of her.

"Jon," Mack said pointedly, jabbing him in the side with a sharp elbow.

"Oh," he glanced sheepishly at Katherine. "Well, I mean, Bastian is sure to win, of course."

Katherine rolled her eyes.

"Boys," Agnes muttered, following suit.

"Anyway," Melanie trilled before Jonathan had the opportunity to cram more of his foot in his mouth, "you came just in time, Katherine. Leander was just telling us about a race that's been planned for tonight."

"A race?" she asked, her interest mildly piqued.

Leander, who'd been quiet since Katherine had arrived – it was nothing new; she hadn't heard him speak more than a handful of words to anyone since she'd met him – nodded. "Some of the alphas are interested to see who the fastest of the upcoming recruits are. I heard Rip talking about it – complaining about how he couldn't participate, what with his hand and all."

Katherine had seen Rip at school since the locker room fiasco a few weeks back, of course. She wasn't sure how she felt about the cast that'd been present around his right wrist ever since. He'd been ignoring her though, so she couldn't deny that she was grateful for that at least.

"You're such a good runner, Katherine. You should definitely compete. Jon, Agnes and I are going to."

She blushed a little at Mack's praise, but wavered on her answer. "I don't know. I don't think Bastian wants me to stray too far from him."

What she *didn't* say was that she didn't think she wanted to stray too far from the man either. The anxiety that overtook her whenever she allowed herself to think of his upcoming fight with Rogue made Katherine more than a little hesitant to leave his side for too long. She wasn't sure what worried her more – that Bastian could get seriously hurt, or what would happen to her if he somehow lost.

"Oh, come on," Agnes attempted to persuade her. "You can't possibly pass up the opportunity to show up some of the dunces in our class."

"Yeah, and think of the alphas that'll be watching. You're pretty fast – you stand a good chance of impressing a few of them," Jon added.

"I don't care about that," Katherine mumbled, glancing at the faint sheen of moonlight that was beginning to creep in through the tops of the trees. She sighed. "I should probably go find Bastian."

"I think you should compete too, Katherine," Melanie pointed out, ignoring what Katherine had just said about finding Bastian. "The alpha fight won't start until midnight, if that is what's stopping you," she continued, correctly guessing what Katherine's hold up was. "The race is scheduled to start pretty much as soon as the moon hits its peak and should be long over by then, right, Leander?"

Leander bobbed his head up and down.

Katherine still hesitated. "Maybe..."

"Please?" Mack practically begged. "It'll be fun."

"Imagine the look on those boys' faces when we girls kick their butts," Agnes tried to entice her.

And with all of her friends looking at her with pleading eyes, she couldn't just say no. "Okay, okay. I'll race." Paying no mind to the cheer that met her announcement, she looked back up at the sky.

Katherine's heart nearly leapt straight out of her chest. The full moon – round and impossibly white against the near blackness that surrounded it – was already beginning its ascent over the trees.

Before she could think too much about the trouble she knew she was going to be in with Bastian, it started – *the change*.

It was almost exactly like the first time. Her body temperature rose to such a degree that it almost felt like her insides were burning. And then with a disjointed twist of her spine and a sickening crack, the edges of her vision blurred until there was nothing.

* * *

When Katherine forced her eyes open moments later, she was surrounded by five unfamiliar wolves.

Unfamiliar, yet *not*.

She knew immediately that the wolf furthest on her left – the one whose bright eyes gleamed intelligently as he stared down at her – was Mack. And the slightly larger, dark one right by him was undoubtedly Jonathan. The next – he was covered in shaggy, russet fur – could only be Leander. Then Agnes, or the wolf version of her anyhow, who was about the size of Mack with a coat a similar shade of gray as Caleb's. And finally, Melanie, whose wolf form was small and black with equally dark eyes.

Mack and Jon began yipping excitedly when they noticed Katherine stirring. A nudge from the former had her shakily getting to her feet – or paws rather.

She didn't know if she'd ever get used to transforming into a wolf. Thus far, Zane had been unsuccessful in teaching her how to do it voluntarily. And she could attest that transforming involuntarily wasn't a whole lot of fun.

Although this transformation had been easier than the first, she still wished that Bastian had been there to help ease her into it – to help her get used to her wolf form again liked he'd done for her the last full moon.

But, of course, he wasn't there. And she had no one to blame for that but herself. She allowed her eyes to wander back to the iridescent moon hovering above them all in the sky. *Bastian was going to kill her.*

The guilt that thought brought on made her shrink into herself a bit. She wasn't allowed to dwell on it, however, as her friends quickly began prodding her and encouraging her to follow them into the thick of the forest.

What was going on? Where were they going?

They didn't make it far, though, before they came upon a relatively small group of wolves, and Katherine remembered. The race. Of course.

Including Katherine and her friends, there were perhaps a dozen or so wolves. Three, who were larger than the rest and gave off auras of power, were obviously alphas. She strongly suspected that the light brown one with the mean eyes was Rip's father. He smelled horrible – like decaying rot.

Before she could bring herself to be truly bothered by his presence, however, Mack began butting his head into her side, attempting to move her towards where the other young wolves were forming a sort of line. Melanie and Leander scurried off to the side, clearly having chosen to observe, but not participate in, the soon-to-begin race.

Katherine let Mack lead her to where she was supposed to go, but was feeling more and more uneasy about her decision to compete. Bastian was probably looking for her – likely worried to the point of anger. Not to mention the fact that her friends hadn't had time to tell her the route of the race before the moonlight had shone down upon them and they'd all been turned into giant, hairy beasts.

Glancing at Agnes, who was readying herself on her right, Katherine supposed she could just follow her. She knew she'd be able to keep pace with her easily enough and besides, like she'd professed earlier, it wasn't like she actually cared what any of the alphas thought of her. If she got last… oh well.

So why had she even agreed to race in the first place? Katherine really didn't know.

Before she could consider the question too closely, however, the wolf she suspected to be Briggs was lifting his head and howling loudly into the wind. The other wolves who were lined up with her dashed off.

Okay. So clearly the howl was meant to serve as the starting signal of the race – like an air horn of sorts.

Springing into action, Katherine leapt forward a beat after the others. She quickly worked to spot Agnes's gray coat in the blur of furry bodies that rushed through the trees. And… *there* she was.

Katherine swiftly fell into step behind her friend, though it didn't seem like Agnes really noticed her new shadow as her full attention was dedicated to moving her powerful limbs. Agnes *was* fast.

But the fact of the matter was that Katherine was faster. And within minutes, she was fighting the urge to dart past her. Although the results of the race hardly mattered to Katherine, she longed for the feeling of joy – of freedom – that nothing but running could bring her. She yearned to fly through the trees like she had the last full moon. The temptation to do so was strong, but she managed to resist. Barely.

It wasn't worth the risk of getting lost.

But, of course, Katherine's intentions of sticking to Agnes like glue ceased to matter when another wolf – large and fur close to the same color of chocolate brown as her own – knocked her off balance and sent her body careening straight into the trunk of a nearby tree. She couldn't stop a pained yelp from escaping when her torso met the rough bark, but forced herself to stay on her feet. Paws. Whatever.

Her assailant had stopped to watch her as she stumbled, and she growled at him, attempting to discern his identity as she snapped at his ankles in retaliation to the harsh shove. She knew it couldn't be Rip because Leander had said he wasn't competing in the race. Maybe it was one of his friends?

Before she could decide for sure – though she was fairly certain it was Jason Collins, one of her more boorish classmates – he pushed her back into the same tree. This time, she *did* fall, and the other wolf took off, howling as he did so. The sound was high-pitched and sounded suspiciously like laughter. All too soon, he was out of sight.

And Katherine was alone.

With no real idea of where she was.

Exactly the situation she *didn't* want to be in.

Growling in frustration, she ignored the painful twinges coming from her rib cage and gave chase. Katherine ran in the direction that Collins had gone, but it didn't take long for her to realize that she wouldn't be able to catch him. *Or* Agnes, for that matter. She attempted to make her way back to where Collins had jumped her, thinking that surely there were some paw prints on the ground she could follow to the finish line of the race.

Unfortunately for Katherine, the wind had picked up since she'd arrived at the clearing with her pack more than an hour earlier and the only paw prints to follow were her own. It didn't help that everything was white and every tree looked the same as the last.

Nevertheless, she tried to find her way out of the forest and back to the clearing. It took a long while of fruitless searching for Katherine to finally admit that she was lost.

Why, oh why, had she agreed to participate in the stupid race?

As Katherine looked for a way out of the woods, her eyes frequently traveled up to gaze at the full, glowing moon. She watched apprehensively as it loomed nearer and nearer.

Bastian was going to be taking on Rogue soon and Katherine was terrified. Terrified that her absence would somehow cause him to lose and what that loss would mean for Bastian. What it would mean for her.

She was also more than a little afraid of what it would mean for her if she couldn't find her way out of the forest and back to the moon gathering by daylight. She would transform back into a human when the sun rose, and Sophie had the backpack that contained her change of fresh clothes. If she didn't make it back to the clearing by the time the sun rose, well… she'd be both lost and naked in the dark, cold forest.

How utterly humiliating.

It was right then – when she was on the verge of panic and all these horrifying scenarios were running through her mind – that Katherine saw a strange marking on the trunk of a nearby tree. It was almost as if some of the bark had been ripped off by… claws? *Werewolf claws?*

Was it possible that the alphas had marked a trail before the race had begun?

Heart palpitating in her chest, Katherine ran up to the tree, scrutinizing the mark. Yes, it had definitely been made by werewolf claws. She quickly examined surrounding trees, hoping to see a similar mark on another trunk.

And she did.

Hoping that she was right about the alphas marking the racing route, Katherine took off, following the marked trees as she saw them. She hadn't been at it for more than ten minutes when she began to vaguely recognize the landscape. Five more minutes, and she heard a howl.

Eager to find whoever was howling – she didn't even care if it was Rip's dad at that point – Katherine ran full tilt to where the sound was coming from.

She couldn't describe the relief that nearly overwhelmed her when she saw Caleb waiting for her where the race had begun hours earlier. Her friends were there too, looking as apologetic as any group of wolves possibly could.

Caleb, whom Katherine crashed into mid-howl, yelped in surprise before recognizing exactly who it was that'd pounced on him. When he did, he began nuzzling her, digging his snout into Katherine's soft fur in a faux hug. Then he was pulling back, checking her over to make sure that she was unharmed.

Once he was satisfied that she was none the worse for wear, he playfully bit her ear – almost like he was chastising her for disregarding Bastian's earlier instructions and getting herself involved in such a mess. As soon as he had her attention, though, all he did was gesture westward with his head. He took off, clearly expecting Katherine to follow.

She did, her five friends trailing after her.

Within minutes, they were out of the forest and had made it back to the clearing where the tall fire still burned brightly in its pit. Katherine expected to see wolves everywhere, mulling about, much like their human counterparts had been earlier. Instead, nearly all of the wolves were gathered together, many of them yipping excitedly.

It looked like they were surrounding something.

The fight!

Feeling her stomach plummet, Katherine sprinted to catch up with Caleb. Leaving her friends in her dust, she followed her pack mate's lead, slinking around bodies until she was at the forefront of the action. She recognized Sophie, Markus, and Zane in her peripheral vision, but she didn't acknowledge them.

She spotted Bastian immediately. *But then, how could she not?* There were only two wolves in the center of the circle that had been formed. There was the large, sinewy one with an almost tawny colored coat – Rogue, no doubt – and there was Bastian.

Katherine could do nothing but watch helplessly as Rogue jumped on Bastian, obviously trying to take a bite out of him, if his snapping jaws were any indication. Bastian shrugged him off easily enough, but as the moonlight caught his fur, Katherine immediately noticed that it was glistening in places – proof that Rogue had managed to dig his sharp teeth into him more than once already.

The fact that Bastian was bleeding – she couldn't explain how much it infuriated her.

But why wasn't he retaliating? Attacking Rogue in the same fashion that the other was coming at him?

Instead, Bastian seemed distracted. He wasn't focused on thoroughly trouncing his opponent. He was just standing there, seemingly looking out into the crowd for something… or someone.

The idea that *she* could be what he was looking for – that *she* was the reason for his distraction – well, the guilt nearly paralyzed her.

Sophie, apparently, was thinking along the same lines as Katherine. While Rogue was busy picking himself up, she began barking loudly, clearly trying to get Bastian's attention. His head jerked in their direction, his eyes seemingly drawn to Katherine's by some magnetic force field. His serious blue eyes positively drilled into her remorseful green ones.

Their gazes couldn't have interlocked for more than a second, but it was enough – enough to divert his attention – and Katherine watched, horrified, as Rogue once again slammed into him.

This time, though, Bastian *truly* bucked him off – nearly throwing the other wolf into the crowd of spectators and by the time Rogue was able to get back up to leap at Bastian once more, he was ready.

He met Rogue's attack with one of his own. Stretching on his hind legs, Bastian clawed at Rogue's snout. Lurching away from Bastian in obvious pain, he took a moment to compose himself. Then sprang at him again. Bastian jumped at him too. Their two bodies clashed in mid-air with a *thwack*.

Bastian landed on his paws.

Rogue did not.

And before he could roll off of his back, Bastian had placed his big, black body atop of his, paws on either side of Rogue's head as he growled menacingly, nostrils flaring and spittle dripping down his chin as he bared his teeth.

Katherine could recall play fighting with Bastian during the last full moon. He'd pinned her to the ground much the same way he had Rogue. But he didn't look nearly as frightening then. This was different. This was real rage.

Foolishly, though, Rogue refused to surrender and show his neck to the other alpha. He tried to squirm out from under him.

It was a mistake.

As soon as he'd moved, Bastian sunk his teeth into the other wolf's shoulder, not letting go even as Rogue let out a pained cry and began to writhe underneath him. After a minute or two of struggling, Rogue finally cooperated and lay prone. Bastian released him and the tawny wolf grudgingly bore his neck.

All around Katherine, wolves starting barking and yapping excitedly. Sophie, whom Katherine had paid only a minimal amount of attention to up to that point, was hopping up and down and butting her head against Katherine's affectionately.

But she only had eyes for Bastian.

Katherine watched as he stepped down from his position over Rogue and made his way to where she stood with the rest of his pack. His blue eyes were bright with remnants of adrenaline and anger undoubtedly reserved for her. But he didn't snarl, bark, or even glare at her.

He pressed his face hard against hers before he began to brush his side up alongside hers. It could be taken as nothing but the tender gesture that it was.

Obviously, he was just relieved that she was okay. Katherine was glad that he was okay too.

When she attempted to pull away from him, though, he growled – the noise low and originating from deep within his throat. She immediately pressed herself back up against him, whining softly in apology.

Alright, so maybe he was still a little mad. Somehow, Katherine doubted she'd be let out of his sight any time soon.

CHAPTER SEVENTEEN

"Please, Katherine. Please, please, please."

The small brunette sighed, trying hard not to let her aggravation show as she leaned back against Markus' red truck and listened to Melanie plead with her for the umpteenth time that day.

Monday and Tuesday she'd been forced to endure her friends apologizing every other minute – apparently they'd felt responsible for her getting lost in the woods at the moon gathering. Once she'd convinced them that she didn't blame them, however, and that she wasn't in *that* much trouble with Bastian, they'd moved on to begging her to go out with them on Friday after school.

They'd launched their campaign on Wednesday, cajoling her every spare second they had. Even Penelope, whom Katherine strongly suspected didn't even *like* her, was insistent that she tag along. And today – Thursday – they had moved on to phase two of their little operation…

"*Please* Katherine."

… which basically involved wearing down her defenses with the overuse of the word "please."

"Melanie, you know I can't go."

The girl in question frowned – though it would have been more of a pout if her lips weren't so thin. "Can't or won't?" she demanded.

"Can't," Katherine answered honestly, crossing her arms over her chest. While it was true that Bastian hadn't been nearly as mad at her as she'd thought he'd be after her disappearing act at the moon gathering, he'd still been quite obviously upset. Even more obvious was that he didn't want her wandering far from his sight.

Not only had he driven her to school every day that week, he'd picked her up too – even though Markus was already there and could have easily done it. Today, in fact, was the first time since the incident that he was actually allowing his beta to chauffeur her home.

And Katherine assumed the only reason Bastian was even permitting it was because he had some sort of important meeting scheduled with Cain that afternoon.

Katherine didn't want to admit it, but she'd been getting used to Bastian's constant attention and had been a little disappointed that morning when the man had informed her he wouldn't be able to pick her up after school.

Thankfully, her excitement at the prospect of Markus and Zane being able to resume her secret fighting lessons had quickly overshadowed it.

She just wished that Markus would hurry up with whatever he was doing in the gym so she could escape her friend's probing gaze, and they could get going.

Melanie's eyes narrowed at her answer. "Have you even asked Bastian if you can go?"

Katherine shifted uneasily, her fingers fiddling with the thick hair of her ponytail as she debated what to say to the girl. The short answer was no, she hadn't asked Bastian.

She didn't doubt what he'd say if she did, but the truth of the matter was that she didn't *want* to go.

"Come on, Katherine," her friend whined when she took too long to reply. "It'll be a blast. We hardly ever get the opportunity to leave town."

And that was precisely why she didn't want to go. Her friends weren't just going out anywhere after school tomorrow. They were actually leaving Haven Falls altogether to hang out in some other city. Fort Something or Another. According to Melanie, it was about three hours away by car.

From what Katherine understood, they were planning on eating out before, as Penelope put it, they hit the clubs.

It all sounded so… *normal*. Like something her friend Abby would have tried to coax her into doing before Miller Road – before she'd been bitten by a gargantuan wolf with sharp teeth and piercing blue eyes.

But she *had* been bitten by that wolf. And for whatever reason, the very idea of doing something so normal in an ordinary, *human* town made Katherine uncomfortable. Nervous, even.

And thus, she'd said no each and every time her friends had urged her to go with them.

"Sorry, I just can't. Maybe next time," Katherine finally offered.

Melanie allowed her shoulders to slump. "Fine, okay," she muttered, looking down and making patterns with the toe of her boot in the sludgy snow that covered the parking lot.

Both girls startled when the sound of a door banging open echoed throughout the nearly empty parking lot. Katherine glanced at the school, sighing in relief when she saw Markus heading toward them, shrugging on his worn, plaid jacket as he did so.

About time.

"I guess that's my cue," Melanie sulked for a moment before abruptly changing her demeanor and offering Katherine one last smile. "But, hey, if you change your mind, we're heading to my place right after school tomorrow. I have a couple of outfits that would fit you if you don't have anything club appropriate to wear. See you!" she called as she walked away.

As fond as she was of her friend, Katherine barely managed to stop herself from rolling her eyes at Melanie's exuberance. Apparently, however, she couldn't completely mask her incredulity from Markus, who smirked when he saw her expression.

"Ready to go, princess?" he asked, digging the truck's keys out of one of his jacket's many pockets and unlocking the vehicle's doors.

"Definitely," she agreed, not even bothering to object to the man's ridiculous nickname for her as she pulled herself up onto the beige passenger seat.

Markus had the truck started and was darting out of the parking lot before Katherine even had the chance to pull the safety belt across her chest. "What's the rush?" she asked, struggling to pull the strap free from the loop over her shoulder.

Huffing in mild annoyance, Markus reached across the cab, buckling the seat belt for her with his right hand while his left remained firmly on the wheel.

Katherine struggled not to blush. She must have successfully kept the red that threatened to blossom across her face at bay as he refrained from commenting on her complexion. Instead, he smirked at her. "No rush. I just thought you'd want to fit fight club in before Bastian got back from his uncle's place."

Katherine beamed.

* * *

Katherine glared.

When the words "punch me" had escaped Markus's mouth, she'd been suspicious. Especially when she'd spotted Zane's amused half smile.

Despite her reservations, however, Katherine had listened to the man. She'd balled up her fingers and swung. And then, when her fist was inches from his face, Markus caught it. Raising an unimpressed eyebrow, he easily shoved her fist – and as a result, *her* – away from him.

He'd pushed hard enough to knock her over, and she landed on her butt. *Of course.*

Hence, the glaring.

"That had to have been the saddest excuse for a punch I've ever seen someone throw," Markus scoffed loudly as Zane, whose half smile had transformed into a full-blown grin, helped her to her feet.

Flat out ignoring the way she glowered at him, Markus grabbed her right wrist as soon as Zane had pulled her up.

"Hey!" she objected.

"Thankfully, I'm here to teach you the right way to do it. Now, make a fist."

Katherine rolled her eyes at the man's abrasiveness, but did as she was told, curling her fingers around her thumb just as she had moments before.

Markus frowned, using the hand that wasn't holding her wrist steady to quickly unbend her fingers. "Never tuck in your thumb like that. If you'd actually managed to hit me earlier – and your thumb was like that – you probably would have broken it."

Katherine blinked. "Oh."

She applied his correction, making sure her thumb stayed on the outside of her fingers this time as she made a fist.

"Better. Now, do you see how your knuckles protrude a bit when you ball up your hand? When you throw your next punch, make sure you don't lead with them, alright? Lead with the flat your fingers instead." Markus released her wrist. "Zane, fix her stance."

Jumping into action, Zane helped her separate her feet so that they were a good fifteen inches apart, her left foot well ahead of her right. "The key to putting your weight behind a punch," he explained, "is to shift your weight from your back leg to your front as you lean in to hit your opponent. There's no need to actually wind up and pull your fist behind your head. Think jabs, not swings. Got it?"

"Got it," Katherine assured, replaying both men's instructions in her head. *Shift weight forward. Jab, don't swing. Don't lead with knuckles.*

"Alright," Markus said, stealing her attention, "now let's try this again. Punch me."

Wary after what had happened the last time she'd complied with that particular request, Katherine hesitated. When Markus sighed impatiently, however, she forced herself to disregard her misgivings and once again took aim.

Just as before, the man stopped her fist well before it could connect with his face. "Wrong," he sniped, making his displeasure clear.

Tearing her hand from his before he could push her over again, Katherine furrowed her brows. "Wrong? What do you mean *wrong*? I was following *your* instructions."

"Sure," he agreed, "but you went for my face – easy to anticipate and block."

"I was aiming for your nose. You're the one who taught me that it's one of the body's main weak spots," Katherine argued.

"You're right. But while a broken nose would hurt, it would only incapacitate your opponent for so long. If you could even connect your hit at all, that is. Not only is it easy to anticipate, but a nose is a pretty small target. A much smarter move would have been to go for the throat."

Katherine brought a hand up to her slender neck. "But couldn't that seriously injure someone?"

Markus looked exasperated. "Yeah, Katherine, it could. Even if someone as little as you was doing the punching. So if you're ever really in trouble, you don't question it. You go for the throat, alright?"

"Alright," she stammered, forcing her hand to move back down to its place at her side.

"Good. Now tell you what, princess? You actually manage to land a hit on me in the next five minutes and I'll let you choose what you want to learn next. Deal?"

Katherine narrowed her eyes, recognizing a change of subject when she heard one, but she wasn't about to pass up on that offer. Maybe she could sweeten the pot first, though? "I land a hit and not only do you let me pick what you teach me next, but you go a whole week without calling me that nefarious nickname."

Markus grinned. "Deal."

As Katherine sized up her opponent, she was only vaguely aware of Zane groaning and muttering to himself not far away. "Not a good idea, guys."

Ignoring Zane, Katherine aimed low, attempting to kick Markus's legs out from under him instead just punching wildly. It didn't work, of course. And as the first and then second minute ticked by, she resorted to doing exactly what she had wanted to avoid – punching wildly.

She'd punch left and then right, adding in a cheap shot here and there, like a shoe to the shin or a knee to the groin. Unfortunately, the infuriating man managed to block all of her attempts with ease.

As the fourth minute withered away – Zane, acting as their official time keeper, kept them well informed – and one of her punches came a hair's breath away from connecting with Markus's ribs. However, he'd clearly had enough. Grabbing first her right fist and then her left the next time she jabbed them at him, he quickly spun her around so that he had her hands trapped behind her back.

"That's not fair!" Katherine protested, trying to hit him in the nose with the back of her head like she'd been taught. But, of course, Markus was ready for it and already well out of reach.

Refusing to give up, she lifted her leg and stomped down hard on the man's toes. With a startled curse, Markus let go of one of her wrists. Caught off balance and with one arm still restrained behind her, Katherine squealed and fell forward, somehow managing to drag Markus with her.

It would have been entirely hilarious if the brunt of the man's weight had not have landed on her, knocking the wind right out of her lungs.

"Damn it! Are you alright-"

Concerned with the way Markus had cut himself off so quickly, Katherine looked up from where she'd been inadvertently pinned.

And immediately understood why the man had been unable to finish his question. Why Zane was staring, his usually dark-skinned face downright ashen, at the same exact spot as Markus.

Bastian stood in the entryway.

They hadn't heard his SUV pull up or the front door open over their noisy tussling, but his presence was impossible to miss now.

With his jaw clenched tightly shut and his attractive face quickly turning a fiery shade of red, he looked the very definition of angry. Katherine could even see a vein throbbing on his right temple from where she lay, helplessly trapped under Markus.

Zane was the first to react. "Bastian, it's not what it looks like."

It became evident that Bastian thought it was *exactly* what it looked like, however, when he crossed the floor before Zane had even finished his sentence. He grabbed Markus by the scruff of his shirt, lifting him off of Katherine and throwing him against the nearest wall.

"Bastian, man, seriously-" Zane tried again, but a sharp look from his alpha had him hastily shutting his yap.

Katherine picked herself up from the floor, but her voice was stuck hopelessly in her throat.

"You have one chance to explain to me what I just saw before I beat the snot out of you," Bastian snarled, shoving Markus against the wall again when he made a move to approach him.

"Really?" Markus scoffed, sounding awfully confident for someone who found himself being threatened by a man as powerful as Bastian was. "And what is it that you think you saw?"

"You were hurting her," he spat, obviously enraged. His whole body was tense, the muscles of his arms straining against the sleeves of his white shirt.

Markus actually laughed at that – the disbelieving chortle ringing throughout the room. "You actually believe that? That Zane and I would hurt her on purpose? What – that we torture her while you're away? Pick on her, push her around?"

"Shut up!"

"She's *pack*. Why would we hurt her? Listen to yourself." This time it was Markus shoving Bastian.

"I never would have believed it if I didn't see it with my own eyes," he said, stepping into Markus's space. The difference in the two men's heights was miniscule and as they stared each other down, they were nose to nose.

Zane's eyes were imploring Katherine to intervene. And finally finding her voice, she did. "Stop!" she demanded, reaching out to grab onto Bastian's taut forearm. She attempted to pull him away. "Markus wasn't hurting me."

Those words seemed to have a calming effect on the man. He relaxed his stance some, allowing her to tug him away from Markus. But he still didn't look entirely convinced.

"If that's true, then what was going on when I walked in?" he demanded.

Katherine licked her suddenly dry lips. Of course. *This* is how he had to find out about her secret fighting lessons. "Uh, well. You know how I asked you to teach me how to fight a few weeks ago and you said no?"

Bastian frowned. "Yes."

It was now or never. "Well," she paused, glancing once at Markus and then at Zane before finally allowing her eyes to land on Bastian's. The admission spilled out so fast the words nearly blended together. "I asked Markus to teach me afterwards and he said yes."

It took a moment for him to digest the words. To Katherine's surprise, he remained calm – deceptively so. "And that's what I walked in on? Some secret rendezvous where Markus and Zane were teaching you how to fight."

Katherine took a deep breath. "Yeah."

"And how long has this been going on?"

"A couple weeks," she admitted.

To be honest, Bastian's non-reaction to the entire situation was beginning to freak her out. She couldn't stop herself from babbling nervously. "I just wanted to learn how to defend myself. I know that you're the protector of the pack and everything, but I felt it was important that I learn a few techniques, you know? I mean, it makes sense that-"

Bastian stopped her rambling with a raised hand before bringing it to the bridge of his nose, which he pinched between his thumb and fore finger. "No, Katherine, it's okay."

Katherine almost didn't believe it. Apparently, she'd been worried about Bastian finding out about her lessons for nothing. "*Really?* That's great. Because Markus promised to let me pick what I wanted to learn next since I totally kicked his-"

"No. You misunderstand." He turned to look at her. "I'm not mad, but these little meetings you three have been having? They have to stop."

Katherine gaped. "But why? As much as it pains me to admit it, Markus and Zane are actually pretty good teachers. I've learned so much already."

Bastian leveled his gaze at the two men. "Of that, I have little doubt," he muttered before turning his eyes back on her. "But the fact that you feel the need to learn how to defend yourself? It's infuriating – downright insulting to me. I am the protector of this pack – the protector of *you* – and you need to learn to accept that. Now, the lessons stop."

She probably shouldn't have been, but Katherine was amazed by the man's nerve. She narrowed her eyes at him. "You can't tell me what to do," she argued, glancing at Markus and Zane, a little annoyed that they weren't backing her up. "Them either."

"Actually," he quipped, "I can."

She looked to the other two men in the room again, hoping they'd speak up. Neither would meet her eyes. She turned back to Bastian, disgusted at their apparent cowardice. "But that's not fair!"

"I don't care if you don't think it's fair," he roared, the first sign of his temper making itself known. "I'm the alpha and I make the decisions for this pack – for *you* – based on what I think is best. And I said no more lessons."

Katherine was well aware of the heat spreading across her cheeks. She struggled to find the words to display how she was feeling. What she came up with was this: "You're a real asshole, Bastian Prince."

Then, without further ado, she ran, heading straight for her bedroom and slamming the door shut behind her.

She heard him follow her, evidenced by three sharp raps on her door. "I wasn't done talking to you."

"Well, unless you've changed your mind about letting me learn how to fight, then *I* am done talking to *you!*"

For a long moment he didn't respond. Then she heard the telltale sound of feet shuffling across the carpeted floor and knew he'd retreated.

Unfortunately, his absence didn't make her feel any better. She just couldn't believe how completely chauvinistic he was acting. She had perfectly valid reasons for wanting to learn how to fight, and Bastian wasn't even willing to listen to them. The man had more ego than common sense.

And Markus and Zane – they hadn't even stuck up for her!

She was just so... *mad!* Who did Bastian think he was anyway? He couldn't dictate her life.

Katherine stewed. She paced the hardwood floor of her room.

It was then that – quite suddenly – an idea came to her.

She'd show him. She was perfectly capable of making decisions for herself. She didn't need his permission for anything.

He wasn't her keeper.

Katherine yanked open the doors to her closet, raiding through her clothes until she found what she was looking for buried in the very back – a flimsy, black dress that she'd nearly forgotten about.

* * *

She didn't wait long the next day to approach Melanie. The girl was digging in her locker – she was notoriously unorganized and no doubt looking for a misplaced textbook or stack of notecards – when Katherine tapped on her shoulder.

"Yeah?" she asked, obviously distracted.

Katherine took in a deep breath. "I'm in."

Looking up from the black abyss that was her locker, Melanie raised an inquiring eyebrow. "In... what exactly? Trouble?"

Really? *That* was where her friend's mind went?

Katherine supposed she couldn't blame her.

"Uh, no," she said, "I meant I'm in as in I want to go out with you guys tonight... well, if the offer still stands anyway."

Melanie squealed, seeming to forget about her hunt for her book – or whatever it was she was looking for – as she pulled Katherine into a tight hug. "Of course it does! This is going to be so fun. I *really* can't wait for school to be over now."

Katherine forced a smile, hoping it looked sincere. And ignoring the smidgen of guilt threatening to turn it into a frown, she agreed.

"Yeah, me either."

Just as Melanie had hoped for, classes flew by quickly. At lunch, Katherine announced to the rest of the gang that she'd changed her mind about going out with them, and they reacted in similarly excited manners. Especially Jon, who apparently subscribed to the theory that the more attractive girls a guy went out with, the more attractive girls he could pick up.

Yeah.

Before Katherine knew it, her last class of the day – P.E. – had come to an end.

"Hey, princess," Markus called, stopping her before she could disappear into the locker room.

Princess. *Ugh.* So much for their deal.

"Yeah?"

"Bastian can't pick you up this afternoon so just hang out by my truck for a few minutes while I put this crap away, alright?" He gestured toward the two goals and pile of sticks that they'd been using to play indoor hockey.

"Okay, sure," Katherine agreed, not quite believing her luck. She'd had no idea how she was going to sneak away undetected after school, especially since Bastian had been dropping her off and picking her up lately. But with Bastian out of the picture and Markus preoccupied, it would be laughably easy.

Still, Katherine wondered why Bastian had bailed. She figured he probably didn't want to sit through another car ride of hostile silence. She'd made it a wee bit obvious that morning that she was still mad at him.

Katherine hurried out of her gym uniform and into the baggy sweatpants and t-shirt she'd worn to school. She rushed Melanie and Agnes through their routines as well. If her friends thought anything of her odd behavior, they kept it to themselves.

Sparing a glance at Markus as she exited the locker room and gym with her friends, Katherine made her way to the parking lot, where she, Melanie, and Agnes met up with Penelope and the boys.

It was quickly decided that the girls would hop in with Melanie in her tiny two door car, while the guys would ride with Mack in his slightly larger – but infinitely rustier – four door vehicle.

Katherine loaded her satchel, which was stuffed not only with her school books but with the black dress she'd thrown in there last night, into Melanie's car before squeezing in the back seat with Penelope.

She couldn't resist peering out the rear view window as Melanie pulled out of the lot, wondering how Markus would feel when he realized that she wasn't where she was supposed to be. That she wasn't at the school at all.

He'd probably be angry. Maybe even worried.

No.

Katherine forced that thought away.

Who cared how he – or more importantly, how *Bastian* – would feel? If he couldn't respect her enough to allow her to make her own decisions – well, she wouldn't feel the need to inform him when she made them anyway. Why should she? He may have been her alpha, but he wasn't her mother.

She didn't have one. Not anymore.

Thankfully, Melanie forced Katherine out of her spiraling thoughts when she began to talk, explaining to Katherine where it was she resided as she navigated through Haven Fall's narrow streets. "I only live a few miles west of the school. Well, not just me – Mack and Jon too. You probably didn't know this, Katherine, but Mack, Jon and I all live together in the same house. There are two other boys who stay with us as well, but they aren't in our grade. We're all changed werewolves, but we haven't been claimed by a pack. Not like you have been."

For the first time since she'd been introduced to her, Katherine detected a hint of envy in the other girl's voice.

"Anyway," she continued, "a man named Luther – he's an alpha, but a lone wolf – takes care of us. He's in charge of us until we're old enough to be recruited. If he's around, I'll make sure to introduce you before we take off."

"I've met him a few times. Don't worry, he's really nice," Agnes assured from where she sat in the passenger seat.

"Yeah," Penelope agreed noncommittally.

Not a moment later, they'd arrived. Katherine couldn't help but be relieved that Melanie's house was on the opposite side of Haven Falls of where Bastian lived.

Melanie parked her little car and the girls unloaded, the boys not far behind them.

Like most of the residential buildings in Haven Falls, the house was two stories tall and made mostly of brick. Melanie skipped to the front door, pulling it open and ushering her friends in.

"Come on, Katherine, I'll give you the abridged tour before we girls head upstairs to get ready."

She proceeded to show her the kitchen, living room, and downstairs toilet before grabbing the other girls and heading up the stairs. After quickly pointing out the upstairs bathroom to Katherine, Melanie led them all to her room.

Katherine couldn't help but smile when Melanie tugged open the door. Her first observation was that her bedroom was as disorganized as her locker and her second was that it was very… *pink*.

Melanie grimaced when she saw Katherine's expression, mistaking her amused smile for something more jeering. "Yeah, I know – I think this wall paper has seen one too many centuries."

"Nah, it has character," Katherine assured, eyeballing the pale pink slabs of paper. "My old bedroom back in the states looked a lot like this one," she lied, hoping to make her feel better.

"Really?" Melanie asked, seemingly intrigued, before abruptly shaking her head. "Sorry, I'm sure you don't want to talk about that. Anyway," she heaved a pile of laundry away from what must have been her closet door, "I have the cutest outfit for you to wear."

Katherine bit her lip. "Actually, I brought something of my own."

"Really?" Melanie asked, giving her rumpled sweatpants a long look. She shrugged. "Well, if you're sure."

"Quit dawdling, girls," Penelope interrupted from where she

lounged on the bed. "We only have half an hour to get ready, tops, if we want to have time to stop for supper at Fort Saskatchewan."

With no more warning than that, Penelope began to pull her top off.

Katherine quickly averted her gaze, gesturing vaguely at the door. "I'll go change in the bathroom."

Without waiting for a reply, she grabbed her bag and exited.

Fumbling out of her clothes and into the scrap of fabric that was her dress was a little difficult in the enclosed space of Melanie's bathroom, but Katherine managed. With more than a little apprehension, she looked at herself in the mirror.

She saw a lot of skin.

The dress was even shorter than she remembered it. The flowy skirt hit her a few inches above the knee and while the neckline was somewhat modest, the bust was only held up by two tiny, lacy scraps.

Katherine twisted a bit. And had it always been nearly completely backless?

So much for wearing a bra.

Steeling her resolve, Katherine pulled on the rubber band that held her hair back in a ponytail and watched as the wavy mess tumbled free. Brushing her hair to one side so it cascaded over her right shoulder, she examined her reflection in the mirror.

Despite her discomfort in the revealing dress, Katherine had to admit – she looked good.

Hoping that her outfit wasn't too much, she reluctantly let herself out of the bathroom and headed back to Melanie's room.

She realized as soon as she opened the door that she needn't have worried.

Melanie was wearing an orange sweater dress with a sweeping neckline. Agnes was in a leather skirt and red halter top. And Penelope – well, Penelope had squeezed into a skin tight, leopard print dress, out of which her breasts threatened to spill.

"Wow, Katherine, you look really good," Penelope offered when she spotted her lingering in the doorway.

Katherine refrained from commenting on how surprised the girl sounded. "Uh, thanks. You guys look good too."

"What shoes are you planning on wearing with that?" Melanie asked from where she sat in front of a cracked vanity, fluffing up her short hair.

It was then that Katherine realized she'd only brought her sneakers. And wouldn't that be a fashion statement? Pairing her sneakers with the dress she had on. A statement that she had no idea how to dress herself, but a statement nonetheless.

Melanie must have recognized her deer in the headlights look because she immediately bounced over to her shoe rack. "Don't worry, I have the perfect shoes for it."

Katherine shoulders sagged in relief. Before she could thank her friend, however, Melanie had pulled out what had to have been the most dangerous heels to ever be created. Five inch tall, lime green stilettos.

The color would blind all those who dared to look upon them and the pencil thin heels guaranteed bodily harm to all those who dared to wear them.

Thankfully, Agnes came to her rescue. "She's liable to kill herself in those," she scolded Melanie before offering Katherine a pair of plain black ballet flats. "Here, I brought an extra pair."

"Thanks," Katherine breathed in relief before quickly slipping them on.

"Fine," Melanie pouted, "but at least let me do your make-up."

Katherine reluctantly agreed.

Ten minutes later, she was completely done up.

Truthfully, she hadn't worn any make-up since arriving in Haven Falls so the foundation felt a little heavy on her face. And while she thought the mascara helped her green eyes pop, the red lipstick was a little – okay, *a lot* – much. Unfortunately, when she'd tried to discretely wipe it off, Melanie had admonished her and applied even more of it to her lips.

Katherine and Melanie waited patiently for Penelope to finish

French braiding Agnes's hair before finally reconvening with the boys in the kitchen. They were munching on some barbeque flavored potato chips and the fact that they were still in the same clothes that they'd gone to school in – jeans and t-shirts – made Katherine feel more than a little ridiculous in the get-up she was wearing.

It didn't help when the boys turned around and their eyes practically bugged out of their heads. "Looking lovely as always, ladies." Jon complimented them, throwing one arm around Agnes's shoulder and the other around Penelope's.

"Who are you and what have you done with my friend Katherine?" Mack demanded, bumping shoulders with her.

"Hardy, har har," she muttered, rolling her eyes.

Melanie snatched the bag of chips off the counter, folding the opening shut before throwing it back into a random cupboard. "You guys shouldn't ruin your appetites like that."

Before she could continue to chide them for it, the sound of the front door creaking open and slamming shut reverberated throughout the room.

Katherine's whole body tensed, completely unfounded paranoia flooding her. The man that turned the corner into the kitchen, however, wasn't Bastian – *why would it be?* – and Katherine allowed her shoulders to sag in relief.

The man – well above six feet tall, but rather haggard looking overall – stopped short when he saw the small crowd in his kitchen. "Hey, kids," he muttered, stepping around Nathaniel and Leander to get into the refrigerator and pull out a cold beer. "I thought you were going out after school."

"We are. We just needed to change first," Melanie volunteered, waving Katherine over. She reluctantly stepped forward.

"Luther, this is my new friend, Katherine. *Bastian's* Katherine."

Bastian's Katherine, was she?

Trying to ignore the way her friend had emphasized her alpha's name, Katherine focused on determining if the man had been at the council meeting she'd been forced to attend not long ago. She wasn't sure.

Luther offered her a tired smile. "Good to meet you, Katherine."

"You too," she mumbled.

"Anyway," Melanie continued, "we were just leaving. See you later, Luther."

"Yeah, you kids have a good time. Try to be back before midnight."

"Of course," Melanie agreed.

"Yeah, right," Penelope snorted. Mack and Jon smirked at each other.

Without further ado, they all took their leave.

Just as they had after school, the group split up – the girls with Melanie again and the boys with Mack – for the drive to Fort Saskatchewan. Despite the fact that Penelope spent the whole three hours it took to get there gushing about a boy she'd met the last time they'd visited the city, the time passed relatively quickly.

It was nearing eight o'clock when they arrived, and they decided on having supper at a bar and grill that Agnes insisted served the best steak ever. After trying it, Katherine wasn't sure if it was the best *ever*, but it was certainly delicious. Rare and filled with succulent red juices, she was tempted to order another. Mack and Jon both did.

The pork that Melanie and Nathaniel ordered looked tasty as well.

Katherine paid for her meal with a credit card of some sort that Bastian had given her months ago when she'd first arrived at Haven Falls. She didn't feel the least bit guilty about it either. Well, maybe a little.

As they left the restaurant, Katherine had to admit that she was having a good time despite her initial reservations about going out with her friends to Fort S-Whatever. Not even the horrible pick-up lines that Jon was testing out on her – he planned to use them on the girls at the club they were walking to – could sour her mood.

"Okay, okay. How about this one? If this was a meat market, you'd be the prime rib."

Katherine groaned. "Really?"

"What was your last one?" Agnes chimed in. "If you were a steak, you'd be well done? I just got done eating some *awesome* steak, and it still makes me throw up in my mouth a little."

"Maybe you should try one that, you know, doesn't mention meat," Melanie suggested.

"But why? I'm a pretty meaty guy if you know what I mean." He actually wiggled his eyebrows.

"Gross," Penelope scoffed.

"Sounds to me like you're a guy who is pretty *into* meat, if you know what *I* mean," Katherine retorted.

The comment had even quiet Leander in titters.

Soon, they arrived at the club her friends had insisted didn't check its patrons for ID's. Katherine was pretty sure she didn't even *have* a Canadian ID so any other club was out of the question.

The club's name – Vertigo – was illuminated in bright, neon lights over its entrance. Just as she'd been promised, they got in without any trouble. The inside was exactly what Katherine suspected most night clubs were like. There were flashing lights, a fog machine, and loud, fast paced music that blared from speakers above the bar. Booths lined the walls, boxing in a packed dance floor.

Penelope, spotting a "hunk" getting down, abandoned them nearly immediately. After setting her purse on the plastic table of the booth they picked out, Melanie joined her on the dance floor. Mack and Jon left not long after, taking off to go chat up some "hotties" they saw sitting at the bar.

Katherine and her other friends – Agnes, Nathaniel, and Leander – were all perfectly content to lounge in the booth and talk, sipping on the sodas they'd ordered. It wasn't long, though, before Melanie was back and dragging all four of them out on the dance floor with her.

At first it was a bit awkward, lifting her arms in the air and shaking her hips to the beat. Soon, however, she began to enjoy herself. She got used to dancing by her friends without ever actually dancing *with* them.

After they'd been dancing for the better part of a half hour, Melanie hip checked her, immediately getting her attention. "Cutie at six o'clock," she stage whispered.

Glancing behind her, Katherine quickly averted her gaze when her eyes locked with the baby blues of a blond man. He certainly wasn't bad-looking – cute in a boyish sort of way – but Katherine wasn't interested in hooking up like most of her friends seemed to be.

What were they thinking anyway? Sans Penelope and Nathaniel, they were all *werewolves*.

She cringed when she felt the man press his chest to her back, boldly digging his fingers into her hipbones as she danced. She stepped away from him. "No, thanks," she declined as politely as she could, deciding it was time for a break from dancing anyway.

He seemed disappointed, but let her go easily enough, eyeing Melanie like he might try sneaking up behind her next. Katherine didn't think the girl would mind.

Making her way through the maze of people on the dance floor, Katherine decided to head over to the bar to check on Mack and Jon – see how they were doing with the ladies.

They were both chatting up the same girl.

She was pretty, with long hair that ended near her waist, but she suspected the boys were more attracted to the goods that threatened to pop out of her low cut top.

"Katherine," Mack called, gesturing for her to join them. She hopped up on a bar stool. "This is Emily."

"She's a college student," Jon offered, seeming particularly enamored with that fact.

"Hey," Katherine greeted her, nodding her head in acknowledgement.

"Hi," the girl replied, her bubbly personality immediately apparent. "Katherine – that's such a pretty name! A little old-fashioned though. I mean, I think I have a great-great-grandma who was named Katherine or something. Oh, I know. Have you ever thought of going by a nickname? Kathy? Kate? What about Kitty? Oh, I like it! I have a kitty, you know. His name is Mr. Snuggles, though, not Katherine. Sorry."

The girl had obviously had one too many of the little pink drinks she was holding. Maybe even five too many.

"Uh, that's okay."

Before Emily could share more of her wit with them, though – the results of a clearly sophisticated college education – a loud squawk from the dance floor caught all of their attention.

"Get your greasy hands off of my boyfriend, you tramp!"

Katherine's eyes landed on the source of the commotion. Penelope.

Well, Penelope and another girl, who had a very pink bob of hair upon her head.

They were arguing rather heatedly and from what Katherine could tell, Pinkie had just shoved Penelope.

"Tramp?" Penelope screeched. Katherine watched as Melanie grabbed her elbow to stop her from flying at the other girl. "Really? Maybe if you learned how to satisfy your boyfriend's needs, he wouldn't have to look for his kicks elsewhere."

"Well, I can certainly see why it was he was looking here," Pinkie spat, eyeing the bust line of Penelope's dress. "Do you know how to spell easy? Your name."

Pinkie took another step towards Penelope and Melanie – she was nearly in their faces – and Katherine knew she had to move. She unglued herself from her seat at the bar, intent on helping Melanie try to defuse the situation.

"If you got it, flaunt it, honey!" she heard Penelope retort.

And just when Katherine got to them, it happened.

"Flaunt this," Pinkie yelled and doused all three of them with whatever kind of drink it was she was holding in her hand. All Katherine knew was that it was extremely sticky and judging by the awful smell it shrouded them in – *very* alcoholic.

Lovely.

And then, as if things couldn't get any worse, Penelope lost it.

And by “it”, Katherine meant her marbles. Every last one of them.

She shrieked and with no one holding her back, launched herself at the girl, toppling her over. She swung an arm wildly – totally the wrong way to throw a punch, as Katherine was now well aware – and somehow connected with Pinkie’s mouth. Her bottom lip began to bleed.

Fortunately, that was when the oh-so-diligent bouncers finally made an appearance and pulled the furious Penelope off of the girl. Unfortunately, they swiftly kicked Penelope – and Katherine and Melanie, who were apparently her cohorts – out of the club.

Agnes and the boys – minus Jon – immediately found them where they sat sulking on the sidewalk outside of Vertigo. There, Penelope explained that she had, in fact, met up with the boy she’d gushed about the entire drive to Fort Saskatchewan, only to find out he had a girlfriend – that’s right, Pinkie. Or Kristin as Penelope had called her.

By the time she’d recounted the entire sordid tale, Jon had finally joined then, looking entirely too pleased with himself. Apparently, he’d weaseled a kiss out of college girl Emily.

Mack wasn’t too impressed.

The drive back to Haven Falls seemed to take forever – much longer than it’d taken them to get to Fort Saskatchewan. She didn’t know if it was because it was well past ten o’clock by the time they’d finally left and she was tired or because she was covered in sticky alcohol and extremely uncomfortable.

Or perhaps the most obvious reason of all was the culprit – Bastian. She had no idea what awaited her back in Haven Falls.

But she was about to find out.

As soon as Melanie’s tiny car was parked safely in the gravel lot outside of her house, the front door smacked open. Luther stepped out, looking grim. Behind him followed none other than the man who’d occupied her thoughts all night.

“He looks mad.”

And the award for understatement of the century goes to you, Melanie.

Agnes kicked the back of Katherine's seat, snapping her out of her momentary stupor.

"You did get permission to go out with us, didn't you?" she asked.

Steeling her resolve, Katherine shook her head. She wasn't going to allow herself to be intimidated by Bastian – even if her friends were. "I don't need his permission for anything," she spat, wrenching open Melanie's car door. She marched across the lawn, towards the two men, only vaguely aware of her friends scrambling to catch up to her.

The closer she got to Bastian, however, the more she realized that her wrath was no match for his.

He was the angriest she'd ever seen him. The air around him positively crackled, like a lightning storm. Both terrifying and beautiful.

Her proud march turned into a much more subdued shuffle.

That made no difference to Bastian, however, who was more than willing to meet her halfway across the yard, grabbing her by the crook of her elbow when he reached her.

"Hey!"

Ignoring her protests, he dragged her to his parked SUV, which had gone unnoticed by Katherine until then.

Still holding onto her arm with one hand, he yanked the passenger's side door open with the other. Finally, he let go of her. "Get in," he ordered.

"But what about my friends? I should say-"

"Get in," he repeated slowly, stressing each word between clenched teeth.

Biting down hard on the soft tissue of her inner cheek, Katherine did as she was told. Bastian slammed the car door shut as soon as she'd pulled her seat belt across her chest and was in the driver's seat, starting the SUV, in the blink of an eye.

He hit the gas, and tires squealing, they were off. The sound of the engine purring softly beneath the hood made the edgy silence between them seem somehow more intense to Katherine.

When he finally parked the vehicle beside his house, she prepared herself for a fight. Instead of yelling, however, he remained frightfully silent, ducking out of the SUV as soon as he'd turned the ignition off. He pulled Katherine's door open. "Out," was all he said.

But Katherine had had enough of being ordered around. "No."

A disbelieving – almost *feral* – grin transformed Bastian's handsome face into something dangerous. "No?"

"I don't have to listen to you," Katherine once again defied him.

Grin abruptly wiped from his face, Bastian reached across her lap to unbuckle her and grabbing her by her hips, easily lifted her up and out of the SUV. Before she could react, he'd set her back down on her feet and slammed the door shut again.

"What's wrong with you?" Katherine demanded, furious at the thought of being manhandled – treated like a doll.

"What's wrong with me?" he repeated incredulously. "What's wrong with me is that I have a reckless little girl under my care who takes great pleasure in worrying me to the point of insanity whenever she gets the chance!"

"I'm not a little girl-"

"No," Bastian cut her off. "Be quiet and listen for once. I couldn't find you!" His already bright eyes were blown wide, the blue and black nearly overwhelming the white. "All these scenarios were flying through my head," he cut himself off, obviously not willing to share what exactly those scenarios were. "You're always running – running away from me! Do you really hate it here that much?" He took a deep breath. "Do you really hate *me* that much?"

"No!"

"Then why?"

"I just wanted to prove to you that I'm responsible enough to make my own decisions – that only *I* know what is best for me, and that I can take care of myself. That's all."

"That's all, huh? Well, I have news for you, little girl. All you've managed to prove is how utterly *irresponsible* you are!"

Bastian's continued use of that particular phrase – "little girl" – was getting on Katherine's last nerve.

"Why is it irresponsible to go out with my friends? I had fun." *Sort of.* "Nothing bad happened."

"And you're damned lucky," Bastian spat. He ran an agitated hand through his hair and for the first time, Katherine noticed the man's obvious preoccupation with her current outfit. "Dressed like that, you're just asking for trouble. And I can smell the liquor on you from here."

And that was it for Katherine.

She'd had enough.

The connotations of what Bastian had just said – the implications behind his words – finally pushed her over the edge. She wasn't some drunk floozy!

And so she took the only action that made sense to her at that moment.

She threw herself at the man. And kissed him.

As soon as her lips made contact with his, Bastian froze. But that made no difference to Katherine. She pushed all of the emotions pulsing through her into the kiss – anger, frustration, her goddamn reluctant affection of the man. What she didn't expect was for the softness of his lips, combined with the roughness of his stubble, to send a powerful tingle shooting down her spine.

It was like nothing she'd ever felt before.

She pulled away with a breathless gasp. "Do I taste like liquor to you?" she challenged, feeling more brazen than she ever had in her entire life.

For a long moment, Bastian remained as still as stone.

But then he shook his head. And slowly wrapped a callused hand around the back of her neck, allowing his fingers to entangle themselves in the fine hair he found there. "You are absurdly beautiful," he muttered, and slammed his lips back onto hers.

Hands grasping either side of his face, Katherine kissed him back, responding with equal fervor. He swiped her bottom lip with his tongue, begging for entrance into her mouth, which she immediately granted him. Their mouths clashed in a battle for dominance that he easily won. Every sensual lick and twist of his tongue set her body afire – a heat that was only amplified as he used his free hand to caress the small of her back and press her body closer to his.

And then, as quickly as it had started, it was over.

Bastian retreated, tearing his lips from hers and digging his face into her hair, breathing in deeply, like he couldn't get enough of her scent. Not the alcohol that covered her dress, but *her*.

She'd never wished so zealously to know what she smelled like to him than right at that moment.

For a long minute, the only sound that filled the air was their noisy breathing. Then, he spoke. "You have no idea, Katherine. When Markus told me you disappeared this afternoon, I… I lost it."

Still feeling lightheaded from the kiss they'd just shared, Katherine offered her first breathless apology of the night. "I'm sorry."

"Just promise me you'll never do anything so reckless again. You have to tell me when you're planning on going somewhere. This world we live in – the one I dragged you into – it's a dangerous one. I can't stand the thought of something happening to you."

Swallowing around the wad of guilt that suddenly made itself known in her throat, Katherine offered another apology. "I'm sorry." But she couldn't allow herself to be completely swayed by him. "But, Bastian, I still think-"

"I'll allow you to learn how to fight, if that's what you really want," Bastian interrupted, knowing exactly where she was going with the protest. "I still don't approve, but I understand that it's not something you're willing to give up. But you have to compromise with me. Let *me* teach you, Katherine. Please."

Didn't he realize that was what she'd wanted in the first place?

Nothing could have stopped the giddy smile from creeping onto Katherine's face just then. "Okay."

CHAPTER EIGHTEEN

For the next week, kissing Bastian was all Katherine could think about. The feeling of his lips pressed against hers – the heat of his body as it enveloped her own – haunted her every waking thought.

Non-waking thoughts too, if she was being perfectly honest.

She became aware very quickly, however, that she was the only one who'd been so utterly consumed by what she referred to in her head as *the* kiss.

Bastian, on the other hand, was acting as if it had never happened. As if he'd never gripped the back of her neck and slammed his mouth onto hers. Never held her close afterwards, burying his face into her hair and breathing her in.

He treated her as he always had.

Well, that wasn't exactly true. He became more distant. He stopped driving her to school. He didn't boss her around. He merely offered her a courteous "good morning" when she awoke every sun up and bid her an equally polite "good night" when she retired at sunset.

He was merely... cordial.

It was exactly what Katherine thought she'd always wanted from him.

But it wasn't. Not anymore. Not after *the* kiss.

Now his behavior just left her cold. Still, she played along. Made believe, like Bastian, that their lips and tongues had never met. That, even if they did, it didn't mean anything to her. She didn't know what else to do.

Katherine was pleased, at least, that the man had kept his word about helping her learn how to fight. After talking to Markus and Zane and discovering what they'd already taught her, Bastian decided that teaching her how to voluntarily transform into her wolf form would be the next logical step in her education. He took her outside to practice nearly every day, always traveling a ways into the woods before beginning.

Unfortunately, no matter how hard she tried, she just couldn't seem to do it. Without the powerful pull of the moon, Katherine's wolf seemed content to lie dormant inside her.

She grew more and more frustrated as their sessions lagged on. And it was just the afternoon before, in the midst of such a session, that she'd finally cracked.

Katherine didn't know when Bastian had turned into some Zen-loving guru, but this whole meditation business was getting on her last nerve.

After a week of attempting to teach her how to voluntarily transform – and utterly failing at it, she might add—Bastian had apparently decided that meditation was the key to unlocking her inner wolf. He was fixated on the idea.

Thus far, however, no amount of introspection or reflection had helped.

She could sit there with Bastian, trying to picture her inner wolf until kingdom come and she was convinced that absolutely nothing would come of it.

It didn't help that whenever she thought of her wolf form, she thought of Bastian's wolf form. Which, of course, led her to thinking of Bastian. Which led her to thinking about, well... the kiss.

"I can tell you aren't focused," she heard the man mutter from where she knew he sat, cross-legged on a snow covered stump in front of her.

She risked peeking open an eyelid. He was staring at her. She immediately closed it.

He released a frustrated sigh.

"I'm trying," Katherine pointed out defensively, eyes still clenched shut.

"Well, try harder."

Gritting her teeth, Katherine did just that. Concentrating on her breathing, she pictured her wolf form in her mind – dark brown fur, sleek build, sharp teeth. She managed to do it successfully for all of five minutes before images of Bastian and his infuriatingly perfect lips began to once again invade her thoughts.

Katherine sighed in defeat, snapping open her eyes.

Her bright green orbs landed on Bastian. Bastian, the wolf, to be specific. So focused on not focusing, she hadn't even heard him transform.

And yet, there he sat – flaunting his ability to do exactly what she couldn't, no matter how hard she tried.

Katherine stood. Her hands curled into fists, and she could feel what she knew to be irrational anger rising from the pit of her stomach, burning up her esophagus and throat until she had no other choice than to spew it out – in the form of words – from her mouth.

"You think you're so much better than me, don't you?"

Somehow it was easier to talk to Bastian the wolf than Bastian the man. And as she looked into the beast's eyes, she couldn't stop herself from bringing up what she promised herself she wouldn't.

"You kissed me," she said, the ire in her voice making it seem as if she was accusing him of a crime. "You kissed me, and yet you make it so *obvious that you don't even care about me."*

The wolf growled – the noise low and originating from deep in his throat. The sound should have scared her – startled her at the very least – but it didn't.

"You think that I'm some pathetic girl that you can jerk around — use as some form of sick entertainment. Sure, you've felt obligated to protect me since dragging me into this demented fairy tale months ago, but you don't care. Not really."

The growling grew louder.

Katherine's fists loosened at her sides as she lost some of her steam. "I guess that someone like you could just never like someone like me," she continued, her voice lowering an octave. "Not little Katherine Mayes. Not like that, anyway."

Before the last sentence had even fully left her mouth, Bastian was changing. In a nearly instantaneous blur, the man stood in the space that the wolf just was. And, of course, he was as naked as the day he was born.

N-A-K-E-D.

Momentarily stunned, Katherine allowed her gaze to dip inappropriately low before she realized what she was doing. Her face positively burned as she hastily turned around, forcing her eyes to stay locked on a nearby evergreen tree.

"Christ! A little warning would have been nice," she choked out, listening to him shuffle around behind her, no doubt changing into the spare clothes he always insisted each of them bring to these little sessions.

After all, if Katherine did actually manage to transform into her wolf form, she'd need some clothes to dress into when she changed back.

She heard Bastian snort. "It's nothing you haven't seen before," he pointed out, seemingly amused.

Katherine was all too aware of that fact. She shifted uncomfortably as she recalled her first transformation and waking up trapped under Bastian's arm – how she'd ogled his bare backside.

She didn't think he had known about that.

"That's not the point," she sputtered, crossing her arms over her chest. "Traipsing around naked... it's – well, it's indecent!"

That little gem prompted a chuckle from Bastian, and Katherine turned around, ready to defend herself.

The half-smile on his face stopped her in her tracks, however. He was being the most open he'd been with her since their meeting of the mouths over a week ago.

"Bastian." The name left her lips entirely without her permissions. It was said softly, pleadingly. Entirely too pathetically, in her opinion.

The half-smile fell from his face. A hard, unyielding line took its place. "We should get back to the house. It's already getting dark."

The sun was still visible above the tree line.

"But, Bastian-"

"Katherine," he interjected sharply, shutting her down. He ran an agitated hand through his hair. "Let's just get back to the house."

Without further ado, he turned his back on her, gathering both of their bags and heading in the direction Katherine knew led to the Prince house.

He didn't look behind him to make sure she was following even once.

She knew with certainty then that Bastian understood perfectly what she was saying when he was in his wolf form.

He just didn't have anything to say back to her.

Katherine had never felt more rejected than she had in that moment. Humiliated was another apt description. She had been all too willing to avoid Bastian the rest of the night – much like he'd been avoiding her the entire week.

The next morning – *this* morning – he hadn't been around to ignore. According to Sophie, he was doing some sort of research – investigating was the word she'd used – at the city hall. Apparently, at their last meeting, Cain had given him some information he'd received about the potential whereabouts of his parents' – and her parents' – remaining killer. Markus and Zane had disappeared too, though she had no idea if they'd gone with him or not. Markus, she knew, still hadn't completely forgiven her for disappearing on him after school on that Friday over a week ago.

He'd made that rather obvious with his increased use of the abhorrent nickname he had for her – princess.

As a result of the trio's absence, Sophie had been rather insistent that Katherine join her and Caleb on their preplanned shopping trip into town. Apparently, a new shipment of women's clothing had been delivered to The Closet and Sophie wanted to check it out. Caleb needed to deliver some venison to the local butcher and pick up some baking goods at the farmers' market.

Katherine, rather intent on staying home and throwing herself a pity party, adamantly refused.

Eventually, the blonde had given up on her and with a cheery wave good bye had taken her leave. After flashing the despondent girl a quick smile, Caleb had trailed after her.

Which brought Katherine to where she was now – completely alone in a depressingly empty house, staring forlornly into a bowl of soggy cereal she'd poured herself over a half hour ago.

"And let the party commence," Katherine muttered to herself sarcastically.

Wasn't she just a big old ball of sunshine?

Fierce pounding on the front door knocked her from her stupor. Somewhat alarmed, Katherine abandoned her cereal – it wasn't really edible at that point anyhow – and hurried to the door. She hadn't locked it after Sophie and Caleb. Surely if they'd forgotten something, they'd have just come straight in.

Twisting a knob, she opened one of the double doors.

It was Melanie.

Her features were warped into a panicked grimace and her short hair was disheveled, but there was no mistaking it was her.

"Are you okay?" Katherine asked, eyeing her friend's unkempt appearance as she waited for the girl to catch her breath.

"Katherine, you have to help me!" She grabbed the edge of the small brunette's shirt sleeve, nearly yanking her through the open doorway and onto the porch.

Startled, Katherine jerked away from her. "Just calm down and tell me what's wrong," she demanded.

"It's Mack," Melanie began to blubber. "We were playing around near the falls, trying to climb on the rocks and he fell! He's unconscious, and I think one of his legs is broken. It's all crooked and bent at a weird angle. I'm not strong enough to move him by myself. Your house was the closest. I ran all the way here. Please, you have to help me get him into town to see a healer. He's all by himself out there!"

Melanie grabbed onto her again, hysterically trying to pull her along, and for a moment, Katherine almost allowed it.

But she remembered all too well the plea Bastian had made to her a week ago – on the night of *the* kiss. She had to let him know somehow where she was going. "Hold on," she insisted, tugging her arm free from her friend's grip. "Just let me leave a note. That way if someone gets back here before we're able to get him into town, they can come help us."

Melanie paused for a moment before quickly agreeing. "Okay, but please hurry! Mack needs our help."

Katherine quickly scribbled a note, explaining the situation. She left it next to her unfinished bowl of cereal before grabbing her coat and throwing on a pair of oversized boots – they were probably one of Markus's many pairs. Then she finally allowed Melanie to drag her away.

The two girls dashed through the trees, dodging branches and leaping over upturned roots as they did. "Exactly how hurt is he?" Katherine asked as they ran. She wondered if it would even be safe to move Mack – maybe it'd make more sense for one of them to run into town and bring the town healer, Gabriela Atkins, to him instead?

"I don't know! When he fell, I called out to him, but he didn't respond," Melanie explained between breaths. "By the time I could climb down from the rocks and get to him, his eyes were closed and he wouldn't open them, even when I tried to shake him awake!"

Katherine refrained from blurting out her thoughts – that shaking an unconscious person probably wasn't the best idea the other girl had ever had.

She decided she'd follow Melanie to the falls and check out Mack's condition for herself. If she didn't think they should move him, she'd run back into town and get Gabriela herself.

Less than ten minutes later, they were nearing the falls – Katherine could have gotten there sooner, but made herself to match Melanie's slower pace, not wanting to leave the girl behind.

She forced her legs to slow to a stop as she reached the small, frozen pond at the bottom of the equally frozen waterfall. As she rested her hands on her knees and attempted to catch her breath, she looked around for a prone body.

She saw snows. Trees. And, of course, the waterfall. But no Mack. She didn't see him anywhere.

He couldn't have gotten up and walked away with a broken leg though.

She turned to Melanie, who'd stopped to rest some feet beside her. She, too, was attempting to recover from their run. "Where is he?" Katherine asked.

But the girl wouldn't meet her eyes.

"Melanie, where's Mack?" she demanded more firmly.

"He's not here, Katherine," a voice answered her. But it wasn't Melanie's high-pitched soprano. It was a lower timbre – one she'd only heard once before and just barely recognized.

She could hear rustling in the greenery behind them and turned to watch as the owner of the voice emerged from the trees. "Your little friend isn't here. Just me."

Katherine forced her facial expression to remain neutral – to not give away her surprise – as she stared at the man.

It was Cain.

CHAPTER NINETEEN

The head alpha of Haven Falls stood in the clearing, his dark eyes drinking in Katherine's form.

And Katherine, of course, didn't know what to think. She was beyond bewildered. Ignoring Cain's words and the horrible feeling they instilled deep in her gut, she turned to face her friend, who was still avoiding eye contact.

"Melanie, what's going on? Where's Mack? You said he was hurt."

A bark of rough laughter escaping Cain's mouth forced Katherine's attention to jerk back to the man. "I'm sorry, my dear. Did you not hear me? I said that he's not here."

Narrowing her green eyes at the man, Katherine addressed her friend once more, forcing out her words between gritted teeth. "Melanie, *what* is he talking about?"

"Yes, Melanie darling. Just *what* am I talking about?"

Twirling her brightly colored scarf with suddenly nervous fingers, the girl attempted to explain. "I… well, you see, he said that…" she trailed off, biting her lip. Melanie briefly met Katherine's eyes before swiftly lowering them once more. "I'm sorry."

"For what?"

No answer was forthcoming.

"For what, Melanie?" Katherine demanded more urgently, an angry edge to her voice.

What in God's name was going on?

"Now, now," Cain chided, taking a step closer to the two girls, which immediately caused Katherine to take a step back. The alpha grinned, his smile all teeth. "There's no need for such hostility, my dear. I merely asked your friend to bring you here so that we might speak privately about something that's been troubling me."

Katherine continued to eye the man suspiciously. "Why all the way out here? And why trick me? Couldn't you have just asked Bastian to bring me into town?"

Cain's smile – insincere as it was – grew wider. "Aw, your naiveté – it's surprisingly charming. And you really are a pretty girl. It's not hard to see why Bastian's so taken with you."

Cain moved closer to her still, and Katherine backed up another two steps, incredibly wary of the man who was making very little sense. Danger was thick in the air. "What does that have to do with anything? You said you wanted to talk."

"Yes," the man agreed, halting his movement for a moment, "but, you see, that is precisely what I wanted to talk to you about. It's unfortunate, but your arrival here has... *interfered*... with plans I've set into motion long ago."

Katherine licked her dry lips, sparing a glance at Melanie, who was worriedly watching the action unfold from where she'd planted herself under the shade of a nearby evergreen. "What plans?"

"Why, my plans for Haven Falls, of course," the man said as if the answer should have been obvious to her. "You've been here for a few months. I'm sure you realize the trouble you've caused in that short time."

Katherine furrowed her brow. "If this is about what happened with Rip-"

Cain released a derisive snort. "Don't be absurd. What Brigg's pup gets up to hardly concerns me. No. I'm talking about your alpha – Bastian – and the changes I've seen in him. He's more involved than ever in the community here. He no longer acts like a rabid dog, bothered only with finding the murderers of his parents. It's very... *disconcerting*."

Katherine just didn't get it. "Those sound like positive changes to me."

That was when Cain began to lose his composure. His very real temper revealed itself. "Do you know nothing of werewolf tradition, you stupid girl? Of politics? His behavior concerns me because any day, at any time, your Bastian could challenge me for the title of head alpha. He could take control of the entire village. It is his *birth right*, after all," he sneered, making his opinion of *that particular* fact clear.

Katherine refused to let herself be cowed. She crossed her arms over her chest, glaring at Cain. "Well, maybe you should save yourself the trouble and give him the title then."

The man laughed incredulously. "Give it to him? *Give it to him?* Do you have any idea how hard I've worked to secure this position for myself? How many people I've bribed? Manipulated? How many I've *killed*? Do you, Katherine?"

Her breath hitched when that word, that horrid word – *killed* – escaped Cain's mouth. Ignoring how her palpitating heart was now thundering in her chest – and somehow in her ears – Katherine forced herself to ignore the instincts that were screaming at her to run. "Killed?" she whispered.

"Yes, killed. You don't really believe that the same pair of incompetent hunters who tried to do you in would be able to track and kill Bastian's parents without a little inside help, do you?" he scoffed.

Air escaped Katherine's lungs with a *whoosh*. "What are you saying?"

"I'm saying," he sneered, stalking towards Katherine like a predator approaching its prey, "that I set those hunters on my brother and his insufferable wife. Paid them a hefty price to kill the both of them. They were basically worthless and didn't even manage to injure Brom. But his wife – Bastian's mother, Margaret – she was grievously wounded. Brom and Margaret were so in love with each other – truly destined mates. Within a week of her death, he too was gone from the world." Cain smirked. "So I guess the hunters did their jobs after all."

"That's sick," Katherine sputtered, completely aghast at the man's confession, her stomach in a mess of knots. She knew she was feeling only a fraction of what Bastian would if he ever found out. "You're twisted – completely warped in the head. How could you do that? You were his brother – and Bastian's and Sophie's uncle! When Bastian finds out, he's going to-"

"And how exactly is he going to find out, hmm?" Cain interrupted, still grinning. "You certainly aren't going to tell him. How could you... when you're dead?"

She knew the man didn't intend for her to leave the clearing alive as soon as he'd admitting to killing others for his head alpha title, but that didn't stop the feeling of panic – of downright hysteria – from nearly overwhelming her for a moment.

Katherine looked once more at Melanie. She still stood under the evergreen. The girl looked horrified at the entire situation, and her face had gone as pale as Katherine suspected her own had at hearing Cain admit to killing his own brother. "Melanie..."

"She's not going to help you," Cain boomed, his irritation with Katherine for refusing to show her fear obvious. "Don't you get it? She *tricked* you. Agreed to help me get you out here alone so that my plans for you could come to fruition. All it took was a promise she'd be recruited into a respected alpha's pack and she was on board."

Katherine ignored the man. "Melanie," she implored one last time, convinced that the girl couldn't have possibly known what she was dragging her friend into. "Please."

But as fretful as Melanie looked – tears in her eyes and hands shaking at her sides – she refused to meet the brunette's eyes. "I'm sorry, Katherine," she choked out.

Katherine's pleading expression hardened. "Fine," she spat, turning back to face Cain, her bottom lip trembling against her will. "So you killed Bastian's parents. Why target me? I'm no one important."

Cain's eyes grew impossibly darker. "Haven't you figured it out yet, Katherine? Don't you get it? When I kill you and show Bastian your mangled body, he'll suffer the same fate as his dear old dad." He offered her one last grin. "*Death.*"

And then he pounced.

In mid-air, Cain's form changed. Where there was once a man, there was a gray blur and then a wolf. The massive animal was coming right at her. Katherine was only half aware of Melanie's strangled scream as she leapt out of the way. She moved just in time, but the beast's claws managed to imbed themselves into the left sleeve of her coat, tearing into the leather and the fragile skin underneath it.

Ignoring the searing sting emanating from the gashes on her arm, Katherine ran. She racked her brain, hoping that an idea – some sort of strategy – would come to her, but nothing that Markus or Zane had taught her about fighting would be useful against a three hundred pound wolf.

She briefly thought about sprinting out onto the icy pond under the frozen falls, but knew it was much too cold out for the ice to be brittle enough to break under the animal's weight.

Instead, she headed for the forest that surrounding the small clearing, hoping she'd be able to find a spot to hide – maybe have time to climb one of the trees. She hadn't made it more than ten yards, however, before Cain was upon her. He sprang at her again, and though she tried to jump out of the way, her quickness was no match for the wolf's speed.

The beast slammed into her back, knocking her to the ground and pressing her body into the snow with one enormous paw. Gasping at how Cain's claws dug into the fabric of her coat and the tense muscles of her back, Katherine forced herself to move. Grabbing a jagged rock that was just within reach of her right hand, she desperately jammed it into the paw that wasn't digging into her.

Letting loose a pain-filled yelp, the wolf immediately shot off of her.

She'd only bought herself enough time to get to her knees, however, before Cain's uninjured paw forced her back to the ground, this time flipping her onto her battered back.

For the briefest of moments, Katherine lost her ability to breathe. The sensation of her bloodied wounds making contact with the ice cold snow was like nothing she'd ever felt before. The pain was excruciating.

Even as the edges of her vision threatened to darken, however, Katherine knew what she had to do. She had to transform. Cain could easily kill her in her human form. If she couldn't change into a wolf in the next five seconds, she was going to die.

She tried to remember what Bastian had taught her about meditation. She willed herself to focus and visualize her inner wolf. But it wasn't working. The painful throbbing of her back was just too distracting. And how could she possibly center her mind and thoughts when there was a giant wolf sitting atop of her, its razor-like teeth bared threateningly and its dark eyes gleaming with menace?

She didn't feel calm or serene or anything like that. Instead, cold, icy fear ran through her veins. And as the extended claws of Cain's uninjured paw came down at her prone form – no doubt aiming to slice her jugular – Katherine could do nothing but stare.

She thought of her parents – despite how much she missed them, she wasn't ready to be reunited with them quite yet. She thought of her sister. Of Abby. Even of Mallory and her gaggle of followers. Her new friends crossed her mind too. Mack, Jon, Agnes, and Leander. And, of course, her pack. Markus and Zane. Sophie and Caleb. And Bastian. It was him she thought of at the end.

But it wasn't the end. Not yet.

Cain's sharp claws were a hair's breath away from connecting with her delicate throat when a blurry form plowed into Cain, knocking him clean off of her.

At first Katherine thought it was Bastian. That somehow he'd known she was in trouble and had come to play hero like he always did. But then the color of the other wolf's coat registered – not black, but a glossy white. And Katherine knew that it was Sophie who'd saved her.

She must have seen her note and come to help with Mack.

Struggling to her knees and then her feet, Katherine took a second to search for Melanie, but it looked like her supposed friend had long since left the scene. Turning her attention to the battling werewolves, Katherine frantically hunted for *something* – some sort of weapon, like the rock she'd used earlier – to wield against Cain and help Sophie, but she came up empty.

She watched helplessly as the two wolves fought. Despite Cain's superior size, they seemed fairly evenly matched as they snapped their teeth and slashed their claws at each other. She suspected the injury she'd inflicted on the head alpha's paw perhaps had something to do with it.

Katherine became more and more desperate to help, however, as Cain slowly but surely gained the upper hand against Sophie. And then, with one powerful blow to her side, she was down, her furry body blending in almost perfectly with the snow on the ground.

And she wasn't getting up.

But instead of returning his attention to Katherine, Cain zeroed in on the fallen wolf who was struggling – and failing – to pull herself up from the ground. *Probably broken ribs*, Katherine thought dazedly, her horror growing.

She was frozen where she stood, forced to watch as Cain approached the incapacitated Sophie. Bastian's sister. *Her* sister.

And without another thought, Katherine was moving. She wouldn't allow her pack mate to die – not without doing her damnedest to protect her.

The change.

It barely even registered to Katherine that it was happening.

One moment she was racing towards Cain on shaky legs and the next, she was a wolf, colliding with the head alpha and falling into the snow with him. Somehow, she managed to latch her teeth into the flesh of Cain's ear, refusing to release the appendage even as the other wolf wailed and tried to buck her off of him.

When he crashed her body into the trunk of a tree, however, she was forced to let go. But not without taking a chunk of his ear with her. Ignoring his furious snarling, Katherine leapt at Cain again.

This time, though, he was ready for her. Cain easily threw her off of him. Katherine landed hard on her side, but wasn't at all deterred. She went at him again. And again. Each time, though, he'd fling her to the ground before she could even really make contact. She was vaguely aware of Sophie's pained whining in the background, knowing it was more out of fear for Katherine's safety than her own undoubtedly aching ribs.

Katherine was tired – her body bruised and exhausted – but as little good as it did her, she kept charging at Cain. At least she did until his tolerance for her persistent attacks came to an abrupt end, and he pinned her to the ground.

Before Katherine could even appreciate the irony of the situation – being pinned down by the vile man yet again even after Sophie's brave interference and her successful transformation into a wolf – sharp claws reigned down upon her. First, a brutal slash to her chest and then another to the left side of her face. Blood immediately gushed forth from the wounds, rivulets of red spilling into her eyes and distorting her vision.

Sophie's panicked barking was loud in Katherine's ears now, but nothing could permeate the blinding haze of pain that befell her.

And then, just as Cain's sharp teeth were about to join his claws in his savage attack, his weight was abruptly shoved off of her. A familiar black snout was pressed to hers for just a moment before the wolf attached to it let loose an enraged howl and dashed out of view.

Bastian.

And another wolf – Caleb, she thought – she could see attending to Sophie.

They had come.

Katherine knew Bastian would defeat Cain – knew, too, that he and Caleb would save Sophie, who she could still hear whimpering softly from where she lay some distance away.

Knowing this as she did, Katherine allowed herself to rest – to close her eyes before the darkness at the edges of her vision could conquer it completely.

As she lost consciousness, she was unaware of her furry body changing back into that of a young woman's. She was unaware of the sight she made – crimson blood soaking into the pure white snow beneath her – and of the fear and panic that such a sight would inflict upon those around her.

CHAPTER TWENTY

For an indiscernible amount of time, Katherine was trapped in a hazy sort of oblivion that allowed only small flashes of consciousness to break through.

A redhead loomed over her – the ends of the woman's flame-like hair gently tickling her face as firm hands applied pressure to her aching chest. A feminine voice – familiar, but only just – demanded furiously that someone leave the room before his temper caused him to do even more damage to her medicine stores.

Then unconsciousness beckoned her and nothing.

Another woman – blonde this time – fondly caressed her cheek, quietly assuring Katherine that everything would be okay. She nearly believed her.

And then more nothingness.

A man sat beside her, his weight causing the bed she was resting on to dip. She couldn't find the strength to pry open her eyes, but she recognized his grizzly voice as he informed her that if she didn't wake up soon he was liable to kick her in her "little, worry-inducing derrière" when she finally did.

His threat, of course, was soon followed by the unyielding grasp of lethargy and oblivion reigned once again.

Large arms encircled Katherine, tucking her safely into the heat of a warm, hard body that lay next to her. She took comfort in the soft, steady breathing that caused her bangs to flicker back and forth against her sweaty forehead.

And then nothing.

She could only break through to awareness for mere seconds before being tugged steadfastly back into unconsciousness.

Until now.

Katherine knew as soon as she was able to crack open her eyes that this time was different. She felt *lucid* as she took in her surroundings. Taking note that the bed she was lying on and the heavy quilt that covered her from the chest down were her own, she took a moment to admire the crackling blaze in the fireplace before turning her attention to the man who was standing – or rather, sitting – guard by her bed. Although the book he was reading did a stellar job of hiding his face, she easily recognized the ashy blond head of hair visible above the impressive tome. Caleb.

But why was he here? And why did her body – especially the left side of her chest and the entirety of her back hurt so much?

It took a long moment for her memories to completely return to her, but when they did, she felt her blood freeze in her veins.

Cain.

Melanie had dragged her out into the woods, claiming that she needed her help with a hurt Mack. But it had all been a trick – a set up – so that Cain could get her alone. Convinced that she and Bastian were destined mates, he'd planned to kill her and lord her mutilated body over Bastian – cause his demise the same way he'd caused his own brother's.

Oh God.

Brom and Margaret – Bastian's parents. Katherine had to tell him what Cain had told her.

She made an uncoordinated grab for Caleb's arm, managing to latch onto the man's wrist. He visibly startled, dropping the book he was reading in obvious alarm. He gaped at her for what had to have been close to a full minute before he was able to regain his bearings. "Holy crap," he muttered. And then louder. "Holy crap! Katherine! You're awake! How are you feeling? Does it hurt anywhere?"

Katherine tried to pull herself up, using her grip on Caleb's arm to bear her weight.

"No, no," Caleb insisted frantically, standing up and gently forcing her to lie back down against the plethora of pillows on her bed. "You have to rest. You've been so sick."

"Bastian," she managed to croak, her voice raspy from disuse, "I have to talk to him."

Caleb's eyes widened. "Bastian. Of course! He'll want to know that you're up. I'll get him right away."

The man sprinted from the room.

Ignoring Caleb's order to stay put in her bed, Katherine hooked her fingers around one of the knobs of the headboard and used it to help herself sit up. Despite her back's painful protesting, she was able to get as far as placing her feet on the hardwood floor before becoming distracted by shouting from somewhere outside of her bedroom, followed by the sound of thundering footsteps in the hallway.

Katherine glanced at the door that Caleb had left wide open when he'd run from her room. And there he was. Bastian.

He was a mess.

His hair looked as if a tornado had landed in the black locks and left behind a wild mane of curls capable only of standing up on end. The dark circles under his eyes seemed almost sinister against the pale alabaster of his skin. And his cheekbones. Katherine knew she couldn't have been out *that* terribly long, but she could have sworn that they were sharper – more prominent – than she remembered, which could only have been the direct result of weight loss.

He truly looked the worst Katherine had ever seen him. He was still unbelievably handsome, of course, but he appeared so ragged and worn down – so frayed at the seams. The man was examining Katherine just as closely as she was him – his eyes zealously roving her form – and she wondered vaguely how awful she must have looked if Bastian looked like *this*.

Then he seemed to realize that she was sitting up.

"What are you doing?" Bastian demanded sharply, a definite note of panic in his voice as he rushed towards her. "You're supposed to be resting. Didn't Caleb tell you that?"

Despite the harshness of his tone, Bastian's hands were gentle as he pushed her back down onto the bed – rearranging her body so that her head was once again lying on soft pillows and she was covered to her chin in thick covers.

A bit irritated at being manhandled – even if he was being incredibly tender with her – Katherine yanked her quilt off once more.

"Katherine!"

"I'll rest as soon as I talk to you! It's about your parents and it's important."

Bastian's eyes softened. "I already know."

Katherine furrowed her brow. "I really don't think you do," she insisted. "Cain told me… well, he said that…" she trailed off, desperately searching her mind for a considerate way to tell him that his uncle had essentially murdered his mom and dad.

"He told you that he was responsible for my parents' deaths, I know," Bastian finished for her, shocking Katherine into momentary silence. "Your *friend* Melanie came forward," he explained, his blue irises darkening. "She even confessed to the part she played in Cain's plot. She'll pay for what she did to you, Katherine. I can promise you that."

Katherine bit her bottom lip, surprised at how worried that statement made her for the girl, even after everything Melanie had done. "Bastian, I don't know how fair that is," she said, the words spilling from her mouth before she could think twice about it. "It was obvious to me – even as everything was happening – that she didn't know what Cain's true plans were when she agreed to drag me out into the woods."

Katherine eyed Bastian nervously as his face turned an angry fuchsia.

"I don't care," he barked. "How can you defend her after she used your friendship with her to manipulate you? Whether she knew what Cain truly intended or not, her actions almost got you killed. She needs to be punished."

"You're right," Katherine quickly agreed, seeing how upset the man was getting. "But the punishment has to fit the crime. Melanie just wanted to be recruited into a decent pack. Despite how questionable her decision to get involved with Cain was, I really don't think she intended for me to get hurt. So punish her as you deem fit, but just... *don't* hurt her, okay?"

The way Bastian's hands curled into fists at his sides made his displeasure at the notion of going easy on Melanie clear. And if it didn't, the way the vein on the side of his forehead bulged and his jaw muscles tensed certainly got the message across. Katherine thought for sure that he was about to deny her request – yell at her for even suggesting it – but he didn't. Instead, his bottom lip began to tremble and she watched in alarm as he abruptly fell to his knees, burying his face into the quilt that sat crumpled on her lap.

Katherine was flabbergasted. "Bastian?" she asked nervously.

"You just don't get it!" he exploded, revealing his face, tears in his eyes as he stared her down. "I almost lost you!"

The small brunette floundered for something to say, shocked by the usually stoic man's emotional outburst. "I didn't know you cared so much," she finally said. "I mean, you've been avoiding me since... well, since that kiss we shared... what? A week ago?"

"That was three weeks ago," Bastian muttered weakly.

Three weeks ago! But that would mean... "I've been unconscious for the past two weeks?"

Bastian nodded numbly. "Nearly – today would've been the twelfth day. You lost a lot of blood and somehow managed to catch pneumonia – the first case Haven Falls has seen of it in decades."

Katherine wet her dry lips. "Oh."

"Yeah."

"And Sophie? Is she okay?"

Bastian mustered up a halfhearted smile. "She's fine, thanks to you. She did suffer two fractured ribs, but they've healed nicely. She said it would've been much worse if you hadn't intervened – transformed and engaged Cain the way you did."

"She saved me first," Katherine insisted. "She protected me as best she could until you and Caleb got there. I couldn't have just left her for dead against that brute." She sank her teeth into her bottom lip as it occurred to her that she still hadn't asked after the man. "Speaking of Cain, is he... did you... I mean, what happened to him?"

"He's dead."

Bastian didn't even twitch as the callous words shot out of his mouth, and Katherine wasn't stupid – she could read between the lines. He had killed Cain. She couldn't find it in herself to feel sorry for the man. Not after all he'd done to her – to Sophie and Bastian. Instead, the news of Cain's death merely brought relief.

And curiosity.

"If Cain's dead," she asked, "then who's going to take over as head alpha? The council – Haven Falls itself – needs a leader, doesn't it?"

"Yes, it does. But for now, the community is still reeling over Cain's betrayal."

Katherine blanched. "Everyone knows what happened?"

"No one knows the exact details of the attack except for the pack, but everyone else has been informed that Cain injured you and Sophie in an effort to hurt me and that he played a significant role in my parents' deaths." Bastian nervously ran a hand through his unruly hair. "I admit that some have been calling for me to take over as head alpha after Cain's treachery was revealed, but I've just been so preoccupied with you, Katherine – so worried that I've barely been able to function – and I haven't given them an answer yet."

Katherine looked down, suddenly finding her fingernails very interesting. "But I'm awake now and clearly on the mend. Won't you need to give them just that – an answer?" She paused. "What are you going to tell them?"

Bastian frowned, refusing to reply for a long moment. "I don't know," he finally admitted. "I really don't."

Forcing herself to meet his azure gaze, Katherine immediately saw the fear and apprehension present in the man's blue eyes. But she could see longing there too.

She knew what she had to do and she chose her words carefully. "Bastian, I know I never knew them, but your mom and dad… they would've had to have been crazy not to be proud of the man you've become. They loved you with all their hearts – you *and* Sophie – and I have no doubt that they are loving you still from wherever it is people go when they die. No matter what it is you decide to do, that won't change." She took a deep breath. "But," she added hesitantly, "I think that your father would have wanted this for you. He would've deemed no one but you worthy enough of being his true predecessor."

Katherine watched Bastian's reaction to her declaration very closely, knowing there was a chance that what she'd said would offend him. She knew nothing of Bastian's relationship with his parents when they were alive, after all. As her words soaked in, however, Katherine could literally see the tension drain from Bastian's shoulders, and she knew she'd said what he'd needed to hear.

"You really think that?" he asked.

Katherine grinned. "Yeah."

Bastian allowed a hint of a smile to creep onto his face. "Maybe you're right."

"I *know* I'm right," Katherine assured him, but her grin drooped a little at the edges as she allowed anxiety to worm its way into her heart. Becoming head alpha was a huge commitment. She knew that mountains of responsibilities and duties came with the job. It would be a major draw on his time. "But will I ever see you?" The question flew past Katherine's lips without permission. She could feel heat flood her cheeks as she realized what she'd asked. "I mean, you'll have so much to do," she quickly explained. "Becoming head alpha… it's a big deal."

Bastian's eyes softened. "Are you kidding? Whether I become head alpha or not, I'm never letting you out of my sight again. Nothing good ever comes of it."

Katherine wasn't sure whether she should have been relieved by the assurance that Bastian planned on spending plenty of time with her or insulted by the insinuation that she couldn't take care of herself. She hadn't quite decided when Bastian caught her completely off guard by tenderly trailing a finger down her left cheek. "You're so pretty when you blush."

Katherine's already red face burned fiercely at Bastian's words, but the unexpected compliment didn't fluster her enough to allow the raised skin she could feel beneath Bastian's lone finger go unnoticed.

"What *is* that?"

Bastian jerked his hand back like he'd been burnt. "It's just a scar. Don't worry; it's faint," he attempted to assure her, "and will fade even more with time."

Katherine wasn't exactly comforted by that. "Can I see?" she asked.

It was obvious that Bastian wanted to deny her request, but he sighed and reluctantly stood. "Hold on." He disappeared into the room's adjoined bathroom before swiftly emerging with a handheld mirror clutched in his hand. He reclaimed his spot on the floor by Katherine's bed and held the small, oval mirror up for her.

Paying no mind to the horrid state of her hair or the feverish look to her cheeks, Katherine stared at the so called small scar. Cain's claw had certainly got her good. The raised line of skin was faint, like Bastian had said, but it was extensive and stretched all the way from the outside corner of her left eyebrow to her chin.

Katherine knew it was stupid to cry over something as silly as a scar, but could feel the moisture begin to build in her eyes anyway. Bastian snatched the mirror away when he saw the tears, grabbing her chin and forcing Katherine to look at him.

"You're beautiful – the prettiest girl in the entire village. The scar only adds to your allure. It's the mark of a fighter – a warrior."

Katherine managed to keep the tears that threatened to fall at bay, but couldn't subdue the surge of emotion that the man's words caused to rise within her. "Bastian?"

"Yes?"

Katherine took a deep breath before asking the question she'd been dying to know the answer to since she'd first met the man. "What do I smell like to you?"

A long nerve-wracking minute passed before he finally responded, but as he spoke, she could hear nothing but sincerity in his voice. "You smell warm and sweet – like flowers blooming in early spring.

Like rose petals as they open and welcome the nurturing rays of the sun. You smell like joy and happiness and home and… just *everything*. Like everything anyone could ever want."

Katherine could feel her heart pounding – threatening to leap right out of her chest – as she let his answer sink in. She thought of Bastian's scent – of the way the man smelled to her. Like the strong pine trees of the forest. Like the freshness of rain somehow combined with the appealing smokiness of a campfire. Like the musky smell of sweat and hard work – *like man*.

"We're mates, aren't we? Destined mates?" The words tumbled out of Katherine's mouth without thought. "Why else would Cain come after me? It's why you bit me and why… it's why I feel this way about you."

Katherine realized that if she was wrong, Bastian's rejection would be swift and harsh, but she couldn't bring herself to take back the words – they rang of truth.

She knew she was right when Bastian gently grasped her hands in his, stroking her fingers with the pads of his. "Yes," he admitted in a near whisper before abruptly pressing the back of her hands to his forehead like some desperate beggar, but imploring her for forgiveness instead of money or food. "I'm so sorry, Katherine. I should have told you right away, but I was terrified. After watching what happened to my parents – seeing my father waste away in front of me after my mom was killed – I didn't want a mate. I thought of it as more of a curse than anything. To have my soul tied so intimately to someone else's that my very life depended on hers and vice versa – it wasn't something that I wanted to deal with."

Katherine jerked her hands out of Bastian's grip. She understood, but the words still hurt. Bastian didn't want a mate. Especially not a destined mate. And really, who would? The concept sounded romantic at first, but her heart had essentially been enslaved to his and his to hers the moment they'd met – before they'd even really known each other.

"I'm sorry that my very existence is such a burden to you." As much as she understood, Katherine couldn't stop the bitter words from escaping.

"No!" Bastian vehemently denied. "No!" He lowered his voice. "Let me finish. I won't deny that I thought of our connection – of you – as a hindrance in the beginning. As misguided as it was, I was on a mission to hunt down my parents' killers when our paths crossed. It was bad enough that I was endangering my entire pack by pursuing those men. I didn't want to have to worry about you too – some girl I didn't even know. But don't you see? I was so ignorant – *so wrong*. You're not just some girl. You're smart, and kind, and so damn brave. I've been such a fool, trying to protect the both of us from this bond. But Katherine, as much as I've tried to fight them, my feelings for you have only grown stronger. I… I *love* you."

So many emotions – a little bit of trepidation, but mostly jubilance and validation – swelled within her at Bastian's unexpected confession. Katherine could have sworn her palpitating heart was so overjoyed that it stopped for a moment, but her response was tumbling past her lips a moment later so it must have kept beating. "I… I think I love you too."

Bastian's answering smile was magnificent. "I can work with that."

Katherine couldn't help but stare as the skin around Bastian's eyes crinkled and the adorable dimple on his right cheek made an appearance. He looked so *happy* – a stark contrast to how he had appeared when he'd first come into the room. And gazing at him, Katherine knew. She knew that despite the trouble she always seemed to stumble into, and despite the heavy responsibilities Bastian faced by becoming head alpha, somehow everything would work out. They would navigate what it meant to be destined mates together.

Bastian gently cupped either side of Katherine's face. "Can I kiss you?"

Katherine smiled at the question, but instead of answering with words, pressed her lips to his. And as their mouths moved sensually against one another's, Katherine knew that she could handle anything that came her way as long as Bastian was always there to smile at her like that and kiss her like this.

END

About the Author

Noelle Marie is a full time stay-at-home mom and a part time writer. When not being driven wonderfully mad by her two adorable (read: deranged) toddlers or staring woefully at her keyboard, she can be found curled up in a comfy chair reading a book or attempting to bake in the kitchen. Occasionally she might be pestered into golfing with her husband, but is largely an embarrassment to the sport.

Made in the USA
San Bernardino, CA
12 December 2019